I Can Dance

REVISED EDITION

A Soul's Cry of Freedom
KIMBERLY MILLARD

5 Fold Media
Visit us at www.5foldmedia.com

I Can Dance, Revised Edition
Copyright © 2010 by Kimberly Millard

Published by 5 Fold Media, LLC
www.5foldmedia.com

Unless otherwise indicated, all Scripture quotations are taken from the Holy Bible, New Living Translation, copyright 1996, 2004. Used by permission of Tyndale House Publishers, Inc., Wheaton, Illinois 60189. All rights reserved.

Scripture taken from The Message. Copyright 1993, 1994, 1995, 1996, 2000, 2001, 2002. Used by permission of NavPress Publishing Group.

ISBN: 978-1-936578-00-9

Cover photo by Liliana Sanches, used by permission.

Dedication

Kim,

Thank you for writing your story. It is not only to honor your memory that we pursued the publishing of your book, but also to fulfill a promise to a dear friend. The prayer is, to get your testimony out there for all those that need to hear it. Your life, faith, testimony and legacy will live on. You are deeply loved and missed every day.

Your Friends and Family

Foreword

Every once in a while, someone comes along that has an incredible faith in the impossible. Kimberly was that type of person. Kim exemplified the true meaning of the word, "faith." As one who had been afflicted with a crippling disease at a young age, she chose not to let her situation cripple her mind and faith. She was an individual who was an inspiration to many people.

I have personally been blessed by her life. Even though she did not receive her miracle here on earth, she never gave up believing. As her Pastor, her presence would be an encouragement to me. She had reason to complain, but she did not. She had reason to be mad at God, but she was not. She had reason to crawl into a hole and forget those around her, but she did not.

As you read this, you will see her heart and the commitment that she had. The years that she lived were a blessing to all. Kim's life could very well be part of the Bible characters that we read of in Hebrews, chapter 11. These people were commended for their faith during difficult situations. Some remained faithful even though they did not receive. Their very lives still speak today to encourage us to have faith in God. Kim's faith in God gave her the assurance of the things she could not see.

Kim did not just have faith that was in word only, but hers was one that she lived. She did not receive what she believed for, but she never stopped believing. Let this story encourage you in whatever you are walking through.

"Each one of these people of faith died not yet having in hand what was promised, but still believing. How did they do it? They saw it way off in the distance, waved their greeting, and accepted the fact that they were transients in this world. People who live this way make it plain that they are looking for their true home. If they were homesick for the old country, they could have gone back any time they wanted. But they were after a far better country than that—heaven country. You can see why God is so proud of them, and has a City waiting for them" (Hebrews 11:13- MSG).

Pastor Mark M. Babin
Celebration Center, Fort Fairfield, ME

Prologue

The little girl's tiny hand desperately gripped the bed rail, struggling to give her lungs more power to drag in any possible amount of air, however small. She had been in that hospital room so often she knew her surroundings by heart, but this night was different from the countless nights she had spent there in the past.

With each small breath she let out, a quiet whimper escaped with it. Alyssa remembered what the nurse had told her: remain calm and take deep breaths. She allowed tears to roll freely from her eyes but forced herself to remain quiet. Terrified by what was happening to her, remaining calm was a hard task for the nine-year-old.

Her hand began to ache from holding the bar so tightly, and her breathing shallowed. Blonde hair clung to her forehead in wet strands of perspiration. Every muscle in her body strained as she fought to take each breath. *God, help me. I can't breathe!*

Alyssa was crying without restraint by the time she reached for the nurse's bell. "I can't breathe." Her hoarse whisper was barely audible over the intercom.

Within moments the nurse entered the room and went to Alyssa. Her desperate eyes were round with fear against her tiny strained face, which was slowly turning a frightening shade of blue. The nurse quickly put medicine into the nebulizer for the child. "Just breathe," she said, putting the mask around Alyssa's face.

The child struggled to inhale the medicine, but the mask only seemed to suffocate her. Her whimpering turned to gasping cries of panic, and she squirmed with each tormented breath. The nurse agonized over the child's misery as she stroked her head. "Ally, I'm going to call the doctor again. OK?"

Alyssa nodded, but her heart was pleading for the nurse to stay with her. Walking out quickly, the nurse left the suffering child alone. The medicine was not helping, so Alyssa tore the mask from her face hoping for more air. But none came. *Am I dying?* she wondered. *Lord, it's OK if I die, if You want me to come to heaven.* She released the bedrail from her deathlike grip and clasped her tiny hands together under her chin. She closed her eyes and prayed silently, having no breath to speak out loud. *Lord Jesus, please help me. I can't breathe, and it hurts. If You have to make me die, that's OK. Do whatever You have to, Jesus. I'm tired, and I can't fight anymore.*

Finally the doctor came rushing in and, taking one glance at the girl, spoke to the nurse that had followed him. Alyssa heard Dr. Matthews's words but only a few registered, ones she did not understand. "ICU...losing oxygen..." the doctor's voice droned in Alyssa's ears.

"It's OK, Ally. Just hold on," Dr. Matthews spoke gently to her. He sounded far away in Alyssa's ears, his voice growing dimmer with each word.

The rest of the night was a blur to the little girl. She awoke the next day, breathing easily. In fact, the big tube down her throat now did the breathing for her, pushing her lungs in and out rhythmically. Her mother sat near the bed and smiled at her as she woke up.

The child's mother talked to her in a soothing voice, reading her stories and telling her that the family was anxious for her to come home. Though secretly, she wondered if her child ever would come home. "Ally, do you know how much Mommy loves you?" The child nodded.

"If I could, I would take your place in a second. I wish it were me lying there instead of you." Catherine meant those words with her entire soul. Her eyes filled with tears at the frightening sight of her child, so small and frail with tubes running into her mouth, nose, and arms. The doctor had called Catherine and told her that Alyssa wouldn't make it through the night.

But Alyssa had made it, grasping at life with what minimal strength she had. Something kept the little girl alive. Something, or Someone, had saved her from the brink of death. There was a much bigger plan for this child's life, and she lived.

One

Alyssa Langer looked up into the heavens at the countless stars shooting beams of light from the night sky. In the backyard of her big, colonial style home, she often sat and watched nature live and breathe all around her. As a little girl, her mother would bring her out and tell her about the God who created every living thing.

Normally, she loved the awesome stillness of the night. A sense of peace, able to invade disturbing thoughts, was often found in the sounds of crickets and rustling leaves. Out here nothing existed but the sounds, the stars, and those things mysteriously illuminated by moonlight, in the otherwise utter blackness of her surroundings.

This night was different, however. There was no joy for her in seeing the sparkling diamonds against the ceiling of coal. A slight, ironic smile appeared on her lips as she remembered times of innocence and fascination in years long past.

She'd had many dreams as a child. One of her happiest aspirations was to be a dancer. The memory pierced her now like the sudden prick of a needle through tender skin. She had been foolish then; foolish to think the sickness that plagued her body would somehow disappear. Though she had been born with a rare muscle disease, her childlike faith had never imagined that weakness would hinder her dreams.

"Where are You?" The vast darkness beyond the moon stared back silently. "I know You're there. Why don't You help me?" Her whispered plea exposed the broken years of pain and heartache. A single tear made its way down her cheek as she listened. "Will You ever answer me?" The evening breeze blew softly around her face, causing little wisps of hair to dance on her cheek. She waited, as if those strands might whisper back.

This wasn't the first time she had asked such questions. Sometimes overwhelmed by the burdens she carried, she cried out to a God that seemed too far away to reach. She had been through much in her short twenty-four years of life, and she sometimes wondered if it was worth the trouble.

Scolding herself for being so morbid, she reached up and pulled out the clip holding her hair. Masses of long, golden strands fell around her shoulders, happy to be free. As her fingers combed through the tresses, her thoughts reflectively traveled over her life, pondering why she had been chosen to carry such a burden.

Eventually her mind slowed and lingered on her last doctor's appointment. "Could you come back on Thursday? The test results should be in by then." The doctor had carefully averted his glance as he spoke earlier that morning. The look he had used frightened her. She noticed herself getting tired more easily in recent days but chose to ignore it until now.

The signs were easy to ignore, since her strength was normally limited. She could walk short distances but was forced to rest when the walk was too long. Yet lately, the distances she walked grew shorter, and the times of resting grew much more frequent.

She had wondered…the question slipping into her thoughts once or twice over the last several weeks…*Am I getting worse?* It was hard not to contemplate the possibility. For half of her life the disease had been degenerative, causing her muscles to waste slowly away as she grew. However, the progression of the disease had seemed to stop before her thirteenth birthday.

With the disease in remission, Alyssa had been determined to prove herself. She went to college and graduated at the top of her class. She now worked for her father as the marketing executive for the family-owned ranch.

She had, or so she thought, succeeded in all she wanted to achieve. Many people admired her accomplishments, telling her how strong she was in spite of her difficulties. People were drawn to her sincere compassion, quick sense of humor, and disarming smile.

Yet nobody saw the emotional wreck she was inside. She wondered what those people would say if they saw her tonight, anguishing over her possible future.

It was times such as these that Alyssa felt completely alone. She longed for someone to confide in, to share her secret scars. But there was no one. She was alone in her thoughts and isolated in her pain.

"Lyssa?" A deep voice called from somewhere in the darkness. Startled, Alyssa quickly brushed away a tear and forced a smile as she turned toward the voice. "Hi. I saw you out and thought I'd stop and say goodnight on my way to the cabin."

For a moment Alyssa forgot her troubles, and a genuine smile emerged for the ranch hand standing before her. Austin Jacobs smiled, and she was slightly astonished once more at how breathtakingly handsome he was. "I'm glad you did. How was your day?"

"Great." He crouched down near her chair and habitually raked a hand through his dark brown hair. "We hired the new foreman, and he seems to be doing well." He looked up into her face intently, with penetrating, deep blue eyes that threatened to pierce Alyssa's defenses and see her hidden pain. "Your brother said you went to see a doctor today. Is everything all right?"

"Yes." Alyssa glanced away, somehow knowing that Austin could read her thoughts as no one else could.

Austin had always shown a special interest in her. Yet, Alyssa was well aware that his interest was that of a friend and nothing more. This had been a disappointing realization for her. But his friendship had become a source of strength she could not fathom living without, and she pushed whatever notions of love she might have had aside. Quickly

12

regaining her smile, she looked back at him. "The doctor wants to see me again, but I'm sure it's nothing."

His concern for her was evident as he leaned closer to her chair. "Are you feeling OK?"

"Yes. I am tired though." She tried to suppress a yawn and, failing miserably, began to laugh.

"I'll get going then." He stood, revealing his towering 6'4" frame, and reached out his hand to her, which Alyssa grasped lightly. "Sleep well, Lyssa." He smiled down and gently squeezed her hand before he left.

"You too. Thanks for stopping by." She watched Austin head back toward the dirt path that would take him to his cabin. With a slight innocent smile, she noticed how appealing he looked in the typical jeans and T-shirt of a rancher. It wasn't just his muscular build and rugged good looks but also the way he carried himself with humble confidence that made him so attractive.

Alyssa shook herself out of her reflections and headed inside toward her bedroom. Relief swept over her tired body when she reached her room. There a massive, four poster bed took up much of the space, and a Victorian flowers and lace look dominated her bedspread, curtains, and wallpaper.

An antique roll-top desk occupied one corner of the room. There she spent time each day pouring her thoughts into a journal. At times like these, Alyssa imagined the small notebook to be the only thing to which she ever revealed her true self.

Suddenly Alyssa's face hardened into a scowl, as her eyes caught sight of the wheelchair sitting beside her bed. Going to it as fast as her tired legs would carry her, she grabbed it and dragged it into the hall outside her room.

"How many times do I have to tell mom not to put that thing in here?" The slamming door punctuated her vehement whisper as she reentered. The wheelchair reminded her of her differences; at times it seemed to laugh and mock her. She only used it when she was too tired to walk or in the past when she had been ill. Even then she despised it.

Holding on to the bed and dresser for support, she made her way to the desk and thankfully sat in the small wooden chair. She took out her journal and wrote:

It seems there is a bottomless pit in my soul, full of excruciating pain. Sometimes I feel strong and capable—like I can handle any tragedy that comes. Tonight, I felt the hands of depression clutch my throat and drag me toward that black hole at such a frightening speed that I couldn't stop them. I try to reach up, to hang onto something, but there's nothing there.

I sought God, but He didn't answer. Are You listening, Lord? I need someone. I can't go on alone—it hurts too much. If I just had a reason to live—someone to love me. But no one even sees me.

My soul is locked up inside of me, invisible to the world. I'm trying to fight, but it's getting harder. Hanging onto the same rope all my life—I'm at the end—getting weaker. I may have to let go soon.

Tears began to fall on the pages, smearing the words she had written. She looked up at the ceiling, trying to see past it and catch a glimpse of the One she called God.

"God help me," she said in a voice that sounded more like a whimper, before dropping her head onto the desk in anguish.

In his small cabin, Austin knelt beside his bed and let out a moan that came from the depths of his soul. He had been in the same position praying since leaving Alyssa. Having looked past her smile and seeing what lay beyond her eyes, he feared for her.

This was not the first time he had prayed for the sweet, innocent woman. He often found himself on his knees interceding for Alyssa.

The burden was strong, unlike any he had ever felt. He frequently saw the pretty face and troubled eyes in his dreams. Then he would awake and know he had to pray.

God began to reveal things to him that were afflicting Alyssa's mind and heart. He felt her pain and desperation, causing him to pray more fervently. An atmosphere of depression entered the room and grew thick around him. He envisioned suffocating blackness leading to the pits of hell. God was showing him the condition of Alyssa's soul, allowing him to experience those things with which the devil attacked her.

Austin trusted God's Holy Spirit, took Him by the hand, and began to intercede with a mighty vengeance. Tears rained from his eyes, and he raged against the evil that was tormenting Alyssa's weary mind and body. Every muscle in his body tensed as heavenly language flowed from his lips until he went hoarse. He was fighting for Alyssa's life, and he knew it.

He cursed the oppression that held her in chains and spoke death to the disease that ravaged her body. He claimed the authority given to him by Christ Jesus and commanded every demon to cease in its attack against her. When the heaviness finally lifted and left his room, he asked the Lord to fill Alyssa with His Spirit, love, and peace.

Some time later, Austin lay on his bed, exhausted emotionally and physically. His normally strong body went limp as he lay there. He felt an abounding peace and victory surround him and knew Alyssa would be able to relax for the time being. He also realized that her rest would not be permanent if she failed to turn to God.

Austin raised his hands toward the ceiling in one more offering of praise and prayer. "Thank You, Jesus. Keep her safe." He closed his eyes then and slept until the sun came up less than two hours later.

Two

The sun shone through the large window in Alyssa's room and woke her from a peaceful sleep. Her eyes opened, squinting as they adjusted to the light. She stayed there for a time, enjoying the comfort of her bed and the panoramic view from the windows opposite where she lay. It wasn't long, however, before the breathtaking scene beyond the glass drew her. Throwing the covers aside, she sat up and pushed her tousled hair from her face.

Almost immediately she noticed that her body felt stronger today. This was not unusual; she had good days and bad. Nevertheless, it managed to spark a bit of hope. Going to the window, she sat on the cushioned covering of the window seat, leaned back, and pulled her slim legs up under her. There she watched the glorious morning bloom into being. The lush green trees, common around Northern Maine, sang their morning song, while blossoms of all colors danced in the gentle breeze, seemingly loving the tune.

"It's a beautiful morning, Lord. Thank You for it." Her serene words caused her to wonder at God's power. He had created such beauty. Couldn't He create something beautiful out of her life?

Alyssa was taught early on about the Son of God who had died for her. She asked Jesus to forgive her sins and live in her heart at the age of four and willingly told of her love for Christ even now.

As a young girl, she had a childlike faith in Jesus. Proudly, she would tell her mother that Jesus was going to heal her. "Then I'm going to be a dancer, Mama," she'd declare. Her mother would look at her little girl with eyes of mingled hope and longing, wanting to believe with such faith.

The day came when reality crushed Alyssa's dream, and her lovely fantasy crumbled around her. She was not getting better; she was getting worse. It took years of struggling before she relented with bitter acceptance. Part of this struggle was with God.

Confusion ate at her; why would God let this happen? Finally a conclusion formed out of twisted human logic; it was because He loved her. She was told by some that God had a special purpose for her: when others saw her peace and joy despite her circumstances they would realize how great God's goodness was.

This rationalization had disturbed her at first. Yet, after years of reasoning, it eventually made some kind of irrational sense. It even brought her a small amount of comfort. So she focused her efforts on trying to radiate a serenity that she did not have.

Suddenly Alyssa jerked herself from her thoughts. How easily her mind could wander from joy to sadness! Taking those familiar thoughts captive, she determined not to let them dominate her on such a fine day.

Alyssa finally stood to stretch and reluctantly headed for the bathroom across the hall. After she showered and dressed, she studied herself in the mirror. Wearing a flattering, light blue dress that framed her small figure, she personified the word *petite*.

Alyssa had a soft, subtle beauty. Her oval face was etched with delicate lines, as if molded by an expert's hand, with large blue eyes and full lips. Her hair was cut in long layers that angled in to frame her face, falling in thick shining masses around her head. Looking at herself now, she saw only imperfection, wondering why she was cursed with such features.

Leaving the bathroom, she headed for the kitchen. At the front of the hall that led to Alyssa's room, the house divided into two main sections: the kitchen and the living room. Just inside the living room rose a majestic staircase with a banister of thickly carved oak. Up above, a balcony-type hallway allowed for a view of one of the rooms upstairs.

Alyssa followed the sound of her sister's loud voice sharing the latest gossip. She reached the kitchen, greeted Elizabeth and her mother, and headed for the stove to spy cooking pancakes.

Catherine watched skeptically as Alyssa turned to talk with Elizabeth. She looked happy this morning. Not long ago Catherine had caught a glimpse of something frightening in Alyssa's eyes. Despair had emptied them of emotion, and Catherine feared she had lost Alyssa to some hidden horror that plagued her. She hadn't seen that look since but nonetheless watched for some small crack in Alyssa's armor that might reveal whatever demons lie behind her mask of content.

Catherine's forty-five years of age showed in the forming wrinkles and white hair that covered more of the dark brown each day. Yet she was still a beautiful woman, with high cheekbones and a full mouth, which she had passed on to each of her daughters.

Alyssa sat at the table with her older sister. "Did you come with Carlos? And where are my two gorgeous nieces?"

"Carlos wanted to get an early start on the ranch today, so he got us all out of bed before it was even light out! The kids are out back playing." Carlos had come to work on the ranch six years ago. Within a year he and Elizabeth had married and moved into a small home of their own nearby.

Catherine dished out plates of pancakes and set them on the table. "Go get the kids and find Rebecca. Breakfast is ready."

Alyssa headed for the living room. "What about Tyler?"

"He left already. It's impossible to track him down lately." Even though her mother tried to sound irritated with her only son, concern was more evident in her voice. Tyler was the pride and joy of Ken and Catherine Langer, yet he often gave them cause to worry. His typical carefree ways had grown dangerous over the last few months.

Alyssa quickly saw that her younger sister was not in the next room. The living room was decorated with a plush cushioned sofa and love seat of soft white, with a glass-topped coffee table between them.

The other side of the room had two comfortable armchairs in front of a brick fireplace. The walls and floor were done in subdued mauve and various other blended colors. Windows made up an entire wall, with sliding glass doors leading to the porch outside offering a breathtaking view of the backyard.

Alyssa could see the garden flowers in full array and Elizabeth attempting to round up her two girls. Paige was skipping around the flower beds as four-year-olds love to do, while Britney watched with a mother-like attention.

Grabbing hold of the thick banister, Alyssa looked up to the second floor. "Becca, breakfast is ready!" After a moment, a striking face appeared followed by a long, perfectly curved body outlined in blue and black spandex.

"You don't have to yell. I can hear ya." Rebecca came around the corner and bounded down the stairs. Alyssa watched her, feeling a familiar stir of pride and admiration. Rebecca was everything Alyssa wanted to be: strong and uncompromising in her beliefs, confident in her personality, and passionate in her relationships.

Nearing her sister, Rebecca graced Alyssa with a dazzling smile. Rebecca's favor was as drops of fresh rain on sun-parched sand. Alyssa drank from her seemingly endless joy, hoping to bottle some for her own lacking soul.

Their kinship was a bond that surpassed blood ties—reaching beyond a family name to grasp at a unique, intimate friendship. Though the older of the two by eleven months, Alyssa had always looked up to Rebecca. Little saddened her more than to realize that at some point in life, she had retreated into herself, leaving out the one person she felt closest to. Not even with Rebecca did Alyssa share the darkness inside her.

"You look nice this morning. You make me look bad." Rebecca swiped at a stray piece of brown hair that had fallen from her short ponytail.

Alyssa laughed at the absurdity of such a compliment. "Nothing could make *you* look bad, Rebecca."

The two sisters walked side by side into the kitchen. Rebecca slowed her pace to Alyssa's but didn't seem to notice; it was as natural as breathing. Since childhood she had been unconsciously matching her pace to Alyssa's, not caring that everyone else was going faster. She stuck close, often rising up as her sister's avenging angel when Alyssa felt too inadequate to fight.

The two sat down, filling the table despite their father and brother being absent. Alyssa smiled at her nieces across from her. Although the girls were nine years apart, Alyssa saw the same love between them that she felt with her own sisters. "Were you having fun outside?"

Paige's blue eyes sparkled with a light only a child's could hold. Her blonde hair fell down her shoulders, matching her sister's perfectly. "We played hide and seek, and I won!"

"That's only 'cause I let you win." Britney's hair was turning slightly darker in places, giving it unique highlights with hundreds of shades of blonde and brown mixed together. She was already as tall as her mother and could easily be mistaken for one much older than her thirteen years.

"I'm going out to see Dancer this morning; do you girls want to come?"

"Yeah! Can we, Mom?" The excitement in Britney's eyes gave away her adoration of Alyssa's pure white stallion, but it quickly diminished when they were told they could not go.

Elizabeth ignored her children's arguments and sought to change the subject. "How are you feeling, Ally? Mom said the doctor wants to see you again next week."

"Fine. You know, I was thinking that maybe I've actually improved." Alyssa looked around the table, hoping to see some support for her optimistic idea. Her mother averted her gaze by looking out the window. Elizabeth pretended not to hear by reprimanding the children for not eating. Rebecca looked at her with a sad smile.

Anger and embarrassment stung hard. Without thought, Alyssa quickly gave an excuse to leave the table. "Well, I have no time to think about it now. I want to see the horses before I head to the office."

With a few quick goodbyes, she headed out the kitchen and through the living room. Before she reached the sliding glass doors, her mother's voice jabbed at her pride once more. "Alyssa, aren't you going to take your chair?"

"No, I'm going to walk."

Catherine came to the archway of the kitchen, her hands on her hips. "You know you have a hard time walking that far."

For some reason the subject was grating heavily on Alyssa's nerves. She didn't want to hear what she couldn't do this morning. She could not deal with the pitying gazes of her family, and she didn't want to use the wheelchair. "I'll be fine. See you after work." As soon as the words were out of her mouth she was out the door, breathing the sweet scent of morning. Yet the stench of the atmosphere inside lingered around her.

She brushed off the nagging tension and walked down the ramp of the porch. Her mother's prized garden of blooming flowers greeted her along the way to the path that would lead through the woods. She stopped for a moment to finger the red and pink petals of some wild roses. They seemed to whisper to her, telling sweet tales of promised love just beyond the dirt path.

She continued on, smiling at the trees lining the little trail. It was only a short way before she reached the crossroad. To the right, the path led to the cabins belonging to the ranchers. If she went straight she would end up at a small lake—her own private sanctuary. She chose the path to the left, leading to the stables.

The walk seemed to be taking longer than she expected, forcing her to stop several times to rest. She enjoyed sitting alone in the woods just to clear her mind and wonder at nature's glory. The massive trees rose high above, protecting her, restraining the rest of the world and all the things from which she longed to escape.

Even though the shade of the woods kept her comfortably cool, she could still tell that Maine was in for another unusually hot day. Spring had come early with the sun taking possession of the land by its fiery heat.

Finally she reached the edge of the woods. The barn was close by, housing some of the finest-bred horses in America. Various breeds, mostly Morgans and quarter horses, were bred for different purposes.

21

The air was considerably cooler inside the barn. Alyssa welcomed the relief from the sun after the long walk and stopped to relish her surroundings. The smell of hay and horseflesh mingled with the sounds of the thoroughbreds. Though vastly different from her wooded haven, the stables offered Alyssa another kind of respite for her soul.

She headed toward the back of the barn, stopping at various stalls to stroke the horses. As she passed, the great beasts seemed to welcome her, rousing at her arrival. Here, she felt accepted–loved by these magnificent creatures that expected nothing from her but affection. They didn't demand that she wear a guise or speak with strength. They simply responded to *her*.

Coming to the last stall, Alyssa saw her beloved friend. "Hi, Dancer." She cooed to the large white Arabian stallion as she unlatched the gate. Gently she began to stroke the horse's soft nose and broad muscular back. His powerful body was such a contrast to her small, weak hand. Her father had purchased the horse several years earlier at a show in the South.

Dancer instantly knew her and nestled his nose against her face. Alyssa laughed and spoke to the horse in soft, loving tones. "I haven't seen you for a couple days. Did you miss me?"

"He sure did. Nobody has been able to get that horse to cooperate since you were here last." As the deep masculine voice washed over her, Alyssa turned to meet Austin's gaze. "Dancer gets stubborn when you don't come around. You should come more often, Lyssa." Austin's gentle chiding was punctuated with the hint of a smile.

Alyssa laughed at his feigned irritation while stilling the slight, heady pleasure that arose when Austin spoke her name in his unique way. "Well, he loves me. And you're right. I should come more often. I miss our little talks."

"The horse is talking now, huh!" Austin leaned his tall frame casually against the gate and folded his arms across his wide chest.

"In his own way." Alyssa's head tilted up high to return Austin's smile. She studied his face, unable to pull her eyes away, and suddenly noticed how tired he looked. His quickly combed through hair and unshaven face gave him an attractive, rugged appearance, but his bloodshot eyes alarmed her. "Are you feeling all right?"

The concern in her voice touched something in Austin. "I'm just tired; I got to bed kind of late last night. I didn't have much time this morning." He ran a self-conscious hand through his hair and over his chin, giving Alyssa an embarrassed grin. "You, however, look very nice."

Austin had noticed immediately the change in Alyssa since the night before. There was a light in her eyes that had been missing, and he inwardly thanked the Lord for the power of His love.

"Thank you. I feel wonderful for some reason, so I'm going to get the most out of it. I don't have too many days like this." A slight flicker of pain crossed over her eyes then disappeared again as her face broke into a radiant smile. "Thank you for stopping by last night. It was sweet of you to think of me."

Austin was drawn by Alyssa's quiet candor. Reaching for her small, delicate hand and engulfing it tenderly with his large, strong one, he fixed his eyes on hers. "Don't ever doubt that someone cares about you. You'll never be forgotten, Lyssa."

The intensity in Austin's voice startled Alyssa. There was no doubt to the sincerity of his words, yet she sensed a veiled meaning that eluded her. They stood for several heartbeats, not wanting to move, until another voice interrupted the thoughts swirling in their heads.

"Well, Austin! Entertaining ladies in the barn?" Their hands dropped to their sides as they simultaneously turned toward the newcomer. At the sight of Jake Cutler, Austin straightened and moved imperceptibly closer to Alyssa.

Alyssa simply stared. The man who had interrupted was of average height and nice build, with black hair pulled back into a ponytail.

"I'm not 'entertaining,' Cutler. This is Alyssa, Mr. Langer's daughter." Alyssa noticed the tone of Austin's voice had changed slightly when talking to the man. "Alyssa, this is the new ranch foreman, Jake Cutler."

"It's nice to meet you, Mr. Cutler." As the man reached out to grasp her hand, she noticed his dark brown, almost black, eyes leisurely travel down the full length of her body.

A shade of pink crept into Alyssa's face, not just because of Jake's bold appraisal, but because of the tiny warm shivers that played on her skin as his eyes touched her. Though she realized that she should be offended, she instead was intrigued by his reaction to her.

Instantly Jake Cutler fascinated her. Something in his eyes, or voice, or overall appearance made him alluring. Alyssa couldn't put her finger on what she was feeling, but it unnerved and thrilled her at the same time.

"Call me Jake. I didn't know there was such a beautiful woman living up in the boss's big house. I may enjoy this job after all." Jake still held her hand as Alyssa stood speechless. She felt like a fool but could think of nothing to say. His black eyes devoured her insatiably, leaving her spellbound. "You don't mind if I call you Alyssa, do you?"

"No, of course not." In fact, the name spoken from his deep, rasping voice sent a slight shiver up her spine. For some reason, her thoughts jumbled, and she felt she must escape the barn quickly. "Uh, I…I've got to go." She stammered and pulled her hand from his. "It was nice meeting you, Jake. Excuse me." She turned and walked as quickly as she could toward the barn door.

Austin followed close behind. "I'll walk you out." He looked back over his shoulder briefly, throwing Jake a glare of warning. He didn't trust Jake Cutler, nor did he miss the way Jake had looked at Alyssa.

Jake watched as the two left. A huge, satisfied smile broke out across his face. Yes, this was going to be a very interesting summer. Alyssa was beautiful, in a sweet and innocent way; he would enjoy watching that innocence bow in submission to him.

Three

Austin watched Alyssa make her way back through the path. A smile played on his lips as he lingered where he stood after she had disappeared behind the trees. Finally he turned and headed back, praising God on the way for the obvious change in Alyssa since the night before.

His smile faded quickly when he entered the barn and saw Jake still there. Walking past him without a glance, Austin went directly to the stall marked "Midnight." Midnight–Austin's own pure black Morgan–had a fearfully powerful appearance. Austin grabbed his saddle and hoisted it upon the stallion's back, doing his best to ignore the approaching sound of footsteps.

Jake's voice echoed through the whole barn, slashing irritably at Austin's nerves. "So, Jacobs, is Alyssa your woman or what?"

Austin continued to strap the saddle onto the horse, not looking at the unwanted intruder. "She's not your type, Jake, that's all I can tell ya."

Jake laughed mockingly. "I think she's exactly my type."

Austin had finished saddling the horse and slowly turned around to look at Jake. "Stay away from her. Hurt her, and you'll regret it." His eyes blazed, belying the threatening calm of his voice. Austin didn't stay to catch Jake's reaction but led the horse past him and out of the barn.

It was a little after 9:00 a.m. when Alyssa entered her office in town and sank thankfully into the chair behind her desk. Though a bit tired after all the walking she had done that morning, she felt better than she had in weeks. Her thoughts drifted involuntarily to the intriguing stranger she had met. The way Jake had studied her lingered in her memory, causing her heart to beat with an unfamiliar sense of anticipation.

Almost reluctantly, she forced Jake from her thoughts when hearing a knock on her door. Seeing her assistant through the glass, she smiled and waved her in. The tall woman with short red hair walked briskly in. "Don't tell me—you got a flat tire on the way."

Alyssa laughed and looked up at the woman's amused, lightly freckled face. "I know, Candy—I'm late, and I'm sorry."

"You're lucky I decide to put up with you. Now, we need to discuss today's meeting with Barton." She knew that Candy more than put up with her. Their friendship had grown into one of mutual admiration since the day they first began working together for Alyssa's father.

When the ranch began bringing in record profits several years prior, Ken Langer realized he had more than a ranch in the country; he had a potential goldmine. So he built the Langer office building and made Alyssa the head of marketing.

"I'll get the files." Bracing her hands on the top of the desk, Alyssa quickly pulled herself to her feet. Just as quickly, she fell back into her chair with a surprised gasp.

Hurrying around the desk, Candy knelt next to her chair. "Are you all right, Ally?"

"I'm fine, just a little stunned is all." Red flooded her face in embarrassment over her lack of grace. "My legs seemed to have turned to Jell-O!" Alyssa's attempt at easing Candy's mind with humor failed miserably. "Really, I'm fine. I've walked around too much this morning and just need to rest for a minute."

"Well, OK, but you stay in that chair and don't move an inch! If you need anything, you let me know." Candy ended all arguments before they could begin. "Now, tell me where those files are, and I'll get them."

With Alyssa's instructions, Candy found the needed folder, then grabbed a chair from the corner of the office. Sitting down in front of the desk, she focused her green eyes closely on Alyssa. "Are you sure you're OK? We can put this off for a while if you want to rest."

"You just told me how important this meeting is; besides, I'm fine!"

Candy still looked skeptical but didn't push the issue. "Barton will be here in an hour or so." A twinkle suddenly lit the older woman's eyes. "You know, I hear Barton is available."

"What's that got to do with our advertising campaign?"

The corners of the secretary's mouth hinted a grin. "Nothing, I was just commenting on someone we will be working with."

"Fine, but don't distract him! We are lucky Mr. Barton himself has agreed to meet with us, and we need to remain professional."

"He's also bringing his nephew who's some kind of artistic genius. He's about your age, I think." Candy's mouth exploded into a full-blown smile.

"Enough!" Alyssa's half-hearted warning was met with a self-satisfied laugh from the redhead. The two then managed to go over last minute details and take some notes for the upcoming meeting.

Less than an hour later, Candy ushered in a handsome gentleman in his late fifties. Mr. Barton went to Alyssa and introduced himself. "I apologize, Ms. Langer, for my nephew. It seems Peter's class got out a bit late. He should be here any minute. I'm truly sorry for this inconvenience."

"There's no need to apologize. Have a seat, and please call me Alyssa." Mr. Barton sat in one of the three chairs arranged around her desk, and Candy took the one closest to him. "So, your nephew is still in school?"

"Yes. Peter is working toward his master's degree. He has a brilliant mind and can make any idea you have come alive. If you can put up with his little differences, you'll find it's worth it in the end." Alyssa grew slightly uneasy at the description of his nephew and was just about to question him concerning Peter's 'little differences,' when Peter Barton knocked on the door.

"Hello. I'm sorry I'm late." Alyssa simply stared at the young man as Mr. Barton introduced him.

"Ms. Langer, this is my nephew, Peter."

Peter stretched his hand out to her and began speaking in a jumble of quick, agitated words. "Hi, I'm sorry I'm late. My bike got a flat tire on the way over. I must have hit some glass on the sidewalk or something. I don't know where the glass would have come from. Maybe a soda bottle or something. I didn't even have a chance to go home and change after class. My class ran late, too. My professor just keeps talking and talking sometimes."

"It's OK, please sit down. We were just getting started."

Mr. Barton's eyes traveled to the ceiling, and Alyssa could almost hear him mentally counting to ten. She watched his jaw finally relax, and his eyes return to glare at his peculiar nephew once again. Alyssa exchanged a curious glance with Candy before looking Peter over more closely.

Peter Barton wore a multicolored shirt that hung loosely around his average size build and came down into a v-neck, an old pair of jeans, and sandals. Alyssa scanned all this quickly, but what held her fascination was the little African beanie he wore on his head, which seemed to go with his rose tinted glasses. Peter shifted in his chair a couple of times, crossing and uncrossing his legs.

Alyssa tried to ease her own tension before beginning. "I'm told you're the creative genius, so why don't I tell you a little about what I want to do with the campaign and we can go from there?"

"OK." Peter leaned forward in his chair and looked at her expectantly. "I'm anxious to hear your ideas and will do everything I can to give you what you're looking for." His hands waved at random, accentuating the passion that charged even the simplest words he spoke.

Alyssa's opinion of Peter was changed instantly in light of his sincerity. Her anxiety melted away as she shared her vision for the intended campaign. "As you know, we are advertising horses. We have a couple of different target markets that we want to reach.

The first is those who want to buy our horses for breeding purposes or personal use.

"Our second market is those who want to rent a horse for the day. We have some beautiful land groomed specifically for people to come in and follow one of the trails that lead to various spots."

Alyssa paused to see that everyone understood her so far. Candy was quickly taking notes, while Mr. Barton sat with his arms crossed in front of his chest, looking politely interested. She talked a little more about the expected customers and made sure there were no questions concerning the targeted markets before she explained what she wanted to see in the advertisements.

"I want the commercials, magazine ads, and whatever else we decide on doing, to be different. I don't want them just to say that we have great horses. I want them to show people what riding the horse is like. The quality and breed of our horses speak for themselves. What we need to do is get the Langer name out there, and make it known for its horses. It's an image that I'm looking for—a feeling."

Leaning forward in her chair, Alyssa attempted to clarify her thoughts. "I want something that makes people want our horses not just because they're the best but because they associate our horses with a feeling. There are many ranches in the Northeast alone that have great reputations, so we need an edge."

Peter leaned forward, resting his elbows on his knees, and clasped his hands in front of him. He was staring intently at her as his head bobbed like a little windup toy unable to stop. Encouraged by his interest, Alyssa continued her explanation.

"I haven't ridden a horse in a very long time actually, but I remember what it was like. There's a feeling of exhilaration when you're riding." Alyssa's eyes held the sparkle of a lost memory blended with a current fantasy. "It's almost intoxicating."

Seeing Peter's head still bobbing, she went on. "I want to capture that feeling in the ads, make people associate that feeling with our horses." The original zeal she had for her idea began to resurface as she spoke directly to Peter and saw his response. He seemed to actually catch the vision she had.

Mr. Barton's voice interrupted the connection. "What was the feeling you wanted to capture, Ms. Langer—being *intoxicated*?" His voice held an obvious sarcastic undertone, crushing Alyssa's excitement like a boot stomping an insect.

"No, Mr. Barton, not the feeling of being intoxicated." Straining to keep the irritation out of her voice, Alyssa managed to hide her annoyance. "It's more like a feeling of freedom. When you're riding, nothing else seems to matter except the complete freedom you feel. It's a time for letting go of life's problems, releasing all of your stress. It's like…it's like, dancing."

"Dancing?" Mr. Barton made no attempt to hide his cynicism this time.

Alyssa looked directly at him, not restraining her exasperation any longer. "Yes, dancing. Just watching someone dance makes you long for something. If I watch ballet, the grace and beauty of the people make me crave that kind of grace and beauty in my life. There's a freedom in dancing that makes others want that feeling."

Peter suddenly decided to give his own impassioned opinion, stumbling over his thoughts and waving his hands around to emphasize each word. "Yeah, I know what you mean. I mean, it's like you said—it's a feeling. People just get carried away when they dance, like riding a horse, I guess. I can imagine that feeling of leaving the world behind and being free for a while. I mean, I don't think it would be too hard to capture that in an ad. I could. I can come up with something that you'd like, if you would like me to try."

"Yeah, I'd like you to try." Alyssa smiled sincerely at him. "Why don't I give you a week to come up with some ideas, and we'll meet again Friday. Is that good for you?"

"Sure, that's great."

"Actually, I don't think I'll be able to make it on Friday, Ms. Langer." Mr. Barton rose from his chair while speaking in his once again polite and formal tone.

"That's OK, Mr. Barton," Alyssa spoke sweetly while extending her hand to him. "I don't think we'll be needing you. Thank you so much for coming." Shaking Peter's hand, she thanked him as well. "I'll see you soon."

As Mr. Barton and Peter turned to leave, Alyssa noticed for the first time the back of Peter's shirt. In big bold letters the words *Jesus Freak* were printed among the motley of colors. When the door was shut behind them, Alyssa looked at Candy and laughed out loud.

"Jesus Freak?" Candy looked curiously at Alyssa, making them both laugh.

"Well, he certainly was different!"

"Do you think he knows what he's doing?"

Alyssa hesitated briefly before answering honestly. "Yeah, I think he does."

For the rest of the day Alyssa tried to focus on her work while images of Jake Cutler kept slipping into her mind. He wasn't nearly as handsome as Austin, but no man she had ever seen was. Anyway, it did her no good to compare other men to a man she could never have.

She felt completely foolish for dwelling on a guy she had barely even spoken to. Nonetheless, she forced herself to quickly finish up some necessary work and left the office an hour earlier than usual. She suddenly felt the need to be at the stables that afternoon.

Four

Catherine wiped the sweat from her forehead before it was able to travel down her face. Normally she loved working in the garden, but the heat was stifling, making a pleasant hobby into a draining chore. She couldn't remember it ever being so hot, especially in May. She would have waited to pull out the weeds but knew they'd grow quickly, killing the flowers with deep, thick roots, choking out all life and beauty.

Hearing the back door open, she looked up from her work to see Alyssa. "You're home early."

"I just had a meeting. It went pretty quick, so I thought I'd get the rest of my work done and leave." Alyssa left the porch and joined her mother in the garden. "The flowers are more beautiful every year."

"Yeah, I just wish it wasn't so hot."

"You should go inside and cool off if you're that hot."

"I will in awhile."

"OK. I think I'll take a walk." Alyssa's attempt to sound casual failed miserably.

"Take a walk!" Catherine stared as if Alyssa had just sprouted antlers.

"Yeah." A defiant glare emerged in defense of her mother's objection.

"Where are you going? You were walking all over the place this morning. Don't you think you should rest?" The question came as more of an angry command.

"I'm not tired. I'm just going to the stables. Relax, Mom." Alyssa tried to keep her voice level but found her irritation mounting.

"I am *relaxed*!" Her mother spat the word Alyssa knew she detested. "Are you at least going to take your wheelchair?"

"No, I'll be fine."

Catherine ripped out another weed angrily, accidentally taking a few new rose buds with it. "You'll be fine. Then I won't hear from you for hours and find you stuck in the middle of the woods unable to walk home!"

Frustrated beyond words, Alyssa turned abruptly and started down the path. "I'll be home later."

Catherine continued yanking roots from the ground, no longer paying much attention to what she was doing. She was angry and needed something to take it out on—her roses just happened to have the misfortune of being in front of her. At times Catherine wanted to slap the mocking look off her daughter's face.

She had never forgotten the fear that had gripped her seven years ago when Alyssa decided to go for a walk. Catherine assumed her daughter would go to the lake as usual, but Alyssa took off down the path toward the cabins. Instead of going to the end of the path that led to the ranchers' homes, she followed a faintly marked trail that veered off deep into the woods. Though she grew extremely tired as she went, she refused to stop and rest. By nine o'clock that night Catherine had sent Ken and some of the ranchers out looking for her.

The hour it took to find Alyssa was the longest in Catherine's life. She had been waiting in the window, praying silently, when she saw Ken coming with their daughter in his arms. Alyssa had grown so exhausted that she collapsed in the woods, barely able to move. The guilt that had consumed Catherine as she nursed her child back to health never seemed to go away.

Stopping her work, she sat back wiping her forehead again. *Why me, Lord?* The thought brought tears to her eyes as she fought oppressive weariness. *How much more do I have to take?*

Catherine got up and brushed the dirt from her clothes. Breathing deeply, she attempted to ease her anger. Her guilt brought resentment, and resentment brought frustration. She resented Alyssa for being sick and causing her so much work and worry. She was frustrated with herself for feeling such things toward the child she loved. On top of it all lay an oppression that came with the knowledge of a future sentenced with little hope of relief.

Alyssa started to feel guilty halfway to the stables. She knew her mom was just worried, but it made her so angry when Catherine treated her as a child, glaring at her ridiculously. Alyssa was sure that Catherine wished she had never been born and felt guilty for being alive.

She sat down on a nearby stump to rest. Years of heartache came rolling back in her memory; childhood scenes lingered in the recesses of Alyssa's mind. Whenever she looked at her mother—saw the hard stare and felt their struggling, frustrated relationship—she remembered times that seemed ancient and far away.

Her childhood was filled with troubling new experiences she and Catherine shared. She remembered the many hospitals and doctors: She heard her mother singing songs about patience as they sat in waiting rooms. She saw Catherine sticking her tongue out and making faces when the doctor turned his back, making Alyssa giggle delightfully. She felt her mother's hand squeezing hers reassuringly as needles were stuck in her arms.

No, the memories of hospitals and sicknesses were never happy, but her mother's closeness and small gestures of encouragement were sweet. Alyssa held on to those times, for they spoke of love. She smiled slightly and began to softly sing. It was a song she and her mother sang when Alyssa was a tiny girl and she was bored or scared. "Have patience, have patience…God has patience too…"

34

God. How often had her mother talked of God in those hospital rooms? She couldn't count the times. Alyssa was very aware of God as a child; He had been her best friend. He still was, wasn't He?

A bumblebee came swooping by Alyssa's ear, scaring her senseless and breaking the past memory. She got up from her stump and quickly escaped. She would focus her thoughts on more pleasant things, like Jake. What would she do if she saw him again? She wanted him to see her, to look at her as he did before. Surprised at her feelings, she wondered what had come over her with such instant power.

She reached the clearing and saw Rebecca sitting on the grass near the stables, watching Austin work with one of the horses inside the fence. Paige was running around laughing and talking to new insect friends.

Rebecca waved at her as Alyssa made her way to where she sat. Alyssa never tired of her sister. "What'cha doing, as if I didn't know?" She grinned at Rebecca knowingly as she sat next to her.

"Just look at that perfect creature, have you ever seen anything more gorgeous?" Rebecca's green eyes twinkled as they moved toward the rancher nearby. Alyssa looked over at Austin, her mouth dropping unconsciously. He wore faded jeans and a tee shirt, his lean, muscular body dark from the sun. The young stallion with him was yet to be broken in, rearing high as Austin held the reigns tightly.

"No, I don't think I have." She said it so bluntly that both girls began to laugh. "So what are you doing down here really?"

"Paige wanted to come see the horses, although she's more interested in the bugs right now. And I'm much more interested in our favorite rancher."

Paige came running when she saw Alyssa. "Ally!" She fell into Alyssa's lap happily, hugged her tightly, and then sat up. "Come play with me, I found an ant house!"

Alyssa adored the precious face that lit up whenever the child spoke. "Oh Sweetie," she said smoothing the fine blonde hair from her face. "I'd love to, but I'm pretty tired right now. Maybe later, OK?" She brushed at Paige's fine blonde hair as her small mouth dropped slightly.

"Alright." Her smile returned as quickly as it had left before she ran off to play once more.

As they watched Paige, the girls laughed and reminisced over their childhood days. It was the first time they had talked in weeks, as they were now. "I've missed you, little sister." Alyssa smiled when they both became silent.

"I know. I miss you too."

"I don't even know what's been happening in your life."

"There's really not much to tell." Rebecca was silent a moment, then shrugged. "I go out sometimes with a bunch from college. We don't do a whole lot, just hang out; sometimes we party." Sighing in frustration, Rebecca plucked a dandelion and began to pick at the tiny bright yellow pedals. "I don't know. I need something more in my life, and I don't know really what it is."

"Is everything OK?"

"Oh yeah, I'm just kind of restless. I know I'll eventually find whatever it is I'm looking for. I like my friends and have fun sometimes, but I don't think it's really for me anymore. I feel like I'm too old to be partying and doing things that get you absolutely nowhere." Rebecca threw the remaining green stem void of petals.

"You always have been more mature than most."

Rebecca smiled slightly. "I don't know about that. I just know there's something out there for me that I haven't found yet. I'm hungry for it."

Alyssa saw that spark of hunger in her sister's eyes and wished for it in her own. Any kind of hunger, or hope for something, would be better than the nothing that she was living in. However, there was something stirring in her recently, but that hunger scared her, for she wasn't sure where it may lead. The thought caused her to break the silence that had fallen between them.

"Have you met the new foreman?"

"Yeah."

Rebecca's rather flat reply warned Alyssa to tread carefully with her next question. "Why do you say it like that?"

"I don't like him. He didn't impress me."

"Why?" Alyssa was slightly offended by her sister's reaction, and she wasn't sure why.

"It's his whole attitude. It's obvious he thinks a lot of himself, and assumes everyone else should too. He's one of those womanizers who undresses you with his eyes. He's a jerk."

Alyssa sat stunned without saying anything. Jake looked at every woman like he had looked at her? She felt a huge disappointment in that little revelation and suddenly wanted to cry. She scolded herself for letting her emotions get out of control. She didn't really know him, so why should she care? Yet he was the only one who had ever looked at her with such interest.

"Have you met him?" Rebecca's question broke into her troubled thoughts.

"Once. I didn't talk to him long enough to know what he's like." Alyssa purposely evaded any more questions, and the two became silent.

Austin had disappeared into the barn moments before and now came back out. Having put the horse back in its stall, he now walked to the girls who sat staring at his every move. He smiled as he came near. "Mind if I join you?"

Both girls quickly invited him to sit down.

"Alyssa and I saw you with the stallion. How's the training going?"

"The horse is beautiful but not real cooperative yet."

Alyssa smiled a little shyly at Austin. "You're very good with him."

"Thanks." Austin's eyes met hers. "He'll come around."

Rebecca watched as Austin looked at Alyssa with a deep, searching stare. She had seen that look in Austin's eyes before, an easily recognizable interest, always for Alyssa. Casually she looked around to check on Paige and noticed that she was getting quite far from them. "Excuse me while I go get the munchkin." She bounced quickly to her feet and went after her niece.

After a moment of awkward silence, Austin spoke. "So how was the big meeting you had today?"

Alyssa was pleasantly surprised that he remembered. "It went well." She told him about the meeting, making him laugh at her description of Peter.

The sun was going down slowly, getting hotter as it got closer to setting. Paige came over as Austin stood and went toward the child. "Austin!"

37

Paige yelled as she ran straight into his waiting arms. He lifted her high in the air until she squealed in delight. "I found an ant house, wanna see?"

"Paige, we have to go home now. Mommy will be looking for you." Rebecca glanced at her watch. "Give Austin and Ally a hug goodbye."

Paige did as she was told, hugging Austin, then reaching over and hugging Alyssa while still in Austin's arms. He then set her down, and Rebecca led her back toward the house.

Austin looked back at Alyssa. "So what are your plans this evening?"

"I just thought I'd come down and see Dancer again. I didn't get to spend much time with him this morning."

"Why don't you take him for a ride?"

"A ride?" Alyssa looked away uncomfortably.

"Sure. I know he'd love it and so would you."

"Austin, it sounds nice but...I can't ride."

"Sure you can. You'll be a great rider with me behind you."

Alyssa looked up in sudden excitement to catch his playful smile and the gleam in his eye. "You'll take me?"

"I would love to." He held out his hand for her to take. She put her hand in his and followed him into the barn. Dancer was waiting in his stall and seemed to perk up when he saw Alyssa.

Austin grabbed the saddle and got Dancer ready as Alyssa watched him, now getting nervous. "Austin, maybe I shouldn't. I haven't ridden since I was little when dad took me. My balance is really bad if I'm not on stable ground..."

When the horse was ready Austin led him out of the barn, glancing at Alyssa with a knowing grin. Alyssa followed closely, still listing reasons why she couldn't possibly ride.

Austin stopped her before she could continue with her excuses. "Lyssa, trust me. I wouldn't let anything happen to you. I'll be right behind you holding you the whole time, I promise." His gentle voice was followed by an irresistible grin.

His eyes were so sincere and caring as he spoke that Alyssa would have trusted him with her very life. She smiled compliantly and walked over to the waiting horse.

"Put your arm around me, and I'll lift you into the saddle." Alyssa did as she was told, surprised at how broad his shoulders felt beneath her arm. He lifted her as if she were weightless and set her gently into the saddle.

"Oh my goodness!" Alyssa gasped clutching Austin's shoulder tightly. She was instantly scared at how high up and completely unstable she felt. She held on to his shoulder, fearing for her life.

"It's OK. I've got you." He continued to hold her waist until she was comfortable. "I'm going to swing up behind you. Hold on to Dancer's mane, and you'll be fine."

Alyssa did not like the idea of letting go of Austin for even an instant, but she obeyed. Before she had time to get a hold of the mane, he had mounted the horse behind her. He slipped his arm around her waist, holding her gently but securely. Alyssa relaxed at the feel of his strong arm and sat back against his chest as he reached around with his other hand to grab the reins.

With a slight touch of his heel, Austin urged the horse into a slow pace. A tiny squeal escaped Alyssa's lips as she grabbed Austin's arm compulsively. His hold tightened around her with steady reassurance. "You're alright, Lyssa, I've got you." His soothing, confident voice comforted her greatly. "I want to take you someplace special."

"Where?"

"You'll see." Though Alyssa couldn't see Austin, his voice betrayed the smile on his face.

Slowly Austin urged Dancer into a trot. Before long they were galloping far away from the stables. They crossed a great deal of open grassland, passing by forests on one side, until the trees got thicker and spread out around them.

Alyssa couldn't believe how exhilarating riding was. It had taken some time for her to get used to, but suddenly she felt like she was flying. She loosened her grip on Austin's arm but continued to lean against his chest for stability. She stuck her arms out, letting the wind blow over them. For the first time in her life she felt strong. No longer did she have two weak legs carrying her; she had four strong ones that could take her anywhere.

She remembered what she had said, that riding a horse must bring a great feeling of freedom, and now she knew. The feeling was wondrous, and she soaked in every minute of it. "This is incredible, Austin!"

Austin urged the horse on faster, listening to the sweet feminine laughter that rose from below him. Her hair flew wildly, tickling his face. The scent of it mingled with the wind like a soft perfume, bringing an urge to bury his face in the golden tresses and drink in the fragrance. He shook his head sharply, surprised and nervous at such an impulse.

Finally, Austin slowed the horse and turned into the sparse forest, following an old worn path that looked as if it had been forgotten for years.

It seemed to Alyssa that they had come quite far from home. "Where are we going?"

"It's my secret place. It looks as if people used to come here at one time but not anymore."

The trees grew thicker then ended abruptly, opening to a small clearing. It was here that Austin pulled the reins, bringing the horse to a halt. Alyssa looked around, wide-eyed, surveying the breathtaking view. Thick green grass covered the area and was divided by a small bubbling stream. Wild flowers grew everywhere among big oak trees.

Austin slid off the horse, making sure not to let go of Alyssa. She turned and put her hands on his shoulders as he took her by the waist and lifted her easily to the ground. For a fraction of an instant they stood holding each other before awkwardly pulling away.

Alyssa turned and looked around. "This place is so beautiful. How did you ever find it?"

"I was exploring one day, hoping to find some secluded place to pray. I like to pray in the middle of God's creation."

Alyssa looked up and saw that his eyes were very serious. She had never heard him talk about praying before.

"I've never brought anyone here until now."

"Why did you bring me?" she asked softly.

"I don't know." A boyish grin that Alyssa found adorable spread across his face.

"I'm glad you did." Alyssa smiled back at him, then headed toward the stream.

Austin tied Dancer's reins around the tree, allowing him room to graze. Walking over to the stream's edge, he sat down beside Alyssa. They remained quiet as they listened to the brook babble incoherently.

Alyssa broke the sacred silence in a hushed, serene voice. "Thank you for taking me riding and for bringing me here. It's been so long since I've been this happy. I can't tell you what this means to me."

Austin discerned the sincerity in her voice without seeing her face. He also heard the longing laced in her words. His heart reached out, and he prayed for words that would give her comfort. "I'm glad you came with me. You deserve joy, Lyssa."

She smiled bitterly and grew reflective. "Sometimes I don't think I do."

"What do you mean?" Though inside he felt a sudden urge to punish whoever might dare hurt her, he kept his voice calm.

Embarrassed by what she had revealed, Alyssa attempted to lighten her voice. "I'm sorry. I've never said anything like that to anyone before. Let's change the subject."

"Everyone needs to talk sometimes. Whatever you've been holding in seems to be eating you up inside. Talk to me." He watched her carefully, raked his hand through his thick hair, and waited for her to speak.

"Thank you for caring." She looked deeply into his eyes then turned again to the traveling stream. "I've just been going through some things lately. My mother and I aren't getting along, and it gets worse all the time. There are other things that I have to deal with that I really don't know how to explain."

"Just speak from your heart."

Austin's gentle probing threatened to destroy Alyssa's wall of resistance. She wanted so much to open up to him. He cared; she could see it in his eyes. But what would he say if he knew her whole heart? She couldn't possibly pour out all her thoughts and fears to this man, could she?

"I guess I just get scared sometimes."

"Of what?"

"Mostly my future." Feeling completely foolish, yet yearning to find compassion from someone, words began to pour from her disquieted soul. "It seems like all my life I've been alone. That probably sounds stupid coming from someone with such a big family."

"It doesn't sound stupid at all."

Alyssa looked at him. "I know there are people that love me but not in the way I need them to. My family and friends have no idea who I really am. There's so much inside of me that I want to share with someone."

"Share it with me." His gentle smile embraced her, breaking the last of her reticence.

"I have so many dreams and desires but worry that I'll never experience any of them."

"God says to ask in His name, and He will answer. Delight in Him, give Him your life, and He will give you the desires of your heart." Austin spoke with an overwhelming intensity, which fueled his words with authority.

She looked out at the lowering sun. "I have asked God for many things in my life, few of which He has given me."

"Don't give up on God, Lyssa. He has many blessings for you; you just have to seek Him."

Discussing God with Austin made her uncomfortable for reasons she chose not to ponder, so she steered the subject away from God. "I want to share my life with someone, but what if my disease starts to progress?" She glanced at him but didn't wait for an answer. "I've seen what having to care for a person can do to another person. I've seen the resentment in my mother's eyes. It would kill me if the man I loved had to end up taking care of me and eventually came to resent me." Her delicate face held a sad, distant expression of defeat.

Austin sat silent, stunned by what he was hearing. Impulsively he reached out and took her hand in his. Her small hand grasped his willingly, drawing strength from it. "Real love, the kind that God gives, holds no resentment. It places a desire in you to serve the person you love. Someday a man is going to rejoice in each moment he has with you, no matter what he has to do to get it." Austin's deep voice was husky with emotions that he couldn't identify.

The conviction in his voice startled Alyssa. "Thank you, Austin." She squeezed his hand, then let go. "I appreciate your encouragement."

Wanting to get the focus off of herself, she asked him about his own life. "Tell me about yourself, about where you came from."

"Well, let's see, I came from Dallas, was raised on a ranch, and was an only child. Any more questions?"

"Yes!" Her face suddenly split into an enchanting smile. "I want to know all about you, every last sordid detail!"

Austin laughed with her. "I suppose you'll find out the whole truth someday anyway. I certainly wasn't an angel, at least not when I hit high school." His joking grew reflective as he remembered his childhood. "My parents were great. I was very close to them." Alyssa watched as his face lit up. She could easily see the love he had for his mother and father.

Austin looked out past the stream, his face sobering. "When I was fourteen they both died in a car accident. After that my world went downhill. My aunt and uncle came to run the ranch. I used to love working with my father but couldn't bear the thought of it without him." He sounded so distant that Alyssa wanted to cry for him.

Coming back to the present, he looked over at Alyssa and continued his story. "In school I started hanging with a rough group of kids. I did every drug going, drank constantly, and stole to support my addiction. By sixteen I ended up in a juvenile facility. I was determined to show God how much I hated Him for taking my parents away."

A chill went down Alyssa's spine. She was stunned by the story she was hearing. Austin didn't seem like he had the capacity to do anything that he was describing. "What happened?"

"I was in and out of jail until I was twenty-two. I remember the day exactly. I was up for parole when this preacher came to my cell. He looked at me as no one had ever looked at me before. His eyes shone with some kind of brightness that I didn't understand. Now I know that it was the light of God shining through him. It was like God just walked into my cell, and I immediately fell to my knees sobbing before this preacher."

Austin stopped for a moment, remembering the scene that had changed his life seven years ago. "I cried and begged God, right there in my cell for forgiveness. All I knew was that I had to come clean of everything before God. And that preacher stood there looking at me with love, not speaking a single word! When I finally confessed everything I could possibly think of to confess, I just stayed there on the floor crying softly, hoping God still loved me.

"Then the preacher knelt next to me and wrapped his arms around me. He spoke for the first time, saying, 'Jesus loves you. He forgives and forgets everything you've just repented of. It's all gone! You've received your pardon from Christ!'"

Austin's words poured out of him with gleaming eyes. He spoke as if he were reliving it all again. "Later that day, Preacher Mike helped me get parole. My life was never the same after that. I went back home, worked the ranch, and got my life straight with God. I've belonged to Him ever since and have never been happier or more blessed in my life." He looked at her, hoping she would glean some hope from his testimony.

Alyssa was quiet for a moment, letting his words sink in before she spoke. "I find it so hard to believe that those things happened to you! We never know what another person has been through in life. It's weird how you just broke before the preacher even spoke a word."

"It's not that weird really, that's just the way God can work. His Spirit can saturate people's lives to the point that others are affected if they even enter the same room as a Spirit-filled Christian."

Alyssa was somewhat confused by his "spirit" talk. She searched for words of support, or understanding, or just something to say. "I didn't realize that you were so religious. That's great for you." After speaking she felt incredibly stupid, somehow knowing she said exactly the wrong thing.

"Religious!" Austin grabbed at his heart, moaned, and fell backward as if he had been shot. He lay there on the ground with arms sprawled out on each side. "You make me sound like those monks who take a vow of silence and poverty." Alyssa stared at him in shock until he started laughing without restraint, then she felt laughter escaping from her own mouth. After a moment they were both roaring with laughter for no real reason.

It took a few minutes before they each caught their breath. When they did, Alyssa wiped the tears from her eyes and spoke through

44

giggles. "I promise never to call you religious anymore." Both of them began laughing again.

Eventually Alyssa noticed how quickly the sun was disappearing. Long shadows were stretching from the trees, while the sky was on fire with brilliant pinks and oranges. "I have to go. Mom's going to be mad. She usually waits for me to get home, and I didn't tell her where I was going."

"OK, come on." Austin stood and held his hand out to her. "We'll get you home, Ms. Langer."

"My, aren't we the Southern gentleman! I guess Becca was right about you." She took his hand with a smile and walked with him to where Dancer stood.

"What else did Becca say?" Austin was immensely enjoying the deeper level of friendship they now shared.

"I'll never tell," Alyssa laughed playfully up at him.

He grinned back as he lifted her once again in his arms. "You know, instead of putting you on the horse, I could carry you down and throw you into that stream."

"No you won't!" She tried to sound severe, but her laughter took over. Austin lifted her into the saddle and climbed up behind. Alyssa quickly resumed her previous position resting against his chest. More than she would admit, even to herself, she enjoyed being in his arms.

The ride home went too quickly for both of them. Austin rode to the backyard of her house and helped her off the horse. They stood for moment looking into each other's eyes.

"Thank you again. I will remember this day as one of the happiest ever." She spoke softly from her heart.

"We'll go again soon. I'm glad we got to know each other a little better." He wanted to say something intelligent or suave but only came up with words that sounded hollow. It frustrated him when he had been so at ease moments before. Impulsively, Alyssa gave him a quick hug, then backed away, saying goodbye as he watched her go.

Entering through the glass doors, Alyssa was relieved to see that her mother was not in the living room. It really wasn't how late Alyssa came home that angered Catherine. It could be five in the afternoon, and her mother would still seem irritated. It annoyed Alyssa to no end, for she had no idea how to appease Catherine.

Despite her foreboding over the coming confrontation, her elation over the evening she had spent with Austin eased any fear. She wanted to shout her excitement and hoped her mom would share her joy. It might give the two something to talk about without yelling.

She took a deep breath and headed for the kitchen. "Mom, I'm home."

She found Catherine sitting at the kitchen table cradling a cup of coffee in her hand. Alyssa's elation quickly evaporated when greeted by the glare she had come to easily recognize. As children, Becca and Ally would joke about Catherine's stare that could cause grown men to cry and little children to die. They had even made up a little song about it, which they were very proud of at the time.

Her mother's voice cut in on the thought. "Where have you been, Alyssa?"

"With Austin." Alyssa was greatly vexed when her voice mumbled in humility. She hated that she regressed to acting five-years-old again whenever her mother used that tone.

"Do you realize that I had no idea where you were? How am I supposed to know if you've fallen and hurt yourself or if I should go looking for you? You have no consideration for what I go through when I don't know where you are!"

Alyssa's anger started taking over, and she looked her mother in the eye. "I told you I was going to the stables." She tried not to raise her voice. Alyssa had a great deal of respect for her mother, but there were times she felt that Catherine was being totally unreasonable.

"That was almost five hours ago! What were you doing for five hours at the stables with Austin?"

The implications draped in her mother's voice caused Alyssa's temper to flare. She knew that Catherine didn't believe anything improper had gone on but rather implied it simply to upset Alyssa.

She gritted her teeth trying to control, rather than hide, her anger. "He took me for a ride on Dancer." How badly she wanted to scream at her mother for being so impossible.

"He what?" Catherine's eyes bugged out of her head. "You could have been hurt!"

"Oh jeez, Mom! Let's not start that, OK?"

"Start what, Alyssa? I'm just wondering if you ever consider the consequences of what you do! What would have happened if you had fallen off the horse?" Catherine's loud voice echoed in the kitchen. She couldn't believe the ignorance and total lack of responsibility of her daughter.

"There was no chance of me falling off the horse. Austin had total control over the horse and me. I'm going to bed now." She effectively ended the conversation before her mother could continue and turned to head for her room, leaving her mother staring after her.

Five

Thursday came quickly, bringing a growing anxiety in the pit of Alyssa's stomach. There had been very little conversation between herself and her mother over the past few days, but Catherine did say she would meet Alyssa at her doctor's appointment.

Rows of trees passed by, separated by potato fields, as Alyssa stared through the windshield. Usually the simplistic beauty of her surroundings fascinated her, but today her mind was too cluttered, too anxious to see any beauty.

Big, run down farmhouses sat isolated in the country. The familiar sound of rusty screen doors squeaking open, then slamming shut as children ran out to play, could be heard in one's imagination. Clotheslines filled with sheets hung along front porches. Cows grazed in pastures that spotted the brilliant green landscapes. In some places in Northern Maine, time had ceased years ago, yet life still breathed beyond the fringes of progress.

Fidgeting in her seat, Alyssa realized that her previous hope of good news had waned since her last appointment. She pulled into the driveway of the doctor's office just as her mother was getting out of her own car. They began walking toward the building together, saying nothing for several minutes. Finally Alyssa broke the silence with the only words she could find.

"I hope the appointment doesn't last long. I'm sure he'll tell me I'm doing well. Don't you think?" Desperate for encouragement, she looked at her mother.

"I don't know." Catherine's flat answer stung Alyssa, bringing unseen tears to her eyes.

The two were ushered into the doctor's office and sat in chairs facing the massive oak desk. Alyssa folded and re-folded her hands while looking around at the familiar room, trying to get her mind off her growing nausea. *Everything is fine Ally. Don't be nervous. So you've had a few bad days—you've just been pushing yourself too hard.*

Dr. Matthews walked in, pulling Alyssa from her thoughts. "Hello, Ally, Catherine," he greeted them warmly. Closing the door, he came to sit behind his desk facing them. "How are you?"

"Fine," they said in unison. Neither had much of a desire for chitchat but were anxious to hear about whatever had brought them here. The doctor seemed to understand and wasted no time with small talk.

"Ally," he began slowly, uncertain as to how he should break the news. "We did some tests last week and have been watching your progress over the last few months. I've been your doctor since the day you were born, and we both know I'm no expert in the field of muscle diseases, but I do know your situation better than anyone." Dr. Matthews flipped through the thick chart in front of him, then looked at her once again with sincere compassion.

"Up until you were fifteen years old, you were in and out of the hospital constantly. As Catherine can relate, I told her on several occasions that you wouldn't survive another year." The doctor spoke gently as Alyssa's fear of impending doom heightened.

"At ten years of age, you had the rods put in your back to straighten your spine. That seemed to help considerably. You got stronger, you were healthy, and you had more energy. We have seen no muscle deterioration in almost fourteen years." The doctor paused a moment and looked directly at Alyssa. "Ally, the muscle disease you have doesn't behave in any kind of normal manner—it has a mind of its own. Unfortunately, after looking at your test results and seeing some of the things that are happening to you physically lately…I'm afraid that, um…it appears that your disease has…gone out of remission, if you want to call it that. The test results show deterioration of the muscles in almost every muscle group."

Alyssa felt every fiber in her body go numb, and her ears deafened. No, she couldn't have heard what he had just said. Her brain was melting and wouldn't register the doctor's words. What did he mean? Deterioration?

"What exactly are you saying, Dr. Matthews?" Her voice sounded cold and far away in her ears.

"Alyssa," Dr. Matthews said as gently as possible, "your muscles have started to deteriorate."

Each time he used the word *deteriorate* Alyssa could feel her nerves suddenly screeching, causing her to cringe. She got a mental image of her body decaying like a corpse. "Deteriorate?" she snapped, failing to calm the sudden wild rage that wanted to escape. "What exactly do you mean?" The hostility in her voice was not meant for the doctor, whom she had respected and grown fond of over the years, but she knew of no one else at whom to direct it.

Dr. Matthews took a deep breath and continued to speak. His voice was pained as he anguished over the fate that Alyssa was dealt. "Basically, the muscles in your body are wasting away, little by little. In effect, it will cause you to grow continually weaker."

"Waste away" rang in Alyssa's ears as her stomach turned and convulsed. Her hand flew to her mouth and remained there for a moment until the threat of vomiting had subsided.

Catherine was still in somewhat of a shock, yet a part of her had expected this kind of thing to happen to Alyssa's condition eventually. "What's going to happen now, Dr. Matthews? Is there anything we can do?"

The questions bombarded Alyssa's mind, making her stomach tremble again. She didn't want to hear the answers but was compelled to listen, like someone drawn to a gruesome car crash. The doctor's words ran together, and she wasn't quite sure if she was hearing him correctly.

"Well, the disease is going full force right now; the deterioration is progressing rapidly." Tears sprang to Alyssa's eyes, and she made no effort to stop them. Frozen in her seat, images of her future state clouded her mind with each word the doctor spoke. "That's why you have been experiencing so much fatigue and the reason for your falling spells."

"No," Alyssa's voice interrupted shakily. "No, I've just been working too hard. You know when I push myself those things happen. I can take it easier, I'll rest more…"

"Ally," he said, cutting off her desperate attempt to change the circumstances. "I'm afraid nothing you do will change what's happened, and nothing you did caused it. Yes, you will rest more, but it will be because you won't have the energy you used to."

"How bad will it get?" Alyssa had the awful impulse to slap her mother each time she asked those horrifying questions. What was wrong with her? Didn't she feel Alyssa's pain?

"If the progression continues, then Ally's strength will gradually weaken until she is unable to walk. She will eventually have to have an electric wheelchair—she won't have the strength to push a manual one. She will come to the place where she will need complete assistance with anything that requires physical strength." Dr. Matthews choked out the words. "We really don't know how far the disease will progress, but if it doesn't stop it could lead…to death," he finished quietly.

The room was silent for several moments. Alyssa closed her eyes as the tears rolled freely down her cheeks. On the outside she looked to be handling the information rather bravely, but in reality she was so overcome that she could not respond.

Catherine's next question broke the silence. "How long before these things happen?"

The doctor took a deep breath before answering. "If it continues to progress at this rate, it could be less than a year before she will require the wheelchair and assistance with daily routine activities."

For an instant Alyssa had the wild impulse to laugh hysterically. This whole thing was so ridiculous and sickening. What else could she do but laugh?

51

"We would like to do a muscle biopsy. It would give us a better idea of what we are dealing with, and it may help prepare us for future complications," Dr. Matthews explained.

Suddenly Alyssa was jerked from her frozen state. Her anger started to boil, and her eyes went wild. "Excuse me?" she almost shrieked. "You tell me I'm going to become a complete invalid in a year, and you want to do surgery to see what other complications there might be?" All attempts to control her rage dissolved as she teetered on momentary insanity.

"It may help us understand better what is happening to you. It will help us to help you," Dr. Matthews explained.

"Help me!" She bellowed back at him, not caring who might hear her in the waiting room. She stood to her feet and looked down on the only one at whom she could aim her anger. "How are you going to help me? I'm *deteriorating*," she spat the word with contempt. "All your other little biopsies didn't help me when I was young."

Tears streamed until Alyssa's face was soaked with them and she screamed each word between choking sobs. "How can you sit there and tell me I'm deteriorating and then say you want to take out more muscle so you can study it? I can't believe this! After fourteen years this thing starts progressing and you had no idea what was happening? You don't even know what it is!" Catherine sat dumbfounded watching her daughter.

"Why can't you fix it?" Alyssa paced around the room not really knowing what she wanted to say but wanting to scream at someone. Finally she stopped and turned back to look in the doctor's eyes.

"Give me a name for this, Dr. Matthews." Her voice suddenly became quite. A fierce fire burned in her eyes, yet if one looked beyond the anger at that moment, they would have caught the desperate look of a child pleading for help. "You just tell me what's destroying my body, and I'll let you do whatever you want to me."

Silence filled the room at Alyssa's challenge. After what seemed like an eternity, Dr. Matthews lifted his glistening eyes slowly to meet Alyssa's. "I'm sorry," he said almost inaudibly. "I can't...I don't know."

"Alyssa, sit down!" The sound of her mother's reprimand broke any reserve Alyssa had left. Wildly she flared her hands in the air accentuating each frenzied scream.

"Stop treating me like a child, Mother! You already treat me like some cripple. I'm a woman! A woman who will be completely useless and shriveled up before long! How in the world do you expect me to behave right now?" She stopped pacing and attempted to wipe some of the tears from her face. "I've got to get out of here." She suddenly opened the door and left as quickly as she could.

"Alyssa!" Catherine got up and started to go after her until Dr. Matthews stopped her.

"Let her go, Catherine. She needs time to deal with what she has just heard. So do you." Catherine sat back down and blinked her eyes several times. She would not allow anyone to see her cry. *Oh God, the pain.* She could feel the swell of hurt rising into her chest. She didn't like that kind of pain, for it made her feel helpless. She managed, as always, to suppress the pain, pushing it deep within her soul until she almost couldn't feel it anymore…almost.

Dr. Matthews's voice broke into her rage of emotions. "What are you going to do, Catherine?"

She looked up and eyed the well-meaning doctor. "What do you mean?" she asked shortly.

"Sooner or later you have to think about the future. Ally's needs are going to increase as time goes on. Eventually she'll need constant care."

Hot anger flashed in her eyes as she responded to his insinuation. "I intend to take care of her. I am her mother."

"You may need help, and it's best to look into those kinds of things early."

Catherine stood, fed up with where the conversation was going. "If you'll excuse me, I really don't feel like talking about this right now." She turned and stomped out of the office, slamming the door on her way while Dr. Matthews sat staring after her.

53

Alyssa drove aimlessly, wanting to escape from civilization. She saw a small dirt road that led through a potato field and headed down it. She drove until the road turned to lead back to the main street. There, in the middle of nowhere, surrounded by fields of silence, she stopped her car and got out. The numbness that had frozen her slowly slipped away and left a painful ache. Fresh tears coursed down her face, and she looked up into the brilliant blue sky.

"Why?" It was a cry that rang from the depths of her soul and flowed across the open fields. "Why have You done this to me? I thought You were supposed to love Your children. What have I done? Whatever it is, I'm sorry...I'm sorry for whatever sins I've committed. Please God, forgive me, and don't let this happen to me!" She continued to beg, as if her very life could be saved by it. Her pleas met with quiet stillness. Frustration grew until she felt crazed. She let out an ear-piercing scream and pounded the car.

When all her energy was spent, she slowly lowered herself to the ground and leaned against the car. She allowed her thoughts to drift to the future. The images she conjured were much worse than a grisly corpse in a horror flick. The more she thought about it, the more her stomach threatened her to stop. It wasn't long before she was vomiting what little she had eaten that morning.

Finally, she got up from the ground and climbed back into her car. She checked in the mirror to make sure she had cleaned herself up well enough. She wanted no one to know what a fool she had just made of herself. She would go home and show everyone how strong she was; that she was happy despite the death sentence that had been handed to her.

Before she left, she said a short prayer. "Forgive me, Lord, for questioning You. Thank You for choosing me for Your special purpose."

When Alyssa got home she found her mother in the kitchen sitting alone with an open Bible. Catherine looked up and saw the exhausted look on her daughter's face.

"You OK?" She tried to sound comforting but was unsure of the right words.

"Yeah, I'm just going to go lie down for a while." Alyssa left the kitchen and went to her room. Catherine watched her go, hearing her bedroom door close moments later. Slowly she closed her Bible. A heaviness pushed down upon her shoulders even as she tried to draw strength from the scriptures she had read.

Catherine's heart ached for her child and for the future. It also ached for herself. Life would only get harder from here on out. She could feel herself being closed in; the fence that kept her trapped was getting taller and closer. She prayed for the strength to take care of Alyssa as she grew worse and for the grace to glorify God in every situation. Though the torment was great, she did not cry.

Alyssa sat alone in her room, pressing a shaky pen to her journal.

I wish I had never been born. I feel so alone right now, like there's no one in my life who's worth living for—no one who cares. My life has been destroyed. Why, God?

I feel the darkness closing in again. I think I'll go to sleep before it catches me.

55

Six

"Peter Barton is here." Candy poked her head through the door.

Alyssa looked up from the papers on her desk. "Uh…give me five minutes, then show him in." Candy smiled and closed the door softly. Alyssa sighed at the coming appointment. She was in no mood to discuss marketing strategies or advertising projects.

She touched the clip holding her hair in a flattering twist at the back of her head and wondered if she looked as bad as she felt. She had no time to find a mirror, for Peter knocked on the door and came in sooner then expected. "Hi, how ya doing?"

Alyssa was instantly surprised at his appearance. He wore a comfortable-looking, dark teal suit and tie. He was actually handsome, looking not at all like the young man she had met a week ago.

She stood and welcomed him with a warm smile. "Why don't we sit over here? It will be more comfortable." She motioned to the small sofa and chairs in the corner of her office. When she was seated in one of the chairs, Peter sat on the sofa. "Did you come up with anything?"

"I think so. I'm kind of excited about it." He started pulling several large posters out of his bag and spread them on the table. "I just took what you said, about dancing and what you wanted for advertising, and came up with these."

Alyssa looked at the pictures in front of her. She was astonished at the obvious talent in the drawing and painting of the posters but was more amazed at what the scenes depicted. The first was of a beautiful woman riding a horse. The whole image revealed the wild abandonment that Alyssa had hoped for. She went through a couple different pictures similar to that one, marveling at the intricate detail of the horse and rider.

"These are wonderful, Peter," she said honestly, amazed that anyone could capture such emotion, bringing a picture to life.

"Thanks. I thought they would be great for magazines or even a good start for commercials."

Alyssa continued to look over the drawings, then stopped suddenly to inspect one more closely. She stared dumbfounded at the scene colored before her. It was set in a meadow with brilliant yellow wildflowers all around. A white stallion stood rearing high and powerful in one half of the picture. In the other half was a woman—a woman that looked exactly like Alyssa! The woman seemed to be dancing: Her hair was flying around her head in beautiful golden waves. Her arms were stretched wide as she twirled. And utter joy filled the woman's face.

"Peter, this girl…?" Alyssa tried to ask who it was but was speechless.

"I drew the woman to look like you," he said, slightly embarrassed.

"Why?" Alyssa's eyes remained riveted to the picture.

"That's what I saw while I was praying."

She looked up at him then, confusion evident in her eyes. Peter laughed slightly and tried to explain. "I always pray before starting this kind of project. Really, I can't do anything on my own. God gives me the inspiration and the talent to do what I do. While I was asking God to give me some ideas, these were the things He gave me. I saw you very clearly in that last one, dancing around like a child."

She again looked down at the picture. Peter's words and the lifelike picture mingled around in her head, and she was struck by the cruel irony of it. If God showed him this scene, then why? Why would God want her to see this right after she was told there was no hope of her ever dancing? She forced her mind back to the present meeting.

"Peter, I am so pleased with these. I couldn't have asked for any better. They're going to be wonderful for our advertising."

"It's only a start. I'll continue developing them for commercials and magazines."

"Good. I'm anxious to see what else you come up with."

They talked for awhile longer, coming up with several possibilities for the sketches he had done, while Alyssa kept up a cheerful outward appearance. In any other circumstance, she would have enjoyed talking with him a great deal. Peter had proven himself intelligent, friendly, and easygoing. But Alyssa was finding it hard to be around anyone. As soon as the opportunity arose, she ended the meeting and scheduled their next appointment.

After he left, she took the poster that had so captured her attention and quickly made a photocopy of it. After folding the copy up and putting it in her purse, she took the other pictures and went out to find her secretary.

"Candy, would you take these sketches to Bryan in the art department? Tell him they're for the new ad campaign and to work some ideas off from them. I'm going home. You can call me there if you need me."

"OK, sure." Candy eyed her curiously but refrained from asking why Alyssa was leaving early.

"See ya," Alyssa called as she stepped into the elevator.

She got home quickly and heard the yelling even before stepping through the door. Her mother's shrill shouts bombarded her senses as she slipped quietly across the kitchen to the table. She leaned against the table's edge listening while her curiosity turned to sickening fear: her mother's rage was not one of annoyance but of desperation.

"How could you do this, Tyler? When are you going to learn?" Catherine's loud voice echoed into the kitchen.

Tyler! Alyssa's skin crawled as trepidation enveloped her heart. *What has he done now?* A million possibilities went through her mind when remembering his foolish actions of the past.

"I don't know how to help you, Tyler. Tell me what can I do!" Catherine's voice sounded wild and urgent, as if her son's life depended on her words.

"I don't know," came Tyler's typical mumbled response.

Alyssa could see her brother slumped on the sofa while Catherine paced around like a caged animal. Alyssa's hand went unconsciously to her mouth. *Oh no, I thought he stopped drinking.*

"Do you realize you could have killed yourself?" Catherine screamed.

"I wasn't that bad," Tyler said weakly.

"Not that bad! You took a wild horse and tried to ride him while you were drunk!"

"I didn't drink that much."

"You didn't?" she yelled as her arms flailed wildly. "You're still too drunk to walk or talk straight. Just look at you!"

"I'm fine," he slurred unconvincingly.

"I can't take it anymore, Tyler! Get out of my sight until you're sober enough to hold a conversation," she said in disgust.

Alyssa watched Tyler stumble up the stairs to his room with his head hanging low. She shared her mother's anger. How could he have done something so dangerous? Didn't he consider those who loved him? Yet, as she watched him ascend the stairs in defeat, she saw the shame and remorse on his face and wanted to cry for him.

Catherine went out onto the back porch. Alyssa waited but a moment and then followed. She found her mother sitting on the stone bench among the flowers with tears in her eyes.

Alyssa sat down quietly next to her, wishing she and Catherine were closer so that she would know the right words to say. She wanted to comfort her mother but felt immensely inadequate. Catherine broke the awkward silence with a shaky voice.

"What am I going to do?" The tears finally flowed down her redden face. "Where did I go wrong?"

Alyssa could feel her mother's pain and wanted to erase it for her. "You didn't do anything, Ma. It wasn't your fault—you can't blame yourself."

There was another long silence. Alyssa put her arm ineptly around her mother's shoulder. After awhile Catherine restored her composure slightly, stood up, and paced around the garden as Alyssa watched.

"Where did he get the horse, anyway?" Alyssa asked.

"Oh, that Richards kid. Apparently his father bought this mustang. He's always buying crazy horses! They both started drinking and decided they would ride it. Tyler got thrown off."

"He wasn't hurt?" Alyssa was surprised; such a fall could have been life threatening in any number of ways.

"No." Catherine stopped pacing and looked at her watch. "I've got to go to town and get something for supper. I'll be back in a little while."

Alyssa could tell that her mom was searching for a way to end the conversation. She wasn't much for discussing her feelings. She followed Catherine inside and headed for her own room. She felt the need to get away from the house as much as her mother. After slipping on a pair of comfortable white jean shorts and red tank top, she slipped out through the living room, to the backyard.

Soon she was on her way down the familiar path to the lake. Reaching the point where the paths crossed, she sat down to rest on a tree stump circled by small wildflowers. She almost wished she hadn't stopped, for the moment she sat down, her mind began replaying the last couple of days in detail. She longed to turn off her brain, shut out her thoughts, but they tormented her without ceasing. Briefly her whirlwind of thoughts paused on the wheelchair sitting outside of her bedroom. The doctor had said she would need an electric wheelchair. She visibly cringed as his words echoed through her skull. Tears stung her eyes but none came. She was tired of crying.

The poster that Peter had drawn arose now in her memory. She was completely confounded by the image he had created. Dancing was a dream forever beyond her grasp, and soon walking would be but a faint remembrance, so what message was God sending? She supposed it was meant as some form of encouragement—that she remain joyful in spite of her circumstances.

She attempted to fight off the depressing mood by thinking of something uplifting. Her thoughts drifted to the evening she had spent with Austin. A wonderful moment in time! He was so kind and sweet to her, making her feel worthy and whole. It had been nice to feel like a woman instead of some ugly "thing." Her feelings for Austin went deeper than any emotion she had ever known. He was as light in her darkened world.

Yet she consistently refused her thoughts from traveling that road. It didn't matter what she felt for Austin or even how incredibly good he was to her. What mattered was that she would never be the kind of woman he deserved. A man like him would never love her, and she wouldn't make a fool of herself by hoping for that which would never come.

Thoughts of Austin brought a small bitter smile. Her eyes stared softly as she sat thinking of him. Though times with him were sweet, they rubbed raw her longing for love when, inevitably, she would find herself alone again. She desperately tried to fight the terrifying fear of never being loved. He had said it could happen. He said someone would love her someday…

Alyssa looked up suddenly, a sound snapping her out of her reflections. Her mouth dropped open at the sight of Jake Cutler's approach. She was once more caught off guard and speechless in the presence of this man, who now stood smiling over her.

"I must be the luckiest man in the world. I'm just walking back to my cabin and run into the most beautiful creature in these woods." Jake's silky voice seemed to match his almost black eyes. He leaned up against a tree and stared down at Alyssa.

Alyssa laughed lightly at his comment. "You obviously haven't seen many of the creatures in these woods."

Jake smiled. Her voice was sweet in his ears and her laugh intoxicating. He moved closer and lowered himself in front of her. "I've seen enough to know what's beautiful."

Alyssa looked away briefly. Knowing that his words were spoken more out of a habit for flattery rather than sincerity did not negate the fact that she did indeed feel flattered.

"You looked as if you were deep in thought. I'm dying to know what was going on in that gorgeous head." His brown-black eyes narrowed as he grinned.

She looked at him then. His long black hair fell freely to his shoulders, and his clothes contained a mixture of dirt and sweat. "I was just thinking about some things going on in my life."

"Was I in any of those thoughts?"

"Actually, no." Alyssa was thankful that she was able to answer honestly. If he had asked that question at any other moment since they had met, the answer may have been different.

"No!" he exclaimed sounding devastated, making Alyssa laugh again. "I would have enjoyed knowing you were thinking about me."

Alyssa's heart fluttered wildly at his words and at the way he boldly watched her. She didn't understand why her insides went crazy when Jake was near or why she enjoyed the way he looked at her now. His last comment caused her to get up from the stump where she was sitting.

Jake's presence was overwhelming, almost suffocating Alyssa. Her thoughts were jumbled and slow, yet her senses seemed to be frantically racing. She walked a couple steps from him before turning back. "I was going to go down to the lake. You're welcome to join me."

Jake jumped up with a huge smile. "I can't think of anything that I'd like better." Amidst her somersaulting stomach, Alyssa couldn't help but consider how little she knew of Jake Cutler. She had met him once briefly and was now inviting him to the lake while contemplating forbidden things.

Jake and Alyssa walked without saying much. Jake watched her as she moved slightly in front of him, pleased with what he saw. Growing impatient already, he wanted to do away with the pretense and satisfy his desire.

"Isn't it beautiful?" Alyssa interrupted his thoughts when they had reached the lake.

"Yes," he said, looking at her. Alyssa did not turn away this time. She stared back at him boldly, questioning his meaning. It was Jake who turned away first. "The water looks too good to pass up!" He stripped off his shirt and ran to the lake. Diving in, he disappeared for a moment.

Alyssa sat down on the grass. She was disturbed with how tired she felt but shrugged it off, unwilling to think about it. She wanted to think of Jake—just Jake and her. She craved his eyes to look at her again.

She knew that she had been acting innocent and immature with him up to this point. She wasn't sure how, but she determined that she would no longer act like a child when he was near. She was a woman and would let him know how she felt. If Jake wasn't interested, she'd get over the embarrassment, but her intuition told her he wanted her.

Could a man really want her? Her mind seemed confused with the concept, incapable of accepting the possibility. She watched Jake come out of the water dripping from head to toe. He slicked his long hair back and, grabbing his T-shirt, wiped his face and chest before throwing it aside. "That was great!"

"You cooled down now?" Alyssa remained unable to tear her eyes from him.

"As much as can be expected under the circumstances," he said seriously, testing Alyssa's response.

"What circumstances are those, Mr. Cutler?" she asked coyly.

He smiled easily at her question. She was playing his game now. "A beautiful woman is sitting in front of me."

She searched his eyes. Had he said beautiful? Yes, she saw the telling look as he watched her reaction. Suddenly there was no doubt in her mind—he wanted her. The revelation startled her for a moment.

She had to decide if she was going to dive into the shaky, unknown territory this stranger was leading her into. There was something dangerous and forbidden about him, and she knew the right thing to do. But he made her feel something she had never felt before; he made her feel desirable. No man had ever shown such an interest. No, she couldn't allow her last chance to be with a man to pass her by. An expectant smile played on her lips, and a new spark entered her eyes.

Jake broke the silence abruptly. "Come swimming with me."

"I don't think so." She didn't want to tell him that she wasn't able to swim. As far as she knew, he knew nothing about her illness. Jake stood and walked toward her slowly with a devious smile on his face.

"What are you doing?" Alyssa asked half laughing.

"I want you to come swimming with me." He grinned dangerously, and quickly bent down and scooped her up in his arms. When he started heading for the lake Alyssa grew alarmed.

"Jake no, really, I don't want to," she said urgently.

"Sure you do."

He was knee deep in the water now, and started swinging her in his arms. "Jake! I can't swim!"

"My father always said the best way to learn is to get thrown in," he said casually, still swinging her. "I think it's time you learn."

"No! Really, I can't. I won't be able to! I'm not strong enough, Jake!" He suddenly heard the desperation in her voice and quickly took her back to shore.

"OK, OK, I won't throw you in." Setting her back on her feet he looked down at her for an explanation. He saw the panic on her face, and his eyes widened slightly. "Hey, I'm sorry, I wasn't going to drown you."

She saw his confusion with her reaction and knew that she should explain. She turned away and walked down to the small wharf her father had built when the children were young. Sitting on the edge of the wharf, she was silent for several moments.

Jake watched her, waiting for an explanation. He finally followed her and took his place on the wharf. Alyssa almost wished he hadn't sat right beside her. His nearness closed in on her, and she felt as though she was breathing it in, like thick smoke in a small room. It was all the harder for her to think clearly and say what she must.

"Jake, I'm not really sure why I'm telling you this, but I feel like I should, I guess." She was quiet for another moment, and Jake waited until she began again. "Um…I have a muscle disease…so I'm not quite as strong as most people. That's why I can't swim." Immediately she realized how pathetic it sounded and wished she could snatch the words back from the air where they hung.

Jake was silent, not really sure what her declaration meant. His mind whirled with questions. *If I touch her will I hurt her? Is she able to have a physical relationship?* If she wasn't, he might as well not pursue her any longer. What was the point if it wouldn't go anywhere?

"Jake, say something." His silence was agonizing.

"I'm just wondering what exactly that means. Are you sick? I mean, did I hurt you?"

"No! Not at all. I'm not sick, I just don't have the strength of most people. There are some things that require a lot of muscles, which I don't have." She worked to keep her voice light and unconcerned. She looked at him carefully before speaking again. "You don't have to be afraid of hurting me—you won't." She gave him a breathtaking smile, with the spark of a promise in her eyes.

Jake was taken with that smile. It was beautiful. He decided to set aside his worries. He was intrigued by her and even more so by this new information. Lowering his mouth nearer to her ear, Jake's low voice consumed Alyssa's senses. "I've always found new things exciting."

Jake slid off the wharf and stood in the waist deep water in front of Alyssa's dangling legs. "What do you say we try something new right now?"

"What?" she asked expectantly.

"Come in the water with me." He slipped his hands around her small waist, causing her heart to race. "I'll hold you." She held onto his shoulders and allowed him to slide her off the wooden planks.

"The water feels good, huh," he said as he held her in the water.

"Yeah," she said absently. She could think of nothing but his closeness. He held her firmly as he moved around in circles causing small waves to wash against them as they floated.

Jake watched her closely. Her huge blue eyes were clouded with uncertainty and longing. Experience told him that she was close to complete submission to him. Yet, as hard as it was, he knew he must take his time. She was not only fragile in her body but in her emotions as well. Like a doe easily frightened, he could scare her away. But if he was smart and coaxed her just right, she'd be running after him.

Her lips begged him to kiss them now, and he wanted to. But he knew if he did, he wouldn't be able to stop. After a moment he pulled his eyes away, turned, and lifted her back onto the wharf, making Alyssa look at him in confusion. Jake's breath caught for a moment at the sight of her long, half-wet hair and flushed face. He cleared his throat and forced a casual smile.

"I wouldn't mind staying here all evening with you, but I'm afraid I've been gone too long already." If it had been any other woman, he would have taken advantage of her obvious eagerness and left without much thought. But somehow Alyssa was different. She seemed much too pure to take advantage of in such a way—too quickly. He pulled himself up onto the plank beside her and started back toward the grass.

"I was on my way to change my clothes and head back to the barn when I met you," he explained as he slipped on his T-shirt. "One of the mares is getting ready to give birth."

"Oh," her small voice sounded disappointed. "Which mare is it?"

"Sally, the brown quarter horse."

"I know Sally," she said with a familiar smile.

"You want to come?" He didn't want to leave her, and the fact that Austin would see them together hadn't escaped him.

Alyssa rewarded his offer with a brilliant smile. Though she longed to go, it would take her awhile to walk all that way for she was already tired. "I better not. I would just slow you way down. I'm kind of tired."

Jake hesitated a moment until a playful smile spread across his mouth. "So I'll carry you!"

"You're not going to carry me all that way!" She laughed at the insane picture such a suggestion created.

"Sure I am." He hunkered down in front of her. "Climb on my back."

"What!" she laughed in surprise.

"Haven't you ever had a piggyback ride?"

"Not for quite some time."

"Well then, it's about time for another one. Climb on my back."

She thought of what others might say if they saw her, but she quickly dismissed the thought and did as he asked. She put her arms around his neck, and he reached behind and grabbed her legs. Standing, he took off quickly, reaching the clearing at the end of the path in no time and set her gently back on the ground. Taking her hand, they walked to the barn.

Before they had reached the door, Rebecca came hurrying out to meet Jake. She stopped dead in her tracks and stared with mouth dropped at the two of them. She eyed them both from head to toe, probing Alyssa's eyes before she spoke to Jake. "Lady decided she was going to have her baby too."

"She's not due for a few more weeks," he said, already releasing Alyssa's hand and starting for the barn.

Alyssa entered the barn behind Jake and was immediately greeted by Austin. Much like Rebecca, Austin looked them both over and met

Jake's grin with his own hard stare. Alyssa saw the fire in Austin's eyes as he glared at Jake. She had never seen him look like that before and wondered what could cause such dislike.

"Nice of you to show up, Jake," Austin smiled sarcastically.

"Yeah, I guess I got sidetracked," Jake answered, briefly eyeing Alyssa all too intimately. Austin looked at her, his expression softening into more of a pained look. Then he turned back to Jake.

"Sally's doing fine. Just keep an eye on her with Rebecca in case there are problems. I'm going to stay with Lady." Austin spoke calmly, though he felt he might explode at any moment. "Lyssa, would you come with me in case I need your help?"

"Sure," she said, leaving Jake's side. Though Jake's anger flared at how quickly Alyssa followed Austin, he chose not to object and went back to the birthing quarter horse.

Alyssa followed Austin to the last stall in silence. She had sensed his tension and was sorry she had come with Jake looking as she did. Did she always have to be so completely thoughtless when it came to matters such as these?

Austin's mind whirled with thoughts as he led her to the horse's stall. The picture of Alyssa and Jake soaking wet and smiling was burning in his mind. What had happened between them? And that cocky, triumphant glare of Jake's! Oh, how he wanted to knock that look off his face. How he so desired to hit him right in the...*God, I'm sorry! What is wrong with me? Why do I hate this man so much? Father, forgive me, and help me to see him as You see him. And Lord please keep Alyssa away from him.*

They reached Lady's stall where the beautiful, deep brown Morgan lay on its side making painful moaning sounds. "Is she going to be alright?" Alyssa spoke for the first time. Austin could hear the concern in her voice, and his anger at Jake was momentarily forgotten.

"We'll do everything we can, and God will do the rest." Austin's voice held the hint of a gentle smile. They went in, and he knelt near the mare's stomach, rubbing it gently.

"What can I do?"

Austin looked up at Alyssa standing nearby with fear in her face. Her voice touched his heart in a way that was unfamiliar to him. "You can talk to her. Your voice will help her stay calm." Alyssa allowed her eyes to hold Austin's for a moment. His approval meant more to her than he knew. Giving Austin a hesitant smile, she knelt down where Lady's head rested in the hay. The mare's head came up instantly, allowing Alyssa to gently caress it.

"It's OK, Lady. Austin is going to take care of you now." She spoke in a quiet loving whisper. "You'll have a brand new baby soon! It's OK,..."

"It's breech." Austin's surprisingly calm but firm voice cut in on her soothing melody.

"What?" Alyssa looked up at Austin, praying she had heard wrong.

"It's breech. I'm going to have to turn it. Keep talking to her." Alyssa began to speak to the horse more urgently. She stroked her while watching Austin work. His strong arms pushed and turned the unborn horse while he prayed earnestly. "Lord God, help me, give me strength. I pray this horse will be born healthy." His prayer continued, urgent yet confident. Alyssa had never heard someone pray like that before, like he was talking to a friend, asking for help. She closed her eyes and said her own little prayer but somehow felt it wasn't quite as good as Austin's.

He worked unrelentingly for what seemed like hours before his voice rang out triumphantly. "It's alive! Thank you, Lord!" Alyssa moved to get a better view of the miracle taking place, still keeping her hand on Lady's head. Austin's strong gentle hands guided the new foal into the world as Alyssa watched.

She half spoke, half laughed in joyful relief. "You have a girl, Lady! A brand new baby girl." She kissed the horse and stroked her as she spoke.

Just then Rebecca came up quickly to the stall. "Is everything all right? She's beautiful," she said watching the deep brown filly nestle her matching mother.

"The baby is fine." Austin's voice held a hint of something that made Alyssa look up with concern. He saw her questioning stare and gave her a tender look. "Lady has lost a lot of blood. I'm sure she'll be fine with rest," he said, his voice betraying his fear.

"I'm going to stay with her tonight, just to make sure. She'll be fine by morning, back to her old self."

Alyssa watched him as he rubbed the mare with long soothing strokes. "I'll stay, too."

"Lyssa, you've been a big help already. Go home and get some rest. I'll let you know how she's doing in the morning."

"No, I want to stay. My mind is made up, so you might as well not bother arguing with me." Seeing her flint-like face, Austin decided not to argue. He'd let her stay for awhile, then take her home before it got too late.

"Becca, tell Mom what happened and that I'm staying here to tend to Lady."

"Alright."

"How is Sally, anyway?" Austin asked.

"Great, she's got a new colt."

"So our little girl already has a little boyfriend," Alyssa laughed. She looked at Rebecca, swallowed hard, and forced her voice to be casual. "Ah—is Jake with Sally?"

Rebecca studied her sister before answering. She didn't like what she saw in her sibling's eyes. "No, he left."

"Oh." Alyssa was unable to keep the disappointment out of her voice.

Austin glanced at Rebecca briefly before he spoke. "I think I'll go down and check on the new colt. You keep an eye on these two. I'll be right back." He gave Alyssa a departing smile.

"OK." Alyssa was relieved to have a moment alone to feel sorry for herself. Why did Jake leave without a word to her?

"See ya." Rebecca waved at Alyssa then followed Austin.

When they were a safe distance away from Alyssa's ears, Rebecca quickened her pace to reach Austin's long stride. "Austin," she whispered loudly. "You've got to talk to her about Jake."

"Me?" His frustrated look told her how he felt about her suggestion. "You're her sister."

"She won't listen to me. You're the only one she might listen to. That guy is a jerk, and he's going to hurt her bad if someone doesn't stop him."

69

"I know, Rebecca, but what makes you think she'll listen to me?"

Rebecca rolled her eyes. "Austin, it's obvious that you two have a special relationship. She cares very much for you, and I know you care about her." She looked at him pointedly.

"Of course I care about her. She's a friend. I don't want to see her get hurt any more than you do."

"*Friend?* That's like saying Jake wants to just be her pal."

Rebecca's dripping sarcasm stopped Austin dead. He stared at her for a moment, his feet rooted to the floor. "What's that suppose to mean?" he finally demanded.

"Look, you're in love with my sister, and for some reason, you refuse to admit it. Now, I don't care what the reason is or what you do about it. I just know that you may be able to get her out of the hole she's digging if you'll stop playing stupid and talk to her."

Austin was stunned into silence. He couldn't believe what he had just heard. He could believe whom he was hearing it from; Rebecca was known for speaking her mind. But…in love with Alyssa?

"I don't believe you said that." He had no clue what else to say.

"Believe it, and deal with it." She looked him boldly in the eye, daring him to lie to her.

"Alyssa's important to me. I care about her, but I care about you too. I care about a lot of people," he fumbled foolishly for words.

"You don't look at me the way you look at her." A satisfied smile slide across her face as heat flooded Austin's.

He had lost his voice and could speak no retaliation for her comment. How did he look at Alyssa? He was sure that if he asked Rebecca she would tell him honestly, but he thought maybe he wouldn't like the answer.

When Rebecca spoke again, this time more gently, Austin was extremely relieved that she didn't press the former issue. "Just suggest to her that Jake isn't good for her. Be honest with her about him before it goes too far. I'm afraid maybe it already has."

Suddenly Austin found his voice again. "What do you mean?"

"I've seen the look in her eyes. She's hooked already."

Austin nodded, slightly comforted that she hadn't meant any more than that. "I'll talk to her."

After checking on the horses, he made his way back to Alyssa. His mind was swimming with Rebecca's words. *That girl has opened her mouth too often. In love with Lyssa! Where does she get off saying something like that? He didn't look at others the way he looked at Alyssa. How do I look at her? God has placed a special burden and godly love on my heart for Lyssa; that's what Rebecca sees.* Satisfied that he had figured it out, he put it out of his mind for the time being.

Seven

Alyssa sat absently stroking the Morgan lying at her feet. Her mind was not in the stall with the new mother and baby; it was at the lake. She relived each moment she and Jake had spent together that afternoon. Jake thrilled her, yet with the excitement came fear. Each time she felt as though her life was turning around, fear of the beast would step in and hold her back.

She would never dare speak of the beast living inside her soul. Surely someone would lock her up if she mentioned the force which compelled her into darkness. She rightfully named this thing "the beast." It was pain that drew her into tormented sobs while alone in her room; it was depression that tied her in chains of bondage until she could not move; and it was thoughts that made the reality of life all the more frightening.

Each time a little joy came along, the beast was pushed down and buried, but not gone. She could still sense it there, waiting like a rapist in a dark alley. Her joy never seemed real to her, it was superficial—a facade to please anyone watching.

Jake. For a moment he had made her forget the awful thing inside. In one afternoon she felt her whole world turn upside down. Her brain ached with questions she could not answer. Where was Jake? Was he thinking about her? Did he truly want her? These questions so consumed her that she forgot Austin sitting across from her until he spoke.

"Lyssa?" She snapped out of her thoughts and looked up at the gorgeous smile Austin had won many hearts with. "Where were you?"

She blushed slightly. "I'm sorry. I was just thinking."

"About what?" Though his voice was quiet in the stillness of the barn, Austin's words probed Alyssa's thoughts mercilessly.

"Oh, just about my family." Alyssa said nothing further and turned her gaze from his, lest he read in her eyes the lie she had just spoken.

Austin persisted in his gentle attempt to get at Alyssa's heart. "How is your family anyway?"

"The same, I guess. Mom and I haven't been getting along, and I don't know what to do about it. She sees me as some ungrateful, selfish child. I don't know how to make her see differently."

"Have you talked to her about it?"

"Talking is a problem in our family. None of us really know how to talk or to show love for that matter. We've never been taught how." Alyssa's voice grew sad as she let down her guard to reveal pieces of herself to Austin.

"My mother closes up behind a defensive wall when confronted with anything. She has trouble showing love, though I've known she's loved us. There are a lot of things in my family that seem to be passed on down the line." She smiled faintly then looked at Austin, who was watching her closely. She loved how he listened to her. "I'm afraid I'm talking and can't shut up!"

He laughed easily with her. "I like hearing you talk," he said, quickly wishing he hadn't, until her pleased smile and shy laugh brought a warm glow to his heart. *Sometimes she laughs so easily, why not always?*

They grew silent, each with their own thoughts. Austin watched as Alyssa smiled and softly stroked the horse. Then she graced him with that smile. *Lord, she is so sweet, sometimes like a child with a spark of hope in her eyes. I don't know if I can stand to see her get hurt.* His throat caught at the thought of anyone hurting Alyssa. Emotions washed over him, ones that he chose not to decipher at that moment. She was so gentle; why was life so cruel to her? *Why Lord?*

Circumstances have been cruel, but I have not. I will lift her out of the hurt, and she will know joy.

Austin closed his eyes, and thanked God for His promise. He would hold on to that promise for her. He opened his eyes again and saw her watching him. His mouth tipped slightly, and she returned his smile. "I've been meaning to ask how your doctor's appointment went." He saw her face change in an instant. Her mouth dropped, and her eyes darted quickly away from his.

She didn't say anything for a long time. Why did he have to ask her that question? She had been able to forget for awhile, and now Austin wanted to drag it all up again. Maybe she just wouldn't answer.

"Lyssa?" Austin's voice pried gently.

She looked at his searching expression, full of sincerity, and knew he would not leave it alone until she answered. She reached up and pushed her still damp hair out of her face. "Not great." Her flat voice was void of emotion. "Apparently, my muscles have started to deteriorate." The word was like poison in her mouth. It caused her skin to crawl a short distance over her body. "I'm not just 'not able to get stronger' anymore, now I'm officially getting worse." Alyssa laughed a quiet, harsh laugh that made Austin shudder. "In about a year I should be a complete cripple." The word cripple made her cringe—she despised the word and declared that she would never be one. *Cripple.*

Austin sat motionless. She couldn't be serious. *Lord? Is this true? No, God. Please, not Lyssa! Don't let this happen to her.* What could he say? He saw the pain in her eyes and heard the anger in her voice. How could he make this better? *I am so useless! Why did You put me in her life, Lord, and not someone who could give her hope?*

You've got the hope she needs, Austin. I've chosen you.

He got up and moved closer to Alyssa. Sitting beside her he took her hand gently in his and held it. Her eyes moved slowly to his. His simple act caused her reserve to fall, and slow tears trickled down her face. "I'm so sorry, Lyssa." Austin's quiet voice was full of anguish. "I'm so sorry that you have to go through this."

He saw her small shoulders shake gently as she cried, and impulsively he reached out and pulled her to him. She lay in his embrace gratefully, with her head resting on his broad chest and his strong arms enfolding her. His strength felt good in the midst of her own weakness. She closed her eyes and attempted to draw that strength from him. She would need it in the days to come.

They were still for a long time as he held her. He prayed silently, allowing her to draw what comfort she could from him. Looking down, he saw the damp golden tendrils fall in thick strands down her back as she rested against him. He tentatively moved his hand and caressed her head, down the length of her hair. Lovingly he let it curl around his finger, marveling at how soft it was, and how much he loved touching it. He rubbed a piece between his fingers and had the insane impulse to feel it on his face.

"I use to wish my mother would hold me like this." Alyssa's soft, shaky voice startled him, and he dropped the strand from his fingers. "When I was young, I would pray that somehow she would see my need for her to hold me, but she never did."

"Did you ever ask her to?"

"No." Alyssa knew that she could have asked, and perhaps her mother would have gladly held her while she cried. Perhaps, though, she would have gotten angry and told Alyssa to stop pitying herself and be strong. "This is all I've ever wanted from anyone really."

Austin could feel his emotions breaking; his soul mourned for her. His heart was melting like gold in a fire. Everything covering that piece of gold was falling away, all his reasoning and explanation were slipping far from his understanding. He looked at himself as he really was. He looked at his heart and saw something he hadn't seen before.

He saw love.

Love that was purer than the purest gold and as bright as a lighthouse in a storm. He loved Alyssa. This woman who was but a child in so many ways and ancient in so many others. This woman who cared and dreamed and hoped and prayed through all her life and all her pain. He loved her for all that she was, for all that she wanted in life, and for all that God was going to make her. Oh God, how he loved her! These revelations washed over him in such a rush that he felt engulfed by them.

This newfound knowledge brought an indescribable joy and excitement, with it immense dread following close behind. Oh no, he loved her! His arms tightened imperceptibly. How could he ever let her go now? What would he do with this new information? Should he tell her? *Oh God. Oh no, I love her.*

Alyssa's tears subsided, but she didn't want to move. She loved feeling a man such as Austin holding her. "You're a good friend, Austin," she said softly, "I don't know what I would do without you." The word *friend* suddenly grated slightly on Austin's nerves. "It's probably the closest I'll ever get to having a boyfriend," Alyssa laughed jokingly. Austin laughed flatly in return.

"Is that why you're interested in Jake?" Austin was surprised at the question, which seemed to arise out of nowhere, yet not as surprised as Alyssa.

Her head shot up, and she quickly pulled from his embrace. "Who says I'm interested in Jake?" Alyssa eyed him defensively, accusing him with her tone.

"Lyssa, it's obvious the way you two came here tonight." Austin's voice was more irritated than he meant it to sound. "I can see it in your eyes," he added more gently. She averted her eyes quickly, and he was sorry he had brought up the subject of Jake, for she was no longer lying in his arms. His arms immediately felt empty when she pulled away. He wanted to reach out and pull her back into them. "What is it you see in him? He uses women—is that what you want?"

His words shocked and offended Alyssa as she stared angrily at the man in front of her. She was ready to rain down a few choice words on Austin's head when she realized what he said was true. She looked at the barn floor, speaking in a low mumble. "What if I like him? At least he shows an interest in me, which is more than I can say for any guy I have ever met."

He touched her chin forcing her head up gently to meet his gaze. "You can do better, Lyssa."

She scoffed, rolling her eyes. "What do you know? You're a friend who's trying to be nice." Alyssa's voice held accusation, though she wasn't aware of it.

"I know more than you think," he answered softly, realizing his words held more meaning than she could possibly understand. "I know you're scared of being alone. I know this disease terrifies you, though for some reason you try to hide that fear from everyone. I know you think no one could love you because of it." His words sunk in deep and caused tears to flow freely from Alyssa's eyes. She turned away and tried to hide them. She would not look at him—she could not, for he knew too much of her heart.

"I know," he continued more gently, "that you see Jake as your only chance at love." He paused for a moment wanting to tell her that he loved her, but he held back. "I know, too, that you will find a wonderful life with someone, but it's not with Jake. I know Christ can heal you, and you don't have to face the fear of this disease. There's so much for you if you would just reach out and take it."

"What if God doesn't heal me?" Her challenge was spoken in frustration.

"Lyssa, I don't care what happens to you, if you were void of legs and arms, there would still be a man who would love you." *I would, Lyssa. I would love you no matter what disease ate away at your body. I would look upon your sweet face and think it the most beautiful in the world.* "There is someone God has chosen who will come and love you no matter what the circumstances." *Me, Lord?* "I know, too, that God does have a plan to heal you."

Alyssa stood then. "You can't possibly know what you're talking about. You can't know what I'm going through or what I'm feeling. Jake looks at me like no man has ever looked at me." The intense emotion in her voice tore at Austin's heart. Alyssa paced around the stall while Austin looked up at her. "He makes me feel like a woman. I don't think I've ever felt like that before." She thought about that for a moment, than paused in her pacing to look down at Austin where he sat. "Except with you." She suddenly grew quiet, fixing her eyes on his for a moment. "You've always made me feel special." She gave him a small grateful smile that made his heart ache for her.

"But it's different," she sighed, looking away again. "He's interested in me. I like someone being interested in me. I want to know what it's like to be with a man who desires *me*." Looking back toward Austin she spoke in a small but determined voice. "Nobody is going to take this chance away from me. I need this. It's all I've got right now."

"No, Alyssa, he'll use you and hurt you." Austin's tone begged her earnestly to hear. "That's not all there is, Jesus Christ…"

"Austin, stop!" Alyssa yelled in exasperation. She didn't want to hear anymore about Jesus, as if she were some atheist who needed conversion. "You don't understand! I can't handle my life as it is. I've got to hold on to every moment of happiness I can get." Her voice threatened to give over to sobs as she covered her face with her hands.

Austin reached up for her hand and gently pulled her down to him. She came slowly, falling down at his side and allowed him to enfold her in his arms once more. "OK," he whispered, "we don't have to talk anymore."

They were silent as Austin stroked her hair until he felt her crying subside and her breathing lighten. She fell asleep as he held her. He prayed silently for this tiny woman he held in his arms and in his heart and for himself in the days to come. He struggled over the things she had revealed. He understood her needs well and wished that somehow he could be the one to meet them. But as he sat in silent prayer holding Alyssa, he knew God was speaking and instructing him not to reveal his newfound love.

Alyssa slept in Austin's arms for over an hour. He was reluctant to let go, savoring each precious moment that she was so close. She was so beautiful! In the light of the moon through the window high above the stall, Austin could see her perfectly etched, untroubled face and lips parted slightly, letting in the sweet breath of life. He wanted to hold that striking face in his hands and tell her he loved her. But he couldn't.

Finally he decided he had better get her home. Lady was faring much better, and Austin knew the mare would be fine. Not wanting to wake Alyssa, he carefully slipped an arm under her legs and around her back, picking her up in his strong arms. She stirred slightly, nestling her head close to his neck, and he paused. After a moment's hesitation, he continued reluctantly out of the barn with his sleeping beauty.

He carried her the distance to her house easily. At her back door he spoke softly near her ear. "Lyssa…" Alyssa stirred slightly, then was still again. He hunkered down, resting her on his knee. His now free hand brushed her cheek, pushing back the soft hair that now lay dry against her face. "Lyssa, time to wake up." Alyssa's hand moved unconsciously to her cheek as if to chase a bothersome fly. Austin grinned, amused at the annoyed expression that crept into her face momentarily. He cupped her face and softly rubbed her cheek with his thumb. "Come on, you're home now." Finally her eyes inched open, and she laboriously sat up from his shoulder.

Alyssa looked around confused before realizing where she was. She gave Austin a sleepy, embarrassed smile and rubbed her half-opened eyes awake. "How come you brought me home?"

Austin was surprised at how much her quiet, scratchy voice pleased him, how much everything about her suddenly delighted him. "Lady is doing fine; she'll be just like new by morning. I thought you should get some rest."

"Oh, good. I'm glad she's OK." She stood up from his lap and smiled at him gratefully. "Thanks for bringing me home." She paused a moment than continued more seriously. "And for being a good friend."

Austin stood up to his full, towering height and gave her a crooked smile. "It was nothing."

"Well, it means a lot to me." She stepped closer and reached up high to embrace him. Austin held her tightly but only for a moment before letting go. "I'll see you tomorrow," she said.

He watched her walk into the house. The lights were on in the living room briefly before they were out again. Turning, he walked down the path and back to the barn. His arms felt empty, but he could still feel the warmth of her in them with her head resting on his shoulder and her breath on his neck. He felt the aching in his heart for her and was afraid that those feelings were not going away for a very long time—if ever.

Eight

A week had gone by since Alyssa had seen Jake. Curled up on her window seat, she stared out at nothing with her journal open and pen twirling slowly through her fingers. Her thoughts were jumbled and confused. Her emotions wreaked havoc, and her desires were out of control.

Her eyes looked absently toward the rainy Friday evening. A heavy sigh escaped her lips, accentuating her mood. Just as the flowers outside were soaking in the cool May rains, so she soaked in the drizzle of depression. Not one word had come from Jake since she had last seen him. She had gone to the stables often over the past week, but Jake was nowhere to be found.

Breathing another sigh, she picked up her journal and wrote slowly.

Nothing matters to me anymore—nothing except one very important something. For so long I've struggled to hold on to life, looking for a reason not to simply disappear forever.

Alyssa looked up for a moment. Why had she always felt so lost, so unloved? What had sent her on this downward spiral into the darkness she now felt almost sickeningly comfortable in? She had no answers, only questions.

Suddenly, a man comes along and I grab tight to...to what? A look he gave me? A smile? A tone in his voice? Were these real? Was the look in his eyes really a desire for me? I have, for whatever reason, grabbed on to the hope of Jake Cutler, and I am powerless to let go. Why didn't I fight harder against the temptation of my heart?

I think the beast inside of me likes Jake, for thoughts of him are all consuming now. I wake up and hope the day brings word from him. I go to bed and yearn for him to come and lay beside me. The thoughts I have are out of control.

Suddenly my morals do not seem to matter in the least. I can't even remember what kind of morals I had before Jake. I will give myself to him totally if he'll have me. He already possesses my mind.

She slammed her journal shut when she heard a knock at the door.

"Alyssa?" Rebecca called in a soft voice from behind the door. Quickly shoving the journal behind one of the overstuffed decorative pillows, she invited her sister in. Rebecca entered, radiant smile in place, and sat with Alyssa on the window seat. "Hey, what'cha doing?"

"Nothing." Alyssa's eyes darted to the pillow hiding her secret thoughts. "How about you?"

"Nothing. I was just wondering how you were doing." Rebecca looked at Alyssa carefully as she spoke.

"I'm alright," Alyssa said quietly with a small smile. What else could she say? *I'm dying inside. I can't get the picture of the grotesque, deteriorated me out of my mind unless thoughts of Jake fill it. I wish I'd never been born and feel guilty that I was.* "It's hard sometimes, but I'm fine."

"You're so strong, Ally. I don't know how you do it." Rebecca's words stung slightly. If she knew the truth of what lay within Alyssa's soul, she would not think her strong. She would think Alyssa weak for pitying herself.

Alyssa shrugged in false humility. "The Lord helps me through it." Even as she spoke, she inwardly cringed. Part of her believed the lie and felt a certain pride at knowing that she had brought glory to God with those words. Another part of her, however, did not understand it at all. How was God helping her? How was He going to get her through this? *Jake! God has given Jake to encourage me.*

"Huh, yeah," Rebecca scoffed. "I'm having serious doubts about God."

"What do you mean?" A sudden nervousness struck Alyssa at her sister's words.

"Ever since I was old enough, I have prayed that God would heal you. When we were little I prayed that you would get better and be able to run like the rest of the kids. I guess I thought He answered some of my prayers when you stopped getting so sick. Now this happens." She stopped for a moment. Bitter tears stung her eyes but did not escape. "I just don't know what to think anymore. How can a God that loves you make you sick?" Her question demanded an answer.

Alyssa felt a strange fear crawl along her spine. Was her sister committing blasphemy? She was questioning God out loud, even angrily confronting Him. Alyssa could not let that happen; she was to glorify God to others in spite of her disease, not cause people to turn from God because of it. "Becca, it is not for us to question God. Everything that He does is for our benefit. We may not see it right now, but God will use this disease for some greater good." Her words sounded ridiculous in her ears.

Did she believe what her own mouth was saying? By the blank look on Becca's face she could tell that her sister wasn't getting much from the speech. "I don't understand it all," she continued, "but I know that God is good. He has heard our prayers but has a greater purpose than we can understand right now."

Rebecca managed a smile for her sister. "I know what you're saying, I just have to figure it all out." Didn't Rebecca always have everything figured out? Wasn't she the strong one? Even in Rebecca's weakness and confusion she was sure and bold in her words. She spoke of her anger and confusion without fear. *Sometimes you speak too boldly Becca.*

Rebecca changed the subject. "I saw Lady's filly today. She's so cute. Austin was able to name her since he delivered her. Guess what he named her." Becca smiled mischievously, the sparkle coming back into her eyes as quickly as it had left. "You'll never guess!"

Alyssa's eyes narrowed in curiosity. "Just tell me!" she laughed, lightly hitting her sister in the arm.

"Alright, alright! He named her Lyssa." Rebecca's satisfied grin spoke volumes.

Alyssa's mouth dropped slightly and her heart skipped a beat. "Lyssa? Why?"

"He said it's because you helped him deliver her, but I think it's more than that." Rebecca's smile turned smug. Alyssa's surprised pleasure turned to confusion at her sister's less-than-subtle-hint.

"What do you mean?"

"Come on, you know he likes you."

"Austin doesn't like me. We're just friends!" Alyssa was shocked at the suggestion.

"Sure, if you say so."

It was Alyssa's turn to laugh. "Really, we care about each other but not in the way you think."

Rebecca looked her sister squarely in the eyes. "You honestly don't care for Austin beyond friendship?"

Alyssa was silent for a moment. There was a time when that question would have been harder for her to answer. "No." Whatever she felt for Austin didn't matter anymore, for there was another man in her life now, one that might actually prove attainable.

Rebecca looked momentarily doubtful before her expression altered. Alyssa saw two beautiful green eyes narrow and search her own. "Is it because of Jake?" she asked slowly.

"No," Alyssa answered quickly, turning away from the eyes that saw past her instant lie.

"Alyssa, stay away from Jake. He's the lowest form of scum imaginable."

Alyssa gasped at the harsh words. "He's not either!" In an instant her defense of him gave her feelings away, and she regretted her unthinking declaration. What made it even worse was the pitying look Rebecca now gave her.

83

When Rebecca spoke again, the pity was evident in her voice. "Listen, I know his type. All that guy wants is sex. He'll use you, then toss you away like a piece of trash. You're too good for him." Alyssa listened to her sister's bold words with fire darkening her blue eyes.

"You listen." She spoke in a low voice that was seething just below the surface. "I'm not stupid, Rebecca. I know Jake better than you think I do." She paused for a moment, letting her subtle insinuation hit its mark. "I'm a big girl and can make any decision I choose. Did you consider that maybe I know exactly what he wants from me? The fact is I'm enjoying him right now." If she had thought about it, she would have wondered in what way she had been enjoying the last couple of miserable weeks. "As for doing better, why don't you show me someone better who wants me."

Rebecca was obviously shocked by Alyssa's words, and she enjoyed knocking the all-knowing look off her younger sibling's face. She got up, walked toward her bed, then turned to face Rebecca once more. "I'm so sick of you acting like you know everything. I know you've had more experience than I have. I know you want what's best for me, but I'm sick of it!"

"Excuse me for caring!" Rebecca stood to face Alyssa. Alyssa was already sorry she had said such hateful words. The last thing she could stand was hurting the one person who had forever been her best friend. "I just don't want to see that jerk take advantage of you. I'm really surprised to hear you talk like this. It's not like you."

Guilt pricked at Alyssa, but she angrily pushed it away. Why should she feel guilty for feeling as she did about Jake?

"Becca, I'm sorry. I didn't mean what I said. I guess I'm just kind of screwed up right now because of all that's happening." *That's good. Blame it on the disease.* Rebecca's face softened as pity returned to her eyes. Though it annoyed Alyssa, she kept her feelings under wrap while returning Rebecca's smile with her own.

"Just promise me you'll be careful, OK?" Alyssa heard the concern in Rebecca's plea.

"I promise."

"Good." Rebecca went and hugged her older sister briefly. "Well, I've got to go. I have a blind date with a guy a friend hooked me up with."

"Oh, so that's why you're all dressed up." Alyssa had noticed her sister's black flared skirt and close-fitting black cotton shirt. It was simple but attractive. Rebecca didn't need fancy clothes as some women did; she could wear a potato sack and still cause every man to beg for a moment of her time. Her shoulder-length hair was pulled up into a simple flattering twist. Jealously got the better of Alyssa as she wondered why Rebecca had gotten every perfect feature, while she felt like a freak of nature. She pushed the thought from her mind. "What's this guy like anyway?" she asked, now playing the part of big sister.

"I'll find out soon enough." Rebecca laughed easily, already forgetting the harsh words spoken to her moments ago. Alyssa loved her laugh, missing it if she didn't hear it regularly. It was a sound that seemed to burst forth from somewhere deep inside her gut. It was loud and untamed, beautiful and striking, and matched the rest of Rebecca perfectly. Such laughter made some feel as though they had never known joy themselves.

Alyssa watched as Rebecca's skirt brushed a couple inches above her knee and her perfectly shaped, long legs carried her effortlessly out the door. Alyssa yearned for that kind of effortless grace and beauty in her own life.

Walking back to the window seat, she sat down and pulled her journal from behind the pillow.

Rebecca, my little sister, so full of experiences I've never had. She is bold and strong and beautiful—everything I'm not. Would she hate me for wanting just a small piece of her beauty and charm? Would she think me stupid and weak if she knew my immeasurable fears? As children she'd laugh and say I was feeling sorry for myself when I cried. Would she laugh now?

What has my disease cost Becca? Forced to grow up and help care for me at times. Forced to fight for me when I was too *pathetic to fight for myself. Forced to deal with my guilt trips and jealousies for things she has no control over. Yet through it all she has loved me.*

Alyssa closed her journal and put it back in the drawer of her desk. She left her bedroom and headed down the hall. Her father's voice echoed angrily from the kitchen. "So what am I supposed to do, Catherine?"

"Talk to him! Forbid him to drink! We have to do something!" Catherine's reply was desperate. Alyssa glanced in the kitchen and saw the large frame of Ken Langer sitting at the table across from his wife. His gray hair was thinning considerably, but this made him look even stronger. The years he had lived and worked showed in the lines around his eyes and forehead and in the thick arms that had built up an entire ranch single-handedly. Alyssa thought better of going into the kitchen. Instead she went to the living room and sat in one of the overstuffed chairs in front of the fireplace to listen, unnoticed.

"Forbidding him doesn't do any good." Alyssa could hear several cupboards slamming before Ken spoke again. "Look, I will talk to him, but I really think he's going to grow out of his drinking. He's just an eighteen-year-old boy trying to have some fun."

"I hope you're right. If you're not, we're going to end up with another child that we have to take care of for the rest of our lives." Catherine's words, spoken out of a need for her husband to understand, reached the ears of an invisible listener.

Alyssa felt the painful sting of her mother's plea. Quick tears came, and she brushed them away angrily. Getting up, she slipped out the sliding glass door to the back porch. She didn't want to give her mother the satisfaction of knowing that she had heard her words. No. She would harden herself and pretend she didn't hear. She sat down on the porch swing, thinking of Jake as she rocked back and forth. She needed him now. She wanted him to come and hold her in his arms, to comfort her and take away her pain.

The rain had stopped, but the thick clouds were almost black, threatening a big storm. Alyssa scanned the huge expanse of sky, marveling at how evil and angry it looked. She wrapped her arms around herself against the slight chill in the air, which had replaced the intense heat of the day before.

A few moments later her mother came out onto the porch. "What are you doing out here?" she asked pointlessly.

"Nothing." Alyssa did not try to keep the resentment out of her voice.

Not seeming to notice Alyssa's hostility, Catherine explained her plans hurriedly. "Your father and I are going to get something to eat. Then we're going to play cards at Jim and Karen's. Do you want me to make you supper before I go?"

"No, I'm not hungry," Alyssa mumbled, still not looking at her mother. *I'd rather starve than be an inconvenience.*

"Alright, I'll be back later tonight." Catherine went back in the house and slid the door closed. Alyssa took a deep breath, relieved her mother was gone for awhile. She would enjoy some time alone.

She got up and went back into the house just as Tyler was bounding down the staircase. "Ally!" He jumped over the last four or five stairs and came quickly to where she stood staring at him. "Can I use your car tonight? My truck is in the shop."

She didn't say anything for a few moments. She simply stared at him like he had asked to borrow two million dollars, unaware that she had perfected her mother's death stare exactly.

She looked up at her dark blond, 5'11" brother, amazed once again at how old he looked. To Alyssa he would always be her little brother, but standing before her now she realized he wasn't little anymore. He was well built and attractive, but what stood out most were his sky blue eyes and black, thick lashes. Lately however, his eyes were often bloodshot and glazed over.

"Where are you going?" she asked at last.

"Just over to Kristen's house."

It had been over four years since Tyler had first started dating Kristen. "Alright," she said reluctantly. If nothing else, she was glad she would be alone in the house.

She gave him her keys and watched as he hurried out the kitchen door. Fear for him often welled up in her. How she wished she could stop the horrible things he was doing to himself. She wanted as much as her parents to believe that he was fine.

They had never been really close, but she loved him. He, like the rest of the family, had often resented her in the past. She remembered once when she was too weak to stand, and he had to help her do various things. He had actually gotten so mad when asked to get her a glass of water that he dumped the entire glass over her head.

Thunder boomed loudly, causing Alyssa to jump and the house to rumble with the noise. She turned to the tall windows in the living room and watched nature rage against humanity. All at once the clouds opened, and water poured from the sky in rivers. On such a dreadful night she was glad that she was home, safe in her house where the angry thunder couldn't touch her.

Alyssa turned away from the scene and went to her bedroom. Going into her room she sat down on her bed and suddenly realized how tired she was. Her head hurt, her muscles were sore, and her heart was in pain. She decided that a hot bath would help ease the tension in her limbs. The thought of relaxing in the steamy water when no one else was home to pound on the door and demand she hurry perked her up a little. She could stay and soak in the tub for hours if she chose.

She slipped off the bed, grabbing the bedpost for support when her knees shook slightly. She was more tired than she realized. Fear instantly grabbed at her stomach. No! Not so soon! Was she getting worse already? Maybe she would go to bed early and get her strength back. Surely that was all she needed, a good rest.

She rummaged around in a dresser drawer for a moment before pulling out a big elastic band. Gathering the mass of hair that she had styled into loose curls earlier that day, she wrapped the elastic band around to hold it in place. With this done, she grabbed the cordless phone and headed across the hall.

In the pretty, rose-colored bathroom, she shut the door, sat down on the edge of the tub, and filled it with water. She stripped off her clothes and stepped in, slowly lowering herself into the steaming liquid. She relaxed with a relieved sigh. Leaning back, she rested her head against the cool porcelain tub and closed her eyes, while stray curls floated around her shoulders on top of the water.

For a few minutes she forced her mind to go completely blank and allowed her tired body to soak in the soothing heat. A content smile played on her lips as her arms floated weightlessly around her. It wasn't long, however, when thoughts of Jake seeped in to her peaceful contentment. She willingly allowed her mind to wander over what had happened between them in the not-too-distant past and what she hoped would happen in the near future. Her thoughts continued with bold freedom, until she was forced to pause and calm her racing pulse.

She sat up and grabbed the soap and washcloth, trying to forget her previous obsession for a moment. She thought of what Rebecca had said about Austin. Of course she knew that Austin did not care for her in the way Becca had suggested. But she wondered how deep her own feelings for Austin truly went. She was glad Jake was in her life now; she no longer had to fight feelings for Austin very long. She wanted Jake. She would do anything for the opportunity to give herself to him. Once again her mind belonged to Jake Cutler.

She noticed the water was cooling off, so she turned it back on, letting hot water run briefly before shutting it off again. She wasn't ready to relinquish the tub of relaxation and her thoughts full of Jake. Before she was able to enter back into the solitude of her mind, the telephone rang. She reached over the side of the tub and picked up the phone she had left on the floor.

"Hello?"

"Alyssa?" asked a deep male voice.

"Yes."

"I'm glad I caught you. I've missed hearing your voice."

Alyssa's heart leaped into her throat as she forced herself to breathe. It was Jake! She couldn't believe it. He had actually called her!

His rasping voice spoke again when she remained silent. "Do you know who this is?"

"Uh, I think so. Is this Jake?" She didn't want to be too obvious and let him know that she would recognize his voice in her dreams.

"Yeah. How ya doing?"

She forced herself to answer in the midst of her swirling thoughts. He had actually called her! That meant that he had been thinking about her. They made small talk while she drank in the sound of his voice. She ate his words up as if they were her very life source.

Carefully she finagled her way out of the tub and to her room, throwing on some pajamas, while not dropping the phone. Being out of the tub and dressed, she felt less nervous and began to talk halfway intelligently.

"So what are you doing, anyway?" They had been talking for some time, so Alyssa sensed that Jake's question was more than casual.

"Well, my whole family went out, and I'm home alone. I'm just sitting here in my bedroom. I guess you caught me at the wrong time, huh?" She had gotten her tongue back in control and was playing the part of a desperate flirt beautifully. Though her tone was apologetic, she was confident that her words would have the desired effect.

"Actually, it sounds like I called at the perfect moment," he said roughly. She smiled as her words had hit their mark. "I just wish I was there." Suddenly the bedroom disappeared. All that existed for Alyssa was Jake's voice and the phone in her hand that she clung to. The phone was her lifeline, her connection to Jake. Her fingers began to ache from holding it so tightly. Alyssa listened to the deep, husky voice, speaking the very thoughts she had been having moments before. Her hand moved unconsciously to her racing heart as if to slow it and catch her shallow breath. Finally, mercifully, Jake's voice paused.

"Alyssa, are you still there?" Jake asked laughing, obviously pleased with himself.

"Yes," she whispered almost inaudibly.

"You know what I think? I think you should come over to my place. We'll have our own little party," he said softly.

Alyssa's stomach flipped several times, and her eyes went wide again. *Go over? Yes, go over!* The thought made her excited and fearful at the same time. "OK," she said with little thought. "Oh, no...wait, my brother took my car. I have no way of getting there." The deep disappointment was obvious in her voice. She instantly began searching her brain for any possible way of getting there. She turned to peer out the large window in her room. If anything, it was raining harder, and she was already tired. She'd never make it to his cabin if she tried to walk.

She felt slightly insane, crazed with desire. Like an addict who would steal or sell their body for the drug that fed their need, she would risk the wrath of her family for satisfaction. "Why don't you come here?"

Her question met with brief silence before Jake replied. "Alright, I'm on my way." The line went dead before Alyssa could respond.

Alyssa's heart stopped, and fear swept over her. "Jake? Jake!" *Oh my God! He's coming here! What am I going to do?* She froze with the telephone in her hand and what-ifs racing through her mind. Then, suddenly she realized that several minutes had passed, and she hadn't moved. "Shoot," she muttered and threw the phone heedlessly aside, quickly sliding off the bed. Jake was coming over, and she had to make herself presentable. She glanced in the full-length mirror briefly. Standing there, seeing what Jake might soon see, she bit her lip fearfully. "Oh no," she cried softly, before heading to her vanity to fix her hair.

She forgot about the possibility of being caught by her family in a rather compromising situation. She forgot about all the dangers of being with a man like Jake. She forgot about everything except her ever-increasing need. It was all that truly mattered after all.

Nine

Jake jumped on his motorcycle and headed for the wooded path. The harsh rain forced him to go slowly as he squinted his eyes to see. He was anxious, too anxious, and forced his raging hormones to calm. He must be careful least he scare her. She was innocent, and innocent women had to be treated gently at first. He smiled to himself. She wanted him so bad that she wasn't thinking straight. He had already won. He was just on his way to collect his prize.

Alyssa looked at herself in the mirror. She had hastily put on a simple, but pretty, lavender dress. It shaped her body nicely and fell a couple inches above her knees. She had combed her hair until it lay straight and shining around her shoulders.

Finally she turned from the mirror. She was sure Jake would not want her when he saw how horrid she looked. She went into the living room where she paced nervously. Suddenly she was no longer the bold woman who flirted seductively moments before; she had become an anxious girl, unsure of what to expect. Sitting down near the fireplace, clenching her shaking hands in her lap, she forced herself to breathe as her mind vividly predicted the coming events. She wasn't sure if she could tolerate the wait.

As she held her stomach and willed it not to be sick, an unpleasant thought snuck in unexpectedly. A voice, almost a whisper, asked a simple question inside her.

Is it sin?

Her mind and body instantly retaliated and screamed, *Who cares!* However, the thought remained, and she could not throw it away.

Is it sin?

She allowed herself to ponder the question. She had grown very fond of Jake since their last conversation and thought she was falling in love with him. She had learned a great deal on the phone and liked what she learned, and that was just a stepping stone to love.

She was surprised that suddenly she felt she loved Jake. But who could define love? Who could say at what moment love begins for each individual? Then if she loved him, how could giving herself to him be so wrong? No, God would understand her need. God would allow her this happiness.

Are you sure?

Yes! She was sure…sort of…almost positive.

Alyssa stood up and paced around the room again. She was angry at her conscience for adding this little problem to her night. It was too late now anyway. Jake was on his way, and she couldn't turn him away after he had come all the way to her place. Besides that, she needed him. If she refused him now, she would either die from such an unfed hunger or at least go mad.

A knock on the glass doors pulled her from her thoughts. She turned, seeing Jake standing in the door, and her heart stopped. He opened it slowly and walked in, his hair and black leather jacket dripping wet. "Hi." He smiled as his eyes traveled the length of her. That familiar look made her feel she might jump out of her skin. She placed a shaky hand over her stomach, praying her nervousness would ease before she vomited.

"Hi." She cringed inwardly at her shaking voice. "Come in…uh…make yourself at home. Would you like something to drink or…something?" It was settled in her mind, she was a complete idiot.

"Sure." An amused grin cropped up on his unshaven face. Alyssa turned quickly so he would not see her turn red from embarrassment, and so she could tear herself from those piercing eyes. She went to the kitchen, and he followed close behind, watching her small hips sway and her hair lay thick down her back.

She opened the fridge, grabbed two sodas and handed one to him, managing a smile. "I hope Pepsi is alright."

"Perfect." He quickly opened the can and downed a few gulps without taking his eyes off her.

As she watched him, she was overcome by guilt. Somehow she felt this was not right. Somehow she knew that maybe he should not be there. *What's the problem?* she asked herself desperately. *Why are you suddenly feeling guilty? Stop it. This isn't the time to be feeling these things!* Jake set the can down on the table, still staring intently at her.

After a moment, Jake slipped off his wet jacket and threw it on the chair. He took a couple steps closer to her and spoke in a low, hushed voice. "Sweetheart, you seem a little nervous. You sure you're alright?"

"Yes." She turned away from him, feeling she might pass out from sheer anticipation. She needed a minute to think, to figure out the new things crowding her brain. She went to the cupboard, reaching for the handle. Suddenly Jake's hand covered hers and pulled it away slowly. "I was just going to get a glass," she breathed a weak explanation.

Jake's hand was hot over her own, like fire. Instantly her mind whirled back to her mother's childhood warnings, "Don't touch the stove. It's hot!" and "Don't play with fire, or you'll get burned!" The knot in her stomach tightened painfully. Her heart beat so fast she believed she would faint. Jake pulled her arm down until it encircled her waist under his arm. He was so close to her now.

Her mouth tried to make a sound. *Wait, maybe we should talk about this. I need to think. Maybe this is not right…*but her lips simply moved with no sound coming out. She felt his hot breath on her neck. *Maybe…*the arguments died as quickly as they came when his fingers lightly brushed her neck, gently pushing her hair off her shoulder. Each voice that had dared protest was now gone.

He looked down at her with a knowing smile and saw the look: she was indeed enslaved to him. Their eyes met in an unspoken understanding as Alyssa turned to face him. Jake strove to keep his desire under control so he would not scare her. "You're so beautiful," he whispered near her ear. Alyssa closed her eyes and allowed his words to become real to her. She had never been told that before by a man, not like Jake had said it. She believed him, and she felt beautiful.

"Jake." Her whispered plea was breathed from a region that went much deeper than her flesh. Though her physical need was all that she was conscious of at that moment, her heart cried out for fulfillment even more loudly. She felt an urgency she had never known consume her. Her voice was desperate. "Jake, I need you," she pleaded shakily. "I need you."

Jake's smile broke out across his face. Victory was sweet to him. He was ready to claim his prize. "I know, Sweetheart. I'm going to take care of you," he said, ready to release his own desire upon her completely, until a knock at the door froze them both.

Jake cursed violently and let go of her while Alyssa called out in a voice that seemed not her own. "Who is it?"

"Alyssa! It's me, Austin. Can I come in?"

"No!" she yelled out too quick and urgently. She slid out from between Jake and the cupboard. "I mean, just a minute."

Jake quickly clasped her wrist. "Send him away!"

Alyssa looked with uncertainty toward the door. Thankfully the shade was drawn so Austin could not see in. "I'm kind of busy, Austin. Maybe you could come back tomorrow?" *Please come back tomorrow. Please leave now!*

"Lyssa, it's really important. I need to talk to you. It's about Tyler. Something's happened, and your parents asked me to find you."

Cold fear blended with the fiery heat of desire as Austin's words sunk in. She pulled her arm free from Jake. "It's Tyler." She looked at Jake, pleading for him to understand. "I've got to let him in." Jake cursed again as she went to the door.

95

Alyssa opened the door, letting Austin in. "What happened, Austin? Is Tyler OK?" Austin did not reply, but simply stared past her to Jake. Alyssa's face turned deep red as she groped for some explanation to give Austin, but he waited for none.

Alyssa saw the anger burning in his eyes as he looked at Jake, even before hearing it in his curt tone. "He's been in an accident and is in the hospital. They're not sure how he is yet. Your parents tried calling, but apparently there was no answer. They got worried." He paused meaningfully, glancing again at Jake. "They wanted me to see if you were alright and to bring you down there if you wanted to go."

Jake walked over and wrapped an arm around Alyssa's waist. "I'll take her in a little while." He punctuated his statement with a possessive squeeze.

"No, Jake." Alyssa spoke quickly, wanting to avoid any possible conflict at the hospital. "I should go with Austin."

"I'll wait for you outside." Austin did not spare another glance at Jake as he walked out, shutting the door behind him.

Once Austin had gone outside Jake turned her around quickly and cupped her face in his hand. "Come on," he said with his enticing smile and fire-filled eyes. "Let's go to your room. He can wait."

Alyssa pulled away from him abruptly. When she spoke, her resolve was less than convincing. "My brother is hurt. I need to go."

Jake's promising smile did not disappear. "Just for a few precious moments, Alyssa. You can't leave yet," he whispered in a seductive voice.

Alyssa's breath caught in her throat, and she closed her eyes unwillingly. He took her hand and brought it to his lips. His mouth touched her fingers and for an instant she felt her insides melt. She didn't pull her hand away; instead she stepped closer to him. *A few precious moments. What's the harm?* She was a slave to his expert touch.

"Alyssa!" Austin called from outside. "You coming?"

She opened her eyes quickly and backed away from Jake, horrified at herself for forgetting her brother so completely. "I'm sorry," she choked, her eyes begging him to understand. "I'm so sorry, Jake."

Jake heard the finality in her voice and decided not to press further. There would be other nights when they would not be bothered;

he would make sure of it. Cursing several times, he grabbed his jacket and left without another word to Alyssa.

She went to her room and quickly changed her clothes. How would she face Austin? She was still shaking from the memory of Jake's touch. The sensations had not died when he left. In fact, they burned strong and impatient, crying out for him. She tried to push aside what had just happened as she went outside to where Austin waited.

Ten

The silence between Austin and Alyssa was thick and frightening. Alyssa still longed for Jake, but dread and guilt rose inside of her as well. Was her brother seriously hurt? She had almost let that question slip from her at Jake's touch. Now she felt like the lowest person on earth, and it didn't help that Austin was driving in complete silence. She could tell he was angry. The thought of him being upset with her disturbed her beyond reason.

Besides not talking, Austin tried to look at Alyssa as little as possible. The image of her when he had walked in on something he wished he hadn't seen was stuck in his mind. Her flushed cheeks, shaking hands, and breathless voice. Her eyes full of desire—for Jake.

Austin was angry but not at Alyssa. He was angry with Jake for taking advantage of an innocent girl to serve his selfish desires. Alyssa didn't know where it would lead. Jake didn't care, and she couldn't see beyond her longing for love. Austin knew where it would lead—farther away from Christ and closer to death's door.

He was also angry with himself. When he walked into the kitchen and saw her with Jake, the ugly spirit of jealousy sliced at his heart. Alyssa's desire wasn't for him; it was for Jake. For a moment he silently willed her eyes to look at him that way. However, deep down he didn't want Alyssa to desire him that way, for that wasn't love. He had to keep reminding himself of this as he drove and prayed for God's peace and wisdom.

Finally Alyssa took a shaky breath and braved a question in the thick silence. "Is Tyler alright?"

Her quiet voice was full of humility, and Austin softened, regretting his coldness, and tried to speak gently to her. "I'm not sure. A moose ran out in front of him, and his car went off the road and hit a tree." He glanced sideways at her, worry replacing his anger, then continued. "Your Mom said that he's unconscious."

Alyssa bit her lip as tears filled her eyes. Had he been drinking? She didn't even want to ask. He had been caught once in the past for driving drunk and had just gotten his license back a few months ago. Alyssa closed her eyes and rested her head against the window. Suddenly she was very tired. Her head, arms, and legs all felt heavy and awkward. She wanted to sleep, to forget, to not think for awhile, and to not feel scared or guilty for things she couldn't control.

Austin spoke softly. "He'll be OK, Lyssa. He's strong. He'll make it."

Alyssa's voice was washed with tears. "I just wish there was something I could do. If I hadn't let him use my car..."

"This is not your fault," Austin said firmly. "You can't blame yourself. All you can do is pray and trust God."

"God doesn't hear my prayers." A single tear punctuated the hopelessness in her voice.

"Yes He does! God knows every thought before you even know you're thinking it. He hears every word you speak."

Alyssa cringed inwardly at that declaration. God knows all her thoughts. Surely He would overlook a few little thoughts that weren't so pure, wouldn't He? Yes, God knew her thoughts and her needs and had answered them with Jake. She felt better once she had reasoned out that twinge of guilt. "I know. You're right."

"Come on, we'll pray together right now." He held out his free hand and took her hand in his. "Father, we come before You, in the name of Jesus Christ, believing that You are the God of heaven and earth, the God of all power and all authority. We thank You that we can come before You on behalf of Tyler, knowing that You hear us and will answer. Father, You are the God who heals us. I pray, Lord, that You would fill that hospital room with Your Holy Spirit and power and touch Tyler. I pray he will wake up perfectly whole and healthy. And, Lord, I pray You grant Alyssa and her family Your peace. Amen."

Alyssa smiled at Austin in gratitude. She did feel better, though wondered if they should have prayed longer or harder. As if reading her thoughts, Austin answered her question.

"Just believe. He sees your heart and knows what it's crying for." Alyssa was comforted, not just in believing Tyler would be all right but also that the Lord would grant her Jake's love.

When they reached the hospital, Austin jumped out of his truck and walked around to open Alyssa's door for her. She stepped nervously to the payment. Her legs had started aching halfway through the drive, and she knew it wouldn't be long before they gave out if she did not rest awhile. Finding her knees wobbly but able to move, she gave Austin a tentative smile and started toward the hospital.

Austin noticed her carefulness and touched her arm tentatively. "Can I help?"

"Maybe I could just hold on to you, my legs are a little tired," she mumbled in embarrassment. She despised asking for help. She saw over the years how it frustrated her family, and she hated putting anyone through the trouble. But sometimes she had no choice.

"By all means m'lady." Austin smiled and gallantly held his arm out. Her embarrassment vanished as she laughed up at him and slid her arm through his for support.

Once inside, Alyssa led Austin around the familiar surroundings. She had practically lived inside the whitewashed walls covered with their nature paintings when she was a child. She found the ward easily and went to the nurse's desk.

"Alyssa! How are you?" the plump, gray-haired nurse asked with a pleasant smile. "I haven't seen you for so long, which is good, I guess!"

"Yeah it is, but I do miss you." Alyssa smiled in return at the nurse she had called her second mom years ago.

"We miss you, too." The nurse glanced at the tall handsome man holding her arm as she spoke. "I'm sorry about Tyler. He's in room 303. He's unconscious but has no internal injuries. We'll know more if—when he wakes up."

Alyssa thanked the nurse and headed for Tyler's room. She carefully took her arm from Austin's before going in. Her mother sat on the bed beside Tyler's unconscious body. Upon entering the small, sterile room, she saw a rocking chair and thankfully sank into it before studying her mother's haggard face.

"How is he?" Alyssa felt the need to ask, to somehow fill the deathly silence pervading the room. Austin stood quietly beside Alyssa's chair.

Catherine turned her mournful gaze back to her son. "The doctor won't know anything until he wakes up." Her voice was dry and brittle, lifeless. Alyssa cast a worried glance up at Austin, who returned a reassuring smile. Catherine suddenly looked old to Alyssa. She had never thought her mother old, but as she watched her stroke Tyler's arm, she saw hands that were wrinkled and worn. Her eyes were tired, and her hair looked more gray than Alyssa remembered.

"He's going to be OK, Mom," she said softly, though she felt somewhat desperate. Her mother was always so strong, but now she looked weak. It scared her to see Catherine looking frightened and hopeless and would rather she was angry and screaming.

Catherine sighed as her rough looking hands went up to brush away the quick tears that came. "What if he doesn't wake up?"

"He will." Austin did not flinch, but looked directly into Catherine's eyes as he spoke with certainty.

"We prayed," Alyssa added. "God hears our prayers. We just have to have faith and believe." She repeated the words Austin had spoken previously.

Austin, unsure of what to do, went over to where Catherine sat. He placed a gentle hand on her shoulder and spoke quietly but with an assurance that caused Catherine's tears to stop. "Mrs. Langer, Tyler is going to be fine. I know it." Catherine looked at the man before her.

He spoke his words firmly, leaving no room for question, and his eyes held a comforting light. She reached grateful arms around him in a hug. Austin held her for a moment before letting go.

Catherine laughed slightly, a little embarrassed by her show of emotion. "Thank you." As if suddenly noticing Alyssa's presence in the room, she turned to her. "I see you found my daughter. I appreciate you checking on her for me." She thanked Austin again while succeeding in humiliating Alyssa. "I tried calling for an hour. I thought you fell or something with the phone off the hook."

Alyssa's concern quickly flipped to angry frustration at her mother's demeaning words. Did Catherine have to say such things in front of Austin, of all people? "I was talking to someone."

"Who?"

"Someone from work." Heat flooded Alyssa's cheeks at the question and her quick reply. Afterward, Alyssa felt as though Austin's eyes would burn right through her soul if he looked at her any harder. She quickly changed the subject. "Where's Dad?"

"He's around somewhere. He can't stand to sit still in any one place. I told Elizabeth not to bother coming and dragging the kids down here."

Silence filled the room, with each of them in their own thoughts. Alyssa rested her head on the back of the chair and closed her eyes in exhaustion. Her heart lifted a continual plea before God. *Please let him be all right, Lord. Please let him live.* The quietness of the room and her silent pleas lasted until the total exhaustion she felt crept in, causing her to sleep.

During this time Austin felt he didn't belong but wanted to remain available in case they needed him for anything. Ken came back and began talking with Catherine in hushed, worried tones. Austin slipped from the room unnoticed, attempting to give the family some privacy. He felt peace in his stomach and had no doubts Tyler would wake up healthy. As he walked the hall he prayed fervently to God. *I rejoice, Lord, that You will raise Tyler up. Lord, I pray Your name would be glorified for this family. That when You raise Tyler up, they will have no opportunity to doubt that it was You that saved him, healed him, and raised him from the grip of death.* He continued walking and praying silently, not noticing or caring that the nurse behind the desk was watching him peculiarly.

Finally he went back to Tyler's room to see if they needed him further before he left. It was still quiet when he entered, with both parents watching their son. Austin's gaze rested on Alyssa's sleeping form in the rocking chair. His breath caught in his throat when he looked upon what he thought must be a sleeping angel. Her sweet face was so completely untroubled, so completely beautiful. Her eyes were hidden behind thick black lashes resting on perfect skin. *She's not real. She's too beautiful to be real.*

"She looked exhausted when she came in." Catherine's voice drew him from his thoughts. "She should be home resting. I don't want her getting sick." There was a touch of gentleness in Catherine's expression as she looked at her daughter. "Would you mind taking her home, Austin?"

"No, of course not."

"Could you stay at the house until Rebecca gets home? Ally doesn't like to admit it, but when she gets this tired she really does have a hard time getting around. I would feel better knowing someone was there."

"No problem."

"Thank you." Catherine got up and went to her daughter's sleeping form and gently shook her awake. "Austin is going to take you home. We'll let you know if there's any change."

Alyssa, feeling foolish for falling asleep, nodded, realizing she was no good to Tyler anyway.

"Would you pray with us before you leave?" Catherine asked. When they both agreed, Catherine took her son's hand and prayed while Alyssa, Austin, and Ken bowed their heads in silence. "Lord Jesus, I thank You for sparing Tyler's life. I pray that if it is Your will, You would allow him to come back to us. But Lord, if You chose to take him, give us strength." Catherine stopped to wipe a tissue across her nose.

Austin grew increasingly uncomfortable with the prayer. His spirit rebelled at the words *if it is Your will.* Catherine wasn't praying the prayer of faith but one of acceptance to whatever devices the enemy may use. She continued through sobs, "Lord…"

"Mrs. Langer," Austin interrupted suddenly. Every eye opened and turned to him in surprise, waiting for him to speak. Listening to the prayer caused a holy fire to stir inside of him until it burst forth from his mouth. Righteous anger rose against the lies instilled into these people. "God is not willing that any of His children die or be sick," he said firmly, his eyes blazing at them. "God is the Healer, Deliverer, and Savior." His words gained him strange stares from the others in the room.

Austin turned away from the looks he received from Tyler's family and went to the bed. He laid his strong hand on top of Tyler's head and spoke a quiet command. "In the name of Jesus Christ, I break the hold of the enemy over this man. Tyler, wake up!"

There was complete silence in the room while each stared in amazement. Catherine was too dumbfounded to speak but felt offense rapidly growing within her. Alyssa was scared of what her mother might say to Austin's well-meant prayer and felt bad for how foolish he was going to look when Tyler didn't wake up. Ken almost laughed at the rancher's eccentric religious ways.

When there was no response from the unconscious figure lying in the bed, Austin bent closer to him and spoke fiercely. "Tyler! In the name of Jesus, wake up now!" Chills went up Alyssa's spine at his voice. It wasn't a prayer that Austin prayed; it was a command that he spoke with a zeal that startled her. Suddenly she almost expected Tyler to wake up, for Austin spoke with such authority.

"Austin…" Catherine's voice began to put an end to the show. But her objection was interrupted by a moan coming from Tyler. His eyes slowly opened and looked around at the shocked and amazed expressions of his family. Gasps, shouts, and tears of joy mingled together to form a joyous sound.

Catherine excitedly jumped and hugged her son while Ken stood dumbfounded. Alyssa looked up as Austin's eyes met hers. His eyes seemed to shine like blue fire and his expression was calm yet radiant. A slight shiver of awe and fear ran through her as she watched him. Then a small smile spread humbly across his face as he reached out a hand to her. "Come see your brother." Alyssa did as she was told, walking over to Tyler.

She stood near the bed and smiled down at her brother in amazement while Catherine asked him about what had happened. Tyler answered hoarsely, saying he had hit a moose before even realizing what it was.

"I was so scared, Tyler. They said you were thrown from the car, and my heart just stopped."

"I wasn't thrown from the car, Mom," he croaked.

"But they found you a ways away from the car."

"Yeah, but I wasn't thrown from it." Tyler's eyes got big as he began to tell the untold story. "I wasn't wearing my seatbelt, but when I slammed into the moose I didn't get hurt." Tyler stared, as if he were remembering the scene vividly in his mind. "It was like these two hands were pinned to my chest keeping me in my seat. I could feel them," he whispered with his own hands on his chest. He looked around to see if anyone believed him. "I know it's weird, but it's true. After I hit the tree, I got out of the car and started walking. That's when I got dizzy and fell. The fall knocked me out I guess."

"Praise God!" Catherine voiced her thanksgiving to the Lord.

"Tyler," Austin's voice broke in. "Jesus Christ was with you in that car, holding you in your seat. He saved your life for a purpose."

"I know." Tyler's humble amazement was undeniable. "I don't know why. I haven't done anything for Him. But I'll change—I promise. No more drinking." His eyes clouded with guilt, like a man who had tasted death and suddenly had a chance to start over.

"The important thing is giving your life to Christ," Austin insisted. "Invite Him into your heart and live for Him, and you will see more joy than you ever thought possible. Don't wait until it's too late." Austin pierced Tyler's eyes with his own fire filled gaze.

"I'd like to. What do I do?"

Austin led Tyler in a prayer of repentance and salvation. Alyssa was amazed, and rejoiced that such a thing was happening. Catherine cried happily until the prayer was over.

Everyone started talking again, telling Tyler how glad they were that he was OK and how thankful they were to God. After a short time

105

Ken demanded that Alyssa go home and rest, seeing how tired and drawn she looked.

Austin walked her to the truck, lifting her effortlessly in the seat when she failed in her attempt to step up, her strength completely sapped. She prayed she would at least be able to spare her pride and walk into her home.

Looking over at Austin, she studied him in the darkness. Lights from the passing street lamps flashed across his face, revealing his strong jaw and full mouth. She felt a new sense of awe for this man whom she had always respected. There was a strength and assurance that radiated from him, and it drew her. Though he had always fascinated her, that night she saw something different. He wasn't just kind and gentle and handsome, he was also strong, fierce, and commanding. He was sure of himself, yet so humble at the same time.

"It was really amazing what you did tonight, the way you prayed for Tyler." Though she spoke quietly, her voice seemed loud in the stillness of the truck.

He glanced at her with a shy grin. "I didn't even know what I was doing. The Spirit of God just started speaking. That's how it should be with God's people all the time—speaking death and disease away with one command. Jesus said we would do greater things than He did while He was on the earth." Austin was excited now, and Alyssa could see his face shine in the dark truck.

He finally realized what God had done through him and was in awe of the awesome Lord of his life. "God is so amazing!" He let out a loud yelp and pounded the steering wheel, then laughed at the strange look Alyssa gave him. She laughed with him, marveling at how excited he got over God.

"I don't know about you, Austin. You get stranger all the time."

He flashed a brilliant smile back at her. "Yeah, but you love me anyway right?"

"Of course!" She laughed lightly at his supposed teasing.

They talked a little more then grew quiet as each recounted the events of the evening in their thoughts. Austin tried not to think about seeing Jake and Alyssa together. He simply allowed the Spirit of God to stir joy within him, and blessed God for using him in such a mighty way. He felt so unworthy of God's goodness. *Lord, I am so small and pathetic. I want to be the man of God You want me to be. I want to be used by You.*

When he pulled into Alyssa's driveway and turned the truck off, he saw her sleeping once again. Smiling to himself, he watched her. Without thinking, he reached out and touched her hair lightly. He studied her small, graceful features, causing his heart to overwhelm with emotion. *Lord, I love her so much that it hurts. I want to tell her, to show her. I want to hold her forever and take away all the pain in her life. Jesus, why can't I tell her?* He wanted to speak the depths of his heart to her and risk her laughing in his face.

But he couldn't. He didn't know why, but God was strongly keeping him from doing so. Austin had spent many hours in prayer since the revelation of his love for Alyssa and clearly heard God warning him not to speak of it to her. He prayed once more what he had already prayed a thousand times. *If she is not the woman You have for me, Lord, then take this love away from me. Must I suffer for nothing?* Like always, his heart answered back stronger than ever with throbs of pure love.

He finally got out of the truck and went around to her side. He didn't want to wake her; it was plain how exhausted she was. *I wonder why,* his mind asked sarcastically. He gently lifted her into his arms and shut the truck door as quietly as possible with his foot. He blocked out her nearness as best he could and went inside the house.

He somehow managed to get in, shut the door, and turn on the light with his hands full. Then he realized that he didn't know where her room was. While he wandered around, she began to wake up. "Is this your room?" he asked her quietly, flicking on the light of the bedroom.

"Yeah," she mumbled, embarrassed to have fallen asleep on him again. "I'm sorry, Austin," she said as he set her down on the edge of the bed. "You should have woken me up."

He knelt down at her feet and began to untie her shoes and slip them off. "Either you're working too hard, or I'm a very boring person." An irresistible grin dimpled his face. Her light laughter rolled over the strings of his heart like music. *If everything I said made her laugh like that, I would never stop talking.*

"You are anything but boring."

When he had removed her shoes she stood up while he pulled down the blankets on her bed before helping her back in. "Why is it that such a small person has such a huge bed? I'm not sure if I could even climb into it." Somehow his words made her feel much less foolish for needing his help, and she was grateful.

"I like it." She lifted her chin stubbornly as he drew the covers up over her. When he had tucked her in and stood looking down on her, she spoke softly while looking into his eyes. "Thank you," she said sincerely. "You always seem to be taking care of me, and you do it so well." Something old and familiar tugged at her heart, only it seemed to pull harder than it ever had. *Oh, how easy it would be to love him!* He was so good, so sweet and gentle with her. Suddenly she felt a deep shame wash over her, remembering his face when he walked in on her and Jake.

"Good night, Lyssa," he said in almost a whisper.

"Austin." Austin turned back, and seeing how her face had become troubled, sat down on the edge of the bed and waited for her to speak. Tears welled up in her eyes and she looked away from him as she spoke. "I...I'm sorry," she said in a quivering whisper. "I'm sorry for...for..." she couldn't bring herself to say the words. *I'm sorry for not listening to you about Jake. Please understand Austin. Please don't hate me. It would kill me if you hated me. You're the only friend I have.*

"Lyssa," he spoke before she fumbled over any more words. He instinctively knew what she was apologizing for, and his heart nearly broke. "You don't need to apologize to me. That's something you'll have to talk to Jesus about."

Alyssa looked into his eyes then and saw them filled with love and compassion. Her soul rejoiced that he did not resent her, so much so that she forgot the last part of what he had said. Impulsively she reached out and touched his face. "You're so good to me. I love you, my friend."

Austin cringed inwardly at her words, knowing it wasn't the kind of love he wanted to hear come from her. He put his hand over hers and turned his face slightly. He brushed a gentle kiss in the palm of her hand before pulling it away and letting go. "Me, too." He rose quickly from her side after choking out the words in return.

"Why did you name the horse Lyssa?" Alyssa's question was blurted suddenly as Austin started once more for the door. She watched him intently, waiting for his answer.

He couldn't help but smile at her curious expression, which to him was adorable. "Well, because you helped me deliver her, and because I think it's a beautiful name." Alyssa grinned at his response. "I also named her that because she was the prettiest darn filly I ever did see," he said in his thickest southern drawl, causing her to lavish one more glorious giggle upon him.

With that he walked to the door, looked at her once more, and turned off the light. "I'll be right out here if you need me. Good night, Lyssa." His voice came to her in the darkness.

"Night, Austin. Thank you." Somehow she was unable to keep sadness from coming, taking the place which Austin had filled moments before. The room suddenly felt empty. She lay in the dark a long time thinking about him. Each time she talked to Austin, she felt a void inside afterward. He seemed to fill the void when he was near, giving her strength. But when he left, his strength and presence left with him.

She was comforted, however knowing that he was close, watching over her. Finally she closed her eyes and her thoughts drifted back to Jake. Thinking of him brought excitement instead of the hopeless longing she felt with thoughts of Austin.

Austin sat in front of the fireplace, silently lifting up his heart before God. He had been there since leaving Alyssa's room twenty minutes earlier. His soul was so full of emotions that he couldn't speak, even if he wanted to. He didn't know what he could say to God that he hadn't already said. God knew his feelings, his hurt, and his desire.

As soon as he left the room he had spoken to the Lord in a hoarse whisper choked with emotion. "God, You know how I care for her. You know my prayer, Lord. Take this love from me that I may better serve

You. Lately, she consumes my thoughts and prayers. But Lord, I trust Your will. If You will not take this love from me, than grant me peace and strength to be her friend."

Now, as Austin waited for Alyssa's family to come home, he felt the Lord reach into his soul and impart peace. He was drawn into the beautiful presence descending in the living room. His burdens suddenly became light and easy. Joy replaced longing. The Spirit of God spoke to him, bringing peace to his troubled soul.

Trust Me!

Austin knew he had to lean on God and not his own understanding. God was not going to remove his love for Alyssa, but somehow He would use it.

Eleven

Alyssa slammed the phone down, frustrated when Jake did not answer. She hadn't woken up until about noon the morning after Tyler's accident and since then had stayed close to her bed. Nighttime had come slowly, leading into another day, and now she sat staring at the inanimate object, praying it would ring. All day long she had hoped, and prayed Jake would call her. Finally, she gave in and called nervously, only to hear ring after ring with no voice answering.

She leaned against the pillows piled behind her back. She was still tired and forced herself to rest as much as possible for the whole day. She was determined not to stay down long! But her spirits plummeted downhill each minute she didn't hear from Jake. At times her entire being was so consumed with her need for him that she felt she might simply die of pain. At other times she just sat motionless, letting the miserable depression have its way.

Where was the happiness that had poked through her cloudy soul two days before? It had died as suddenly as it had come. She had time to consider Jake's motives and convinced herself that he had been completely unsatisfied during their brief moment together. She didn't blame him. As she glanced over to the mirror she could see how disgusting she was and knew no man would ever want her. After all, what man would want a cripple?

Bitter tears came as she gave her reflection a hard look. She was nothing but a joke. She took out her journal and wrote slowly.

Have people looked inside their souls as deeply as I have? If so, are they as frightened by what they find? I find such darkness to the deepest recesses of my soul. If I were to walk around the darkness I'd breathe it in like thick air.

Death consumes me, yet I live. Somewhere there is a voice, so deep inside that often I can't hear it. A small voice whispering hope below the roar of the beast. "Someday!" the voice whispers. Someday there will be joy in my life.

Jake stirs that sweet voice. Or maybe the voice is a curse. Without it, I would cease to have false hope and cease to be disappointed. I would cease to live.

Alyssa paused and looked at herself once more in the mirror. A face stared at her strangely from the glass reflection. She studied herself briefly then continued to write.

I look at myself and am disgusted by what I see. Sometimes I don't even recognize the face looking back. As much as I have searched myself, I still have no idea who I am. I have a million and one faces that I put on for others, but who is the real me? I can't find myself in the midst of the darkness inside.

I'm afraid there is no me. What if all the darkness were washed away, and I no longer felt pain? What would be left? Nothing. Rebecca once said that depression was better than feeling nothing.

Now I must begin to play the part of an accepting, happy cripple. Another layer is added to the many that confine me. What if all those layers were stripped away—what would be left? Nothing.

It hurts to think of the reality of what I am, or what I will become. I have to hold on to the small glimmer of hope or else be overwhelmed by these things. Maybe. Maybe Jake does care. Maybe he will love me...

Is it possible to be addicted to a man or a physical need? My heart, mind, and body cry out for Jake. My flesh demands satisfaction so intensely that it's frightening.

Even as I write I am startled and embarrassed by the truth of my words. I'm not sure what's wrong with me.

Alyssa dropped her pen inside her journal and threw it on the nightstand. She sank under the covers and curled up on her side. Holding her pillow tightly, she closed her eyes and prayed sleep would come mercifully again. But it didn't until sometime later, after visions of Jake had succeeded in tormenting her as they did constantly now. Sleep was Alyssa's only escape.

Twelve

"How are you feeling?" Catherine asked as she entered the living room.

"Extremely bored." Alyssa's mother had talked her into staying home from work to rest, but she was tired of resting. She sat on the couch looking out at the beautiful summer day. She was itching to take a walk to the stables and look for Jake but knew her mother would flip if she dared mention such a thing.

"Be thankful you have time to rest. It won't hurt you to be bored for awhile." Catherine scolded Alyssa as she opened the sliding door to let the warm breeze blow inside.

"I've been doing nothing but sitting around all weekend. I'm going crazy." Alyssa made sure her face showed her misery as she sulked.

Catherine stepped onto the back porch. "Do you want to come sit outside?"

"No," Alyssa mumbled childishly. Annoyed, she got up and went to her room. Upon entering, her eyes narrowed in anger as they rested on her wheelchair sitting idly at her desk. She went to it, meaning to push it into the hall, and then she stopped. Her face fell then brightened at an idea that arose in her head.

She grabbed the chair and pushed it through the living room and onto the backyard porch where her mother sat. She knew Catherine wouldn't be thrilled about her leaving the house, but she couldn't object if Alyssa offered to take the wheelchair. "Mom, I'm going to go for a short walk, or ride I should say. I'll stay in my chair, I promise."

Catherine's forehead wrinkled in concern, but she reluctantly nodded her head. "Don't go too far. You don't want to get run down all over again." Alyssa didn't wait for her to say more but pushed her chair down the ramp then got into it. She pushed her way down the familiar path, wondering why her mother always seemed so angry.

Alyssa soon realized pushing a wheelchair wasn't as easy as she thought it would be, for her arms tired quickly. However it was still quicker than walking, and it satisfied her mother. She hoped no one would come along the path. She hated being seen in the chair. Somehow it almost felt as though she were admitting defeat against the disease.

There had been times in the past when she was forced to use her wheelchair. When she had fallen in the woods was the worst; for over the next two weeks she was too weak to walk and had to be pushed everywhere. During that period, Elizabeth had taken her shopping and Alyssa suddenly felt like she was part of another world—the handicapped world.

In Alyssa's mind there were two kinds of people: the normal and the handicapped. Not many people would admit to seeing the world in this way, but it was obvious to Alyssa that day as she rode through the department stores. Suddenly she felt a huge split dividing her from all the people walking by. She saw herself through the eyes of those who looked at her with careful averted glances, or those who dared to stare openly. She heard it in the strained voices of sales clerks who were forced to wait on her. She could sense the wall built up against her.

She understood that somehow in people's minds, handicapped individuals are separated from healthy people. The problem was that she felt God had made some colossal mistake. She wasn't meant to be on the handicapped side of the great divide. She was supposed to be on the normal side. But things got mixed up, and she was given the wrong body. She didn't feel like a cripple, didn't know how to act like one, and hated being seen as one. She felt like a normal person trapped inside an abnormal body.

Since that time she had hated the chair she now rode in, and she didn't allow herself to be seen in it. The problem was there were times when she was caught off guard, as she was now. Deep within her thoughts she failed to hear Austin approaching, and squealed with surprise when he grabbed the chair and tilted it backward so he was looking down on her face from behind.

"Hey, Lyssa!" he laughed. "Want to do a wheelie?"

"Put me down!" she demanded; though she was laughing too. He did as she commanded and started pushing her down the path, which she gratefully allowed him to do. "See? I told you. Every time you see me you end up doing something for me."

"I guess I'll never learn." Alyssa could hear the smile on his face.

They talked easily as they made their way toward the stables. Alyssa pondered how different Austin was from most people. The first time they met, a little over a year ago, Alyssa had been sitting at the lake in the wheelchair. Austin had been exploring when he found his way there.

She was immediately uncomfortable when he introduced himself to her that day. She could only imagine what she looked like sitting there. But quickly she realized that his eyes did not hold the same fear she had seen in others. It was as if he didn't even see that she was sitting in the chair. She remembered the easy smile spread across his face and his eyes looking into hers intently as he crouched before her and talked. She smiled gratefully thinking of it now.

They reached the end of the path and Austin parted company with her. He ran off toward an older rancher who stood waving at him urgently. Alyssa got out of the wheelchair and walked leisurely toward the stables, not noticing Jake who stood outside of the barn.

Jake watched Alyssa carefully as she walked his way. It had surprised him to see her in a wheelchair, suddenly realizing he hadn't taken her physical situation seriously. Guilt pricked him slightly as he thought of how close he had come to possibly hurting a cripple woman.

Alyssa's eyes caught sight of Jake, and he saw her face light up. Slowly he smiled back and started walking toward her. She seemed to look smaller. Jake's eyes traveled over her, but his new revelation of Alyssa's physical condition held his desires in check. He wasn't quite sure how he would handle the slight complication that now confronted him.

Alyssa suddenly forgot her entire miserable weekend. The endless two days of depression vanished instantly at the sight of Jake's smile. She went through the wooden fence and walked around to where Jake stood waiting.

"Hi, beautiful." Jake slipped his arms momentarily around her waist and kissed her lightly on the cheek. She returned his hug gratefully. "I've missed you," he said looking down at her.

"You have?" Alyssa felt her stomach tighten in a wild kind of joy.

"Of course." Jake attempted to look hurt at her disbelief.

"I missed you. I tried calling this weekend but wasn't able to reach you."

"I went downstate to visit my mother for the weekend," he lied easily. "But I thought about you the whole time." Jake's mind briefly went to the beautiful dark-haired woman he had spent the weekend with. Samantha had been a pleasing and willing distraction and, though he would not see her again, he had happily used her to quench the fire that had not been satisfied after Austin's interruption.

"Yeah, right." Though Alyssa tried to laugh lightly, doubt still laced her words.

"How could I not think of you?" He took her hand lightly in his. Alyssa felt she may faint at his touch and had an intense impulse to pull him into the barn and throw herself at him.

"So how are you doing?" he asked her carefully.

Alyssa didn't miss his glance across the field where she left the wheelchair. "I'm fine," she said quickly. "Come with me. I want to see the filly. Austin named her after me, you know." She nervously led him to the barn, wanting him to forget about the chair that now screamed after her.

"Yes, I know," Jake replied with obvious irritation.

They entered the barn and went to Lady's stall. Alyssa went in and knelt next to the small horse that nestled close to her mother. She stroked and cooed softly to the little filly before looking back up at Jake who watched her. She blushed as her body grew warm under his eyes. Her hands began to tremble slightly as she stood to face him. Grasping her hands together to still them, she wondered at how quickly her emotions flitted from one extreme to another.

"Uh, Jake I…I wanted to apologize for Friday." Alyssa stumbled awkwardly over her words. "I didn't mean to kick you out of my house. I mean, I'm sorry if…" her sentence trailed off miserably when she found no suitable sounding words.

"It's OK. It's not your fault. I saw Tyler this morning riding with the other men. He wasn't in the hospital long." Not wanting to discuss anything too personal until he got things figured out in his mind, Jake strove to change the subject.

Alyssa however wasn't through discussing what had happened and continued her train of thought. "He was out the next day. Anyway, I wanted to let you know that I'm glad we were able to spend some time together. It was nice to be with you." Why did she transform into a nervous child when discussing her feelings with Jake?

"It was nice." Jake glanced around toward the barn door as he spoke.

Alyssa tried to push aside her disappointment at his reaction. His response certainly wasn't the declaration of love and affection she'd hoped for. She tried once again to gain his desired response. "I hope we can see each other again soon. Maybe we could go somewhere or… whatever." She wrung her hands until her knuckles turned white. *Please tell me you enjoyed the time we spent together Friday. Look at me with those black eyes of fire, touch me, kiss me, anything!*

"Sure." His eyes fastened on the filly. "I'll call you." Alyssa's heart sank, and she felt she was being dismissed. Her mind whirled over what could have happened to suddenly make him so indifferent to her. He led her out of the barn into bright sunlight. "I've got to get back to work."

"OK," she said softly, trying to smile.

Jake stopped as though a thought struck him. "Are you going to be home tonight?"

Alyssa's face brightened. Maybe all hope was not lost. "Yes, I'll be home."

Jake's eyes finally found hers again. "I'll call you tonight." He smiled as he bent and kissed her cheek before walking away to join the ranchers on the other side of the field. Alyssa watched him go, trying to identify one of the thousands of emotions flooding her. She wasn't sure if she should be happy, sad, excited, or afraid. All she knew is that she was confused. She didn't feel any better than the day before, only different. For a brief instant she felt such joy at the sight of him. Is that what her life was destined to be—brief moments of utter joy amidst a life of confused pain?

Suddenly very weary, she headed back to the waiting wheelchair. Austin had seen her part with Jake and now watched her as Jake rambled on about an upcoming horse show. Only when she was out of sight did Austin turn his attention back on the present conversation.

"...so we have to start planning for it now," Jake instructed. "Mr. Langer wants to go all out for this year's summer festival. He figures it will be a good time to make some big money."

When Jake had finished, the ranchers dispersed and Austin headed toward his waiting black Morgan.

"Austin." Austin stopped at the sound of his name and turned to face Jake. He stood waiting silently for whatever Jake had to say. "Langer said to have you work with Alyssa arranging some events on the ranch."

"He told me." Austin strained to keep his voice calm. Even as he spoke he could feel his heart harden against the man in front of him. "I'll talk to Alyssa." He started to turn away again when Jake's voice caused him to stop.

"As long as that's all you do with Alyssa."

Austin's eyes narrowed imperceptibly at Jake. His voice was low and almost threatening. "What's that supposed to mean?"

"I'm just reminding you who she belongs to," Jake smiled arrogantly. "Of course, I guess you got the hint the other night." Jake's smile widened triumphantly. He had never detested anyone as he did Austin Jacobs and knew exactly how to hit him where it hurt. Though nothing had happened between him and Alyssa, Austin didn't know that.

119

Austin forced his hands to unclench the fists they had tightened into. *God, help me not to kill him,* he prayed halfheartedly. He raked his hand through his hair and smiled sarcastically at Jake. "I don't know what you're talking about, Cutler. If you'll excuse me, I have work to do."

Irritated at Austin's lack of reaction, Jake started speaking without thought. "You want Alyssa and can't have her. But I have— many times." Jake's harsh laugh rubbed raw Austin's nerves. "She's pretty good, you know." Austin shook his head in disgust and stepped toward his horse.

"I'll tell you what Jacobs. When I'm done with her, she's all yours." Fearing Austin would not play along in his little game, Jake spilled out remarks without thinking. "You can have her. All you've got to do is whisper in her ear just right, and she'll do whatever you want. That is, if you don't mind leftovers." Jake laughed wildly at his own joke, reveling in the intense fury which finally appeared on Austin's face.

Austin didn't even think about what he was doing. Anger flooded him and took over, causing his large fist to slam hard into Jake's face. Jake's laughter died instantly as he fell backward, flat on the ground. His hand went up to cover his bleeding nose and mouth as his eyes flashed heated resentment up at Austin.

Austin's unusually menacing voice spat at the sprawling, bloodied man on the ground. "If I ever hear you say anything like that about Alyssa again, I'll rip your tongue out of your mouth." With that he jumped on his horse, leaving Jake seething by himself.

Jake had never been afraid of any man before, but something in the way Austin's eyes had flashed and the way his nose now throbbed made him take the threat seriously.

It was later that night after work when Austin entered his cabin. Sinking thankfully into the recliner, he closed his eyes and habitually ran a hand through his thick hair and over his rough face. Conviction seized him soon after he left Jake lying on the ground. His anger managed to drown out the guilt for awhile, but he was now left with raw feelings of remorse. He had failed God and knew it. That realization had caused his heart to beat with an ever-increasing dull ache.

He had allowed his old ungodly nature to arise and take over. He wouldn't allow himself to forget what God had brought him out of, changing him into a new creation. There had been a time in his life when he was constantly consumed with hate and took it out on everyone who didn't appeal to him.

But God had redeemed him and forgiven his past. The Lord took the heart that turned to stone when his parents died and replaced it with a heart of flesh. He had vowed never to use violence against others again. He had made a promise to the Lord that he had kept until earlier that day.

All day long thoughts had spilled unwillingly into his mind, causing his spirit to waver doubtfully. *You haven't changed, Austin. You think you're some spiritual Christian now when really, you're no better than when you held that knife on the store clerk. You've failed God, just like you've failed everything else in your life…* On and on the thoughts came all day, until he felt he was too wretched to pray.

Not knowing what else to do, he got up and went into his bedroom. There he sat down on the floor near his bed and reached for his Bible lying on the nightstand. He sat the Bible in front of him and began to flip through the scriptures until he found the one he sought. His broken voice read aloud from Psalm 51.

"Have mercy on me, O God, because of your unfailing love. Because of your great compassion, blot out the stain of my sins. Wash me clean from my guilt. Purify me from my sin." Sobs of repentance washed over him at once as he read David's words. "For I recognize my rebellion; it haunts me day and night. Against you, and you alone, have I sinned; I have done what is evil in your sight. You will be proved right in what you say, and your judgment against me is just. For I was born a sinner—yes, from the moment my mother conceived me. But you desire honesty from the womb, teaching me wisdom even there. Purify me from my sins, and I will be clean; wash me, and I will be whiter than snow. Oh, give me back my joy again; you have broken me—now let me rejoice. Don't keep looking at my sins. Remove the stain of my guilt."

Austin's voice died as he allowed David's words to sink in. He knew just how David must have felt at that moment. David had committed adultery and was made to face his sin. That man, chosen and anointed of God, had failed. Yet even after such a failure, David was called a man after God's own heart. David went to God in repentance and God bestowed mercy and grace to him.

He continued reading more fervently, "Create in me a clean heart, O God. Renew a loyal spirit within me. Do not banish me from your presence, and don't take your Holy Spirit from me. Restore to me the joy of your salvation, and make me willing to obey you. Then I will teach your ways to rebels, and they will return to you. Forgive me for shedding blood, O God who saves; then I will joyfully sing of your forgiveness. Unseal my lips, O Lord, that my mouth may praise you. You do not desire a sacrifice, or I would offer one. You do not want a burnt offering. The sacrifice you desire is a broken spirit. You will not reject a broken and repentant heart, O God."

Flowing tears of joy mingled with sobs of repentance. God would not turn away from his broken spirit and contrite heart. God saw every tear of repentance, counted each one, and held them close to His heart. Austin's weight of guilt he had carried all day was suddenly and wonderfully lifted. He placed every sin before God, asking for forgiveness and a pure heart.

That night Austin learned more wonderful truths about God's love, mercy, and forgiveness. His eyes opened a little more to the most awesome God that he called Lord.

Though he had little sleep, Austin felt like a new man the next morning as he headed out for work. The rising sun was warm on his face as he rode his massive stallion to the field where the ranchers were to meet that morning.

He thought about what his words should be to Jake. He knew what he had to do and was prepared to do it. He would have to humble himself before the man who was such a thorn in his side and ask forgiveness.

As Austin rode, he played the words he would say over in his head. He wasn't looking forward to apologizing. In fact, part of him felt Jake had deserved what he got. But it wasn't his place to judge anyone. It was his place to love—even Jake Cutler.

He slowed his horse as he approached the small group of men, talking and laughing loudly. Jumping down, he walked over and joined them. He noticed Jake carefully avoiding his gaze and flinched slightly at the sight of the foreman's bent and swollen nose.

"Now that we are all here, let's go over your duties." Jake's speech was slightly slurred. He continued talking, giving each man several jobs to do throughout the ranch that day. Finally he addressed Austin. "You go to South Field, check the horses, water supply, fences, everything."

Austin was surprised at his assignment. South Field was the largest field, spanning over thirty-five acres and usually having twenty-three horses or more grazing there. Mr. Langer had bought up large portions of land over the years and owned more acres than any of the ranchers knew. South Field was also the farthest field from the ranch. The size alone usually warranted more than one rancher to go at once.

Despite this, Austin simply nodded without objection. The men broke up and mounted their horses while Austin stayed behind. He spoke sincerely as Jake's dark eyes finally bore into him. "Jake, can I speak with you?"

When Jake did not answer he continued. "I want to apologize for hitting you. It was way out of line, and I'm sorry." Jake's hard face broke into amused astonishment. Austin continued despite Jake's triumphant smile. "I hope you can forgive me," he said honestly, though the words were difficult.

When Austin had waited for several seconds, Jake suddenly burst into ridiculous laughter. Austin remained calm. But his chin rose slightly, and his back straightened so that he towered over Jake even more.

"I can't believe you!" Jake exclaimed incredibly. "You want me to forgive you? You're a bigger jerk than I thought."

"Like I said, I'm sorry." Austin remained calm. "Maybe we can put this behind us. I know I haven't been very civil, and I've had to answer to the Lord for that. I now ask for your forgiveness."

Jake's smile widened again. "Oh yeah, you're some kind of religious nut," he scoffed.

Jake's laughter grated on Austin's nerves. However, he didn't get angry, he suddenly felt sorry for the man in front of him. He stood tall and erect against the laughter, not ashamed of his faith, yet his face softened in pity as he extended his hand to Jake. "I was wrong. Will you forgive me?"

Jake's laughter died as his eyes narrowed at Austin's outstretched hand. Anger and indignation shot through him. Who did this religious idiot think he was? Why did he make Jake feel less than a man, when it was Austin who was so strange? In his rage, Jake threw his fist and hit Austin squarely on the jaw, causing his head to jerk back slightly.

Austin's hand went up to gingerly touch his jaw after the shock wore off. As he did, he checked his emotions, relieved to find no desire for retaliation. He found instead that God had honored his humbling himself by giving peace and compassion for the man. He turned his eyes back to look directly into Jake's, and once more held out his hand to him.

Jake stared in complete speechless amazement at the extended hand. He shook his head unable to speak, then spit vehemently at Austin before turning and walking away.

Austin's hand dropped to his side as he watched Jake get on his horse and ride away. He knew he had done all he could yet still felt regret. He had seen only hatred in Jake and somehow felt he was responsible. He prayed the hatred would not be aimed toward a God Jake did not know.

Thirteen

Alyssa was relieved to be back in her office working. After seeing Jake, the rest of her time home had been plagued with confusion, dying hope, and disappointment. She sat by the phone for several days, waiting for him to call, but he didn't.

She was able to stay somewhat distracted by throwing herself into advertising for the upcoming festival. She looked around her office at the three people waiting for her to speak. Peter Barton was enthusiastically prepared for the new campaign, Candy sat waiting with her pen poised over a notebook, and Bryan Davis rummaged through some papers stacked in front of him. Bryan was a member of the advertising division and was working with Alyssa on ads for the town's festival.

Alyssa looked at Bryan as she explained what her father's plans were for the summer's events. "Dad wants to do some heavy ads, starting right away. I'm working with Austin, our rancher, putting together some of the events we'll be hosting on the ranch. We've got to get the word out, really hype it up."

She handed Bryan some sheets of paper before continuing. "It's a list of things you should be sure are in the commercials. I'm meeting with Austin tonight to plan the schedule, so I'll get you the exact events and times. Candy, would you call the chamber director and get a schedule of the festival events that are planned so far?"

"Sure." Candy scribbled herself a note.

"Bryan, you start working on the ads—generic stuff for now, until I get all the information for you. Call the TV stations and see what kind of deal you can work out." Alyssa shuffled through her papers again.

"No problem," Bryan agreed.

"Pete, the work you have done so far is fantastic. I want to start working on the commercials. We have all your layouts, we've got the crew to film the commercials, and you've agreed to help out with directing them, right?"

"Yup." Peter bobbed his head.

"Good." Alyssa gathered her papers, shoved them into a file, and then smiled at the others. "I guess that's it for now. I thank all of you. I know this time of year is pretty crazy, especially this year! But you've all worked so hard, and I really appreciate it."

The small group dispersed, leaving Alyssa alone to sort out the pile of papers on her desk. She looked dismally at the stack, feeling the weight of despair closing in. It was easier when other people were around. Then she could almost forget about her situation. But when those people left, when she was alone, the silence was deafening upon her soul.

Shaking her head, she began pushing her way through the paperwork after remembering she had planned to meet Austin after work. Time was running short, and before long the festival would have come and gone with nothing to show for it if she didn't get moving. She looked at her calendar; the festival week started on July 6. This gave her less than four weeks to prepare.

As she shuffled through papers, feverishly scribbling notes, she heard a soft knock at her door. Looking up, she managed a smile for Candy as she came in.

"It's quitting time, Boss."

Alyssa glanced at the clock and was surprised to see how quickly the time had passed. "I've just got a few more things here to work out…"

"Go home!" Candy's interruption was almost a demand. "This stuff will still be here in the morning. Go get some rest. You look tired."

Alyssa heard the concern in her secretary's voice, though she didn't take it too seriously. "Alright, Mom. You win."

"Don't I always?" Candy's worried expression broke into a smile. "Come on, I'll walk out with you."

The two reached the parking lot and went their separate ways. Alyssa drove quickly, making it home just in time to change before heading down to meet Austin. He was to meet her where the paths crossed and then walk with her to his cabin. Alyssa had suggested it might be quieter there than at her house.

After changing into jeans and a purple T-shirt, she got her wheelchair and left the house. She had decided it was easier to take her chair whenever she went around the ranch. It eased her mother's misgivings and allowed her to save some of her energy.

Austin was waiting for her when she reached the meeting place. He greeted her with his breathtaking smile and quickly took over pushing her chair. She had learned early in their friendship never to argue when he wanted to do something for her. He was always a gentleman, managing somehow to make Alyssa feel like a lady.

"I hope you weren't waiting long," she said over her shoulder.

"Not at all," he answered easily. "I was just enjoying a moment of rest."

Alyssa noticed his voice held a hint of fatigue. His voice was always so strong, gently flowing up from his soul, speaking directly from his heart. It was the rare kind of man's voice that caused a woman to fall in love simply when he spoke.

"Did you have a hard day?" she asked.

"Just long, I guess." Austin avoided mentioning the extra work Jake had given him. "How about yourself?"

"Oh, my day was fine."

"What about your life?"

"My life," she laughed. "What about it?"

"I was just wondering how you were."

"Everything's fine." The sincerity of his words caused Alyssa to grow pensive.

"With Jake?" Austin didn't want to know but felt he should ask, as her friend. His tone was deep with the effort of voicing such a question.

Alyssa was surprised at the question. She knew Austin wasn't fond of Jake and wondered how much she should say. After him walking in on them not long ago, she was uncomfortable with the subject altogether, but she could not lie to Austin. "I'm not really sure."

"What do you mean?" He was curious now and felt an old sensation of resentment stirring. *Did you hurt her, Jake?*

"I don't know." She hesitated for a moment, then continued nervously. "I really like him, Austin." She waited for some sound of shock or horror to come from behind her. When none came, she spoke again more softly. "I just don't know if he likes me."

Austin was at a loss for words. Her statement sliced deep into him. *I really like him, Austin,* her voice seemed to echo over in his head. What would he say to her now? How could he comfort her knowing Jake cared for no one? "What makes you doubt that he would like you?" he finally managed to ask.

"There's nothing to like," she said flatly.

"Lyssa, you are a beautiful, sweet woman any man would be blessed to have. Don't let Jake make you feel differently." He struggled to keep any anger toward Jake out of his admonishment.

"OK, I'm sorry. Besides that—I don't know—sometimes he's distant or something. I mean, sometimes he looks at me like he's interested, and sometimes he won't look at me at all." Her voice ended deflated. She surprised herself for sharing such things with him but was desperate for advice or encouragement.

"To be honest, if a guy cares about you, he'll show it." Austin didn't want to hurt her, but he couldn't lie either.

"I know." Tears stung Alyssa's eyes as she whispered her response.

Feeling guilty, he tried to lighten her mood. "I'm not certain of his motives, and I pray you're careful. But it's pretty obvious seeing you together that he's interested." Austin again had to fight to keep his sarcasm from showing.

Alyssa's face reddened as she quickly explained. "Oh, that wasn't anything. I mean, nothing happened. You got there right after him, so there wasn't time to...we didn't really have much time to spend together...to talk..." her voice drifted before continuing. "He was pretty mad when I told him he had to leave. Maybe that's why he's acting like he is."

"You're brother was in the hospital. What did he expect?" Austin allowed his irritation at this point.

"That's the problem." Alyssa bit her lip remembering the night vividly. "He was expecting something and didn't get it." Alyssa didn't even realize what she had said. She was lost in her own thoughts, speaking out loud.

Austin's heart skipped a beat or two. The overwhelming sensation of mingled relief and elation he felt surprised him. Nothing had happened! He silently thanked God—for Alyssa's sake, of course.

"If that's his problem, then he needs to grow up and get saved."

Alyssa grinned reluctantly. In the midst of her hopelessness, Austin could make her laugh while still being bluntly honest. What better friend could she ask for?

They reached Austin's cabin, and Alyssa got out of her chair and walked inside as Austin held the door for her. Sometimes she was able to forget the wheelchair, especially when she was with Austin. Though at times some incident would throw the fact that she was different back in her face. Today however, the chair would stay outside, and she would be able to forget and feel normal for awhile.

Austin ushered her into his small, roughly-put-together living room. The tiny space held a deep hunter green couch against one wall, and a matching armchair took up most of the adjacent wall. Austin sat next to Alyssa on the small couch and grabbed some papers lying on the coffee table in front of them. "I wrote down some ideas after your dad talked to me."

Alyssa took the papers from him and looked over his notes. "These are good. Where did you come up with them?"

"We did lots of events like those back home, only on a much bigger scale."

"We need at least one event happening every day of that week, and several for the weekend."

"Is this festival really that big of a deal?" Austin asked skeptically.

"The festival is the biggest thing this county sees all year! The last few years we've had over thirty thousand people in town on that weekend. People come from all around to see the big parade and to go to Family Night."

Austin was trying hard to picture what she was so excitedly describing. In his mind he just couldn't imagine the tiny town holding thousands of people along the small sidewalks. Alyssa saw his doubtful look and laughed.

"Really! The town has a bunch of different stuff going on all week. It's really quite fun if you get involved. It makes me kind of proud to be part of such a close community."

Austin tried to suppress the stirring within him as he watched her face fill with emotion. Her eyes sparkled in excitement, and her full lips were spread in a soft, ravishing smile. Turning away abruptly, he almost croaked out his next words. "I'll be sure not to miss it. Would you like something to drink?" He stood and walked to the small kitchen, looking for an excuse to get some distance between them so he could catch his breath.

"Sure, a soda if you have one."

Austin took his time getting two sodas from the fridge and pouring them into glasses before returning to his place beside her.

"Thanks." Alyssa smiled as she took her glass from him and set it on the coffee table after taking a drink. "OK, now some of the things I was thinking." She turned toward him, showing him some of her own notes. "There are trails all over the woods that lead to different clearings and ponds. Dad has them all mapped out so that people can go with the horses for picnics, swimming, or whatever." She stopped and took another sip of soda before continuing.

"I was thinking that we could have tours or guides to take people around. We could have free trail guides all week for guests."

"That's a good idea. I don't think many people realize what you've got out here." Austin finally found himself being able to forget

Alyssa's nearness long enough to get excited about her ideas. "I remember God speaking to me, telling me to come to Maine. I thought I would never find a horse here, let alone a horse ranch." Alyssa joined his laughter.

"I've heard that from many people."

"I'm amazed at how well your father is doing with the place. Living on the ranch makes me forget I'm in Northern Maine, except of course when winter comes."

Alyssa rolled her eyes. "Don't remind me!"

"We should be just about done with the haying by the time of the festival. We could have hay rides for the kids with an old fashioned wagon, if we could find one."

Austin's suggestion brought a spark to Alyssa's eyes. "Yeah! But it doesn't have to be just for kids, some people find it very romantic," she said smiling coyly.

"Oh really?" Austin played along with her flirting. "I guess I'll just have to find out, won't I?" He grabbed her hand and spoke in a deep southern drawl, "Ms. Langer, would you care to go for a hay ride with me?"

Alyssa fully enjoyed Austin's humor. Though she knew their flirting was in fun and never meant to be taken seriously, it still caused her spirits to glow with pleasure. "Why, Sir, I would love to!" she answered between giggles. "But first we have to finish our work."

They spent over an hour discussing everything from square dancing to horse shows. Finally, with piles of notes in her hand, Alyssa breathed a sigh of relief. "It looks like we've got everything set."

"I think so. I'll work with Rebecca on the horse shows. She's amazing in the saddle."

Alyssa smiled her agreement and brushed aside the twinge of jealousy that pricked her over the admiration in Austin's voice. Why should she be jealous? Austin did not belong to her.

"I'll get in touch with Jake and go over this with him." Alyssa was careful to avoid Austin's eyes. This would give her a perfect excuse to call Jake.

Austin said nothing in return, not trusting his voice or the reoccurring impulse for sarcasm. Though God had removed Austin's

131

intense anger toward Jake, he still had to fight his occasional disapproval and jealousy. *But for the grace of God, I would be just like Jake,* he reminded himself.

"Well, I would love to stay and talk all night, but if I do I'll be late for church. I'll walk you home," he offered.

"Church? On a Tuesday?"

"Actually we have church Sunday through Thursday." Austin's matter-of-fact explanation gained an expression of horror mixed with confusion, causing him to burst out laughing.

"Whatever for?"

"God is moving! People can't get enough of His power. We are in revival, and it's only the beginning. We haven't even begun to see what God can do," Austin said excitedly through his dwindling laughter.

"I knew you went often but, every night?" Alyssa was finding the concept rather hard to grasp, not quite believing someone would go to church so often.

"Every night I can." His eyes suddenly took on a new light. His mouth tipped in a grin as his eyebrows rose slightly. "Why don't you come with me?"

"Tonight?" she asked incredibly. She shouldn't have been surprised at his invitation. He had been inviting her for months now. The church she and her mother attended had split over a year ago after a disagreement concerning the color of the rug in the entryway. The board members had gotten so angry that they voted the pastor be fired.

Neither Catherine nor Alyssa had wished to stick around while the church members looked for a more pliable pastor. They determined to find a new church; they simply hadn't gotten around to it yet. Alyssa had promised to go with Austin sometime, but tonight she was all psyched up to call Jake.

"It will be fun!" Austin looked so excited that Alyssa almost agreed.

"I've got so much to do tonight, and I'm kind of tired…I don't know…"

"Lyssa," he coaxed. "I would love for you to come with me."

Alyssa looked into his deep blue eyes filled with promise. His face wore a pleading, I-know-you-want-to look, and his mouth curved

132

into a half grin, half pout. Alyssa's will slipped away as she watched his pleading expression. *He's got to be the most irresistible man I've ever seen.* She wondered if she would always be so completely incapable of saying no to him.

"Alright," she mumbled reluctantly, though she couldn't resist smiling at the look of pure delight that sprang into his face. It made her feel good that he wanted her with him. "I'll call Mom and let her know."

After she had made the call, she began to have doubts. What if Jake called while she was gone? He hadn't called her yet, and he might try tonight. If he called and she wasn't there, he would probably never call her again.

It was too late, however, to back out. Austin ushered her out the door and to his truck. "Do you want me to bring the chair?"

"No, thank you."

After helping her in, he walked around and got in the driver's side. They were on their way to a church Alyssa knew nothing about, while her heart longed to stay home and wait for the possibility of hearing Jake's voice. She knew she was pathetic but weren't all people who were in love?

"Have you ever seen the church?"

Austin's question broke into her thoughts. "No, I don't think so. What's it called?"

"Center of Rejoicing."

"Huh?" she breathed crinkling her nose. "That's a weird name for a church, isn't it?"

"It fits," he smiled.

"How so?"

"Well, it's a place where we go to rejoice in our God, to celebrate Jesus."

"Oh." Alyssa considered Austin's words, thinking that his church might not be so different from the one she used to attend. They drove for about twenty minutes, talking and laughing, when Austin finally pointed to a large, two-story building. "That's the church's youth center."

Alyssa studied the building, noticing the big sign in the front with the words RAY of Christ. Under that, Rejoice All Youth of Christ was written out. She was impressed by the size of the building but quickly realized that it was small compared to the size of the church they were approaching.

"The RAY Center has a small gym and game room, a sanctuary, a fellowship hall downstairs, and a bunch of other small rooms for different things. The kids love it," Austin was saying as she stared at the huge church.

She noticed the church wasn't magnificent in statue, like some churches its size, but it was quaint and well built. *Inviting* was the word Alyssa would use. It spread across the expanse of the huge field on either side. "It's so big," she said incredibly. "I think I've heard of this place. Is this the church that everyone talks about? It's been on the news, hasn't it?"

"Yeah, they've had some stories on different preachers that have been here."

"How big is this place anyway?" Her mouth gaped at the large building they were approaching.

"The sanctuary seats over two thousand. That's the big part on the right. The part on the left is the Bible school."

Alyssa was amazed—did the entire town hold enough people to fill such a church? "What's that place?" she asked pointing to the small building not far from the church.

"That's the church's radio station."

She sat quietly taking it all in as Austin pulled the truck into the parking lot and found a spot to park in. The number of vehicles alone was enough to amaze her. Though the parking lot spanned some distance, cars were still lined up along the road as far as Alyssa could see on either side.

"I think we're late." Alyssa was about to apologize as Austin opened her door and gave her a hand out.

"The service won't start for thirty minutes or so." He led her to the double glass doors at the front of the church.

As they stepped inside, Alyssa was suddenly nervous. What was she doing here? Had Jake tried to call her yet? She somehow had to put Jake out of her mind and concentrate on not making a fool of herself. It was instantly obvious that Austin was very well liked among the people that crowded the seemingly too small outer room. He introduced her proudly to each person they spoke to.

Austin eventually led her through the lobby and into the sanctuary. Her mouth dropped slightly at the sight of the aisles of two thousand plus chairs—almost all of which were occupied. Her mind was still trying to grasp the reality of so many people going to church on a Tuesday night.

"There's usually a couple chairs down front." Austin leaned toward her, pointing down the aisle. Alyssa stayed close to his side, following his lead. Looking around she found that the deep blends of burgundy, mixed with lighter shades, gave the church a very warm, inviting atmosphere. It was beautiful, but what fascinated Alyssa more was the people.

As she walked among the crowd to find a seat, she had trouble not staring at the faces around her. Voices mingled with laughter floated around from all sides until the sanctuary filled with it. There were those who stood, worshiping with hands raised and tears streaming as if they were completely alone with God. Some seemed to have trouble not jumping or running from sheer excitement or anticipation. Alyssa was unsure of what they found so exciting.

Various scenes unraveled before her, each as mesmerizing as the next for, wherever she looked, Alyssa found the same radiance beaming from the faces of the church members. Whether sitting quietly alone, praying fervently some unspoken prayer, or simply visiting with others, everyone seemed happy. Though she couldn't quite pinpoint its origin, Alyssa could not help but sense the spirit of freedom and peace that reigned inside the church.

Finally making it to a couple of seats in the second row from the front, Austin offered Alyssa a seat before sitting beside her. They had just sat down when a man came toward them with a smile.

"Pastor!" Austin smiled, stood up, and took the man's hand. "I'd like you to meet a friend of mine—Alyssa Langer. Alyssa, this is Pastor French."

Alyssa stood to greet the pastor, noticing his dark hair and brown eyes as he took her hand. *He doesn't look like a pastor.* She noted his handsome features and relaxed, sincere manner as he spoke to her. She liked him immediately.

"You have a beautiful ranch," Pastor French said. "I've been meaning to bring my family out to ride one day."

"Oh, please do! Just let us know when and I'll make sure you have the best horses we have." Alyssa wasn't sure why she had just made such an offer but felt strongly to do something nice for this man's family.

"Thank you. I'll have to take you up on that." Pastor French smiled, just before reaching for the hand of a woman who came to stand beside him.

"Alyssa, this is Pastor's wife, Cloe," Austin introduced.

The woman's eyes sparkled as she extended her hand to Alyssa and smiled warmly. "It's nice to meet you. I'm glad you could come." The warmth in the woman's voice left no room to doubt her sincerity. Alyssa felt as though she had walked into a shower of love. "We've heard a lot about you," she added with a twinkle in her eye.

"It's nice to be here, thank you." Alyssa smiled. She was drawn to Cloe immediately, while wondering what exactly Austin had said about her.

Pastor French's wife was an attractive woman in a quiet, humble way. Her beauty was not just outward but radiated from within. As Cloe asked simple, unobtrusive questions, Alyssa couldn't help but believe the woman cared.

"Austin." Pastor French's voice broke through Alyssa's thoughts. "Jeff just called. He has some emergency and wasn't able to get a hold of you in time. I know it's your night off, but would you mind leading the song service?"

"Oh…uh, no." Austin glanced apologetically down at Alyssa. "No, of course not." Turning toward Alyssa, he gave her a tentative smile. "I'm sorry, Lyssa. I hate to leave you sitting alone, but I'll be back down after the song service. Would you mind?"

Alyssa could see the concern in Austin's face and tried to reassure him with her smile, though she wasn't certain she wanted to be alone. "You're on the worship team?"

"Yeah, but I have a couple days off a week usually. There are two others who lead as well. You don't mind, do you?"

"No." Alyssa's eyes darted to the ever-increasing number of people crowding the sanctuary, making it almost overwhelming.

"Would you sit up front with us?" Alyssa's eyes snapped back to the pastor's wife. Cloe, however, did not wait for an answer. "Austin, get your Bible and bring it up here with us." Her light French accent commanded gently.

Austin gratefully led Alyssa to a seat next to Cloe in the front row, then headed for the platform. Alyssa wanted to hug the woman for rescuing her. Cloe and Alyssa continued to talk each seeming to laugh easily with the other. Alyssa felt an instant bond with the woman, as if she could reveal her deepest secrets to her. She wondered what it was that was so very special about Cloe French.

A young woman who had been sitting a couple seats down from Alyssa got up and came over. Cloe introduced the woman as her sister-in-law. Alexandra smiled a brilliant welcome to the newcomer.

"She and her husband are the youth group leaders," Cloe explained. The two women talked to Alyssa for several minutes, making her feel she had known them for years. Though she was conscious of the thought that she in no way measured up to them, their sincerity and love pushed aside her inadequacy.

Just then a boy came running up to Alexandra and hugged her fiercely. Alexandra knelt next to the boy and looked at him adoringly. "This is my son, Caleb." The boy had the same olive-colored eyes and thick brown hair as his mother. Caleb, whom she judged to be about five years old, charmed Alyssa.

"Hello, Caleb." Alyssa gave the child her warmest smile.

"Hi!" Caleb exclaimed back, his cheek dimpling in a grin. His brown eyes grew large, and his voice quieted slightly. "Are you sick?"

Alyssa's face felt hot under Caleb's wondering eyes. Was it becoming obvious so soon? Fear choked her as she tried to swallow and search for an answer she could give.

Alexandra pulled her son closer, speaking gently. "Caleb, why would you ask such a question? She's not sick, sweetheart."

"Jesus told me He's gonna heal her, so I wondered if she's sick." Unconcerned about his apparent mistake, Caleb continued watching Alyssa with an eerie wisdom.

Alyssa was stunned into silence. Caleb's mother smiled softly at her with eyes that held a small apology, though no embarrassment. Her face was calm and understanding as she attempted an explanation. "I'm sorry. Caleb didn't mean to pry. Sometimes the Lord speaks things to him. My husband and I aren't even surprised anymore with the things that he says."

Alyssa wasn't sure how to respond. Certainly God didn't really just speak to the boy. So how did he know that Alyssa was sick?

"Caleb is young," Alexandra continued. "He's still learning how and when to speak what he hears. I hope he didn't offend you."

"It's OK. I understand." Alyssa smiled through her white lie. She was saved from any more questions when music began to flow through the sanctuary. Alexandra ushered Caleb excitedly back to their seats as the service started.

Alyssa looked curiously around her and saw the entire room overflowing with people standing to their feet expectantly. The worship team was together on the platform. Alyssa guessed there to be about 150 people on the team, with every kind of instrument imaginable.

She stood up with everyone else and turned back toward the stage after eyeing the excited congregation. Austin was seated at a piano, moving his fingers easily over the keys. "Are you ready to praise the Lord?" he yelled into the microphone sitting near his mouth. Alyssa was surprised at the overwhelming volume that exploded in her ears at his question. "All right then—let's praise Him!" The eruption of noise as the people reacted to Austin's challenge caused the very building to rumble.

Austin's hands began to dance over the keys like Alyssa had never seen before. She was instantly in awe of his talent; she hadn't even known he played. It wasn't long before the entire front of the church was filled with people dancing in praise to God.

Alyssa was as enraptured with Austin's singing as she was with his playing. His skilled tenor voice drew her ears to listen. It was a throaty, soulful sound that rose up from the core of his heart and flowed out his mouth. As the music went on in its fast, upbeat pace, she couldn't help but clap along with it.

Suddenly Alyssa got a little nervous at how she was feeling. She was used to getting tired and feeling weak but this was different. Her whole body felt heavy—like the air or atmosphere had suddenly become thick. Noticing that her hands were trembling slightly, she quickly grasped them together, willing them to stop. She swallowed the fearful knot in her throat and prayed for strength and peace.

Alyssa noticed that the pastor looked to be less excitable than his congregation. He clapped and tapped his feet to the music but didn't look too rowdy. Though most of the people looked completely ridiculous in their dancing, it was obvious that they didn't care. There was an appearance of rapture on every face as they danced with all their might before the Lord.

They were having so much fun! *If only I could dance like that!* she thought wistfully with a smile. The smile quickly faded, however, as she realized that she would never be able to be so free. Moving her eyes to Austin once again, she saw that same look of intense joy.

Tears that seemed to forever linger behind her eyes threatened to announce themselves suddenly. She watched Austin—strong, handsome, and full of energy—and knew there was no way such a man could desire her. What a cruel thing it would be to tie a vibrant man to an ugly cripple. She had always known this, but seeing him almost dancing at the piano, and knowing that she'd never dance, slapped the fact in her face like a cold, wet rag. It wasn't just the dancing, it was everything—everything a strong healthy man would want that she couldn't give.

But she could give one man something before it was too late and she lost her only chance. Alyssa finally admitted to herself that she had, in fact, held out some hope, way back in her heart, of knowing Austin's love one day. She realized that Austin had been a kind of surrealistic dream for her. Now she let that dream go sadly and gave her whole heart to something more attainable—Jake.

After what seemed like a very long time, the pastor walked up to the podium. The music died to just Austin playing a spirited song quietly in the background. Even these soft, soulful notes touched the people. Alyssa smiled to herself at the glow on Austin's face. It was easy to see that he loved what he was doing.

Finally managing to tear her eyes from him, Alyssa focused on the pastor. She waited for him to speak, anxious to hear what he would say after such a song service. As he stood silent, he looked like he was listening to something no one else could hear or seeing something no one else could see. Alyssa was fascinated simply by the look on his face as he stood there, experiencing something Alyssa could not feel.

It was a long time before Pastor French spoke. When he did, he spoke three words in a calm direct voice. "God is here."

At that moment people all over the congregation fell. It was like the very words out of the man's mouth were a command that sent the entire crowd to their knees. The pastor disappeared behind his pulpit. Everywhere people bowed before God with upraised hands and raptured faces, worshiping a God they knew was in that very room with them. The worship team dropped their instruments and bowed on the stage, with streaming tears loudly proclaiming their adoration of the Lord.

As she looked around, Alyssa saw only a few poor souls like herself left standing. She felt incredibly out of place and wished she had stayed home. Sitting down, she scolded herself for not bringing a watch. Wasn't it time to move on with the service yet?

After some time, people began to pull themselves up and make their way back to their seats. The pastor reappeared at his pulpit and praised God for the work that He was doing. Alyssa wasn't too sure what exactly it was that God was doing.

The musicians on the stage were excused and Austin came down and took his seat next to Alyssa. "How ya doing?"

She had meant to immediately ask him how much longer the service would last, but his warm whispered breath near her ear caused her to forget her purpose. "Fine." The sudden fluttering in her stomach almost caused her to forget her earlier resolve. *No, Alyssa. He's an impossible dream.* Did he notice how he affected her? She decided he hadn't a clue as she looked up into his smile.

She settled back in her seat and tried to focus on Pastor French's words. She felt much better with Austin beside her. Her hands had stopped trembling for the most part, but she still felt a little heavy. Austin opened his Bible to the scripture from which the pastor read and held the book between himself and Alyssa so she could read along with him.

"I'm going to begin reading with Romans 12:1." Pastor French's voice rang out strong and sure. "Therefore, I urge you, brothers, in view of God's mercy, to offer your bodies as living sacrifices, holy and pleasing to God—this is your spiritual act of worship. Do not conform any longer to the pattern of this world, but be transformed by the renewing of your mind. Then you will be able to test and approve what God's will is—his good, pleasing, and perfect will."

The pastor stopped reading and expounded on the verse, but Alyssa had already lost her concentration. She was still contemplating the first words he read about offering your bodies as sacrifices. She found it hard not to think that it sounded slightly promiscuous. Each cell and fiber in her brain was now finely tuned and ready to twist a word or thought into a forbidden fantasy. As Pastor French talked about offering their bodies to God, Alyssa slipped away and dreamed of offering herself to another.

She didn't even realize when it happened any longer. She could retreat inside herself for long periods of time without anyone ever knowing. On the outside she stared toward the platform the preacher stood on and looked to be listening intently.

"Would you like a piece?" Cloe's whisper startled her out of her thoughts. Alyssa's mouth tipped in an embarrassed grin as she accepted the offered piece of candy.

She sucked on the candy nervously. She didn't know how long the pastor had been preaching. She didn't know if anyone had noticed her total lack of attention or her now red face. All she knew was an overwhelming feeling of shame. She was in a church! Sitting in the house of God, she had allowed her mind to fill with unthinkable thoughts. Normally she would find nothing wrong with harmless fantasies, but this was sacrilegious.

I'm sorry, Lord. Alyssa flinched inwardly at her great sense of guilt. How demented was she? She swallowed hard, turned her eyes to Pastor French, and demanded her ears to listen and her mind to be still.

The pastor's deep, even voice asked them to turn to another passage. Austin flipped through his worn Bible quickly, obviously familiar with the verse's location. "First Corinthians 6:19 says, 'Don't you realize that your body is the temple of the Holy Spirit, who lives in you and was given to you by God?'"

Alyssa reflected on that verse as she read along with the Pastor's voice. *My body is the temple of the Holy Spirit.* It sounded nice to her. She listened as the pastor explained.

"God dwells within you, if you are a child of God," he was saying. Alyssa figured it applied to her; she was a child of God. "You are a vessel that the Spirit of the Almighty God—the Spirit that raised Christ from the dead—lives in. Imagine, the power that caused Jesus to rise up from the grave lives in you."

The concept was never presented to Alyssa quite that way before. She knew Jesus lived in her, but Pastor French was talking of something more.

"So why, if God lives inside us, if we are the vessels of the living God, do we treat Him with so little value?" he asked the congregation. "Who, or what, are we allowing to touch the vessel of God? How clean are we keeping God's dwelling place?"

Questions poured from the pulpit and hit Alyssa squarely in the face. She quickly searched herself for answers to these questions and was able to reason away most of them, at least for the time being. She looked down at her hands in her lap, not wanting to catch the pastor's eyes. She moved her eyes and focused her attention on the open Bible that Austin held. At least she would look like she was reading the Word.

Her eyes skimmed the page and found the verse Pastor French had read from. It was highlighted in Austin's Bible. She moved her eyes up a few lines and read: Run from sexual sin! No other sin so clearly affects the body as this one does. For sexual immorality is a sin against your own body. Don't you realize that your body is the temple of the Holy Spirit?

Alyssa read the verses over several times with a sickening sense of nausea. Out of all the verses in that huge book she could have read, she had to see those. They leaped out at her and burned painfully in her temples. Turning away from the condemning words, she no longer tried to listen to the rest of the sermon but instead focused on willing away an increasing sense of guilt.

Fourteen

The scriptures plagued Alyssa the entire ride home, pricking like an annoying tick, though she tried hard not to think of them. Yet she was still glad she had gone with Austin. She had met people who she missed already and had finally seen the part of Austin that was most important to him. "Thank you for taking me, Austin." Her quiet voice permeated the darkness of the truck.

Austin cast her a glance as he drove. He could hear her sincerity and fervently prayed the Holy Spirit would move in her heart. *God, touch her. Turn her heart to You.* At times his heart cried this so loudly that it screamed in his head and wrenched his soul. "I'm glad you came. Did you enjoy it?" He was almost afraid of what her answer might be.

Alyssa paused before answering. "It was certainly interesting." She laughed lightly and looked at him, her eyes holding more emotion than she realized. "I was completely blown away by you! You are so amazing. The people get pretty excited when you play."

"It's not me. We have a lot to be excited about," Austin said. "We are victors. Christ has won the battle over sickness, poverty, and death, yet so often we choose to live in defeat. We're beginning to see what God has for us, to see God move—to actually see His glory—it's worth rejoicing about." He paused briefly and glanced at her again. "I hope you'll come back."

"I'd like that." Alyssa avoided his eyes, which were her downfall. She wasn't actually sure if she would go back. She had other things to think about.

They spoke little the rest of the way home. Alyssa's head swirled with thoughts of Jake; thoughts of love and lust; sounds of two thousand people screaming Jesus and a pastor preaching about the temple of God; Austin, singing songs that washed over her soul, dancing with freedom and strength that revealed how impossibly far from her he was; and the haunting sight of a young boy's prophetic eyes seeing wisdom she could not fathom.

After Austin walked her to her door and said goodnight, she went inside and found her mother in the living room watching television. "Did anyone call?" Though she strained to keep her voice casual, Alyssa was shaking inside with anticipation. When Catherine spoke a distracted no, her spirit crashed to the floor.

She went to her room and shut the door before tears spilled over. She brushed them away angrily and threw herself on the bed like a child. Sitting up against the intricately carved headboard, she pulled her legs up to her chest and looked over at the phone. Why must it hurt so bad when Jake didn't call? Because she loved him. She wouldn't desire him so much and so completely if she didn't. She closed her eyes and buried her face against her knees, allowing visions of Jake to torment her.

Finally, her tears stopped, and she stared at the phone as if it were the source of her pain. "Oh God...please hear me," she barely whispered. Closing her eyes she continued, "God, I ask—I beg You— make Jake love me. Make him want me as I want him." She knew that it wasn't right to pray for such a thing, but desperation overruled her better judgement.

"Forgive me, Father, if it is wrong to ask that, but Lord, I need him so badly. I'll die if he doesn't love me." Her hoarse voice held all the pain wrenching her heart. "God, I need him. Please, make him want me. Please Lord, I've never needed anything so badly." She broke into pained crying. She fell on her side, curled up in a ball, gripped her bedspread and pulled it to her mouth to stifle her sobs. She felt as though she were a heroin addict going through withdrawal. Though her mouth dared not speak such a prayer before God, her body cried out its own plea for Jake.

Part of her wished for death, while another part defied it. If she died now she would never have Jake. There was hope, wasn't there? She couldn't give up without knowing.

After a long time she sat up and grabbed the phone. Swallowing her pride and nervousness, she dialed Jake's number. Her heart raced and her mouth went dry as the phone rang a second time. Already deciding he wasn't home, she was about to hang up when Jake spoke in her ear. "Hello?"

Alyssa was silent for a fraction of a second, which felt like hours. Her mouth froze, and her mind went blank. But she managed an uncertain, "Hi, Jake?"

"Hey Alyssa, how ya doing?"

Relief eased her nerves when he sounded happy to hear from her. "Good, how are you?"

Their conversation went back and forth, staying on a very superficial level for awhile. "It's kind of late," he said after some time. "Shouldn't you be in bed?" he teased.

"I just got home a little bit ago. I was out with Austin."

"Really?" The irritation in Jake's voice boarded on anger. "Where did you go?"

Alyssa smiled victoriously at his jealously and kept her voice light as she answered. "He took me to his church."

"Oh yeah? Did you enjoy yourself?" Jake's humor had returned.

"It was fine." Alyssa was slightly defensive hearing Jake's mocking insinuation against Austin. She let it slide, however, deciding to steer the conversation to other topics. "It wouldn't be my first choice in how to spend my evening."

Alyssa's suggestion was not lost on Jake. "And would Austin be your first choice in who to spend it with?"

"It depends…" her voice trailed coyly.

146

The minutes grew into hours. Alyssa loved Jake's voice, which was fortunate since he enjoyed talking about himself. Alyssa's eyes were opened to many sides of him, all of which made him more fascinating. Several times she tried to steer their conversation to an intimate level. She longed to know his secret thoughts. Was she part of his fantasies?

The longer they talked, the more he considered the possibilities. He was unsure after seeing her in the wheelchair. What if he hurt her? She was so small and innocent. He felt he might break her if he wasn't careful. She was different from other girls—sweet, sincere, and innocent—yet she knew what she wanted and didn't mind letting him know.

But she wasn't concerned, so why should he be? Remembering their brief moment together caused his desire to win the debate. "You should come visit me."

Alyssa looked at the clock. Seeing that it was past midnight, she didn't try to hide her disappointment. "I can't. It's too late."

"That's too bad. I'd like to see you."

Alyssa thought she might cry out for joy. "Jake, why me?" Why was he interested in *her?*

Jake thought before trying to answer her honestly. "You're different. You are who you are, and you're not ashamed of it. You don't care what anybody thinks." The more he thought about her, the more he admired her. "You're also a sweetheart," he said smiling over the phone.

Alyssa basked in the glow of his words. "I wish some guy would notice that and fall in love with me."

"Someday, some knight in shining armor will come sweep you off your feet."

I don't want a knight. I want you! Alyssa cried inwardly.

They talked awhile more, finally saying goodnight after 1:00 in the morning. Alyssa fell asleep smiling, dreaming of Jake.

While Alyssa slept, Rebecca sat sipping warm beer and watching the people at the frat party. She had come with a friend after some serious persuasion but hadn't seen that friend since arriving over two hours before. She was bored and terribly unimpressed with what was happening around her.

She watched a group of guys shaking beer cans, spraying the contents all over each other. Rolling her eyes she looked away only to see two men about to kiss in one corner. Her hand went to her mouth, repulsed at the sight. She set the can down, got up, and headed for the door.

Once outside, she breathed the cool night air, trying to calm her agitation. She was tired of the party. She was tired of her life. Walking down the steps, she strolled slowly across the lawn away from the noise of the house. She cursed herself for not bringing her own car; she was stuck here until her ride decided to leave. Once she was far enough away, she sat under a large oak tree and watched stars twinkling in the sky.

She didn't know how long she had been sitting there before noticing a man on the front porch watching her. He caught her glance and smiled. Rebecca was dismayed and a little excited at the same time, when he stepped off the porch and started toward her.

She watched him watch her as he came closer. He didn't look like all the guys at the party. He was tall and broad with blond, short, well-groomed hair. She noticed he was nicely dressed in navy blue Dockers and tie. Curiosity got the better of her, and she decided to find out who he was. He was quite handsome and looked too old to be a student.

"Hello," he said reaching her. "Is there room under the tree for one more?"

"Sure." She moved over slightly and gave him a reserved smile. "You're not enjoying the party, I take it."

"I wasn't until a few moments ago." The man lowered himself close to her on the grass. "Then I saw the most beautiful woman I've ever laid eyes on, sitting under a tree all by herself." His voice was deep and smooth and his smile easily charming.

Rebecca's eyebrows raised skeptically. "Forgive me," he said smiling at her. "I usually don't make such a fool of myself, but I suddenly feel like a schoolboy who's fallen in love for the first time."

Rebecca couldn't help but smile at that. It was so completely ridiculous that it was funny. She looked at him and saw his face relaxed

148

in a grin. "My name is William Roget." He extended his hand. "May I ask what name is given to such a beautiful face?"

Rebecca laughed at the absurdity of his compliments, while wondering why they seem to be working. "Rebecca Langer," she said taking his hand. "My friends call me Becca."

"Becca," he said as if savoring sweet honey. He held her hand longer than necessary, noticing that she did not pull away.

She tore her eyes away from his and looked up at the sky. Bracing her hands on the grass behind her and leaning back in a relaxed position, she searched for something to say. "So what brings you to a place like this? You don't look like the college party type."

"You mean I'm too old." William laughed at her reddening cheeks.

"No—not at all," she said quickly, afraid she offended him.

"It's alright." His smiling eyes locked with hers. "I'll admit I'm not as young as I used to be, but thirty-five isn't that old, is it?"

Rebecca quickly did the math in her head. He was twelve years older than she but looked younger. As she studied him, she became more aware of just how attractive he was, distinguished, yet very masculine. "No, that's not too old at all." Her eyes met his, and her lips formed into her most ravishing smile.

"Are you sure you want to come here?" Kristen asked.

"I told you I wouldn't drink anything. Can't I have a little fun anymore?" Tyler's frustration with his girlfriend was obvious.

Kristen turned her green eyes back to the house with quiet fear. Pushing her straight blond hair behind her ear and biting her lip were telltale signs of her nervousness. Tyler shut his truck off and turned to look at her. "Don't worry, we won't stay long; and besides, Becca is supposed to be here. She'll keep me honest."

Though the doubt in Kristen's eyes had not disappeared, her face softened. At Tyler's characteristically boyish grin, she relented and gave him a tentative smile. "OK, if you promise to be good."

"Yeah, yeah. I promise," he said over his shoulder as he jumped out of his truck. Kristen got out and followed Tyler up the driveway toward the music blaring from the house.

The music blasted them when they opened the door, along with a variety of other noises all blending together to form a disorienting roar. Tyler's arm slipped from Kristen's waist as he dove into the crowd. Kristen followed as closely as she could, not wanting to get separated from him.

Tyler soon found his friends, who were already enjoying the abundance of liquor on hand. Scott Richards, a tall, thin guy with short, cropped hair and square face, greeted them both while staring too long at Kristen. She had never liked his cocky attitude and bold stares, though she chose not to tell Tyler her opinion of his friend.

"We weren't sure if you'd show up or not, Langer," Scott laughed. "We heard about your accident. What happened, anyway?"

Tyler went into the whole story, explaining everything. Scott listened while other people standing around stopped to listen as well. Before long, Tyler had the attention of a small crowd as he explained how an unseen hand had held him in his car. "I accepted Jesus into my heart real quick when I woke up!" Tyler half laughed in an attempt to lighten the mood.

"Wow, what were you drinking anyway? I think I'll try some of that." Never one to share the spotlight, Scott smirked when his joke received laughter all around. The small crowd dispersed, moving to find the next bit of entertainment.

"I wasn't drinking," Tyler insisted. "I don't think I'll do that anymore." His voice held less conviction than it did moments before in the truck.

"Tyler Langer not drink?" Scott exclaimed. "Impossible. What kind of fun will you be?" Scott laughed again at his joke, grabbed a beer, and held it out to Tyler.

"No thanks," Tyler said eyeing the can.

"A beer is not going to kill you, man," Scott scoffed and pushed it into his hand.

"Tyler." Kristen's eyes pleaded with him as she interrupted softly.

Tyler was suddenly annoyed and looked down at her with a clear warning. "It's one beer." Scott scoffed again before slipping away, wanting to avoid any ensuing fight.

Kristen grew silent, feeling a great sense of defeat. *Oh God, don't let him drink it.* Her heart prayed, though she did not know the One she was praying too. All she knew was Someone had saved Tyler's life. The same Someone who Tyler had asked to live in his heart. She eyed the can and waited for him to raise it to his mouth. After several moments, the can still did not move and Kristen's hope was sparked.

She looked up into her boyfriend's face and saw a look of fear that struck panic through her immediately. "Tyler? What's wrong?"

"I can't move my arm," Tyler mumbled. His eyes grew wide in terror and sudden, fearful tears. Though his voice remained quiet, it bordered on a hysterical note. "I try to lift it, and I can't. It's frozen there."

Kristen looked around to make sure no one was watching, then studied Tyler's stiff arm. Gently, she grasped his forearm and lifted. "My God," she whispered when his arm remained stiffly in place. "Does it hurt?"

"No." Tyler's voice trembled. He looked like a deer caught in headlights.

"Tell me if I hurt you." She grabbed his arm tighter with both hands and tried to move it. As she increased the pressure on his arm, Tyler's hand suddenly started shaking violently. Kristen snatched her hands back and watched with horror as beer splashed everywhere due to the fierce shaking. "Tyler, what's wrong? What's happening?" her now frantic voice demanded.

"I don't know!" Tyler's eyes were wild with fear. "Take the can will ya!"

Kristen quickly grasped the can of beer and pulled it from Tyler's shaking grip. Instantly the violently trembling hand and arm became still as the can was removed from his grip. "God," Kristen breathed in sudden awesome understanding.

Tyler lifted his hand then, opening and closing his fist and moving his arm around. "It feels normal again. I couldn't lift the can. It was like the beer had some kind of power over my arm."

151

"Not the beer—God." Kristen's voice held a new awe-inspired fear for the One she did not know. "I asked God not to let you drink." Joyful tears stung her eyes as she explained. She held out the can to him. "Try to lift it again."

"No!" Tyler quickly stepped back, eyeing the can. "Let's just get out of here." Without waiting for her response, Tyler turned and headed toward the door. Kristen tossed the can and ran after him, a huge smile breaking over her face.

Rebecca became more impressed with William as the night flew by. She learned that he was a professor who was going to be teaching English at the University. She found him intelligent yet easy to talk to. His sense of humor and flattery kept her entertained when they weren't discussing more serious topics.

Finally, around 4:00 in the morning, Rebecca decided she had better head home. "I have to find my ride. Hopefully she's slept off whatever she drank," she said dryly.

"Let me give you a ride."

"OK." Rebecca didn't hesitate in her acceptance, not ready for the night to end. He reached for her hand, and she took it willingly.

They reached William's car and Rebecca stared at the brand-new, shining, white Corvette. "You didn't tell me you were rich." She smiled at him before admiring the luxury car.

"Slipped my mind," he laughed.

She waited, thinking he would open the door for her. Instead, he turned and looked down at her, suddenly very serious. She felt her stomach tighten in anticipation.

William placed his hands behind her, bracing them on the car and trapping her there. If Rebecca had wanted to move, she couldn't have, but she didn't want to. When he buried his hand in her hair, pulling her to him, she responded willingly to his fervent kiss.

"You're so magnificent...I want you, Rebecca. I've never wanted anyone as I want you," he murmured in her ear. She let his words wash over her and mingle with her sudden passion. When they heard people coming from the house, he took one last moment of liberty before pulling away and letting her into the car, leaving her heart racing madly.

They pulled into Rebecca's driveway just as the sun was coming up. William shifted the car into park and was about to get out when Rebecca impulsively grabbed his arm to stop him. "I don't want you to leave." Her eyes held a promising spark as she gazed at him.

William searched her face knowingly. "What did you have in mind?"

"There's an empty cabin on the other side of the ranch. Let's go there." Rebecca didn't even realize what she was saying. She heard herself speaking, and in some ways was shocked at what she had suggested. But she didn't care. All she knew was that she wasn't ready for the night to end.

William needed no further invitation and quickly pulled the car back out of the driveway. They drove a distance before Rebecca directed him to turn down a long dirt road. Coming to several clusters of small cabins, she pointed to the last one. It was set off beyond the others and wasn't visible until they turned up the dirt driveway.

"Pull up behind those trees, beside the house." She hoped to limit the possibility of anyone finding out she had brought a man there.

She forgot about her desire to get home until two hours later. She stood under the hot shower while William lay sleeping in the bedroom. She had decided to leave while he slept for fear she would never want to leave.

William was amazing! In one night she had found the answers she had been looking for in a handsome, distinguished man who left her feeling deliriously ecstatic. She wondered briefly at the speed of their relationship but brushed those thoughts away. It wasn't as though she were a harlot. In fact, William was only the second man she had ever been intimate with.

She dried her hair then went out to find William sitting up in bed. "There you are." He smiled at her familiarly. "Were you going to leave me without a word?"

"I was going to leave a note." She sat on the edge of the bed and kissed him.

"You are amazing," he whispered after returning her kiss. He stopped suddenly and looked at her. "How old are you anyway?"

Rebecca laughed at his question. "Twenty-three."

"That's not possible," he smiled before kissing her again.

Rebecca loved the way he made her feel: heady with power, feeling her sensuality like never before. Suddenly her beauty was a gift rather than an annoying curse. Finally pulling away from him, she smiled with regret. "I've got to go. I've got tons of stuff I'm supposed to do today."

William hesitated a moment before speaking. "Listen, I think maybe it's best if we keep our relationship between us for the time being." At the wide-eyed look of shock mingled with hurt, he laughed lightly. "Hey, don't look so destroyed," he teased. "It's just for a little while."

"Why?" Rebecca's voice gave away her anger.

"I just don't think it would look good if everyone found out that the new professor is sleeping with a student."

He saw her doubts wavering and kissed her with gentle passion. "Now, show me that ravishing smile of yours." Rebecca couldn't help but smile at his gentle coaxing. She decided he was right in wanting to keep a low profile for a time.

Drawing her close, he spoke just above a whisper. "I find your smile absolutely irresistible. Stay with me today," he demanded, convincing her easily. All thoughts of the outside world were quickly forgotten as she surrendered to William's passion.

Fifteen

The clock in Alyssa's bedroom ticked away the minutes annoyingly. Each second rang in her ears over the deadly silence of the house. She pushed her hair behind her ear nervously while tapping her pen on a blank page in her journal. The annual summer festival would finally begin on Sunday—just two days away. Alyssa held little excitement for the coming festivities however, for Jake would be away the entire week, on a trip for her father. Yet an ever-increasing sense of nausea reminded her of her recent resolve; she was going to tell Jake how she felt about him before he left.

Over the last few weeks she had spent time with Jake whenever possible. Sometimes he called her, causing her heart to soar wildly on wings of joy. Sometimes, when she called him, he seemed irritated causing her to plummet to the black depths of her soul. She felt a mass of confusion eating little bits of her brain each day. Soon she may go mad if she didn't do something. She finally wrote:

> I love Jake despite how crazy he makes me. He makes me feel like a woman when he looks at me with fire in his eyes. I feel loved when he calls me Sweetheart; for this alone I would love him. I must know or I will loose all sanity. Does he care at all?

I Can Dance

I needed something to hold on to, to escape from my life of darkness—I found that in Jake. Jake now controls me. I belong to him. He possesses my heart. My soul is surrendered completely.

It was later in the evening when she headed out. She took her time pushing her chair down the tree-lined path. She felt wet and clammy, her stomach tied so tightly in knots that she was ready to throw up. By the time she reached Jake's cabin, she considered turning back. Reluctantly she decided against it—her arms were too tired to go back yet.

Climbing out of the chair and up the steps to his door, she knocked lightly. Jake opened the door and greeted her with a smile. "Hi, Sweetheart."

"Hi." She gave him her most beautiful smile in return as relief washed away a bit of her fear. At least he looked happy; lately she was never sure how he would react to her.

Following him into the small living room, she noticed that it looked much like Austin's, though considerably messier. They sat down at the small kitchen table and talked for some time about the upcoming festival and his trip for her father. Alyssa had almost forgotten her trepidation.

She had been there for over an hour when Jake suggested they go outside for some air. Alyssa agreed though concern about getting tired pricked her mind. What if Jake wanted to go for a walk? It seemed to be an ever more frequent concern for her these days.

They went out and sat down on the front steps. The wheelchair sat not far off, staring silently, it's presence felt loudly by both. "Jake." Cold sweat instantly broke out on Alyssa's skin as she began. "I want to talk to you about something." She paused for a long time, her stomach grew so tight she felt unable to speak. "Actually…I…well, never mind," she mumbled.

Jake looked at her, his forehead creasing in worry. "What is it, Alyssa? Just say what you want to say." He spoke so gently at times, coaxing her beyond her normal senses.

Alyssa glanced at him gratefully. How she loved him! She looked back down at her hands clasped tightly in her lap and swallowed hard, praying her voice would not shake.

156

"I've been wanting to talk to you. I need to tell you my feelings, or I think I might explode." She could feel the heat flooding her face and knew it was turning red. "You mean a lot to me. No one's ever treated me like you do or looked at me the way you do."

"How do I look at you?" His grin and deep voice were irresistible.

She smiled slightly, though she didn't look at him. "You look at me like a man looks at a woman," she said so softly Jake almost didn't hear her.

"You are a woman."

Alyssa's heart pounded at his words. "No one has ever made me feel like one before. From the first day you met me, you seemed...interested in me. Sometimes you make me feel attractive and beautiful...desirable," she mumbled. Even the word was almost impossible for her to speak.

Jake remained silent, taking in her words. He felt a disturbing sense of guilt but wasn't sure why. After all, it was good that he made her feel better about herself. But he never expected to have such an impact with his attraction to her. He was just having fun.

"Jake...I just...well...I love you." Alyssa was shaking visibly now.

"I care about you, too," he said carefully. It was the truth; he had grown to care for Alyssa. She was sweet and would willingly do anything for him, even give him money on occasion when he mentioned he was short. He liked the thought of being loved but worried about the consequences. He really couldn't say for certain if he was in love with her.

Alyssa turned to him but was still unable to meet his eyes. "I really love you. You're all I think about. You're all I dream about. When I hear your voice it makes me crazy. I want to give you anything and everything I have just to make you happy." The words came in a rush. She would say it all before she had time to think about it.

Jake sat in stunned silence listening to her words. He certainly hadn't expected this! Alyssa's words continue to pour out. "When you look at me I feel as though my whole body is on fire. I love you Jake... and I want you more than I've ever wanted anyone. I need you in every way." Her voice was more desperation than she had intended before she finally became silent. Stillness descended like a blanket over them.

157

Jake was speechless and confused. The desperation in her voice startled him, and he wasn't sure how to react. He was confused by the sudden strange sense of morality he was having. He glanced at the empty wheelchair. It wasn't just the physical thing he was worried about; he knew what intimacy would mean to her—and what it wouldn't mean to him.

Alyssa stared up at the sun now casting beams of light through the trees as it went down. Biting her lip she spoke brokenly. "I thought you wanted me too. Was I wrong?"

"No," he said honestly. "I did want you—I still do."

She looked up at him then, though his eyes wouldn't meet hers. "I was so afraid that no man would ever want me like that." Turning away again she continued. "Most men aren't real attracted to wheelchairs." She struggled to keep herself from crying.

He took a deep breath, choosing his words carefully. "Alyssa, it's what's on the inside that matters, and you're the most beautiful woman on the inside that I've ever known."

Alyssa had to close her eyes to keep the joyful tears from coming as his words touched her soul. At another time she would have considered them an insult—she was beautiful inside and horrid outside. But he said it with such sincerity that it made her feel beautiful all over. "I do want you," he continued. "But you deserve more than a one night stand, and I'm not ready to give you more right now. When I am you'll be the first to know." Good words that seemed to satisfy her, but they held little weight with him. "I'm not sure I'd be very good for you," he said with a grin.

"You just need a good woman to straighten you out." Alyssa smiled, trying to lighten her voice.

"Maybe you."

Alyssa's spirits soared, and she got a bit braver. "You know," she said playfully, "until that day I certainly wouldn't mind a one night stand now and then."

Jake laughed, always amazed when her tongue spoke so boldly. "Neither would I." Growing more serious again he went on. "You would though. You may not realize it, but it wouldn't be you."

"You don't know me very well do you?" If someone had said that about her before she had met Jake, they would have been right. But since their first meeting in the barn, she had been willing to sell her soul for one moment with him.

Jake eyed her, amused by her desire. After another short silence he spoke carefully while watching her. "You're so small and dainty." She looked so tiny sitting beside him; he had to admit he found it attractive. "I don't want to hurt you."

"I'm not going to break," she laughed.

"Well, anyway, there's too much going on that I've got to deal with before I can get into a relationship. When I'm finally with you, I want it to be right."

His frankness caused her faced to redden again. Her mind reacted quickly to his words by producing vivid images, which gave birth to her desire. She was deliriously happy that Jake had given her hope for the future but didn't know if she could survive the wait.

"You almost did once," she breathed. "If Austin hadn't come in, we would have..." her voice drifted off unable to form the words.

"I know. But it's different now."

Part of her wanted to convince him, but she couldn't, that wasn't her. She had already said more than she had thought she'd ever dare. "So what's been going on that's got you so distracted?"

Jake hesitated before revealing his past. He didn't want to divulge a side of himself Alyssa might not be so submissive to. "There's this girl I used to go with a few years ago. We have a son together." Alyssa was only slightly surprised at the news but was gripped with an indescribable fear when Jake continued. "She's been calling me—wants me to go see her and my son, J.J. I want to see him, but I'm not sure about seeing Linda."

"Why?"

"She says she wants me to come back to stay."

"Oh," Alyssa choked. "What do you want?" She couldn't help but ask. She closed her eyes as if preparing for a blow to the face.

"I don't know."

"Do you still love her?"

"Yes," he said carefully.

Alyssa opened her eyes and stared hard at the ground. "Do you love me?"

Jake looked away. "Yes."

"How do you love two women?"

"It's hard to explain, but it's possible."

She paused a moment before asking him a final question, still unable to look him in the eye. "Jake, *how* do you love me? There's lots of ways to love someone. You can love like a man loves a woman or like a friend. You could love me like you love your dog."

Jake stood up from the porch abruptly. "Yes, Alyssa, I love you like I love my dog!"

Jake's sarcasm was laced with irritation. She had gone too far and pressed too hard. She decided to back off, afraid she'd anger him. "I'm sorry," she said softly.

He looked back at her and relaxed. Sitting back down beside her, Alyssa noticed he had never actually answered her question. She brushed the thought away and asked about his son. Soon he was talking again, happy to tell her about J.J., which she found out stood for Jake Jr.

She stayed until the sun disappeared behind the far off hills. As she stood to go, she turned to him impulsively and wrapped her arms around him in a hug. He returned her embrace affectionately.

"I love you," she dared to say once more.

"I love you too," he answered lightly. He kissed her cheek then let her go.

Alyssa wanted to say so much more, to do so much more. Instead she smiled at him, wished him a pleasant trip, then turned to the chair, and made her way slowly home through the darkness.

Sixteen

Austin was fascinated listening to Alyssa tell about the festival events. As her face lit with delight, his ears drank in the sound of her laughter. "So," he grinned at her mischievously, "you are going to take me to this festival of yours, aren't you?"

Her eyes widened in excitement. "I'd love to!" Her hands clasped together and eyes sparkled. "It will be so much fun! Before the weekend is over you'll be an honorary 'county man,'" she laughed.

They made their plans around the schedule set for them which involved hosting events held on the ranch. Friday night at 9:00, Austin and his church's worship team were playing in town, so he planned to pick her up around 6:30 to go roam the streets before the performance. Saturday they would go to the morning events in town before the parade.

When Friday afternoon came Alyssa, surprised at how excited she had been all week to go with Austin, carefully got herself ready. With Jake away she was restless and lonely and anxious for Austin's company. She spent a ridiculous amount of time curling her hair, making it fall in soft layers of thick curls around her face and down her back. She painstakingly applied makeup until her complexion looked flawless and each feature was defined beautifully.

Picking out a pair of deep green jeans and a green and white plaid shirt, she dressed and observed herself in the mirror. The casual outfit flattered her figure perfectly. Suddenly she froze at the striking clear blue eyes that stared back at her.

Why did Austin want to go with her? It was the question that had plagued her mind for the last week. She told herself it was because they were friends, and he enjoyed being with her. But even as she declared it to her heart, doubts rose to cast a shadow on her excitement. She couldn't imagine anyone enjoying her company.

Several possible reasons formulated unwillingly in her understanding, none of which had anything to do with Austin's affection for her. Why could she not accept that Austin's friendship was sincere? She had never been able to believe a man could care about her, much less enjoy being with her.

She was brought up believing it was impossible. Hadn't it been engraved on her mind and seared in her soul since she was a child? How was she to believe Austin could desire her company when those around her couldn't believe it? When people who loved her were not only certain she'd never know a man's love but also doubtful that one would choose her friendship, how could she be expected to rise above their skepticism?

Despite the twenty-four-years of quietly and unintentionally being conditioned to believe she was nothing by the standards of the world, Alyssa knew deep down that Austin saw her as something. No matter how hard her doubts fought to destroy the trust she had placed in him, her heart whispered the truth, encouraging her soul. She thought of the many times he touched her gently, smiled at her teasingly, and looked into her eyes with utter sincerity. Her answer lay in those memories—Austin did care.

She smiled and headed out. Opening the door to her bedroom, her mouth dropped at the sight of her new wheelchair. She had almost forgotten the horror of the previous afternoon when her mother brought home the electric contraption.

The same sinking feeling of dread filled her stomach now as she looked at it. It was bad enough having to ride in a normal wheelchair, but that thing? What would people think? Her reasoning was simple: in a normal wheelchair, she didn't look *as* different. She stared harshly at the uncaring chair, getting a mental image of herself 'zipping' down the streets, and cringed. She would not ride through town in that thing!

Her mother's voice sounded through her anger. "Austin is here!"

She went to the kitchen as he came in. She didn't miss the light in his eyes as they quickly moved over her, before riveting to her face, and she gave him a welcoming smile. A surprised and pleased flush tinted her cheeks and her heart missed a beat. She bit her lip, suddenly nervous for a reason she couldn't put a finger on.

"I'll get your chair," Catherine said. Alyssa's eyes did not move from Austin's. He turned away only when Catherine addressed him. "The ramps are on the porch. We'll need them to get the chair in back of your truck."

"I'll take my old chair," Alyssa said quickly. Lately she could stand for no more than fifteen minutes at a time, so she knew she must at least take her manual chair.

"Your old chair?" Catherine gave Alyssa her patented stare.

"It will be easier," she said staring at her mother, willing her to be quiet.

"You're going to be out half the night. You know how tired you get. Austin will end up pushing you everywhere."

Alyssa's face turned crimson in humiliation. She stared at the floor, biting her lip, praying Austin wouldn't notice her eyes watering with embarrassment.

"I certainly wouldn't mind." Austin's sincerity washed over Alyssa's soul like sweet rain in a forest. He did not miss the tension between mother and daughter or Alyssa's embarrassment. His heart went out to her as he spoke gently, "I'll be the envy of every man in town."

Alyssa smiled up at him gratefully, and he caught the watery shine in her eyes.

"So you want the old one?" Catherine's irritation was barely concealed.

"The new one is fine," Alyssa mumbled, unable to defy her mother's wishes.

Alyssa climbed into the truck and waited while they loaded the heavy chair onto the back. She was too humiliated to say anything when she and Austin started for town. He sensed her feelings and wanted to make her forget her embarrassment.

"You look really great," he said with an appreciative smile.

She laughed, feeling instantly better. "I don't know about you." She smiled at him softly, feeling a sting of grateful tears behind her eyes.

"What's that supposed to mean?" he asked in mock offense.

"You always know what to say to make me feel better. Even if you have to lie," she laughed.

"I'm being completely honest when I say how beautiful you look." He wanted to tell her she was more beautiful than any woman he'd ever seen before. *Is this what love does?* he wondered. *Does it make you see beauty in no one but the woman you love?*

Alyssa noticed Austin's quick glances at her and flushed despite herself. What woman's heart wouldn't race with Austin Jacobs? She turned away, forcing the thoughts from her mind as the truck inched along Main Street amidst the bumper to bumper traffic.

They had almost given up on finding any place left to park when Austin caught sight of an empty space in a parking lot. He pulled in, careful not to hit the tightly packed cars. "I'll get your chair," he said jumping out of the truck.

"Thanks," Alyssa mumbled dryly after he shut the door. She closed her eyes and rested her head against the seat. Maybe she should have him take her home. She could say she wasn't feeling well.

"Ready?" Too late. Austin was looking at her expectantly near the opened door. The chair sat waiting, and Austin held his hand out to help her from the truck. She gave him a wavering smile as she took his hand and climbed down. Swallowing her pride, she sat back in the chair, flicked on the power, and followed Austin to the sidewalk.

Moving among the mass of people proved to be more difficult than Alyssa anticipated. All over the sidewalk people stood in clusters or walked in slow moving groups. Those who weren't walking stood blocking the way for anyone who might want to pass. "Come on." Austin grabbed her hand and led her through the thick crowd, off the sidewalk, and out around the parked cars. "This will be easier," he said, smiling at her. He let go of her hand reluctantly after a few moments.

Alyssa stayed close to him as they made their way up the street to find one of the numerous food vendors. A sudden lightness came over Alyssa. Austin had taken her hand as he walked with her. Didn't he realize someone would see them and think he was dating a girl in a wheelchair? He didn't seem to care or notice. Suddenly she cared about the thoughts of others a little less.

They found a hot dog stand and got something to eat. With food in hand, Austin led her to a patch of grass and sat close to her chair. They talked between bites about the number of people and the things to do. As if she could no longer hold it in, Alyssa blurted out what had been on her mind for some time. "I told Jake how I feel about him."

Austin looked up at her surprised. "What did you tell him?"

Alyssa looked down at her half-eaten hot dog shyly. "That I love him."

Austin could feel his heart sinking, along with a certain fear of danger. "What did he say?"

"He loves me, too." But as she sat with Austin, the importance of Jake's love faded.

Anger pricked Austin's nerves. His desire to protect Alyssa could get him into trouble if he wasn't careful. He listened closely as she continued. "He said I was special to him; that he wants me…" her voice trailed, not sure of Austin's reaction to her words. "That he loves me is enough to make me happy," she finished softly.

"Lyssa, don't base your happiness on a man. No matter how perfect you think he is, he'll fail you eventually. Your happiness must be based in Christ—He never fails us."

"I know," Alyssa said, hurt. "I'm not basing my life on Jake." Somehow she knew she was lying but felt the need to defend herself.

"I'm sorry," Austin said gently. "So what do your parents think?"

"I haven't talked to them," she confessed. "Actually, Mom is starting to suspect something. It's obvious she doesn't like him."

"How come you haven't told her?"

"Because she blows everything out of proportion. She acts like I'm carrying on some illicit affair, and it disgusts her." Alyssa's irritation mounted as she spoke. "To hcr, intimacy is a horrid sin that she's afraid I'm committing, which I'm not. Besides, I'm twenty-four-years old—it's none of her business what I do."

"You're her daughter. Your life will always be her business. She's just worried about you." Austin was silent a moment. He gathered his thoughts, then continued, carefully choosing his words. "I think parents try to teach their children certain values. When a child strays from those beliefs, it's hard to accept."

Alyssa knew what beliefs Austin was referring to. "Is it a sin to want to be with—to give yourself to—the one you love? Isn't that what it's all about?" Alyssa was surprised at the direction their conversation had taken but felt she could be honest with him. "I understand that she believes you should wait until you're married, but who says her beliefs are right?"

Austin's eyes met hers boldly yet with compassion. "God. The Bible teaches about the sanctity of marriage, about fornication and sexual immorality. God asks us to wait until marriage."

Alyssa was speechless, not expecting a strong, attractive man to say such things. Her mind was having difficulty comprehending the concept.

Austin continued when met with Alyssa's silence. "God created intimacy, but He laid out rules in His Word so we wouldn't get into trouble. One man, one woman, joined forever in marriage, would be blessed to share such a special gift, becoming one in every way. It is an act of love, a holy act."

He paused to allow his words to sink in. "If we give our bodies in such an intimate way to just anybody, somehow the act that was once so pure and sacred becomes tainted and common. It ceases to be a gift of God treated with respect, and it becomes meaningless. It's no longer a beautiful act of loving and worshiping one another as God intended and receiving pleasure from one another. It becomes a way to selfishly feed the flesh," he said with obvious disdain. Austin fell silent, and his eyes stared far off somewhere in his own thoughts.

Alyssa could find no words to speak, awestruck not only by his words, but the intensity with which he spoke. A part of her wanted to reach out, grasp what he was saying, and hold it close to her heart. The kind of intimacy Austin talked of sounded beautiful and right.

But another part of Alyssa repelled his words for they tried and convicted her. She saw the depth of emotion in his eyes and knew he was relating his own experiences. Though she wished to push the whole conversation aside and forget it, she was compelled to find out what made him feel so strongly. "It sounds like you've had firsthand experience."

Austin spoke with alarming bitterness in his voice. "I don't even remember most of the women I've been with." His self-contempt was obvious as he continued staring at the ground. "I never gave a thought to who I might be hurting. I took pride in pleasing who I was with but never considered the girl when it was over."

Alyssa was shocked at his bluntness and felt her cheeks flush uncomfortably as she bit her lip. Thankfully he didn't notice. "All I cared about was pleasing my flesh and my pride. I was able to do both by satisfying a woman. It was like another drug that took my mind off of my life for a while."

Idly Austin pulled at the grass and tossed it in the air. "I thank God that when we ask for forgiveness, He makes us pure and clean. I'm spotless in His eyes as long as I remain in Christ." He spoke softly now, in awe of the truth of his words. "I know when I get married—it will be new and beautiful and exciting—just as if I've never sinned."

Austin looked up at Alyssa then. "I regret that part of my life more than any other. I only wish I knew then what I know now. I wish I hadn't defiled the gift of God...and taken that gift from so many," he finished hoarsely.

Alyssa saw his torment and wanted to comfort him. "Austin, you took nothing those women didn't want to give. They knew what they were doing." Even as she spoke, she wondered if she were trying to defend her own choices.

Austin looked at her sadly. "I was responsible, Lyssa. There were some who didn't know what they were doing, not really. I knew exactly what I was doing and how to make them willing. They had no idea what they were losing."

Alyssa knew he was speaking directly to her. She knew he was trying to make her see that Jake was the same way and that she was innocent, not knowing what she was getting into. "I know what I'm doing," she said quietly, without hostility.

"No, Lyssa...I don't think you do." Alyssa had to look away from the intensity in Austin's eyes. What was it she saw in them? Pity? Remorse? Fear? Pain? All for her? She wasn't angry with Austin for being honest with her; she appreciated that he cared. But it was obvious he didn't understand what she was going through.

They sat silently, watching the people pass by. Austin's eyes consistently moved back to Alyssa's face. He watched her rather than the droves of people. He studied her eyes and expressions as she searched the crowd of faces. He saw her face light up and smile in recognition of someone heading her way. "It's Peter. You'll get to meet him."

Austin tore his eyes from her to check out the guy she had told him about. He was interested in seeing if Alyssa's unusual description of him was accurate. As he stood, his mouth widened in surprise. "I should have known," he laughed, confusing Alyssa.

"Hey Alyssa, Austin!" Peter reached them, exchanging handshakes and pats on the back with Austin. Immediately they struck up a discussion on the upcoming praise and worship concert.

"You two know each other?" Alyssa interrupted.

Austin's laugh joined with Peter's. "Peter goes to my church. He's on the worship team, too."

Alyssa sat speechless, feeling left out as the two talked about what great things God would do that evening at the concert. Eventually Peter took off, leaving Alyssa and Austin to roam the streets again. They had a wonderful time with each other. All too soon it was almost time for the worship service, so they headed for the place it would be held.

When they reached the parking lot, Austin and the team began setting up and testing the equipment. By the time they had started, the lot was crammed with people. Alyssa was curious as to what kind of songs they would sing and how they would act. Would they act like they do at their church?

She received her answer when Austin spoke loudly into the microphone. "PRAISE THE LORD! Just because we're not in a church building doesn't mean that God's not here. Amen?" His fingers played over the keys, teasing the people's hungry ears. "Let's give Him all the praise tonight!" He began pounding out a fast song, getting present church members dancing immediately.

It was easy to distinguish the members of Center of Rejoicing from people who were drawn in by the music while passing on the street. Soon, however, people who stood listening and watching the free-spirited Christians got excited themselves. The music and charged atmosphere were contagious and people all over began clapping and singing.

By the time the music ended, there were more people crammed into the parking lot than on Main Street. Alyssa was only vaguely surprised when Austin invited to the front anyone who wanted to know Jesus. She was stunned, however, at the great number of people who responded by walking, some even running, to the stage. Those who wanted salvation went in droves, many coming in from the street as church members backed out of the lot to allow room for the staggering crowd.

When all the people received prayer and the musicians had packed up their equipment, Austin went back to where Alyssa sat watching.

Austin grabbed a nearby stray chair and sat beside her, looking over the lingering groups of people around the lot. His eyes came back to rest on Alyssa. "You must be getting tired."

Alyssa gave him a small smile that seemed tinged with sadness. "I am."

"I'll take you home if you're ready."

"OK." Austin rose and led her to the truck. Before leaving the parking lot, Alyssa took one last glance at the ground still scattered with people praying and rejoicing. Somehow—in a way she didn't understand—she wasn't ready to leave. A part of her wanted to stay until the last person got up and left. A sense of loss went with her as she left the place of hope.

Seventeen

Getting in her wheelchair, Alyssa followed her sister as they headed toward the stables. "So what have you been doing lately? I never see you anymore," Alyssa inquired once they were on their way.

Rebecca decided to trust Alyssa with the truth. "Actually I met this guy, William Roget. I spend most of my time with him." She suddenly realized she was spending almost every waking hour in the empty cabin. Even if William wasn't there, she was there waiting for him. In fact, he was demanding more and more of her time lately.

"What is he like?"

"William's wonderful," Rebecca said. "He makes me feel alive. Maybe he's what I've been missing in my life." In some ways she thought this was true, yet lately she had the same feeling of unrest and dissatisfaction she had felt before William. But she figured with time that would fade.

Before reaching the clearing, the girls saw crowds of people scattered around the ranch and fields, taking part in the various activities offered throughout the day. People lined up around the stables waiting to get horses for a tour of the ranch.

The horse show that afternoon went beautifully. The people left the field where the show was held, happy and seeking other activities.

Tyler walked back toward the stables with Alyssa, searching the faces among the crowds for his girlfriend.

"She was supposed to be here," he said, though not sounding concerned. Tyler wasn't one to express much emotion, but when Alyssa asked him if he was in love, his face broke into a goofy grin as he shrugged and said, "She's just too cool."

"Look! It's Pastor French and his wife," Alyssa said, not sure why she was so excited.

"I've heard about him," Tyler said interested. "He's got loads of money. People say he's the richest man in the state. He owns his own airplane," he said with awe.

Alyssa stopped near the fence surrounding the stables and got out of her chair. "I'm going to say hi. You want to meet them?" she asked him.

"Naw," he answered and watched her walk toward them. Part of Tyler yearned to run over there and confide to the man of God what had happened at the party. Another part of Tyler was scared to tell anyone. He and Kristen had agreed to keep it to themselves for fear of sounding completely crazy. Tyler had no idea what had happened to him and was fearfully reluctant to find out.

Alyssa listened to the country music of the county's favorite local band at the dance the ranch hosted that evening. Watching people dancing and laughing made her feel depressed and sorry for herself. Why should they be having fun when she wasn't?

Jake's image came to her vividly. Her desperation had intensified since he'd been gone, at least whenever Austin wasn't around. But there was something more troubling her than the fear of not having Jake. There was the thought of actually having him. Austin's words burned in her mind and were branded on her heart. *Nothing more than a way to satisfy a fleshly desire.* The words irritated her. Who says that it's not right?

God.

171

Austin did not understand. Love makes it beautiful—not some piece of paper saying you're married. Just because he believed one way, what made him think everyone else should believe that way?

God.

She knew God. She was saved as a little girl and had been a Christian all her life. God knew her heart and knew her motives were pure. *Weren't they?* She ignored the fact that she had wanted Jake before deciding she loved him. She loved the Lord and knew He loved her and wanted her to be happy.

If you love Me, you'll obey what I command.

She froze uncomfortably at that thought. Was that from the Bible? Moving her eyes across the crowd of dancing people, she caught sight of Austin standing on the other side of the field talking to a young woman. The woman was very pretty, Alyssa noted unhappily. A moment later another woman joined in their conversation. This one wasn't as young as the other but attractive just the same. The two girls batted their eyes and gave Austin charming smiles, causing Alyssa to instantly dislike them.

Alyssa noticed that Austin was polite and spoke in a friendly manner, but his eyes were locked on hers. He didn't look away when she met his gaze, and her own eyes seemed unable to look away from his. He finally looked down at the younger woman and responded to something she had said. She saw him shake his head, looking politely regretful, then excuse himself.

As Austin slipped from the clutches of the women, his eyes returned to meet Alyssa's amused look. His mouth formed an embarrassed grin, but his gaze was intense—fixed upon her as he wove around the people to reach her.

She chided herself at the warm pleasure that flooded her as she watched Austin dismiss the girls and head for her. She was equally annoyed that her heart beat faster with each step he took closer to her. "I can't stand to see a pretty girl all alone," he said when he reached her and hunkered down close by.

"But you left two of them over there. Completely crushed, I might add." She hoped her teasing would hide the blushing at his compliment.

He grinned unconcerned. "Give them five minutes, and they'll find someone else."

"I wasn't sure you'd be here. This doesn't seem like your kind of thing."

"It's not. Your dad wanted me to stick around in case anyone needed anything. So I'm here for a little while."

"Why don't you dance?"

"Why don't you?" he retorted.

"I can't," she said stating the obvious.

"Of course you can. Come on, dance with me." He stood up and took her hand in his.

The band had begun a knee-slapping fiddle song. "Austin—I can't." She self-consciously looked at the people around them.

"Would you quit telling me what you can't do," he demanded. "When are you going to learn to trust me?" He pulled her out of her chair and led her closer to the dancing people.

Alyssa's face was already turning red. She was going to stand there and make a fool of herself in front of Austin and the rest of the people there. What if she lost her balance and fell?

"Now, come here," Austin instructed. "OK, put your arms around my neck...now step up on my feet."

"Do what?"

"Just do it."

She complied, and he held her waist firmly as he began to dance around. Soon he gave up trying to keep her feet lined up with his and lifted her easily, her feet just off the ground. Alyssa laughed and squealed in delight as he spun her around wildly to the rhythm of the fiddle. She felt like a little girl, remembering her mother holding her in her arms and dancing her around the room as a child.

When the song ended he stood her on her feet for the first time since the song began. His hands did not leave her hips and hers stayed on his shoulders as she breathlessly calmed her laughter. Austin smiled down into her glowing happy face and had to suppress the urge to lean down and kiss her.

The band began to play a soft ballad and the two naturally started moving slowly to the rhythm. Alyssa smiled sheepishly, "You know, I've never danced with a man before."

"Are you tired? You want to sit down?"

"No." She laughed at the concern in Austin's voice. "I haven't been on my feet yet!"

Austin relaxed and pulled her closer. "I find it hard to believe you've never danced before."

"I only went to a couple of dances when I was young. I was always afraid of falling and making a fool of myself, so I would never dance with anyone." She shrugged, looking down.

"You won't fall, not when I've got you," he said huskily.

Alyssa looked up into his eyes, nearly melting at the intensity in them. Impulsively she leaned her head against his chest and closed her eyes. She would remember this moment forever, carving it into her heart and holding on to it in case she never had such a moment again.

Austin stayed by Alyssa's side until the sun had disappeared completely. Then, with a smile, he asked, "Want to go to the rally?" Alexandra and Roger, the youth pastors, had planned a youth service, and Austin had thought it would be great to have it under the stars in one of the Langer's fields.

"Aren't we too old?"

"Too old! I don't know about you, but I'm not too old."

"OK, let's go!"

They took the pickup since the field was a good distance away. Finding Britney standing alone by the bonfire, they asked her to join them, and she agreed with sudden enthusiasm.

Alyssa was once again stunned by the turnout at the rally. "There must be at least six hundred kids here!"

Alyssa fully enjoyed Roger's preaching. Even Britney got excited and cheered "Amens" with the rest of the youth. At the altar call, she went to the front and received Christ as her Savior. Alyssa shed tears of joy as her niece joyously told of her salvation after the service. She watched the girl's eyes light up as she recounted the entire service. The small tug on Alyssa's heart did not go unnoticed, nor did the increasing sense of unrest in her soul.

Eighteen

Jake had been home for a week when he called Alyssa at work. "How are you?" she asked sweetly, tossing her work aside.

"Not great." Jake's voice was heavily dismal. "My uncle in New York was in an accident. He pretty much raised me as a kid. They're not sure if he'll make it." He sounded near tears.

"Oh Jake, I'm so sorry. Is there anything I can do?" Alyssa wanted to cry for him. He sounded like a small boy who had lost his parents but was trying to be brave.

"I just wish I could see him before he dies."

"You should go!"

"I don't have the money."

"I'll lend you the money." She desperately wanted to ease his pain, thinking little of giving him anything he asked. "How much would you need?"

"About three hundred."

Alyssa momentarily calculated her savings. "OK. You need to go visit your uncle," she resolved.

"Really?"

"Of course!"

"Will you meet me tonight at the lake?" Already Jake's voice lightened, Alyssa assumed it was the prospect of seeing his uncle that lifted his mood so quickly.

"I'll be there," she promised eagerly.

She hurried through the day and was at the lake an hour too soon. When Jake finally came she was surprised by how light his mood was, sounding nothing like he had on the phone. He greeted her with a smile and sat with her on the grass.

Alyssa greeted him with a tentative smile. "It's good to see you."

A teasing glint sparked Jake's eyes. "You missed me, huh?"

"I wish you weren't going away again, but I know you have to. I just hate it when you're gone."

"I'll be back soon. When I am, we'll have lots of time to see each other." Jake winked at her before looking out at the lake.

"I hope so. I really want to spend more time with you." Her voice faltered over her words.

Jake ran his hand over the back of his neck. "I know. When I come back I'll make it up to you."

"How?" she asked coyly.

"Any way you want," he grinned knowingly.

Alyssa suddenly got very serious. "You promise?"

Jake was silent looking out at the water. The air seemed hush with anticipation. Not a sound could be heard in the trees around them. Not a sound except the unfamiliar voice of his own conscience. He pushed the unwelcome noise away as the night pushes the sun from the sky. Yet morning would come again, and the sun would rise with blazing fury. But that was tomorrow. Today, Alyssa sat waiting for an answer that would bring her some joy and him relief from the stabs of guilt that accompanied the sadness in her eyes. "Yeah, I promise."

"I'm serious Jake," she said hoarsely, every nerve in her body coming alive at his vow. "You know what I want—not just to sit and talk anymore."

"I know what you want, Alyssa." Jake spoke deliberately. Alyssa swallowed hard and closed her eyes to calm the drunken butterflies in her stomach. The very words made Alyssa feel faint with heady desire. "If that's what you want, that's what we'll do."

She was so overwhelmed she could barely speak. "Is it what you want too?"

"Yes." Jake's answer sounded sincere, and that's all that mattered to Alyssa. All she could do was nod her understanding.

They spoke a short time longer before Jake announced that he had to get going. Alyssa pulled out an envelope and handed it to him. "The money is all there. I hope your uncle pulls through," she said compassionately.

"Me too." He kissed her cheek before heading toward the well-worn path. Turning just before the trees swallowed him up, he smiled and waved the envelope in a final goodbye. "I love you."

"I love you too." She waved back as grateful tears stung her eyes.

Rebecca sat alone in the familiar cabin. She glanced at her bruised wrists, rubbing them absently with her fingers. When she had shown William what his grip had done, he had laughed gently while apologizing.

"Becca," he had chided her, "these things happen." He had kissed her lightly to sooth her look of disbelief. "With passion like ours, there's bound to be a few battle scars."

Being with William was exciting and unpredictable. But his desires had grown strange and demanding. A small part of her began to feel a growing sense of repulsion. Twinges of guilt and emptiness left her cold and unsatisfied after their times together.

She stood up from the couch and went into the bedroom. She was tired and knew she would have no opportunity to sleep when William showed up. She climbed into bed and fell into a light sleep.

It was dark when William woke her, impatiently satisfying his need before she was fully awake. Not long after, he got out of bed and tossed her clothes to her. "Come on, it's a beautiful night. Let's go to the lake." Rebecca watched William as he walked from the bedroom. She wondered where the man she had met under the oak tree was now. The man who had talked and laughed with her. The man who had made her feel beautiful and happy. What happened to the man who made Rebecca feel as though she found her reason for living? Somehow, she had to find him again. Maybe if she held on long enough that joy she knew in the beginning would return.

Rebecca got up, slipped on her clothes and followed him.

Alyssa sat up in bed and flicked on the bedside lamp. It was a quarter to four in the morning, and still she couldn't sleep. Her mind whirled with thoughts, keeping her awake and physically exhausted. Jake had promised. He had said he wanted her and would give her the desire of her heart. When he got back her ever-increasing need would be satisfied. No longer would she feel undesirable or fear missing the knowledge of a man's love. No longer would she be untouched.

That last thought stayed, hanging in the air like a bad odor. A war was going on inside of her; a quiet whispering voice rose up and waged war on her flesh and emotions. The voice sometimes sounded like Austin talking about the beauty of a pure marriage; sometimes it was Pastor French telling her not to prostitute the temple of God; sometimes it was her mother speaking about the evils of fornication.

Alyssa cringed inwardly at that word. *Fornication.* It sounded so—sinful. The voice pleaded insistently with her conscience to do the right thing, while her flesh cried out for satisfaction so loudly that she couldn't think at all. The war plagued her until she felt she might go mad.

She must know: would it really be a sin in the eyes of God? Jake was the first man she had ever loved, and she wanted him to be the first man to ever love her, in every way. However, the thing that weighed heavily on her mind was the fear of never getting the opportunity again.

She glanced at the Bible sitting on her nightstand. She had been stunned when Austin presented it to her and explained that it had been his mother's. He told her that God had put it in his heart to give it to her, and he prayed she would find a deeper relationship with God among the pages.

Already she had searched the Bible several times, rereading the scriptures on sexual immorality. She had looked up the subject in the book's concordance and was nervous to find so many references. However, after reading through each scripture listed, she was encouraged. Many talked about avoiding sexual immorality and lust, but those didn't refer to Alyssa's situation. Her feelings weren't immoral. She loved Jake.

Despite her rational assessment, she was compelled several more times to reread the same scriptures over. She felt she had to double-check just to make sure she was right. Each time she felt less convinced of her resolve. The scriptures that attacked her peace most were those that talked of her body being God's temple.

"...You can't say that our bodies were made for sexual immorality..." *But I love Jake, so it's not immoral.* "They were made for the Lord, and the Lord cares about our bodies...Don't you realize that your bodies are actually parts of Christ?...Should a man take his body, which is part of Christ, and join it to a prostitute? Never!..." *Jake's been around, but that will change.* " Run from sexual sin!...For sexual immorality is a sin against your own body..." *It can't be sin if it's love.* "your body is the temple of the Holy Spirit...Honor God with your body."

These scriptures only caused more confusion and grief. Just when she had it all figured out, the words came flooding back, destroying her confidence in what she was doing.

"Lord, how can I not be with him? It's all I want," she whispered in the dim light of her room. "For one moment to believe I am loved. God, I need this." She clasped her hands together tightly. "Lord, if You would, please make him love me."

Her mind drifted to thoughts of Jake's return, and her flesh won the battle inside. She had no choice. Even if it were wrong, God would forgive her.

Nineteen

Jake was coming home today! Alyssa got little work done watching the clock tick painfully slow. It was pointless to try concentrating; she was too anxious. She had decided that she would be with Jake, though she felt there really was no decision to make.

She had also decided something else: deep inside, she knew it was wrong. Conviction had eaten at her unceasingly, and she finally gave in, admitting it was sin. The real battle began after that admission: whether or not to defy the principles of God. It had been a long and tormenting last few days, but in the end she surrendered to her flesh. Praying God would forgive her, she purposed to be with Jake whatever the cost. She was confident in her salvation and would deal with any repercussions afterward.

Finally Alyssa gave up and left work. She went to the parking lot quickly and got into her new van. She had purchased a van that would allow her to drive while sitting in her wheelchair, though opting to drive in the van's original seat until absolutely necessary.

Her stomach twisted in anticipation as she drove home. Would tonight be the night? That thought caused her stomach to suddenly flip. It would have to be tonight, for she wouldn't be able to bear waiting.

She would call Jake when she got home and make plans for them to meet as soon as possible.

Austin tossed the last bale of hay up to the top of the stack. Having loaded all the hay onto the truck, he jumped down and waved to the driver.

"Sure you don't want a ride back?" asked Big John.

"No thanks." Austin waved again as the rancher drove off. He pulled out the bandana stuffed into his back pocket and wiped his sweating face. Grabbing his shirt, he pulled it over his broad shoulders and started walking back toward the stables.

"OK, Lord, I'm listening."

Something had nagged at Austin all day. Trouble was coming. He could feel it, though he didn't understand where it was coming from. Alyssa's picture burned vividly in his mind while a fierce warning screamed in his spirit.

PRAY FOR HER!

He prayed in the Spirit, not knowing what to pray. "Lord, help me see what's happening, to know what to pray." Austin stopped and knelt in the middle of the harvested hay field, raising his hands to the clear sky, with prayer flowing in power.

Disappointed to see Elizabeth and her mother in the kitchen when she entered, Alyssa sat down at the table, hearing little of the women's discussion. She casually asked if anyone had called for her and hid her disappointment at the answer. Jake hadn't called. She pondered possible explanations in her mind while trying to look interested in the present conversation.

She talked herself into believing that Jake was as excited as she was. She couldn't wait any longer. She could be with him, fulfilling her every fantasy today! That reality hit, and her stomach once more spun out of control. Maybe she should go to his cabin and surprise him.

"Did you hear about the foreman?" Elizabeth asked. Alyssa's head snapped to attention, and her eyes shot to Elizabeth's.

"He's back from Connecticut," she continued, "and he brought his girlfriend and kid with him. Can you imagine Jake Cutler with a son?" she laughed.

Alyssa's face burned, and her mind clouded in confusion. "His girlfriend is here?" Her voice came out strained and hazy.

"And his kid," answered Elizabeth. "They're staying with him."

"I thought he went to New York to see a sick uncle." Alyssa's voice shook despite her effort to control the rising hysteria she felt.

Elizabeth didn't seem to notice. "Carlos tells me all the relatives Jake has are his parents on the Groves Road."

The conversation went on around her as Alyssa's mind wheeled with alarm. Had Jake lied to her? Surely he couldn't have made that whole story up about his uncle—he had been so sad. Why had he brought Linda back?

She stood up and smiled. Explaining that she had to go change, she headed to her room and closed the door. Covering her mouth with her hand as she leaned against the closed door, she stifled a scared sob. No! Jake wouldn't do such a thing!

She shook her head violently as if it would cause the horrible thoughts to go away. Jake loved her! He had promised…when he got back…it would still happen. Nothing had changed. Calming down, she headed out with a quick word to her mother about going to the lake.

Jake would explain, making all her fears go away, and then kiss away her tears. He would touch her and tell her he loved her. Then he would keep his promise. She refused to think of anything else. She wouldn't imagine it any differently, for the possibility scared her too much.

Austin walked around the field praying fervently and crying out to God. His fear for Alyssa was stronger than ever. What was happening? He felt helpless but kept praying.

"God, only You know what's happening. Please, Lord, protect her. Surround her now with Your Spirit."

He knew he had authority over whatever evil the devil might plan. Christ had given His children the same authority He Himself had. But in the end, Alyssa had to choose God to be free. "Lord, do whatever You must to show her You're salvation and hope."

Alyssa rode down the path as quickly as she could; yet her mind was racing a hundred times faster than her electric chair. She would find out the truth, then everyone would know Jake loved her.

She would have him, even if only for a time. Alyssa refused to believe he had brought Linda back for any reason other than love for his son.

She would go meet this woman and stake her claim, so to speak. She and Jake would make plans to meet, maybe that evening once his son was settled. Everything was fine; God would not destroy this for her. *Just for a little while Lord. Even if only for one night. I'll live my life holding on to one night.*

Despite her certainty that Jake still wanted her, she trembled nearing the edge of the clearing. Just beyond the trees and to the right stood Jake's cabin. She closed her eyes and drew in a shaking breath, which only made her more queasy. As she stood from her chair, she heard voices making her stop and listen. She couldn't make out their words but was sure the male voice was Jake's. Without thinking she was compelled to get closer undetected. Stepping over small brush, she made her way through the trees and to the right of the path. As she neared the trees directly in front of the cabin, she saw two figures sitting on the porch where she and Jake had sat not long ago.

It was Jake and a woman Alyssa knew had to be Linda. She got as close to the clearing as she dared and stopped behind a large tree to watch. Alyssa could hear them plainly now and their conversation about J.J. irritated her. Alyssa's heart banged against her ears as she watched them, willing them away from each other. They were too close, too friendly.

"I thought you'd never come," Linda laughed.

"I told you I would once I got some money." Jake's reply caused Alyssa's heart to suddenly stop pounding. Her hand went to her mouth in case she started screaming.

"I missed you," the woman said coyly, sliding closer to Jake.

"I missed you." Jake grinned, moving his eyes over her in a fashion familiar to Alyssa. The look alone sent a stabbing pain of betrayal through her as she watched, frozen behind the tree. *No Jake, don't look at her like that. Please—no!*

"Prove it," Linda demanded.

Jake laughed. "Didn't I already?"

Alyssa felt as if a huge fist had slammed into her face, and she went numb. She wondered if she were in some kind of dream, not seeing what she was seeing, not hearing what she had just heard. It didn't mean what it sounded like it meant.

Proving the intentions of the remark, Linda slipped her arms around Jake. "Prove it again," she said, with a kiss on Jake's neck.

"My pleasure." Jake wrapped his arms around Linda and pulled her close. He kissed Linda with all the hunger and passion Alyssa had dreamed he would kiss her with. After a moment, the two separated long enough to go into the cabin and shut the door.

Austin felt every nerve in his body tighten. He stopped and listened. God was speaking. Suddenly Austin felt death all around him. He saw the vision clearly in his mind: complete darkness lit only by a single flickering match. Then the flame was blown out, and utter blackness was left. God was showing him what was happening to Alyssa.

"God, what can I do!" he cried.

The lake!

Without another thought, he started running. Alyssa was going to the lake, and he needed to be there. But why? He ran as fast as he could in frustration, praying he wouldn't be too late.

Alyssa could not move. How long she stood there she wasn't sure. It was over—everything was over. She didn't cry or yell or moan. She just stared at the closed door, knowing what was going on behind it.

It all had been a lie. Jake had lied: he had never loved her. He had never planned to keep his promise, and she was a fool for thinking he would. She felt dead. Her hope was dead. Her dreams were dead. The small flicker of light that had sustained her was snuffed out. There was no more light in the darkness of her soul. The blackness had won. She knew she had fallen into the great black pit and would never come out.

Her legs began to ache, forcing her back to the chair. The chair was her coffin; she mused with an empty smile. She moved back up the path slowly. There was nothing to hurry for. Nothing. Never would there be anything to look forward to again. Nothing.

What was the point? There was nothing. Impulsively she turned toward the lake. What would her future be? The life of an invalid. A burden to her family.

She reached the lake and sat for a long time staring at the blue waves. Suddenly she had a revelation. *The lake!* Yes, it was her friend. She could hear it whispering a sweet answer of relief. She could step in and all this would be over. No one would miss her. They would be relieved and say a silent prayer of thanks.

She could stop the horror that was her life. She didn't have to deal with a hopeless, dark future. She could do something good for her mother. She could relieve the burden of her family. It made such sense to her; to live made no sense at all.

Alyssa stood from the chair and walked to the edge of the lake. She could still walk. If she walked into the lake now, she would never know the life of a complete cripple. Yes, it was simple, perfect, and gave her a certain feeling of strange excitement. Never to know pain again— how wonderful!

Alyssa stood, allowing the water to crawl slowly over her feet. She stared with blank, unseeing eyes at the pool of blue liquid. The water called her, coaxing her to take another step. She no longer felt fear, pain, or regret. She felt nothing. Focusing on the center of the lake, she listened as it called out to her. *You deserve rest, Ally. You've had a long hard life, and now you can let go of the pain. You've got nothing to live for. Life would be so much easier for your mother and the rest of your family if they didn't have to worry about you anymore. In a way, Ally, you owe this to them.* Alyssa listened closely to the soothing voice, so clear in her ears. *Peace and rest; that's what I offer. Just let go. Stop fighting, Alyssa. You're too tired to fight anymore.*

Her eyes did not waver from her destination as she took slow, deliberate steps toward the center of the lake. She felt the water rising higher up her legs, to her thighs, touching her waist. The gentle waves rippled over her stomach and rose toward her neck. She found the warmth comforting as it saturated her clothes. Stopping just as the water reached her chin, she breathed a final breath of life and closed her eyes in relief. She took one more step, immersing her body in the uncaring water.

Austin reached the clearing just in time to see a mass of thick hair fanning the top of the water, slowly disappearing beneath the surface. "My God," he choked in a whisper. Fear clutched his stomach, cutting off his breath. Without thought he ran with all the strength each muscle in his body contained. With the same amount of force, he found his voice and yelled. "Alyssa!" It was a cry not only to Alyssa but also to God.

By the time he reached the water's edge he could no longer see her hair above the surface. He dove in, reaching her in seconds. Grabbing her around the waist, he lifted her above the surface and headed quickly back to shore. Gently, he laid her on the grass and knelt over her. Cupping her face in his hands, he stroked the wet hair from her eyes. "Lyssa?" He saw she was breathing and knew she would be all right. He lifted her in his arms and held her, praying and rocking her as if she were a child.

186

Slowly Alyssa came to, coughing violently before looking around confused. Austin loosened his embrace as she sat back and looked up at him. "What happened? What did you do?"

"Thank God you're alright. I was so scared when I saw you out there." Tears filled his eyes as he looked at her and then stopped when he saw her expression. The fear he had felt before crawled up his spine once again.

Alyssa's empty eyes bore into his. "You had no right to interfere, Austin. Go home." She spoke as if threatening him.

"I won't allow you to hurt yourself, Alyssa."

"You have no choice." Austin had never seen such lifeless eyes and knew she was well on her way to death. "I want to die. I want to die." Alyssa suddenly screamed in rage and struggled to free herself. "Let me go! I'm going to kill myself! I want to die!"

Austin held her tightly as she fought and spoke in a loud commanding voice. "Alyssa stop! In the name of Jesus, stop." She stilled in his arms and sat unmoving for a long time.

Austin softly prayed over her, for how long he wasn't sure. After a time, he held her chin and gently lifted her face toward his. Relief and anguish washed over him simultaneously as he saw her face contort with unspeakable torment, yet her eyes now held life. Tears sprang up and flowed in rivers over her face as his eyes held hers. A moan rooted in the very depths of her soul poured out from her stomach. She doubled over in Austin's arms as if in physical pain, moaning and sobbing uncontrollably.

Austin held her tightly in his strong arms, stroking her wet hair. He felt each cry and tear that came from her. She cried as if someone were stabbing a knife into her heart, and Austin felt that knife in his own. He had never felt so helpless. He would have given his very existence to spare Alyssa the torment she was experiencing. All he could do was pray with every ounce of his soul and his faith.

Alyssa's cries continued for a long time. She seemed not to hear Austin praying until she calmed down enough to talk between the sobs. "Oh God! Austin, I can't do it anymore. I can't fight and struggle everyday to hold on to some hope that doesn't exist. I've

187

got nothing, no one. It hurts too much to live!" she cried hoarsely. With every tear, it felt like a part of her soul was being ripped from her chest. She turned her tear-drenched eyes to his. The look of pain in them tore his soul into pieces.

"All my life I've fought just to hold on. I'm not even sure what I was holding on to. But I thought that maybe someday I'd have something worth living for. I thought I found someone, but now even that's gone." Her whisper broke into another body-quaking sob as Austin caressed her face soothingly.

Alyssa's voice was barely a hoarse whisper in the midst of her tears. "I'm tired of the pain Austin. I can't do it anymore. I'm in this pit where nobody can see me or find me, and if they could, they really wouldn't care. I can't take it anymore. It hurts too bad to go through life alone facing the things I have to face." Lying back in his arms again she cried more painful sobs.

Austin continued holding her gently and praying. He loved her. That was becoming more and more obvious to him, and he wanted to take away her suffering. But more than that, he wanted her to find Christ. He knew Jesus was her only hope. *Jesus, please let her see Your love through me. Spirit of God, speak through me. Love through me.*

When she quieted he took her face in his hands and made her look at him. "Lyssa, listen to me. You are not alone. Jesus loves you with a real and passionate love and desires to give you joy and peace. He feels all your pain and wants to take it away. He died for you because He loved you so much. Let Him take this pain from you. Give it to Him, and He will set you free and lift you out of that pit and place you in wonderful light. You don't need the strength. He's got all the strength you need. I'll help you, Lyssa. I'm here, and I'll help you find your way to Christ. I care about you and won't let anything happen to you. Let me help you find Jesus."

He held her face gently as she looked up into his eyes. She felt his fingers lightly brushing away the streaming tears from her cheeks. His words didn't hold much meaning for her; her ears were dull to their sound. But she saw something in his eyes as she stared at him. She felt something in his touch as he brushed away her tears.

There was such an abundance of love and compassion in Austin's eyes that it sparked something in Alyssa's soul. Suddenly she became consumed with the need for what she saw in him. Never had she wanted anything more. She never wanted him to stop touching her; she never wanted that look of love to die from his gaze.

Desperately she grabbed his wet shirt and pulled herself close to him. "Austin," her voice cracked with emotion as she drank in the tenderness in his face. "I need you." Sliding her hands across his chest, she leaned toward him and pressed her lips to his. "I need you. Please love me, please," she breathed before kissing him with desperate urgency. She moved her hands around his neck and clung to him.

Austin froze in shock. All his intentions had been mistaken and thrown aside. The fierceness of her kiss stunned his senses, and he felt his body quickly react to her. It took all his willpower not to respond with his own hunger. *God, help me!*

He pulled back as she compulsively devoured his face and neck with her kisses. Knowing he couldn't let this happen, he reached up and grabbed Alyssa's hands, pulling her arms from his neck. "Alyssa, wait. This isn't what you need." His voice didn't hold the conviction it had before. Alyssa's touch had stirred something he had purposely kept under control. Her hands felt so small in his, and as he let them go they immediately went back to rest on his chest.

"Austin, I love you—I need you." His name on her lips, breathed in a pleading voice, broke his resolve. Drinking in the crystal blue of her eyes, he buried his hand in her wet hair and drew her to him. He forgot why he had resisted. The desire he had pushed aside rose up with overwhelming force.

He lowered his mouth to hers in an urgent passionate kiss, tasting the sweetness of her mouth. Every emotion he held inside suddenly came flooding forth. Possessively he pulled her close, not wanting to ever let her go. He kissed her forehead, her eyelids, her cheeks, wanting to erase the pain that had been in her face. Suddenly he wanted her so much that his desire scared him.

Alyssa was startled at Austin's response to her. No man had ever kissed her—never mind Jake's brief kisses, which had always avoided her lips. The pleasure Austin's affection brought her was intense, though in ways beyond physical. *Not even Jake could make me feel like this.* It was a fleeting thought which drew her closer to Austin.

Austin had ceased to think and simply allowed himself to feel. His kisses became tender and searching, reaching deep into her soul with a love that shook the very core of her existence. She longed for him to fill the gaping void where her soul was supposed to be.

"You're all I need," she whispered as he buried his face in her hair. "You're all I'll ever need. You saved my life Austin. You saved me."

Abruptly, reality struck Austin, and he quickly pulled away. He sat back, guilt washing over him. *Oh God, forgive me! What have I done?* Gently tracing the smooth line of her jaw with his fingers, he looked at her with a rueful smile. "Lyssa, I'm sorry." Dropping his hand, he stood up and turned away, raking his hands through his hair while trying to calm the desire he had caused. When he turned back, his stomach tightened at the look of utter confusion on Alyssa's face. That confusion promised to turn to devastation when he explained—and it was his own fault.

He knelt back down in front of her. "I'm sorry; please understand," he choked, taking her hands. "You're searching for something to hold on to, and it would be easy for it to be me. But I can't bring you the peace and joy you need. I would love to be able to wash away everything that has hurt you, but I can't. Only Jesus can. You must reach for Him."

Alyssa's face turned crimson with humiliation as she realized what she had done. She had thrown herself at Austin, and now he was giving her a sermon! Austin nearly broke at the look on her face. *What have I done?* "Lyssa, look at me." Austin touched her chin, lifting her face toward his. "Please forgive me. I took advantage of a situation I shouldn't have, and I'm so sorry. I don't ever want to be the cause of your pain. I care about you too much."

Alyssa turned from his piercing eyes and slowly stood up in an attempt to compose herself. She brushed her hair back and wiped the remaining tears away. "Thank you, Austin, for your help. I'm sorry for..." she searched for the words but couldn't get them out.

She wanted to escape and hide under a rock so she'd never have to face him again. "I've got to go."

She started to leave but Austin caught her wrist, holding her there. "Wait, stay and talk to me. Don't leave like this."

"I really need to go." Feeling another torrent of tears threatening to emerge, she looked directly at him. "Please, just let me go," her voice cracked.

"Promise me you won't hurt yourself."

At her nod he released her wrist and watched her get in her chair and go. When she was out of sight, he looked toward the sky and fell to his knees, praying aloud. He felt as David did when he wrote, *my guilt has overwhelmed me like a burden too heavy to bear.*

"Oh Lord, what have I done? Please forgive me for allowing my flesh to get out of control. Don't let my sin block Lyssa's way to You. Save her, I pray! Don't hold my sin against her. Oh God, how could You ever use a fool like me?"

Twenty

    Austin had not heard from Alyssa since carrying her from the lake. He wanted to go to her and make sure she was all right, to tell her he loved her and would take care of her for the rest of his life. But God restrained him, making it clear that He had work to do in Alyssa, which didn't involve Austin. She had mistakenly looked to Austin as her answer and salvation.

    He prayed unceasingly for her, crying out to God at any given time. All his pride was stripped away as the Holy Spirit drew him into intercession. More than once he'd had to excuse himself from the ranchers when prayer rose so strongly inside him that he could do little but prostrate himself before God.

    Jake said very little to Austin during work hours, avoiding him at all costs. Austin was surprised he felt no anger toward the man, just pity and remorse over Jake's lost soul.

    Austin's biggest problem was in his mind. His vivid memory was merciless. Alyssa's words rang in his ears, *"I love you Austin…I need you…"* Never had he felt so powerful and so totally powerless in one instant just by looking into a woman's eyes.

Alyssa moved through her days absently. At work, she smiled at Candy's lighthearted humor. At home, she interacted stiffly with whoever spoke to her: she smiled when the situation called for humor, listened when someone needed comfort, and responded when questions were asked.

Once free from the facade of living, she locked herself in her room. There she curled up in bed and allowed the pain to wash over her. In the silence of her room, she was free to feel each agonizing emotion inside. It was more real than going about the house as if happy. Her isolated room reflected the utter loneliness she felt of everything inside her.

If not for the anguish that caused tears to flow unyielding during those hours alone, she would doubt the existence of life breathing inside her. The pain was all she had now, and she held on to it. Depression was better than the bone-chilling nothingness she had felt so completely when walking into death.

Her mind endlessly replayed each word Jake ever spoke; each memory produced new tears. She did not understand but desperately tried to make sense out of it all. Had they even had a relationship? Was he sorry for hurting her? Did he care? When she dwelt on such things, anger, mixed with humiliation, rose at how he had used her. She considered going and telling Jake what a jerk he was but knew she would end up crying at his feet, begging him to love her, to touch her like he had promised. *You're such a fool! What man would desire you— an ugly cripple!* She heard the familiar taunting voice of the beast. *You had the audacity to throw yourself at Austin!* It laughed inside her head. Even though she was alone in her room, Alyssa's face turned scarlet with shame and humiliation at the thought of Austin. *The only real man you've ever known, and you thought he'd want you!*

Alyssa sobbed uncontrollably as she looked at herself in the mirror across from her bed. *Look at you! You're disgusting, and it's only going to get worse! You couldn't please a man!* The mocking voice screamed with laughter. *You're pathetic—he felt so sorry for you that he actually kissed you back!* The voice continued its attack unceasingly. She dreaded the day when she would actually have to face Austin.

The look that had been in Austin's eyes haunted her. She had thought it was love—overwhelming, compassionate, pure love. That was what she grasped for when she reached for him. But she had been mistaken. Still, it plagued her thoughts and dreams.

When she tried pushing it from her mind it came back nagging at her. What was it about Austin? She would think painfully of Jake, and the longing he created was always followed by that look of Austin's.

Dejected, she glanced at her Bible. More and more her eyes seemed drawn to it. She could almost hear it speaking, calling her to pick it up. "What do I do now, Lord?" she whispered, staring at the book. No answer came, but her eyes would not look away from the Bible; they stayed riveted as if she might see beyond the cover and find answers among the pages.

Without thinking she reached for the leather bound book. Were there answers in there?

You are My temple, My dwelling place.

He dwells in me. She was taught as a child that Christ lived in her heart, but there seemed to be more to it than that. She opened the Bible in her lap. Where would she look? It fell open to the book of Psalms.

She flipped through until she found something that interested her. She stopped at Psalm 13, which David wrote. She remembered Pastor French mentioning David in his sermon. He said David was a man after God's own heart, even after sinning greatly against God. She smiled flatly. What would David know about the things she was feeling?

She needed something that would speak to her. The Bible was about how awesome God was, but Alyssa felt God didn't even know her. Looking down at the book she read the Psalm quietly with growing amazement.

"How long, O Lord? Will you forget me forever? How long will you hide your face from me? How long must I wrestle with my thoughts and every day have sorrow in my heart? How long will my enemy triumph over me?"

194

Alyssa reread these words with gathering tears. These words were her heart exactly. *Yes, Lord—how long?*

"Turn and answer me, O Lord my God! Restore the sparkle to my eyes, or I will die. Don't let my enemies gloat, saying, 'We have defeated him!' Don't let them rejoice at my downfall."

She would have slept in death but for Austin. The beast now rejoiced within her that he had won. Knowing David's pain, she felt sorry for him. Did God answer? How did he get God to listen?

"But I trust in your unfailing love; my heart rejoices in your salvation. I will sing to the Lord, for he has been good to me."

Confused, Alyssa reread the last part. David just said how God had turned away and allowed darkness to torment him, so why was he now praising God? The Lord hadn't been good to him! What did he have to rejoice about? He rejoiced in God's salvation and unfailing love. What did those things ever bring Alyssa? Why were they so far from her now?

"Lord, I want to understand. I want to praise You and be thankful, but I don't know how." She thought about the people at Austin's church. They knew how to praise Him. Their love for God was obvious. Alyssa loved God, so what was the difference between them and her?

As much as you loved Jake?

She was offended at the question that arose. *Of course—more than Jake!*

Is your desire for Me as strong?

This thought shamed her. Her desire for Jake was dirty and sinful. Her love for God wasn't like that.

But do you want Me as much as you want Jake?

"Yes, I do," she said, disturbed.

What would you have done to have Jake?

The gentle voice reminded her of her sin. "Lord, I'm sorry for what I was going to do." How sorry was she? Her desire for him hadn't lessened. Jake's image still consumed her constantly. She still yearned for him. The bitter truth was, she would still do anything to have him.

Ever since that day at the lake Alyssa had begged God to take away her need for Jake. She wept, telling God how unbearable it was.

She confessed her sin and pleaded with Him to forgive and take it from her. Yet the unbearable need stayed like a raw wound.

What would you do to have more of Me?

She didn't understand this question. She knew God and already had Him. How could she have more of Him? She thought about the people who lingered after the festival concert. They had Jesus. They *knew* Jesus. It was written in every tear rolling down their shining faces. Their love for Him was boldly displayed with upraised hands for all the town to see.

She remembered the strange emptiness she felt watching them worship the Lord. What was the longing that tugged at her heart? She felt it now.

Austin had said something about looking to him to fill her need instead of God. She couldn't remember exactly; she had been too stunned and embarrassed to listen. Frustrated by all the confusing thoughts, she tossed the Bible aside and slid off the bed.

She had to get out of the house and clear her mind. She didn't know where she was going. She just got in her vehicle and drove. Plaguing thoughts harassed her unceasingly; would she ever be free? She was full of pain and longing and darkness, pressing on her like a weight. *God, what am I going to do? Will You ever help me?*

The road suddenly looked familiar to her, and she realized she was heading for Austin's church. Her first impulse was to turn around, but something kept her heading toward it. She knew there would be a service that night and Austin would be there. It couldn't hurt to drive by; she had no intention of going in.

As the church came into view, she saw cars lining the road. That would keep her from going in; she was tired and knew she couldn't walk far. Without thinking she slowed as she neared the church. Her eyes moved over the multitude of vehicles when her heart jumped at seeing one open space near the door.

Before she realized what she was doing, she had pulled into the space. What was she doing? Surely she wasn't planning on going in there! She couldn't face Austin—not in there!

Music spilled from the sanctuary, and she could see through the windows the people dancing joyously, compelling her to go in. She wanted to see, to know from where their joy came.

She could hear Austin's soul-touching voice, and it sent shivers down her spine. What was it about his voice that she loved? Knowing he would lead the song service and then sit in the front of the church, she figured she'd be able to sneak in and out without being noticed.

She tentatively walked into the church and was greeted by several ushers. Thinking to find a seat in the back, she headed toward the loud, rejoicing music and stood just inside the sanctuary, looking for a seat. Suddenly her heart stopped as she caught sight of Austin. He was so breathtakingly handsome! She almost forgot how he made her heart flutter with a smile.

Spotting a vacant chair, she was about to hide in the back when an excited voice stopped her. It was Cloe. Where had she come from? She hugged Alyssa warmly and told her how wonderful it was to see her. "Come sit with us," Cloe insisted. "Does Austin know you're here?"

Alyssa was speechless as she was pulled through the crowd of dancing people straight to the front row! She could feel her face burning as she took her place beside the well-meaning wife of Pastor French. Had Austin seen her yet? She refused to look at him. She couldn't; she was too embarrassed. *Oh God, why did I come?*

Austin saw Alyssa and nearly forgot the words he was singing. His heart soared at the sight of her. Glorious joy swept through him and through the music he played as he praised God with even more power.

He noticed her trying terribly hard to avoid looking his way. It was his fault. He closed his eyes, singing with all his strength, and prayed God would open Alyssa's eyes to His Spirit that night.

After awhile the music slowed to some beautiful ballads sung unto Jesus. The wonderful melody of the piano seeped in and pricked Alyssa's heart uncomfortably. When Austin began to sing in a soft throaty voice, something washed over her that she couldn't define.

Tears sprang to her eyes as Austin sang about God's sweet love. What was wrong with her? She closed them tightly, feeling foolish for wanting to cry. But the feeling would not leave, and her lip began to quiver dangerously. She could feel sobs threatening to erupt as Austin sang with overwhelming emotion, encouraging her to lose control.

Alyssa tried not to listen to the music, but it penetrated to the core of her soul and turned her heart into trembling mush. She was greatly relieved when the pastor stepped up to the podium. However, dismay evaporated her relief when Pastor French spoke. "There are people here crying out for the love of Jesus," he began. "You feel an emptiness inside crying out for something, but you've been looking in all the wrong directions. Tonight you're in the right place, the answer is here."

Pastor French paused, looking around the room. "The Lord wants to set people free tonight. He wants to give everyone here a new revelation of His love and power."

Alyssa bit her lip hard to keep the tears back. The welcomed, self-inflicted pain prevented the flood for another moment. "Tonight, if you desire to know more of Jesus, I ask you to come to these altars and spend time with God. If your heart has been hungry and crying out for something but you haven't been able to find the answer, Jesus Christ is your answer. The power of God's love will set you free."

She could hold the tears back no longer. Several fell down her cheeks, and she felt her face twist in pain.

The pastor asked Austin to play something as the people started lining the altars. The piano began to sing notes that sent more tears down Alyssa's face. When Austin's voice touched her, she looked up at him. He was worshiping the Lord with his eyes raised toward the ceiling. His face was full of powerful emotions, but it was his eyes that caused the desperate, broken sob in Alyssa's throat to escape.

In Austin's eyes she saw the same love and compassion she had seen when he had looked at her after rescuing her from the lake, the unconditional, passionate love that she had reached for. That was the look, the love she had grasped at, now flowing from his eyes as he sang to the Lord. Suddenly she understood that the love she had seen was God's love for her shining through Austin. She broke completely as the revelation struck her.

She couldn't even go to the altar; she slid from her chair and fell to her knees sobbing. Austin's deep voice, hoarse with emotion, sounded through her sobs over the speakers. "In Isaiah 55, the Lord says, 'Is anyone thirsty? Come and drink—even if you have no money! Come, take your choice of wine or milk—it's all free! Why spend your money on food that does not give you strength? Why pay for food that does you no good? Listen to me, and you will eat what is good. You will enjoy the finest food. Come to me with your ears wide open. Listen, and you will find life.'"

Austin's voice pleaded for the hurting to turn to Christ. Alyssa recognized the sound of Christ's love crying out to His people to receive Him. She had heard the plea from Austin's mouth before but had mistaken the love as coming from his own heart and not the heart of Christ. But it was Jesus calling—Jesus was pleading for her to turn to Him.

Cloe knelt and took Alyssa in her arms. Alyssa clung to the woman tightly, crying with abandon, weeping as never before. Layers of bondage were being painfully torn from her, and she could feel a hand reach into her chest, ripping out roots that had grown for so long.

She didn't speak through the wrenching sobs; she simply let go of everything she had been holding onto. Finally she released all her bondage and trusted God to deliver her from the darkness controlling her life.

Cloe held her, stroking her hair while praying soothingly. Alyssa felt like a child in the arms of her mother. Who was this woman that loved Alyssa so much? It was unfathomable. As she soaked in the unconditional love poured upon her, she realized it wasn't just Cloe's arms holding her—it was Jesus's.

Austin watched Alyssa in Cloe's arms and restrained himself from going to her also. He wanted to hold her and comfort her. He wanted to make it all right for her, but it wasn't his place.

Alyssa didn't know how long she cried in the precious woman's arms, but she didn't stop until every last tear was shed and her stomach ceased twisting. Gradually, she quieted in Cloe's embrace, but the woman held on a bit longer before slowly letting go.

Sitting back, Alyssa blew her nose, then turned her tear-stained face to the woman smiling in front of her. "Thank you." Alyssa's hoarse whisper seemed so inadequate. She wished to say so much more to make Cloe understand how grateful she was for her love. Cloe stayed close by, praying quietly while Alyssa leaned back and rested her head against the seat of the chair.

She was spent and exhausted. With her eyes closed, soaking in the atmosphere thick with God's presence, she marveled at how tangible and real the love of Jesus was. She could *feel* it. She thought she might touch it if she reached out. God was in the room surrounding and penetrating her. She breathed in His presence like air. Alyssa's body trembled gently in the presence of God. It was like power going through her—tangible power coursing through her blood.

She felt empty inside. There was no more darkness and pain filling her; she was clean and fresh. God had emptied her of garbage, and the lightness she experienced was exhilarating! The Holy Spirit was seeping in and filling the now empty places with joy, peace, hope, and love.

Daring to turn her thoughts to Jake, Alyssa was newly amazed at what she found: nothing. She had absolutely no desire in the least for Jake! All that was left was compassion that hoped he would find Christ in his own life.

As she realized that she was free from Jake and the beast inside of her, she couldn't help but giggle. It was a small sound that kept bubbling out of her stomach. Cloe and Alex both began laughing with abandon on the floor near her.

She watched the two happily. She wasn't sure about what she saw, but something inside hungered for it. She wanted that kind of joy. She sat laughing quietly at the two and praising God for His deliverance. She was so happy and free, she wondered if others could see her glowing the way that Cloe and Alex did.

It was a long time before the service ended and Austin stepped off the stage. He hesitantly went to where Alyssa sat on the floor. He looked at her, searching her eyes for any sign that she may not want to talk to him. When she saw him she gave him a shaky but welcoming smile.

Reaching her, he knelt down with tears in his eyes to match her own. When he reached for her she quickly wrapped her arms around his neck and held him tightly. "Austin," she breathed, "I'm sorry for what I did. I know now what I needed—you were so right." The words flooded forth as she hugged him.

Pulling back slightly to look into her eyes, he stopped her confession. "No, Lyssa," he insisted. "It wasn't your fault. You weren't thinking; you didn't know what you were doing—I did. I am so sorry." His fingers briefly brushed her cheek before pulling her back into his embrace.

Austin held her close, shut his eyes, and dug his hand into her hair. The joy bursting within him was almost unbearable. "Thank You, Jesus. Thank You, Jesus…" were his only words as he praised God for Alyssa's freedom. Later he would bow at his Lord's feet and thank Him for answering his prayers for the woman he loved.

Twenty-One

Alyssa lay in bed staring out at the bright morning. She had plans to meet Austin later; they had been spending weekends together praying and talking or reading the Bible. She had learned much in the weeks since giving every part of her life to Christ, and the more she learned the more she realized how little she knew.

It was exciting to find new revelations in the Bible that opened her eyes to something she had never before realized. How could she have been so ignorant of God's nature? She had known Him all her life without really *knowing* Him. Reading His Word—which she now did everyday—was the first step.

Alyssa smiled to herself. Austin spent so much time sharing truth and helping her see God's plan. His patience and compassion for her were unending. Lately, her heart quickened with thoughts of him.

When he looked at her she melted. When he innocently touched her arm, her insides quivered. His voice sent flutters through her stomach. She knew, no matter how hard she prayed against it, she was falling in love with Austin Jacobs. The truth was she had always loved him, but suddenly it was impossible to fight. She knew Austin's feelings were not as hers were, and she accepted that. For now, she would hold on to his beautiful, unconditional friendship.

She pushed the blankets aside slowly—they felt like lead weights! Sitting up, along with everything else, was becoming more difficult. She saw the changes as if through a haze, not really noticing the steady decline in strength. She was quick at compensating for the increasing weakness, making it less discernable.

She was using her wheelchair almost constantly now, even around the house. It now sat inside her bedroom; it was quicker, she reasoned. Grasping the nightstand and the bed, she braced herself as she slid to the floor. The moment her feet touched the carpet, her legs went limp and she dropped with a gasp of fear. She lay sprawled on the floor stunned and motionless.

After a few minutes she managed to get herself into a sitting position. Tears bit at her eyes, and she chewed her lip while looking up at her towering bed. *No, God, not yet! Has it happened already? Have I walked for the last time?* She stifled a desperate cry and prayed while grabbing the nightstand and trying to pull herself up.

Her arms were of no more use then her legs, and she gave up after a few struggling tries. Leaning her head on the table in defeat, she let the frightened tears fall. "Lord, help me please."

She thought of the scriptures that Austin had been showing her concerning healing. Pastor French had read Alyssa's thoughts and said that God does not want anyone to be sick nor does He put sickness on people for any purpose. After all, God is our Father, and if we on earth know how to give good gifts, how much more would our Father in heaven give us? Would we ever put sickness on our children to teach them something?

Alyssa had never heard such teaching; but it made perfect sense, and she accepted it readily. She no longer struggled with why God had put this disease upon her, now she struggled with why He hadn't yet taken it away. "Lord, I trust You...I trust Your Word...." She continued to pray until the tears stopped and her spirit calmed.

Gathering courage, she yelled to her mother. Catherine came in and cried in dismay. "What happened?"

203

"I fell getting out of bed. I can't get up." Alyssa's weak reply was soft and shaking.

Catherine quickly lifted Alyssa into her arms and carried her to the wheelchair. Alyssa had lost weight over the last few weeks, making her easier to carry. "From now on, you yell to me, and I'll help you out of bed."

Catherine helped her to the bathroom to bathe and get dressed. It wasn't the first time Alyssa was forced to have help with such personal things, but it always took a small piece of her dignity—if she had any left.

Later that day, as Alyssa sat with Austin at the lake, she told him of her morning, leaving out the more embarrassing moments. Austin felt the pain evident in her eyes, and his heart twisted in response.

"I guess this is it. I'm completely dependent on my mother," she said somberly.

"Don't give up. God has promised healing in His Word and ordained it for you. Hold on to that." Austin prayed his words would spark her faith.

"I know," she said, without conviction. "I'm just scared, I guess."

"Of what?" His voice probed gently into her soul.

Alyssa struggled to find words to explain. "All my life I've worked toward being happy accepting what I am, and what I would someday be. It's engraved on my brain that this is the way I'm supposed to be." She stopped to gather her thoughts.

"I used to pray every day that God would heal me." Painful memories were etched in Alyssa's eyes. "Then I just accepted my fate." She turned to Austin, searching his face for understanding. "I know the truth now. I know God wants to heal me and will heal me someday, but I'm afraid to believe for it now. I'm afraid to be disappointed again."

Austin reached for her hand, holding it tenderly. "I understand."

"You do?"

"It's normal to be afraid. God understands your fear and won't reject you because of it. Believing God is a choice you make. You'll have to choose faith, and faith will come as you seek it."

Something stirred in her spirit. The choice was there in front of her. Would she choose life? Had God ever truly let her down? No, He never had.

She smiled. "I want to be healed."

With new excitement, they opened the Bible and looked up scripture after scripture that proclaimed God's desire to heal His people. Austin read how they had the same power Christ had—could lay hands on the sick and see them healed—and then he prayed for Alyssa.

There was power when they prayed together. Their souls and minds joined as one in worshiping God. They sparked each other's passion for the Lord. They looked forward to the weekends with increasing excitement and weariness. Their love was growing, causing uneasiness to creep in.

Austin was so full of adoration for Alyssa that it hurt. It was agony not to be able to tell her he loved her. He wanted to shout his love on the rooftops. He wanted to hold her as they talked and watched the sunset.

It was late in the fall on one such afternoon. The air was getting cool, forcing Alyssa to dress warmly. She put on a thick tan sweater over her jeans and was comfortable as long as the sun stayed out. Austin had sat her beside him on the grass. She loved being out of her chair; it made her feel free and human again.

They were silent watching the wind bring nature to life around them. The little rippled waves ran along the surface of the water as the trees danced from side to side in perfect rhythm. "I've never seen such beautiful colors." Austin was in awe of God's creation as his eyes traveled over the brilliantly colored trees.

Alyssa smiled her agreement. "I never missed not growing up in a big city. I hope to raise my children here someday." She paused as a flicker of sadness crossed her face.

Austin noticed the change in her expression. "What's wrong?" He asked in such a way that made Alyssa long to be in his arms.

Learning quickly that he saw her every thought, she gave up trying to hide things from him. "I just hope I'll have children someday."

"Why wouldn't you?"

"You need a husband to have children." She tried to sound lighthearted but couldn't meet his gaze with her own.

"You'll have a husband," he said with gentle insistence. Alyssa marveled that Austin seemed genuinely unaware that she was different from other women.

She was quiet for a long time while he waited for her to voice that which tormented her. When she finally spoke he could barely hear her. "What if I'm not healed soon?"

"God has promised it, and you will see it manifest soon." His voice held more conviction than she felt.

"But what if I don't?" Alyssa felt guilty for even having such a thought. *God, forgive my weak faith!*

"God gives us our heart's desire if we delight ourselves in Him. He'll give you a husband. He's got some guy picked out for you already." He hoped this news encouraged Alyssa more than it encouraged his own heart.

"How could anyone want me like this?" She whispered the question to herself, her fear welling up so strongly she couldn't keep it inside.

"How could anyone not?" Austin could not look at her as he hoarsely voiced his heart. If he looked at her, he knew he would break.

Alyssa's eyes stung with gratitude at his quick, sincere response. "You're so sweet to me."

"I mean what I say."

She stared out at the lake and wrapped her arms more tightly around herself. "I want so much to be the kind of wife a man would be happy with. What if, I mean…I want to make him happy…in every way," she said faltering.

Austin knew what she was talking about and didn't hesitate in his answer. "You will. That's not something you have to worry about."

"But I do! I want to please my husband. I want him to be satisfied with me, and I don't know if he could be."

"He'll love you, and being with you will bring him more pleasure than any other woman could." Austin wanted to put her mind at ease, but it was hard to keep his own heart strong as he attempted to reassure her. It would be so easy for him to be satisfied with her. He'd be happy just to hold her in his arms for the rest of his life.

KIMBERLY MILLARD

"It's not that simple." The future seemed to loom at her, giving her glimpses of the hopelessness of her situation. "My body has become useless. What man would get excited over someone who can do nothing but lie there?" she asked with disgust.

Me, came the forbidden thought as Austin raked a hand through his hair. He cleared his throat, gathered his words carefully, and gave Alyssa a pointed look before answering. "First of all, my sweet little friend, I'm quite certain you could do more than lie there." He raised his eyebrows at her as a reprimand.

She shrugged her shoulders, unwilling to relinquish her fears just yet.

"And I happen to know that you kiss well enough to satisfy any man." A huge grin broke out across his rugged features.

"Austin!" Alyssa's eyes went wide. "Are you trying to humiliate me completely?" At the horrified look on Alyssa's face and increasing redness of her cheeks, Austin burst into laughter. She tried not to smile, throwing at him the handful of grass she had been picking self-consciously.

Once his laughter died he spoke again, but his grin stayed. "You give men too much credit, my dear—we're really not that hard to please," he stated dryly.

Austin sobered, his eyes turning to delve into Alyssa's. "I want you to understand how much you have to offer. Don't let satan deceive you with the fear he's tried to weigh you down with. God's healing is yours, and if you don't see it before you're married, you'll have nothing to worry about. If you allow this fear to eat you up now, it will affect your marriage."

A rush of warmth flooded through her, causing her to tremble. She swallowed, trying to keep her senses in check. Austin saw her trembling. "Are you cold?" Before she could answer, he removed his jacket and draped it across her shoulders. "It's getting colder all the time." Alyssa hugged the jacket around her and breathed in the scent of him. Even the way he smelled stirred her. If only she was all that Austin deserved.

He watched her hug his jacket close to her and was frustrated that it wasn't him. Unable to bear watching her any longer without reaching out and pulling her to him, he stood and walked toward the lake. *I don't understand, Lord!* His soul cried for the hundredth time that day. *Is it pleasing You to see me in such torture? Are You trying to test my strength or my devotion to Your will? God, deliver me from this love!*

I will not allow temptation beyond what you can bear. You must wait.

As Alyssa studied him, confusion knit her brow. She couldn't see his face, only his hand moving through his thick hair. She had come to learn this was a habit, common when he was upset or worried about something. It was amazing all the small things she had grown to recognize and adore about this man.

"Austin?" His name from her lips touched him, and he closed his eyes against the longing it caused. "Are you OK?"

"I'm fine," he said over his shoulder.

Alyssa cursed the weakness that trapped her on the ground. In the past month her legs had gotten so weak that she could no longer stand. Her days were now chained to the chair. She longed to go to him and comfort him as he always did when something troubled her. "Are you sure?"

Austin heard her concern and turned toward her with a smile. "Yeah," he said coming to sit down again, though not as close to her as before. He could only imagine the turmoil in her own heart. Was it him she thought about when speaking of a husband? *Would it be so wrong Lord, for me to hold her?*

You would be going against My will and plan for both of you.

Feeling defeated, he tried to push the thoughts out of his mind. The rest of their time together that day was strained. They went home when it became too cold to sit out any longer. Austin insisted Alyssa keep his jacket when they parted on the path. She thanked him with a smile and was surprised and breathless when he bent and brushed a light kiss on her forehead before leaving. It was a gesture that erased all the tension between them. Her relief was so great a single tear made its way down her face as she went the rest of the way home alone.

Church praise and worship had become a vital part of Alyssa's life. It was a time of refreshment and healing and of drawing closer to God. Joy and thankfulness would well up within her with such magnitude that she longed to dance before God with all of her might—but she couldn't.

Each day she grew in God and left more of the world behind. She wanted more. She wanted the glory and power of God in her life. She was hungry for His touch and thirsty for more of His Spirit, knowing they were within reach, but unsure how to grasp them.

She shared her concern with Austin one night as they sat in the sanctuary before a service. "What am I doing wrong? Why isn't God touching me like He's touching others?"

"You aren't doing anything wrong. God is working in you powerfully." He grinned and spoke to her gently. "Keep your heart open, and He will fill you with His glory. It's His promise to you, Lyssa: 'God blesses those who hunger and thirst...for they will be satisfied.' Prepare the way for Him to come into your life in a greater way."

Before Alyssa could ask him what he meant by preparing a way for God, Austin headed for the stage to begin the service. As the music began and the songs admonished God's people to dance, shout, and rejoice in the Lord, Alyssa felt a familiar longing to be free. Part of her spirit seemed trapped along with her body in the wheelchair.

"Lord, I want to dance for You. I want to praise You as You are worthy to be praised." She prayed, raising her hands toward heaven as high as her weak arms would allow.

Dance for Me My child. Dance with Me as You do when you're alone.

Lord! How humiliating would that be? She got a mental image of herself spinning in circles in the electric wheelchair looking like a horrendous idiot.

Who are you dancing for—Me or those around you?

But Father, it's not even dancing really—it's just turning in circles like a moron—God, it's not even dancing!

Dance for Me with ALL your might.

The only might Alyssa possessed was the chair she rode in. *Your desire is my pleasure, Jesus.* She pushed aside her pride and the nagging voices trying to hold her in place and flicked the power button on her chair.

At first Alyssa tentatively moved side to side to the music. She was positive all four thousand plus eyes in the building were riveted on her. Gradually she turned her focus to the One for whom she danced and away from the insecurities striving to restrict her.

As the music went faster so did she, spinning around, no longer caring what anyone might think. She felt free! She could feel her spirit dancing as she had always wanted to dance. Her soul praised in wild abandon as Jesus danced with her. Though her body was bound for the time being, her soul lifted its wings with a new strength and freedom.

"I can dance!" she cried to the Lord joyously. Her voice was inaudible above the music as she shouted to God. "I can dance…I can dance for You, Lord! I love You, Jesus. I will dance for You always!"

Alyssa soaked in the thick heavy presence of the living God. It was so real and strong. God was in the place filling the sanctuary like a dense fog. Then the whole church grew still with a sense of awe.

Suddenly loud, heart-wrenching sobs broke the silence as a woman began running down the aisle. Reaching the altar, she fell on her knees, and with raised hands and streaming face, she cried out, "God, forgive me! I didn't know You! I am such a sinner! What must I do to be saved?" As the woman continued crying out to God, others began running to the front in much the same way.

No one there failed to experience God that night. Alyssa was in awe once again of how *real and tangible* God was. She reveled in the glorious experience, marveling that God loved her enough to bless her. Tears overflowed as she trembled in His presence. With His amazing power came the overwhelming revelation of His love for her.

At some point during the service, Cloe approached Alyssa with a word from God. "The Lord says, 'I'm going to release a fresh anointing to write upon you—words of freedom in the Spirit and encouragement going out to the body of Christ.' In the natural people say you're bound. You're not bound in Him. And the Spirit of a writer is about to come on you. It's going to be a fresh word, and you're going to see the glory of God breathe upon it.

"And the Lord says that you are a lead dancer," Cloe proclaimed, pausing when the place erupted in shouts of praise. "You're a lead dancer, and God says, 'When you dance the angels jump up and down.' You have the same effect on the heart of the Father that David did when he danced before the Lord."

Alyssa had never felt so unworthy. She was nothing, yet God loved her enough to speak such a word to her. He loved her so much that He took joy in her dancing for Him! He trusted her to write words of freedom to the church. Words of *freedom!* All she could do was sit in awe at the feet of Jesus the rest of the service.

Twenty-Two

Opening her journal, Alyssa wrote:

December 12

That I should be blessed with the gift of writing! I know You're calling me to write my testimony, but how? Teach me, Lord.

I've been reading Your Word, listening to tapes, reading books, and praying every prayer I know. Still I'm bound in this chair. The more I read and hear sermons on faith and healing, the more confused I get.

I've had more hands laid on me than I can count! I respond to altar calls and come back the same. Lord, forgive me, but it's getting so I don't even want to respond anymore. I get tired of fighting.

What am I doing wrong? I know the Word—I believe the Word. Lord, if there's sin in me, reveal it and I'll change! Do I lack faith? How do I get this faith that seems unattainable? Lord, I believe—cure my unbelief!

I've prayed that You take away my love for Austin, but it grows stronger each day. I thank You for our friendship. Bless it, make it flourish and grow.

Alyssa closed her journal and went out for her mother. It was late, and she wanted to go to bed. Life had slipped into a daily routine for her and Catherine. Her mother got her out of bed in the morning and helped her get dressed and ready. Alyssa did her own hair and makeup, then went to eat the breakfast her mother made. At night it was much the same routine in reverse.

Though God had moved in Alyssa's life in great strides, the disease still ate pieces of her muscles everyday. If she felt like less than a woman before, she now felt subhuman. What dignity she'd had was stripped ruthlessly away. But Alyssa kept telling herself it didn't matter. Her life was Christ's now. She was free…wasn't she?

A new bruise was darkening on Rebecca's thigh. She touched it tenderly, her face hardening in irritation. She was sick of William's endless passions. She looked across the room to where he sprawled on the bed. Her eyes traveled over the floor at the 'toys' he had brought. The things that pleased him now repulsed her.

Rebecca cringed at the reminder of their latest hours together. William was getting stranger all the time—he didn't even excite her anymore. She now dreaded coming to the cabin, so why did she continue? For the now rare times when he was yielding and sensitive to her needs?

Each time he touched her he took a chunk of her dignity with him. She wasn't herself anymore. He wasn't the answer she had sought; he only drew her away from her search. She had tried to open her mind and follow William's example and had thought she was on her way to reaching some kind of fulfillment for her soul. But she was wrong.

She got dressed and left the room, kicking William's things out of the way as she went. When William awoke, he found her sitting in the living room. "Why are you out here?" He eyed her clothes. "You know I like waking up next to you."

When she didn't answer he shrugged. "As long as you're out here, I want to show you something." William's face took on an expectant glow. "I have a surprise for you."

Rebecca recoiled at the thought of one of his surprises. When he pulled videotape from his briefcase she was only slightly relieved. "William, we need to talk." Rebecca urged him to listen.

"After I show you this." William ignored the urgency in her voice and popped in the video. He came and sat by her on the couch with remote control in hand.

"William, I'm not watching one of your sick movies!" Rebecca thundered, jumping off the couch.

"Then how are you going to learn?" His irritation was quick, and met with Rebecca's cold, menacing glare. "Becca you're too limited in your thinking. This could bring us to a whole other level."

She cursed him violently, loosing all the pent-up anger and humiliation she had been feeling. "I won't sink to your level," she spat before turning toward the door.

William leaped off the couch and roared behind her. "What are you doing? You're not going anywhere!"

When she didn't stop, he went after her and grabbed her arm, whirling her around to face him. His fingers bit hard into her flesh, but she refused to be afraid of him. "I said you're not leaving."

Automatically, Rebecca lifted her knee and drove it up hard. He loosed her immediately. Despite the sudden fierce shooting pain, William tried, and failed, to follow her out the door. Hoarse, he screamed threats after her.

Rebecca entered the cold night, escaping William's rage. She remembered the past months she had wasted with him and was disgusted that she had not seen the truth sooner. How could she have been with such a man?

She crossed her arms over her chest to keep warm. The December night air was bitterly cold, turning to ice in her lungs with each breath. Moonlight shimmered off the freshly fallen snow covering the path, looking like millions of sparkling diamonds.

The beauty of another country winter was lost on Rebecca. All she could see was the filth of what she had become. She felt the familiar longing within: longing for more than what she had, for something she couldn't quite understand.

She was afraid it was too late. Had she messed up her life beyond repair this time? Could she ever be clean after her relationship with William?

"God, if you're real. I need You now." Her voice was little more than a whisper in the frigid air. Alyssa had been talking about the church she went to with Austin. Maybe she would go see for herself what Ally had found that made her so happy.

Catherine fell onto the sofa with a relieved sigh. She was free for the night. Tomorrow she would start all over again. The mornings were the worst. From the time she lifted Alyssa out of bed until she sat her in her chair finally dressed, Catherine struggled.

If she had felt trapped before, she was chained now. Her future loomed into an eternity of having Alyssa to care for. Catherine would never rest again. The problem wasn't the time she spent caring for Alyssa. There was actually little her daughter needed—once she was up and dressed, she was fairly self-sufficient. But the constant tie was there. Catherine was no longer free to come and go as she pleased without considering Alyssa. Every moment she had to be aware of the time and possibility that Alyssa might need her.

Knowing it wasn't for her to question God, Catherine did her best to stifle self-pity. Still, it ate at her, causing roots to grow deeper over the years. *Why me, Lord?*

Guilt dwelt below the surface of her soul, though she didn't recognize from where the oppression came. She hardened herself against it and against any pain too unbearable to feel. The seeds of guilt and bitterness burrowed deep into the once-soft soil of her heart and grew thick roots. Invisibly, the poison seeping from the roots rose, clouding her heart with hints of things beneath the surface. Catherine was hard sometimes, but only because she feared what might happen if she wasn't.

If it hadn't been for God, Catherine would have lost her mind by now. She consistently held on to the hope of glory. Someday she would be free in heaven. Only He gave her the strength to keep walking.

But no one knew of these things inside her. No one saw the years of pain and fighting she had endured. No one cared enough to know. No one saw Catherine.

"Did you know Jake quit?" Rebecca asked tentatively on the way to church with Alyssa and Austin. Alyssa couldn't have been more excited when her sister asked to attend church with them.

Alyssa glanced at her in surprise as she drove. "No…when?"

"A couple days ago. Big John is going to take over as foreman."

Unsure how she felt about the news, Alyssa remembered the last time that she saw Jake. The memory, and the near-death experience that followed, still burned in her mind. She had never heard from Jake again, and God had graciously kept them from crossing paths on the ranch. Now he was gone. Alyssa had given him all she had to give of herself, and he had thrown the gift away like trash.

She felt a strange sadness thinking of Jake. She had cared for him once, and a tiny piece of her still cared. Mostly the uncertainty ate at her. She had no clue as to what Jake had felt, if anything. Alyssa wasn't sure why it was important for her to understand; but because she didn't, the matter seemed unresolved. It haunted her that maybe some man had actually once loved and desired her.

Alyssa was quiet with these thoughts. Her eyes caught Austin watching her carefully in the rear view mirror. *Are you OK?* his eyes questioned. *I'm OK,* her smile answered. She said a prayer for Jake, wherever he was, then pushed the matter from her mind.

Rebecca's excitement grew as they neared the church, and she was out of the van before Alyssa had shut off the ignition. She walked through the door behind Alyssa as Austin held it and immediately knew she had found what her heart hungered for. She didn't know what it was or how to get it, but the answer was there.

Austin ushered them into the sanctuary. The place was thick with the presence of God; the air of expectancy was intense. Alyssa glanced up at Austin and saw him grinning at her. Their eyes sparkled with conspiratorial glee.

I want this! Rebecca's heart cried as she watched people all around her fellowship with God intimately, in their own way. Austin found a couple of empty seats and Rebecca sat, with Austin on the end, while Alyssa stopped her chair next to him in the aisle.

Rebecca was overcome with emotions she never knew she had. The presence of One greater than herself surrounded her in warmth. She closed her eyes and quietly allowed tears of cleansing repentance to flow down her face. God's love was ministering to her—the worst of sinners.

Austin and Alyssa were aware of the work God was doing in Rebecca and left her alone to commune with her Creator. Austin himself was overcome by God's presence and impulsively wished to transfer it to Alyssa and see her healed at that moment. "Can I pray for you?"

"Sure." Alyssa was grateful for those who prayed for her. Yet, when she saw the hope in their eyes, she felt responsible for their faith and dreaded letting them down. As they prayed, she prayed fervently for healing so that the person would not leave disappointed. Each time they walked away without seeing the miracle, Alyssa felt like a failure. What must they think? Did they assume she had no faith or that she harbored sin? Did the Pastor get sick of praying for her?

Austin hunkered down before her, placing his hands on her legs. She felt the power of God flowing through her, but felt no strength developing in her body. She prayed with all her might that God would answer Austin's prayer.

Should she pray and bind the devil? Should she remain silent while Austin prayed? Was there a special word or phrase she could speak to move the hand of God? *Oh Lord, I want this…help me understand what I must do.*

Her legs felt weak. She felt Austin's hands on them as he prayed, but there was no new strength, no new muscle…nothing. She was a failure, unable to receive from a man with as much faith as Austin.

She had let Austin down.

Austin lifted his glowing eyes to hers. "He's going to do it, Lyssa." His smile was full of compassion and confidence. "All you have to do is remember He is the Healer. Just *believe*—it's by His Spirit, not our own power. You try too hard to do something only God can do and has already done."

Alyssa bit her lip, keeping back thankful tears. Did Austin always know her thoughts? He moved toward her and pulled her into a hug. She held him with determination believing that his anointing might rub off on her. "Rest, Lyssa. Be still and see what God will do," he whispered against her ear.

Soon Rebecca's laughter rippled from the aisle and erupted through the sanctuary. Alyssa had never heard such wild, beautiful laughter—so bold and unashamed, unafraid of who might hear. It cascaded from the depths of Rebecca's stomach and poured out in freedom. Rebecca had found her purpose—Christ.

Twenty-Three

The Center of Rejoicing's annual revival conferences came, bringing spring along with them. May was a breath of new life after a bitterly cold winter. God continued to raise up new life in the church as people from every direction came to see the miracles happening. This same phenomenon was taking place in churches throughout the county.

Breathing deeply of the warm air, Alyssa headed down the path and reflected on the wondrous things God was doing. Austin had asked to meet her after church that Sunday. They would stay together all afternoon, then ride to church together that night for the continuing conference services. She mused with a smile on the day to come.

Seeing Alyssa, Austin walked to meet her. Though his smile welcomed her, she immediately noticed something troubling in his eyes. "Can you believe how nice it is today?" His casual question was laced with a tension that only she would have been able to discern. "I checked the water. It's real warm. You want to sit on the dock and put your feet in?"

"Sure." She understood that he was talking to hide whatever was plaguing him—he would share it with her when ready. She had grown to know and love everything about Austin, sometimes feeling she knew him better than she knew herself.

Hunkering in front of her, Austin removed her shoes and socks and rolled her jeans up. He picked her up with ease, carrying her to the wharf where he sat her beside him. She twirled her feet slowly in the water, watching the little waves she created float away. Austin watched her. Her blonde hair was piled high on her head, revealing her slender neck. Loose strands of hair framed the delicate lines of her face and caressed the soft skin below her ear.

She looked so beautiful, how could he live without her presence close enough to breathe? It was several moments before he spoke hesitantly. "How do you like the pastor's daughter and her husband?" The couple had been ministering at the conferences.

Alyssa looked at him excitedly. "They're amazing and anointed! I've never seen God move so powerfully. When she sings, God's glory hits you, and all you can do is sit there in awe."

"I know. They're apostles; they travel all over the world establishing ministries and bringing revival to different areas. They stay in places for however long God ordains, and then go to the next place He brings them." Alyssa wasn't sure why Austin was speaking at length about the ministry of Pastor French's daughter, but she sensed the importance of what he was saying. "She brings her own worship team with her."

Austin went silent before speaking again. When he did, his voice was strained. "They've asked me to join them."

The words hit Alyssa like a bomb. Join them? What did he mean? "Where do they want you to go?" Sudden uncontrollable fear clenched her stomach.

Austin's eyes held hers, watching her reaction carefully. "They've asked me to become part of the team traveling with them."

A deathly sinking feeling descended upon Alyssa as he continued. "They've prayed about it and feel the Lord is calling me to their ministry. Pastor said to seek the Lord before making any decision…but he has released me to go." Each word had to be forced out and caused him more pain than he could have prepared himself for.

Alyssa felt faint at the possibility. Austin leave? The world around her dimmed as she tried to comprehend what he was saying. If he went, it would likely mean never seeing him again. She swallowed the lump in her throat and croaked out the dreaded question. "Are you going?"

"I'm not sure," he answered quietly. He saw the pain written on her face and felt it himself. "I've been praying, and God hasn't revealed His will yet. I have to give them my decision before they leave."

Alyssa nodded in understanding, not trusting her voice. She felt herself shivering with pent-up emotions. But she couldn't break down now; she must be strong and supportive. Forcing her voice to remain even, she smiled up at him encouragingly. "I'm so happy for you. You have a mighty anointing, and I know God will do great things through you." *Oh God, please don't take him from me!* She bit her lip hard to keep from crying.

A slight smile played on his lips as he reached and brushed the wisps of hair lying against her cheek. "And you, my little author." He knew her thoughts all too well. She loved him as much as he loved her. If she only knew how he felt—how very much he adored everything about her!

She blushed under his gaze. *Lord, I can't live without him!*

Unspoken understanding flowed between them as they talked, not mentioning the cries of their hearts. They talked the rest of the afternoon, while the pain of what might come filled their souls. Inside Alyssa knew she would be broken if he went, and there would be no one left to pick up the pieces.

Each night Austin fasted and prayed, determined to know the will of God. This was the kind of ministry his soul had hungered for, but part of him wanted to stay with Alyssa. He had found himself longing for the moments when they were together. Alyssa's hunger for the Holy Spirit had revived Austin's own fire for God. The times they prayed together had become vital to both, seeming to join their spirits, hearts, and minds as one.

He paced the floor, pushing his hands through his hair as he spoke to the Lord. "I've got two days left to decide, Lord. Just tell me what You want, and I'll do it."

What do you want, Austin?

Austin stopped pacing and sat down on his bed. Tears stung his eyes as he looked up. "Lord, I want Alyssa," he choked, his heart aching with the words and eyes closing against the pain.

"I can't help but believe You meant for her and I to be together. Lord, You gave me this love. You put me in her life. Don't take her away from me now."

Love is not self-seeking.

"Self-seeking!" Austin sprang off the bed to pace again. "I've given everything I can possibly give, what more can I do?"

You've been faithful and have given much, but now you are asking for a kind of reward. Love never says, "I deserve a gift for what I've given."

Austin sat down again, his anger depleted. "You're right, Father. Forgive me. I want her so much, but I want You even more. I want Your will in my life and Alyssa's."

My will shall be done in your life, and My glory will be revealed through you. When I speak, you are quick to listen and obey. I chose you to stand in the gap on behalf of My daughter, and you did so with strength and power and with your whole heart. You held on and did not let her slip into to the enemy's hands. Now I ask that you let her go.

Austin felt cold fear grab his stomach and squeeze the air from his lungs. "Lord?" His hoarse whisper betrayed the fear that he had heard God correctly.

You have shown her My truth, and now she follows Me. She will listen and hear My voice, I will sustain her. I will be her strength, joy, hope, and reason for living. But first, you must let her go that she may be free to find Me.

"But Lord," he stammered, unconsciously grabbing the bedspread so tightly his muscles bulged in his arms, and his knuckles turned white. "She has found You. She loves and serves You. She is growing everyday."

She will never become the woman I have called her to be if she continues to rely on man instead of Me. She comes to Me through

you, as most children do. But the season has come for her to grow and stretch. I'm preparing something great for her.

"Without me?" Austin sat devastated, not wanting to believe God's plan for Alyssa didn't include him. His muscular hands dropped limply at his side. Was it possible he would have to leave her forever? Could he give her up?

Will you lay your Isaac before Me? Will you give up that which means most to follow Me?

He didn't have to think about his answer. Though the pain was excruciating, he lifted his now trembling hands in surrender. "Yes, Lord. I'll follow You always."

Then go My son. Go to the nations.

The next day Austin met with the pastor and worship team to share his plans, then made the necessary arrangements for leaving with his new ministry team the following afternoon. The hardest part came that evening. He asked Alyssa to meet him at the lake, saying only that he wanted to talk.

She was waiting for him when he arrived. Seeing her caused him, for one crazed instant, to want to defy God, scream how unfair it was, run to Alyssa, grab her, and never let her go. Instead he took a deep breath and went to her.

Hearing him, Alyssa turned and touched him with her smile. He drank in each feature of the face that he had grown to love so that he might always remember them. "I hope I'm not late." He stared intently into her eyes as he spoke.

"No, I like watching the sun go down." She turned to the glowing ball of fire. "How could anyone look at that and not see God? My life was void of that beauty for so long." She turned back, looking up into his face. "You revealed that beauty to me."

Austin felt a tug on his heart. God was right—Alyssa depended on him. Knowing how she hated being in the chair, he lifted her into his arms. "Come sit with me." He carried her nearer to the lake and sat her down gently before lowering himself in front of her.

He stared into her eyes for a long time before speaking in a near whisper. "Lyssa, I've given them my decision."

Alyssa blinked and glanced away from Austin's intent gaze. Taking a breath in an attempt to loosen the sickening knot in her stomach, she looked back at him, fearing what she was about to hear.

"I'm going." The words felt dry and scratchy in his throat as he choked them out.

Tears quickly stung Alyssa's eyes, and she closed them tightly, striving not to cry hysterically and beg him to stay.

"I've prayed and fought with God, but He isn't seeing this my way." Austin tried to take the pained look off her face with humor and failed miserably. He took her hands in his and spoke gently. "He has a plan. For both of us."

"How long will you be gone?" Though she knew the answer, she felt she must grasp uselessly at false hope.

"Indefinitely." He spoke with as much gentleness he could through his own pain. "God is calling me to go; He doesn't say I'm coming back."

Alyssa pulled her hands from his and covered her face, knowing the tears would no longer obey. Austin pulled her hands down, touched her chin, and turned her wet face to him. Then he folded her in his arms and held her for a long time. She rested her head on his broad chest, closed her eyes, and let the tears flow quietly. She wanted to stay there forever, with his arms holding her and his strong gentle hands stroking her hair.

Without moving, she spoke in a small, defeated voice. "You mean so much to me, Austin. You pulled me out of darkness and showed me Christ. When I was weak, you were there to be my strength. You prayed for me when I didn't have the words to pray. You tore the veil from my eyes when I couldn't see God. Who will I go to now?"

"You'll go to Jesus," he said gently. "You don't need me. Jesus is there waiting to hear each word you speak. The Spirit walks with you, revealing truth and renewing your joy, strength, and peace. If your problems get too hard for you to carry, throw them on Christ, and He'll carry them for you," he said against her ear.

"I need you to remind me of those things."

Austin released her from his embrace and took her face in his hands, forcing her to look at him. "No, you don't." His voice was firm, but his eyes were full of tender love. "God is calling you to a closer place of intimacy with Him. Run to Him, Lyssa. Let go of everything else you hold, and grab on to Him with all your strength."

Alyssa's tears fell, soaking Austin's hands. She wanted such a relationship with Christ, but it pained her greatly to know she must first let Austin go. She wasn't sure if she would make it without him. Fear gripped her, but she reminded herself that she was never alone. *God, help me to remember to draw closer to You. Oh God, help me to let Austin go and not lose my sanity along with him.*

"I'll miss you," she said laughing a little when tears sprang fresh into her eyes. *Oh God, the pain! He's part of me—You're taking part of my soul, Lord!*

With an intense, sobering stare Austin reached out, his fingers tracing her chin. "And I, you," he said in a husky, strained voice. He ached to tell her he loved her. He longed to take her in his arms and spend his life loving her. "You'll always be in my heart and my prayers." His mouth turned up in a familiar grin.

Without thinking Alyssa reached up and traced his lips as they formed the smile she so much adored. Her fingers moved lightly over his mouth, then his face. His smile faded into an intense gaze full of emotion as his eyes held hers.

"I love you, Lyssa," he said, hoarse with emotion.

"I love you, too," she whispered.

Neither was sure of the other's meaning. They had said those words before, but they were common among Christians and friends. Alyssa suddenly became very aware of how close they were. She blushed under Austin's deep blue eyes delving into hers.

Suddenly Austin stopped thinking. He would be gone soon and never see her again. This was his last moment to look at her, to talk to her, to touch her. He lifted a hand and ran it over her soft thick hair, then touched her face—gently tracing every feature.

Alyssa closed her eyes, reveling in his touch. It was so sweet she almost couldn't bear it. Tears wanted to fall and ease the ache in her heart, but she willed them away. When she opened her eyes and met Austin's gaze, she saw his eyes reflecting her own emotions. He buried his other hand in her hair and drew her to him. Leaning down he kissed her softly on the forehead, allowing his lips to stay there for a moment while he inhaled the sweet scent of her.

Finally, he reluctantly pulled away. Too much more and he'd be rethinking his decision to leave. *God, help me—she's so sweet, so beautiful.* He smiled ruefully as his hand remained against her face, his thumb caressing her cheek. Alyssa smiled tentatively, causing more emotions than Austin could manage at once.

His heart overwhelmed, Austin stood and stepped behind her. Sitting down with his legs on either side of hers, he pulled her back against his chest. "I want to hold you for awhile before I go," he said huskily. He wrapped his arms around her and held her close.

Alyssa leaned into him gratefully. His warmth enveloped her, and her love stirred within. His muscled chest against her back made her feel safe and secure. His embrace made her feel whole. How would she feel when he was gone?

They sat, keeping their desires to themselves. They talked about everything except the forbidden topic—their love. They laughed over amusing memories, became thankfully quiet over past tragedies, and shared their future hopes.

"How is your book coming?" Austin asked. He wanted to know everything in her heart and mind before he left. Taking her delicate hand in his strong one, he held it tenderly, caressing her soft skin with his thumb and lacing his fingers around hers. Her hands were like the rest of her, he thought: soft, fragile, gentle, and beautiful.

Alyssa smiled at his question, loving that he cared enough to ask. "I knew that God wanted me to write a book about my testimony— what He has done in my life." She paused, snuggling closer in Austin's arms. "When God began calling me to write a novel, I couldn't believe it." She laughed at her own blindness.

"You'll be a wonderful writer."

"Well, if I am, it's only by God's grace. He's already given me the story. It will be a fiction novel but based on my life. I want it to show what God has brought me out of by His power. I want it to change people's lives, you know?"

"Yeah, I know." He smiled at her excitement.

"I've got it mapped out in my mind. I wasn't sure of the ending, but after praying about it, God showed me how to write it. Between the last chapter and the one before it, the character's healing will take place. It will be like a time-lapse thing, so I won't have to deal with describing it."

"The last chapter? That's a good idea." With a grin she couldn't see but could hear, he asked, "So what about the romance?"

"That's the fiction part," she said dryly then added seriously, "There hasn't been much romance in my life."

Austin's hand closed tightly over hers before he wrapped his arm around her. "Never forget what I told you, Lyssa. God will bring you a husband. A man who will love and want you more than anything." *But he'll never love you as much as I do.* "I know you," he tried to lighten his voice, "You start thinking you're not good enough, but you are."

Alyssa's eyes burned at his words. She would carry them in her heart forever. The sun began to disappear at a frightening pace. Alyssa hugged Austin's arms more tightly as if to prevent him from leaving. Sensing the nearness of night, they were silent, praying God would still the sun a little longer. They had run out of words. All that was left to say were those things that could not be spoken. They both wondered how one moment could be at once so incredibly beautiful yet the most painful of their lives. The bitter sweetness of their last hours together brought increasing dread at their coming separation.

Austin held her and played lovingly with her hair. He wanted to remember everything about the way she felt so near to him. Alyssa held Austin's arms encircling her. She took one of his large hands in her two small ones and traced the lines in his palm with her fingers. She loved his hands. They were hands that folded in prayer for her, hands that were strong and rough from hard work, hands that touched her with heart-melting gentleness.

227

Alyssa wanted to cry as she watched the sky darken. "Will you think of me?"

"Constantly," hc choked. "How about you? I bet it won't take long for you to forget me." His pathetic attempt at joking was lost in the dreaded twilight.

"I'll think of you always." She was finding it hard to speak now. "Besides," she added turning her face toward him with a smile. "A woman never forgets her first kiss."

"First?" His surprise showed on his face. "But I thought…I mean, Jake…"

She laughed. "No! Jake never kissed me—not really."

The sun had gone and stars were shining cold and uncaring upon the two who yearned for time. "We should start back." His tone belied his words.

"Just a few more minutes," Alyssa said fearfully. Austin didn't protest but kept her close in his arms. "Can't we stay here like this forever?"

"I wish we could, Lyssa."

She closed her eyes and smiled, allowing the pleasure of her name on his lips to wash over her. "Did I ever tell you how much I love it when you call me that?"

He grinned down at her and touched her hair in adoration. "No, you never told me." His fingers moved as if touching pure gold. "Lyssa," he breathed. "My sweet, beautiful Lyssa." He spoke her name like a whispered prayer, worshiping the very sound of it.

The sweeter the moment, the later the hour, the more desperate Alyssa became to freeze time, to change the inevitable. "What will I do without you?"

"You'll find your strength in Christ," he said gently. "But if you ever need me, I won't be far from you. I'll stay in your heart as long as you want me to. Close your eyes," he whispered brushing her eyelids with his fingertips as she obeyed. "Remember when we rode Dancer together?"

She smiled and nodded at the image in her mind. "Remember the festival and our dance? Can you see me praying for you? Can you see us here tonight?" As he spoke, Alyssa saw all these things which were engraved in her heart. "When you need me, remember those things."

Alyssa held him tightly, clinging to him. Desperately she held on to the moment and the feeling of love and security she felt. She didn't want to forget anything about Austin—how he looked, how he sounded, how he felt, how he smelled. She wanted to brand it all in her mind. Finally he pulled away. "We should go." The quiet resolution of his voice sounded as a death sentence to Alyssa's soul.

She didn't argue. He slipped one arm under her legs and one around her back, lifting her up against him. She rested her head against his wide shoulders, and in several strides he reached her chair and sat her in it gently.

He walked her home in silent dread thinking about their pending separation. Reaching her house, Alyssa asked him to wait while she got something for him. When she had gone inside to her room, she opened her Bible and found the picture Peter had drawn for the commercial. She studied it now, as she often had in the past, but it had taken on a new significance since she learned of God's healing. The picture was a promise to her from God, and she cherished it.

Grabbing a pen, she carefully wrote across the top of the image of the dancing girl: *"Austin, thank you for believing in me. I will always remember. All my love, Alyssa."*

Austin stood waiting when she came back outside and handed him the picture. Looking at it, his eyes filled with tears, his heart overwhelmed. Gripping it tightly, he whispered, "Thank you." They fell silent, unable to speak.

With a last look, their eyes met, saying everything their words could not say. After a moment he smiled painfully at her, bent to kiss her—his lips brushing hers lightly for the briefest of moments—and then walked away. Alyssa stared down the path with tears streaming down her face long after he had gone.

Twenty-Four

Somehow, Tyler knew he was dreaming. But this dream was too real. He saw himself at a party with hundreds of people caught up in their pleasure. The noise of the party grew louder as people drank and danced freely. Men and women were kissing and touching, going from one person to another indiscriminately. The music, laughter, and screaming pulsed through Tyler's head as fear crawled through his body.

Tyler stood alone and watched the dreadful scene unfold. One man suddenly turned and came to Tyler in the center of the sin-infested room. The man slowly held out a can of beer, his evil grin inviting Tyler to drink. The other people in the room turned to watch, each eye drawing, begging him to join their fun.

Tyler stared horrified at the can, scared of what it contained. The people began to laugh mockingly when Tyler's hand started shaking. The shaking spread to his entire body, violently trembling from some unseen force, and spread until the entire building was quaking. Then a deafening explosive sound blasted through the ceiling as a huge hand reached through, picked Tyler up and lifted him from the room. The hand stopped and held him suspended over the scene, and he watched what unfolded next.

The people at the party quickly forgot the hand crashing through their ceiling and resumed their drunken revelry. They didn't seem to notice when the floor began to cave in. Suddenly the whole room became a massive black pit into which people were falling by the hundreds. Tyler's fear turned to horror as screams and desperate cries for help rose while he sat safely in the hand holding him.

The pit was bottomless and black, with heat rising up, lifting the stench of burning flesh. There were still a few people hanging on to a small portion of the remaining floor, and their eyes turned up to him accusingly.

"Why were you saved while we have to die?" one girl shouted just before her fingers slipped, and she fell into the pit.

"Do something!" another man swore as his piece of floor broke away.

"Please, Tyler," a girl too young to be at the party begged with tears. "Help me up. I don't want to go down there. Please..." Her cries could be heard for several moments as she disappeared into the darkness.

Tyler screamed and reached, but there was no way to save them. They were all gone. "God, help me. I can't reach them. Save them like You saved me!" he cried.

Tyler woke up from his dream, his pillow and face wet with tears, which continued flowing. *It was just a dream,* he told himself, trying to relax. But if it was just a dream, why did he feel such sadness for those who had fallen into the pit? Why did he feel so guilty for not saving them?

For a time, Alyssa stayed away from the lake. It was empty without Austin, the memories too vivid and painful. Why did the Lord take him away? A part of her had left on the plane with the man she now thought about constantly. That part of her felt barren, with a dull ache in its stead. She clung to the last night they shared together. Did it mean as much to him?

231

Jake seemed to come to mind in recent days, her thoughts straying to his deceit. She had been a complete imbecile to trust his words. Thinking about the things she had said to him, the way she had opened up her heart to believe his lies, brought fresh humiliation.

But what if they hadn't been lies? Could Jake's declarations have been true? Had he loved her? She chided herself for caring what lay in Jake's heart. Why could she not let it go? Why was Jake coming back into her thoughts now?

She knew the answer, for she felt loneliness, the old enemy creeping in. She wanted something to believe in. With Austin gone, she was suddenly afraid again. He had consistently shown her love, and she hadn't needed to consider the future. But now it was all she thought about. A future without love—without Austin. Once again her hope had left.

But her fire hadn't died.

She cried out to God endlessly to take the pain that invaded her soul with startling fierceness. She begged forgiveness for her misery, knowing God's will had been done. God was her only hope, and she longed to find satisfaction in Him.

She hadn't felt such despair since before surrendering to God. The old voices started speaking again, telling her she was ugly and worthless. She came against those voices with the Word of God, knowing who she was in Christ, but her voice held less conviction than the beast's.

She had thought she was free from the darkness that had held her in bondage. Why did she now despise her own image again? Wasn't Christ in her stronger than the beast that had once ruled her? She reached out in desperation for the only One who could save her.

Peter stopped by Alyssa's office regularly to show her the latest layouts for the summer ad campaign. They had each grown to value their friendship; she finding solace in their shared bond with Austin, and he finding her to be an increasingly valuable asset in his recent interest. This interest suddenly became clear to Alyssa one afternoon as they visited in her office after work.

Trying to sound casually interested, Peter asked what had been on his mind since arriving. "How's Becca?"

Alyssa smiled. "Why don't you ask her tonight at church? Or maybe you should've asked her last night at church." She tried not to show her amusement over his obvious nervousness.

Pastor French had recently flown a group on a mission trip to Haiti. Rebecca and Peter had both gone, and since then he had taken a new interest in Rebecca. When she saw Peter blush, she tried to put him at ease. "She's fine. She really enjoyed getting to know you on the trip."

"Really?" Peter fidgeted eagerly. "I enjoyed talking with her, too." She could tell his mind was full of questions he was dying to ask, yet he failed to find the courage to question her more on the topic of her sister. They parted soon thereafter, leaving Alyssa to contemplate the possibility of a future between Rebecca and Peter.

Just before leaving, Candy quietly entered Alyssa's office to ask if she needed anything. Alyssa thanked her and encouraged her to go home and relax, but Candy seemed unwilling. Her eyes were troubled as she came in and sat facing Alyssa's desk. "Are you OK? It must be hard dealing with the stuff you go through." Candy's sympathy was appreciated, but Alyssa was unsure of how to respond. She knew Candy was talking about the disease, a subject that she preferred to avoid.

"You learn to handle it."

"I don't think I could. I really admire you. You're so strong. I couldn't live knowing I'd never walk again."

Alyssa smiled hesitantly at the redhead across from her. Why did Candy have to talk about this? "I'll walk again. God promises healing for His children." Alyssa regretted the lack of feeling in her words.

"I hope so. Then you'll have what you've always wanted."

Alyssa looked up from her papers, her eyes narrowing slightly. "What do you mean?"

Candy smiled with compassion. "I know how much you want to get married someday."

Alyssa's whole body grew cold. She couldn't believe her friend was being so bluntly cruel. She strove to keep her voice steady. "And that can only happen *after* I'm healed?"

Candy looked embarrassed. "I'm sorry Ally…I don't want to lie to you," she said awkwardly. "I just don't see how a man could…" she trailed, realizing she was making it worse.

Alyssa's teeth bore down on the inside of her lip. The pain held the sting of tears in her eyes long enough for anger to replace the hurt of her friend's words. Smiling she glanced at Candy. "It's quitting time. Why don't we lock up and go home?"

Candy readily agreed. Alyssa fooled herself into believing she wasn't upset about Candy's thoughtless words. She was already aware that people assumed she was unable to be loved. But to hear the words spoken—to her face—by a friend! She pushed the hurtful words down inside until she couldn't feel their sting anymore.

Finally Alyssa and Rebecca were able to convince their mother to go to church with them. Revival was flowing, and they wanted her in the middle of what God was doing. Catherine enjoyed the service and continued to attend. The girls rejoiced that their mother continued to go on Sunday mornings, but as the weeks went on they saw little change in Catherine.

Alyssa wondered what plagued her mother so deeply, not understanding the chains that bound her. Why didn't she let go of what was tying her down and be free? Catherine seemed unwilling to let God go too deep.

Alyssa remembered how, when she lived in such bondage, she hadn't even realized the depth of what satan was doing. Even now she struggled with old things that crept up ever stronger. But she knew the way out, even if she was too weak to run to it.

She wondered if Catherine could be free while confined to the burden of caring for her adult daughter. Was she the reason her mother was so miserable and angry inside? At times Alyssa could feel the resentment aimed right at her. She felt the unmistakable guilt each time she asked for anything; even the request for a glass of water was mumbled in shame.

She didn't blame her mother for resenting her. How horrible a life did Alyssa's disease create for Catherine? Yet maybe, if Catherine were free in Christ, she wouldn't resent Alyssa so much. She prayed for her mother, forgetting momentarily that her own soul was wrought deeply in bondage. She had to look hard around the plank in her eye to see the stick in her mother's.

After church one morning, Rebecca went into the kitchen as they arrived home. As was her habit, she checked the message board by the phone. This time however, the note she found caused her to gasp and grow pale. It said simply to call William. Folding the note in her fist, she went upstairs to her bedroom.

William! What did *he* want? She sat down slowly on her bed and stared at her brother's messy writing. She fingered the note absently, remembering the last time they had spoken. She hadn't thought about their relationship for awhile and wasn't happy being reminded of it now. Looking at the phone number, her eyes widened in shock. The number was to the cabin they had shared, doing things she wanted to forget! What was he doing there?

Rebecca knew she shouldn't call but was afraid he wouldn't leave her alone until she did. She had grown sorry for William after finding the truth she sought. Maybe she could tell him about Jesus Christ.

Picking up the phone she dialed the number and listened anxiously to the ringing. When the familiar voice sounded on the other end she shivered at the reaction of her fluttering stomach then spoke hesitantly. "William?"

"Becca! I'm so glad you called." William's normally smooth voice was full of emotion.

"What are you doing there?"

"I need to see you. I miss you so much."

"No," Rebecca said quickly, ignoring his plea. "I can't see you. It's over between us." Her voice was too high and urgent for her liking.

"It can't be over. Please just come and talk to me. I need to see you. Can't we talk?"

She had to get this over with no matter how reluctant she was to face him again. "Fine, I'll meet you at the cabin, but understand that it's only to talk."

William agreed and Rebecca hung up, biting her lip nervously. Not taking time to change from her church clothes, she hurried downstairs and slipped out the back door. Her mind reeled in doubt as she headed toward the cabins. "Lord, help me remain strong and bold. Let me be a witness. I pray Your Spirit would surround me, Lord…" she prayed fervently as she neared the cabin.

Her thoughts unwillingly wandered to the last days she had spent with William. Had she really given herself to a man who lusted after such things? In the beginning he hadn't asked anything of her; she had given it all willingly. He had been kind and gentle, fulfilling her every desire before his own demented fantasies took over. She tried not to remember the pleasant times but didn't know how to forget a man who knew every inch of her so intimately.

Rebecca realized that she was a new creation. She felt it, and knew God had changed her. But she wasn't so sure that William would see it. Stopping, she removed the shoes murdering her feet. The soft grass was cool between her toes and refreshingly distracting. She emerged from the path with both shoes dangling from her fingers. Her flowing floral skirt blew softly above her ankles. She unconsciously pushed her hair back from her face.

Rebecca was unaware of William watching her. He had waited anxiously until he saw her. When he did, his breath stopped as her beauty struck him, rendering him motionless. He didn't remember her being as compelling as she now seemed heading toward him, unaware of his presence. He drank in her every feature, his eyes moving from her face down. Small buttons ran the length of her skirt, unbuttoned to just below the knee, revealing a glimpse of her long, shapely legs with each step.

William stared in silent awe. Something was different about her. She seemed innocent, almost ethereal in her countenance. She glowed with an inner light, giving her eyes a look of peace despite her troubled brow. William wasn't sure what had changed Rebecca so much, but knew he had to have her.

As he watched, her eyes finally caught sight of him and widened in surprise. Her gaze lowered, and he sensed a maddening desire to demand those enticing eyes to look upon him again, even if by force.

Stepping toward her, he allowed his gaze to roam freely. Vivid memories had haunted him for months. Rebecca strode through his mind day and night since the moment she had left him. He felt the full force of his longing for her now as she stood before him speechless.

"Becca," he breathed in a deep rough voice. Rebecca recognized the all-too-familiar tone and stepped back as if guarding herself from some unseen danger. Noticing her withdrawal, he forced an even voice. "Let's go inside."

Rebecca's eyes clouded with uncertainty as she followed him. "I'm not sure why you wanted to see me." She finally spoke, wanting to end the meeting as quickly as possible. "I know I left rather suddenly, but I couldn't be with you anymore."

William stared hard at her. What about her was so different and compelling? She had always exhibited a confidence, but it seemed stronger now. She radiated a quiet peace and beauty and…*innocence?* He almost laughed, knowing that Becca was anything but innocent. But she glowed with this illusion of innocence, which he found very enticing.

William seemed not to hear Rebecca's words. "You're as beautiful as ever—even more so. I was devastated when you left me. Don't you know how much I love you?" He stepped closer, his outstretched hand entreating her submission.

"William, whatever we had is over." She needed to make him understand. "You can't love me now. I am not the same person."

"I will always love you." William's eyes shone with the truth of his words. "I'll learn the new things about you and love those as well."

"No," she stated firmly, turning her back to his fire-filled gaze. "I've given my life to Christ." She turned back to face him. "I belong to Jesus—I found what I had looked so hard for." She smiled in wonder at the truth of her words.

William said nothing but stood spellbound by Rebecca's glorious beauty. He had to have her, now more than ever. He had to taste the beauty glowing from her flawless face. He had to consume the light burning in her eyes.

Rebecca continued earnestly. "I thought I could find happiness with you, but it just left me empty. Now I have all I've searched for. Jesus was the answer the whole time!" She walked closer to him, wanting him to see the jewel of life she held in her words. "You've been seeking pleasure and love, but you've been looking in the wrong place. Jesus is the One you should seek—He alone satisfies. He can give you the things your soul lacks."

A smile curved William's face in understanding. So his beautiful little love slave had found Jesus! He had met many Christians before, but their dedication always wavered. He realized that getting her to surrender would be easier than he had hoped.

"What does my soul lack, Becca, but you?"

"Your soul lacks love and fulfillment, joy and peace. It's got nothing to do with me," she spoke bluntly. "Turn from darkness. Allow me to show you God. He's poured out His love and passion on me, fulfilling every longing in my soul. He can do the same for you."

Rebecca could see she was failing miserably in her attempt to win his soul for Christ. Why did everything in her heart come out twisted so that no one could understand what she was truly saying? *God, help me. Give me words to make him see. I pray Your light would shine through me.*

William moved closer and held out his hand, his eyes wide with an intensity greater than Rebecca had ever seen. He spoke roughly past his confident grin. "Yes, Becca, show me your God."

A brilliant smile spread across her face in relief and joy. He wanted the truth! She reached to grasp his hand in sincere Christian affection. As soon as she did she realized just how foolish she was. William's eyes darkened with evil anticipation.

Before she could pull her hand away, he grasped her hard into his arms and held her against him. His mouth lowered in an instant and devoured her soft lips, seeking her newfound confidence. Rebecca struggled against him, but his hold was unrelenting. William's lips slowed, gradually becoming more gentle as he sought her compliance.

"William, stop it!" She flared at him when his mouth finally lifted from hers. "Let me go!"

"Relax, Becca, I'm not going to hurt you." His gruffly spoken demand belied his vow. He held an arm firmly around her waist while his other hand grabbed her hair tightly so she could not turn and avoid his kiss. He whispered softly against her ear trying to calm her. "Don't you remember what it was like in my arms? Tell me your dreams aren't filled with the memory of my kisses. You said no man could make you feel like I made you feel. I *know* you. I know what you want...I can make you happy in ways your God can't," he rasped.

Rebecca violently cursed the stirring of her flesh. William indeed knew her well. His touch and kiss became increasingly tender knowing how Rebecca had always succumbed under his calculated affection. *GOD, HELP ME!* Her soul screamed in desperation against the unbidden desire she fought against. Though she continued to struggle, a tiny voice whispered for her surrender. It had been good with William once.

"You want me...I know you do," William said victoriously. "Come, Becca." William backed her forcefully toward the bedroom. "Show me the power you now possess." He muffled her terrified cry with another long kiss.

Panic flooded her. She feared herself more than William for her lips were tempted to respond to the fire simmering there. Surprised tears gathered in her eyes as she realized how weak and unworthy she was. How could God love her when she was so sinful that her body reacted to this man? *God, forgive me! I don't want this. I don't want him! GOD, HELP ME NOW!*

I am here, Rebecca. My Spirit is within you, take the thoughts that plague you and throw them aside. Rise up in My power, for I will not let you fall. What can man do to you?

Suddenly her fears vanished and a sweet peace flooded her soul. God was not condemning her—she had not submitted. She remembered whose she was, and her spirit rose with confidence. She belonged to Christ. She was not the same, and no matter what William did she would never turn from God.

William pulled away slightly when she ceased fighting. A pleased smile played on his lips, his eyes almost black with desire. "I knew you still wanted me. Only I know how to feed your hunger. Tell me you want me," he demanded. "Say the words before I make you mine again."

Rebecca spoke with surprising calmness as her eyes met William's. "I don't belong to you, William. I never did. I belong to the Lord Jesus Christ!" Her voice grew with an intense fierceness that startled him. "Now take your hands off me for you are touching the Lord's anointed!"

Though he wasn't sure what Rebecca meant, his arms fell from around her, and he found himself backing away with an unexplainable fear. Rebecca stood and looked him directly in the eye as she spoke once more before leaving. "May Jesus Christ have mercy on you."

He watched her leave the cabin without looking back. It wasn't until she had gone that he realized how easily he had let her walk past him. Had he completely lost his senses? He had her right where he wanted her and just let her go.

He cursed himself continually for a long time afterward. He'd never know what had caused him to stand frozen while his greatest desire slipped from his hands. Yet he knew he would not rest until Rebecca was his.

As Rebecca neared home the realization of the miracle God had performed swept over her. In the midst of her weakness, a supernatural strength had come upon her to rise up against her flesh. God had not left her alone; He watched over His beloved child even in the darkness of the moment.

She headed toward the lake, unwilling to go home just then. Reaching the water, she smiled at the blue crystal and hiked up her skirt to wade in its shallow edge. Joy rippled over her and she could not help but dance around like a child who knows no care. Freedom had a new taste, and her soul felt as light as the fluffy clouds overhead.

Until seeing William's phone message, Rebecca hadn't realized her deep-seated fear of seeing him again. She had forced all memories of him away, unwilling to face what feelings they might bring. But today she hadn't had the choice. Not only did the memories come flooding back but they were also reinforced brutally by reality.

Yet God's strength, His grace, was made perfect in her weakness. The thought of William no longer caused her stomach to turn in apprehension. The memories of their relationship were no longer threats to her resolve. She was free!

Leaving the water, Rebecca sat down on the grass and looked up at the bright sky. "Lord, is there no end to Your goodness? Will You always love me, continually setting me free from myself?"

Never will I leave you. Never will I forsake you. No power in heaven or earth can separate My love from you, Rebecca.

Rebecca hugged her legs and laid her head against her raised knees. With closed eyes and a content smile she listened to the sweet voice of her Father flooding her soul.

The Bible pressed against Alyssa's chest as she clung to it and stared out the window of her bedroom later that afternoon. Though the sun was bright enough to hurt her eyes, the day seemed dark and hopeless. She was slipping deeper into herself each day and was helpless to stop it. The world that had opened up before her was suddenly closing in, and she was terrified.

She knew the way—Christ. Yet this knowledge could not help if she was too weak to reach out and grasp it. "God, what am I going to do? I don't know what's wrong with me. I know I'm free in You, but this thing just won't go away."

Each day, every moment, she dragged the memories of Austin with her. At times she could almost feel his touch again. His voice still whispered in her ear, telling her she would find love, but her love had flown to some foreign nation never to return. The memories stabbed her bitterly, offering no joy in their company.

She sat alone for increasingly long periods of time. She couldn't tell anyone; no one would understand. How would she explain the fear of being alone forever? How could she make another person understand the horror of hating yourself and of knowing you'd never be loved?

She recognized the old feelings and warning signs, and she knew what bondage lay ahead if she continued down the dark road she was on. She had been on this path before and knew the way out was God, but which way did she turn to find Him? Her weak prayers went up, bouncing off the ceiling and smacking her in the face as they came back unheard. Reading the Bible brought the memories of Austin back stronger.

She was very afraid of what she was once again becoming. But things were different now, weren't they? She knew God and knew the way now. So why was she in this situation? She who had felt God's power so strong she trembled, she who had laughed in the Spirit under God's anointing, she who was filled with the Holy Spirit—she was being tormented by the devil—the beast.

Deep inside she knew it was her own fault. She was allowing it. The more she prayed the more she felt she knew what she had to do. In the past she had allowed satan's hold on her by locking herself away and feeding the dark beast. It had only been when she reached out that she was set free. She had grasped the hand of a friend who was strong enough to lift her up and see Christ.

She was too afraid not to try, desperate not to fall away from Jesus. She could hear the devil laughing at her as long as she kept the pain inside. "Jesus, I love You so much. I don't want to live like this. Help me Lord, who can I talk to?"

Rebecca had returned from the lake moments before and could not wait to share her miracle with Alyssa. Without knocking, she opened Alyssa's door to find her in tears. "Ally, what's wrong?" Immediately Rebecca shut the door and came to her. She sat on the window seat in front of Alyssa's wheelchair and took her sister's hands in her own.

Alyssa saw the concern on Rebecca's face and began telling her everything she was feeling. She left nothing unsaid, pouring out her soul with an abundance of tears. She told Rebecca of her fear of never knowing love. She told how detestable she found herself and the depression now seeking her heart. With a sob she declared her intense love for Austin.

"I loved him Becca…I loved him so much!"

"I know." Rebecca's compassion poured streams from her eyes. Without hesitation, she enfolded Alyssa in her arms. She held her and spoke soothing words of encouragement.

When Alyssa's tears finally stopped she blew her nose and smiled at her sister appreciatively. Rebecca hadn't said anything Alyssa didn't already know. She hadn't prayed any great prayer or bound any evil spirits, but she had cared. Alyssa saw the love and understanding in Rebecca, and it set her free.

Alyssa laughed in amazement at how little it took to impart new hope to the hurting. One act of love had loosed her from her impending darkness. Rebecca hadn't condemned her or accused her; she had just loved her. How much more was God loving and watching over her every need? God didn't ask much from her, only a simple act of obedience. In return He gave life.

Twenty-Five

Tyler sat on the back porch in the darkness, welcoming the below zero temperatures that froze him numb. Since the summer, many months ago, he'd had the same recurring dream, but the dream last night was different. For the first time, the dream had varied, and he tried now to grasp its meaning.

In last night's dream he had still watched the people falling through the floor into the black hell as he sat safely inside a hand. Yet, this time he wasn't alone. Tyler had turned and saw Kristen sitting in the palm of the giant hand with him. She had looked at him, her face having an angelic quality, and spoke calmly. "It's OK Tyler. We can help them." Her radiant smile had beamed as she held out a rope. "We'll pull them from the pit together." Tyler had taken the rope and examined it. "Don't worry. It's strong enough for all the people. No one is too far away to reach. See?" She pointed to a name inscribed on the rope's handle.

Tyler saw the name Jesus just before waking up. It was the first time he had awakened without a terrible sense of fear and hopelessness.

"God, what do You want from me?" The cold night air did not reply. He still hadn't told Kristen about his dreams, not sure how she would respond. He wasn't ready to risk looking crazy. Tyler stood from the porch and retreated to the warmth of his home. Once more he pushed aside the nagging thoughts of his dream.

February 3

As I've prayed for my family I've seen how much I need to change to be a witness. My attitude is terrible with my mother and has caused a wall between us. I need to be understanding of what Mom goes through. Lord, cause the walls of division and strife to come down!

I know my healing is near. I believe You for it, Lord. I've tried to understand why I haven't been healed and what I need to do to get healed. I think I try so hard that I forget the Healer. But You remind me—it is not by my might or power but by YOUR Spirit!

If there is anything in me that must change before healing comes, then show me. Other than be obedient to whatever You show me, I will stand and see the glory of God. I will wait with faith and see Your promise come to pass!

I have unknowingly limited You by considering my circumstances. I've thought, "God has so much to do and restore in me if I am to be healed." I was somehow thinking that unlike so many other diseases You've cured, mine was more difficult. Though I knew You could do it, I felt You might just skip me because You didn't want to deal with something so complicated. We say, "Nothing is too hard for God." No, I say, "Nothing is hard for God." All You have to do is speak, and I have a new body! You have ALREADY spoken the Word!

Pastor said Austin is in Asia. How I miss him! My heart longs for him, to be with him again. At times I ache for him desperately. But You, Lord, are my all in all. Only You can fulfill my every desire. Help me to realize this truth in a greater way. Help me to still the longing for a man I can't have.

The healing service brought people from all over the county. Alyssa noticed many others in wheelchairs in attendance and went to greet them. She noticed a boy about twelve years old sitting in a wheelchair toward the back. Her heart immediately went out to him as she went to say hello. The boy and the man with him greeted her with a smile, but she was discouraged from making conversation due to the fact that they spoke little English.

As Alyssa turned to go, she heard a hesitant French voice heavily accented. "Good luck," the boy said quietly. Startled, quick tears gathered and her heart wept for the child—paralyzed, yet wishing for her healing. *Oh God, heal this boy!* "You too," she smiled softly at him then went back to her place beside Rebecca.

Her eyes scanned the people, stopping with compassion upon various faces. She saw a man so crippled and disfigured that his eyes rolled in his head and drool slipped from his mouth, giving every indication that he was unaware of his surroundings.

The worship team began to practice for the coming service. Alyssa's eyes went teary as she saw the cross-eyed, drooling man raise his twisted hands as far as he could. His mouth bent in a crooked smile, and his head tipped back awkwardly. He was praising the Lord!

Compassion and love for the man mingled with a fierce anger at the devil. One thought blared in her mind—*the devil had no right to touch that child of God!* She heard the stories of those around her: a two-year-old boy born with half a brain, a sixteen-month-old girl with autism, a ten-year-old boy dying of cancer… The stories were unthinkable and innumerable, each containing some new horror. Yet, they all had something in common—faith. Along with the sickness and disease, she saw the faith of mothers and fathers believing God for their children. Past all the sickness inflicted by satan, she saw the light of Jesus.

As Alyssa was encouraged by the faith of those around her, she began to wonder about the hundreds in the room. Did they all know God desired them healed, that He loved them desperately and would never curse them with sickness?

The pastor preached powerfully, declaring the Word of God. He read scripture after scripture, proving God's will to heal all. He came against popular religious teachings and common beliefs that prevented many from receiving what God has freely given. "If God puts sickness on you—if it's the will of God for you to be sick—then why do you go to the doctor to get rid of your sickness?" he asked.

"He is Jehovah Rapha—the Lord our Healer. He says in Exodus 15:26, 'I am the Lord who heals you.'" Alyssa listened attentively. Every word held life!

"In Exodus 15 we see God making a holy covenant with man. He says if you listen to the voice of the Lord, pay attention to His commands, and do what is right in His eyes, then He will not bring sickness on you. It's that simple. We need to believe the Word of God—know that what He promised will come to pass. God doesn't put sickness on you to teach you something or work something out of you."

The truth of the pastor's words hit Alyssa. "I hear, 'But Pastor, what about this one who wasn't healed?' I don't know," Pastor French said honestly. "What I do know is that this Word is truth." He held his Bible high. "God does not lie! We have to get our eyes off another's situation and onto God: What God says, He will do; what God promises will come to pass!" he exclaimed over increasingly loud shouts of agreement throughout the building.

Something stirred in Alyssa. A persistent nagging pricked her thoughts and refused to be pushed aside. God wanted her to speak to His people. *God, how can I talk about healing when I am not yet healed? Can a bound person speak freedom to others that are bound?*

You are not bound, Alyssa, I have set you free.

But Lord, I am not healed yet.

By your own testimony you are already free. I have spoken My promise over you. Believe that you have received healing, and it will be yours. Declare it as done!

247

Alyssa bit her lip uncertainly. Was she free? Why then did she not see her healing come to pass? Why was she ever sick at all? Even as she asked these questions she remembered a familiar scripture in John. The apostles asked Jesus why a certain man had been born blind. Jesus had replied, "…this happened so that the work of God might be displayed in his life. As long as it is day, we must do the work of him who sent me."

I have created you for such a time as this, Alyssa.

God hadn't made her sick, but He would heal her and glorify His name doing it. She smiled, thinking about the thousands that would be saved when her healing manifested, and the many that would be healed if she declared God's glory now. *You've really messed up this time devil! What you meant for evil, God will use to deliver the multitudes!*

At that moment Alyssa decided that she would speak whenever and wherever she was able. At every opportunity she would declare the promise of God.

Pastor called the sick to the altar that night, and many were healed. Three people got out of their wheelchairs and ran around the church. Alyssa rejoiced with each person's victory, and tried not to question why her healing had not come. *Thank you, Lord, that You will do it soon,* she silently prayed.

Twenty-Six

More and more Alyssa found herself running into the safety of Jesus's arms, for He brought joy, comfort, hope, and fulfillment. She was better at avoiding the pain that came with old memories but couldn't help feeling that something she needed desperately was missing. It was then that memories of Austin came flooding back with such power that she had to catch her breath.

"Austin." She whispered into the darkness of her room as if he might hear.

The nights were the worst; her mind swam with millions of thoughts. In the end, they always drifted back to him. Only when the image of that strong, handsome, smiling man rose from her heart did her mind slow its dizzying pace and fix on one dream.

She closed her eyes. Austin: raw masculine strength, boyishly handsome at times, so sweet and gentle it caused her to ache… She allowed herself the joy of remembering. But eventually she was forced to shift her focus. The memories were good, but if allowed to run too deeply, they cut, leaving scars of loneliness. God had plans for her, and she had realized for some time now that she had to move on. As always, her thoughts turned into words of prayer. "God, how do I move on when he's all I think about? I want You to be my everything. I know I'm to be satisfied in You, but there's such a hunger for someone to love me."

Her voice shook as she prayed. "Lord, I want a husband, a man to spend my life with." Wiping the wetness from her cheeks she continued. "You've promised me a man of God, and I will trust You for him. Lord, until that time help me. Show me, Spirit, how to give every desire over to Christ. Lord, I want to delight in You."

The longing for a husband mingled with the need for Christ. Knowing she was powerless in her own strength, she asked God for His. After a time she stopped praying and listened. The Spirit of Christ spoke clearly to her heart.

I Am your Husband.

Alyssa cried a quiet plea, partly thanksgiving and partly disappointment. She knew the Bible talked of Christ being her husband, but she wanted an intimate, tangible love.

I Am your Husband.

If only the man God had for her was Austin. She still couldn't imagine life without him. The last year had been strange and lonely at times—as if she had expected him to come back. Now she knew he wouldn't.

Alyssa headed home from the stables one afternoon and saw her mother working in her flower garden. Catherine looked up from her roses. "Where have you been?" Alyssa missed the casual tone of her mother's inquiry.

Irrational annoyance swelled in Alyssa as she mumbled a short answer. "The stables." She hated being questioned like a child. Ignoring the still, small voice reminding her that she wasn't exactly acting like an adult, she went inside to her room before her mother could ask another question.

Immediately she felt guilt. Violent mood swings ran in her family, at least in Catherine and herself. At times there was so much unspoken tension between the two that it flowed like an electric current sucking them this way or that.

Alyssa knew part of the problem was their impaired lifestyle. Alyssa was a woman trying to deal with her disease while not losing her independence. Catherine was a mother who had to care for her adult child. Alyssa was striving to hold on to her meager faith while Catherine seemed to accept what she thought to be inevitable.

We're so different, she thought.

Yet so much alike.

The realization startled and shamed her. It was her own attitude that put half of the bricks in the wall dividing mother and daughter. *Father, she needs to know Your Spirit. She loves You, but there's so much she doesn't know. How can I help her be free?*

When you are free, your mother will follow.

I'm always striving for more of You. I haven't arrived, but I'm not as bound as she is.

It is not for you to judge but to pray. Judge yourself. If you want your mother to know My Spirit, let My light shine through you.

Suddenly it was clear. She blamed her mother for resenting her, but she also resented Catherine. She was bitter that Catherine had placed so much guilt on her shoulders. Alyssa knew there was no excuse for her actions.

She prayed for a long time, asking God to change her attitude, heart, and mouth. She wanted to be a new person, showing Christ's nature. It wasn't going to be easy. She didn't know how far the roots of her attitude went or how long it would take to kill them.

Peter finally asked Rebecca out and they had quickly grown fond of one another. One afternoon, a few weeks after they started dating, the two went to the lake and spent a glorious day together. Now they sat quietly, enjoying each other's presence.

When Peter leaned toward Rebecca, she knew he was going to kiss her. His eyes were bright with anticipation, and she gave him a soft smile of encouragement. His lips were tentative at first but became confident with her compliance, testing their affection with tender adoration.

Peter's hands moved through her hair as he pulled her close to him. Suddenly the warm feeling in Rebecca's stomach changed into fear. An alarm went off inside her head and screamed loudly in her ears. Though there was no threat or sinful intention in Peter's touch, her mouth stopped responding to his. Peter seemed not to notice, causing her dread to explode.

Rebecca quickly pushed him away, turning her face from his. "Peter wait," she breathed like a frightened child.

"What's wrong?" His concern was obvious.

Sitting back and pushing her hair out of her face nervously, she looked at him. "We can't do this."

"I'm sorry—I thought—I thought you wanted me to kiss you," he stammered, embarrassed.

Rebecca felt guilty for disappointing him but was more terrified of encouraging him. "Please, it's not that I don't like you. I just—I can't do this." She got up from the ground and walked toward the water with her back to him.

Peter got up and followed her. He reached out and lightly touched her shoulder then quickly pulled away when she flinched. After a span of confused silence, Peter spoke quietly. "If you don't want me touching you, just tell me."

Rebecca turned with eyes pleading for understanding. She knew he wouldn't understand—she didn't fully understand herself. "Don't be upset, Peter, please."

"It's not that I'm upset," he lied. "I'm just trying to understand."

Sudden, frustrated tears filled her eyes. "I'm just not ready for the physical stuff yet."

Guilt overwhelmed him as Rebecca's eyes glistened with confusion and fear. What kind of man was he to make her feel bad about pulling away? "I'm sorry, Becca. I promise, I won't do anything like that again until you're ready. I'm sorry."

"It's OK. I'm sorry. I know I overreacted. I just want to take things slowly." She gave him a beautiful smile, which eased his guilt. He reached out and carefully pulled her into a hug. She returned his embrace rather stiffly and let go.

They talked awkwardly for a short time before she made up an excuse and asked him to walk her home. He left her at the front door with a light kiss on her cheek. When he had driven out of sight, she went to her room and allowed the pent-up tears to come. *What is wrong with me?*

She hadn't had any problem allowing William to kiss her and do everything else. The memory brought blood rushing to her face, and she realized why she had so abruptly pushed Peter away. She had felt a familiar stirring of desire when Peter had kissed her. She had actually responded to him as she had responded to William.

Yet it wasn't the same thing, was it? She hadn't felt the all-consuming need that seemed to drive her crazy as with William. With Peter it had been a gentle, yielding desire that didn't threaten to overtake her. Peter hadn't been demanding with his kisses, only curious and loving. But what if she hadn't stopped it?

William's words rang in her ears, *"I know you, Becca. You belong to me and always will."* No, she couldn't trust herself. She couldn't let her desires burn out of control. She wasn't sure how she would explain herself to Peter. He didn't even know about William; she couldn't bring herself to tell him.

Peter was born and bred a pure Christian, never soiled by unthinkable sins. He would not want her if he knew the sin she had lived in. Having no idea what she was going to do, she prayed, begging God to take all physical desire from her.

How long could she pretend the past didn't exist?

Twenty-Seven

At the lake Alyssa took out the sheets of stationery stuffed between the pages of her Bible and began reading the familiar scriptures she had written. "'He was whipped so we could be healed.' Isaiah fifty-three, verse five." She read these out loud every day, determined that each one would burn into her heart and mind.

Abruptly she stopped and closed her eyes. "Spirit, open my eyes and heart and grant me a revelation of Your promises, that I would believe them and live them." Opening her eyes, she started reading again. "'Daughter, be encouraged! Your faith has made you well.' Matthew nine, verse twenty-two.

"Are any of you sick? You should call for the elders of the church to come and pray over you, anointing you with oil in the name of the Lord. Such a prayer offered in faith will heal the sick, and the Lord will make you well.' James five, verses fourteen and fifteen."

On and on she read, scripture after scripture that spoke of God's healing grace. It all seemed so simple to her. "'Through faith in the name of Jesus, this man was healed.' Acts three, verse sixteen."

God, may my faith be strong and unwavering. I do believe! Cure my unbelief!

"Hebrews six, verse twelve says, '...follow the example of those who are going to inherit God's promises because of their faith and endurance.' I will wait patiently," Alyssa whispered. "I will wait for all You have promised me. I hold on to Your promises, never giving up. Thank You for my healing."

She recalled something Pastor French had said. A problem of any kind was like a mountain he had explained, and each prayer concerning that mountain was like a stick of dynamite being laid on it. There will come a time when one more stick of dynamite laid on that mountain will bring the whole thing crumbling down. "Don't give up," he said. "The next stick might be the one that destroys your mountain!"

As she read the scriptures, she examined her heart. Was there something she was missing? She didn't understand why she hadn't been healed, but she wouldn't stop until she received.

A robin landed nearby, poking at the grass. Alyssa loved her home, yet longed for the day when she would leave it. As she thought of her future, Austin came to mind.

What would her future be without Austin? It seemed too strange to comprehend life without him. He was still part of her soul, no matter how hard she tried to wash him out. More often her memories were turning toward the good things with which Austin had left her. He had taught her about unconditional love. Could she ever love anyone as much as she loved Austin?

I Am your Husband.

Once again Alyssa was reminded to turn her focus to God. God was convicting, drawing her away from her needs and away from Austin's memory. She knew she had to let go of her own desires and live only for God.

Thinking of her family, she prayed for them. She had been trying so hard to change her attitude toward her mother but still wasn't a humble daughter who would gain love and favor with a parent. But God had begun the work, and compassion had begun to replace anger and bitterness. Love was starting to grow where before only seeds of division were rooted.

Rebecca and Peter rode through the big field at the south side of the ranch. Slowing her horse, Rebecca pointed to a patch of trees not far away. "Let's stop over there and give the horses a rest." Peter agreed and followed her.

They reached the trees and tied the horses loosely to the trunk of a thick oak. Walking a short distance from the shade, Rebecca sank down onto the grass and watched Peter untie his backpack from the saddle of the dust-colored Morgan.

Peter dropped the bag in front of Rebecca and sat down behind it. Smiling, he pulled out the contents of the sack. "I want to draw you," he said, digging for drawing tools and paper.

Rebecca looked at him in surprise. "What?"

"Do you mind? I've wanted to draw you for a long time, but I was afraid to."

Rebecca was flattered and amazed. Had she ever known a man so sweet and sincere? Her normal confident reserve melted, and she blushed under his questioning eyes. She crossed her long legs and folded her hands in her lap. "Why would you be afraid to?"

Peter's face was gravely serious as he answered. "It's hard to draw something so beautiful. I'll never be able to capture your beauty on paper, yet I can't help but try."

Though she had heard millions of lines meant to turn her heart to mush, they had rarely affected her. But Peter's words were different. He spoke them straight from his soul, and her heart quivered slightly.

She looked down at her hands and spoke softly. "You can draw me." Her voice seemed lost somewhere within her chest, and it scared her. She wanted him to stop saying things that made her sound perfect and wonderful. She prayed her weakness for Peter would turn into strength to resist him.

The pencil in his hand moved over the paper in his lap. Rebecca's eyes watched as he created the image on the page. His hands were large and strong, not how she would have expected an artist's hands to be.

They were gentle hands, yet held all the passion and intensity of Peter's soul. She felt it when he touched her hair or held her hand.

He hadn't kissed her since the day she had pulled away from him. Rebecca was relieved, though deep inside she felt disappointed. Knowing that her disappointment was a small price to pay for purity, she had kept her distance.

She often wondered if she should tell him of her past. He still didn't know the things she had done or the way she had given herself so freely to a horrible man. Surely Peter wouldn't want her anymore if he knew. As he drew, Peter searched the features of her face. Rebecca felt herself blushing under such intensity. What was he seeing? If he looked hard enough would he see her sin?

"I could stare at you forever." Peter grinned as he ran his fingers over the paper to smooth a line. He spoke bluntly, as if the words were just a fact that couldn't be argued.

Rebecca studied his face, outlining his strong chin and olive eyes, which lifted to meet hers. Giving him her characteristically beautiful smile, she spoke with feigned impatience. "Are you done?"

Nodding his head, he moved around to sit next to her. Rebecca gasped at the startling likeness Peter held out. "It's beautiful!" The image was her own, minus the imperfections she always found in the mirror.

Peter smiled at her laughter. "It's you—you are beautiful, Becca."

Tearing her eyes away from the drawing, she looked into his face. His voice wasn't threatening or demanding, just honest. Where were the typical implications that accompanied most compliments?

When he laid the drawing aside and looked back to search her eyes, she did not turn away. Something held her motionless as Peter slowly and cautiously leaned toward her. He gave her every opportunity to turn away or protest but she didn't. His kiss was so light that she wasn't sure if it was real.

Gradually Peter's mouth grew firmer against hers, but remained gentle and sweet, and she returned his affection conservatively. After several moments he pulled away slightly. Rebecca couldn't help but notice a fire in his eyes that Peter hadn't loosed in his kiss.

She looked down, unable to meet his adoring gaze. "Becca, you're very special to me." Peter stumbled over what to say. When she didn't speak he continued. "I don't want to do anything that might upset you—I just want to know where I stand. I'm falling in love with you."

Rebecca was silent a long time before she spoke with tearful hesitation. "You don't even know me. You know nothing about me."

"What are you talking about? I know how wonderful you are. I know you're someone I could fall madly in love with."

"Peter," she looked at him desperately. "You don't understand. I'm not what you think I am. I've done things in the past that would give you a whole different image of me."

Taking her hands, he held them tightly. "Becca, I don't care about your past. All I care about is who you are now."

She wanted to believe him, to hold on to his words. Maybe it could work. God had made her a new creation; she just needed to make sure that she remained holy. But would Peter agree if he knew about William? Would he want someone that had been used so completely by another man?

"I want to believe that. I want our relationship to work, but you've told me what kind of woman you want. And I can't be that." She referred to a conversation they'd had previously. Peter had fondly described the kind of woman he would like to marry, making it clear that he desired a woman who was pure.

"I want you." Peter sounded so certain. He moved to kiss her again and Rebecca allowed him to press his lips to hers. As he kissed her, her mind analyzed and judged each reaction of her flesh. *Have you really changed, Becca? Don't you want him to kiss you?*

Rebecca pushed aside all thoughts until her mind went blank. She couldn't bring herself to pull away and see the confusion and disappointment etched in Peter's face again. Instead she hardened her heart against any emotion or feeling. She steeled herself from the moment, making herself feel nothing.

She would not allow sin to creep into her soul but would take captive her emotions and desires until they were obedient to her will. When Peter pulled her closer in his embrace, she resisted. "Um—I think we should get going." Smiling reassuringly, she kissed him once more lightly before standing and heading for the horses.

Collecting his paper and pencils, Peter followed, seemingly satisfied that all was well between them. "I have to keep reminding myself to slow down. It's like everything God blesses me with; I see some wonderful gift I want so much, I forget about God's timing."

Rebecca closed her eyes, breathing deeply to calm her nerves. His words, followed by the feel of his hand running through the back of her hair, shook her reserve. Without turning, she quickly mounted her horse. "Race you home!" She laughed over her shoulder, leaving Peter to scramble into his saddle and gallop after her.

Tyler was awestruck listening to Kristen explain her dream. He couldn't believe his ears; his girlfriend was describing his very own dream in detail, only it was her dream now.

"It was so real. I don't know what it all means, but I know God is trying to tell us something. I must sound crazy, but Tyler—God is speaking to me."

Her eyes were plagued with a plea for understanding and a fear of condemnation. "Kristen, I've been having the same dream for awhile." He didn't want to tell her but knew he now had to.

"Don't you see?" She almost bounced off her seat with excitement. "God is speaking. He wants us to do something. We have got to find out what it is, Tyler!"

Tyler grinned in amazement at Kristen. She had no fear or second thoughts. One dream and she was ready to do anything God said. "What do we do?"

"Go to Becca's church. She's told me about it, and I think we'll learn something there. Maybe someone can tell us what it means."

"OK, we'll go." He smiled a little, unable to resist her. Kristen laughed delightfully before jumping up to wrap her arms around him.

Hearing the voices, William stopped outside the stable doors. Peering through the opening he saw two young girls. He recognized Britney, though she was older than he remembered her being in the picture Becca had once showed him. He listened as the two sang about Jesus, and he recoiled.

"OK," Britney said. "I'll get Dancer ready, and we'll go for a ride."

"I love Dancer!" Paige exclaimed running after her big sister.

Britney spent a great deal of time with the six-year-old. God had called her for a reason, and she believed part of her purpose was to teach Paige about Jesus. Paige had willingly said the prayer of salvation and soaked in everything Britney said about Christ.

Britney led Dancer out of the stall. "You ready?" she asked and laughed at Paige's eager nod. They walked out the door, stopping abruptly when a man stepped into their path.

"Hello." William smiled warmly at the girls. "You're Britney, right? And this must be Paige?" He bowed slightly to the little girl.

"Yes," Britney answered carefully. She reached for Paige's hand and held it protectively.

"I'm your Aunt Rebecca's friend." William kept his voice gentle and soothing. "I'm afraid I'm lost. Becca asked me to meet her at some empty cabin. I've been all over, and—well—I'm hopeless." He raised his hands and laughed self-mockingly.

Britney relaxed slightly at William's harmless manner. "The cabin isn't hard to find. You follow the path straight to the end and go to the last cabin you see." She pointed toward the opening in the trees.

William's face masked with confusion. He looked to Britney helplessly. "Would it be too much to ask you to take me?"

Glancing at Paige, Britney chewed her lip in thought. It wouldn't take very long, she reasoned. "OK, follow me." She lifted Paige onto the horse then mounted up behind her. Nudging Dancer with her heel, they went slowly as William walked beside them.

"I really appreciate this." William watched the two girls as he spoke. "I was afraid I'd be late meeting Rebecca."

"Aunt Becca rides best of all ranchers," Paige said proudly.

"Really?" William laughed. "Why don't you tell me all about it." As he listened to the child's enthusiastic story, he eyed Britney with appreciation.

She sat tall and sure in the saddle, holding on to her sister. Her hair hung down her back and shone with multiple sun-streaked colors ranging from brown to bleached blonde. He noticed that Paige had the same striking natural highlights, though hers didn't get as dark in some places.

Britney was growing into a beautiful young woman, William decided. "Are you Becca's boyfriend?" Paige asked, cutting into his thoughts.

William looked at the child indulgently and smiled. "Yes, you could say that. Your Aunt Becca and I have a very special relationship."

"I have a special relationship with Jesus," Paige said, beaming. "Jesus lives in my heart, and I'm going to heaven. Sissy says He gives me joy un-think-able," she said stumbling over the last word.

"I know exactly what you mean." William turned with a strange fire in his eyes as he looked toward the path that would lead them to the cabin. His eyes then moved back up to study Britney more closely.

Alyssa was preparing to leave for church when she heard the front door open, followed by Elizabeth's loud voice. Elizabeth came in and sat down with Carlos in the living room. "Where are the kids?" She spoke to Alyssa while peering out the windows.

"I haven't seen them."

"I wonder where they could be," Elizabeth said, her voice full of irritation. "I told them they could go riding but to be back here by four."

"They'll be here soon."

"They'd better be." Her warning held more fear than reproach. She stood and went outside onto the back porch, straining her neck to see down the path. The prick of fear turned into a dark shadow of dread.

The girls were nowhere in sight.

Twenty-Eight

The music at church that night was intense, compelling Alyssa deeper into worship until she was bowing at the throne of God. She praised Him with unnamed tears and cries of worship as He moved in her heart. Love surrounded her thickly, working within her soul, gently touching things too deep to recognize.

Rebecca also sensed the awesome presence of God. She looked at Tyler and saw him leaning against the chair as if bored into exhaustion with hanging head, oblivious to his surroundings. Kristen was looking around with awe at the raised hands and glowing faces of the congregation.

When Pastor French stepped up to the pulpit, his words confirmed the mighty work the Spirit was doing. "There's power in this place." His voice held a reverential fear and awe. "The power of God is here to set you free and break the chains the enemy has held you down with. Tonight God is going to set people free from hurts of the past."

Though Alyssa wasn't sure what bondage there might be in her life, her soul grasped the words spoken. She felt emotions rising from her stomach, overwhelming her chest. *Oh God, what is holding me back and keeping me from receiving more of You?*

Sweet music continued to surround and lift her deeper into the anointing. Faces of those she loved, or once loved, became clear though she tried to push them aside. Pastor French's past sermon concerning unforgiveness haunted her as she searched her heart. *Lord, do I have unforgiveness in my heart? Am I living in chains of bondage without knowing it?*

The music quieted and a young woman's voice caused Alyssa to open her eyes. "I'd like to testify," the woman said. Alyssa knew the attractive young woman well. Tamera was about Alyssa's age and had recently married.

Tamera's voice was hesitant, though she naturally portrayed authority and outstanding faith. "This is hard for me," she continued, "because it's very personal, but I believe the Lord wants to use this to set people free tonight."

Stopping briefly, she looked around before continuing. "Recently I married a beautiful man. But ever since we got married, I've been having a hard time being intimate. I couldn't understand why because I had repented of all the things in my past. I wanted to give myself to him as a wife, but still it was hard."

Tamera's voice choked precariously with tears. "I prayed and stood on the Word of God. I knew He had delivered me...so I continued to seek God because I knew He would reveal to me what was going on." Her voice grew more confident as the words flowed. "My husband anointed me with oil, and we prayed together. And I knew in my heart that the Lord healed me. Still, I couldn't understand—I would try with all my heart, but it was hard for me to be with my husband intimately."

As she listened, Alyssa felt something pulling from within her. Compassion reached out to the bold woman of God, but more than that, she found herself relating to the testimony. She knew what it was to stand in faith yet not see results.

"Literally—I was bound and deceived," Tamera explained, clenching her fists. "Before, when I was dating—even when I dated Christians—the boyfriends I had expected something from me. Though they never forced me to be intimate with them, because I wasn't willing they would make me feel like less of a person. It got to the point where I didn't want to be touched, and I accepted that: I thought it was a good thing."

Without stopping, Tamera continued her testimony. "When my husband and I were dating, every time we kissed I'd feel like vomiting. I thought that was good because I thought the Lord was protecting me, that it was His way of keeping me pure. I assumed when we got married that was all going to change, but it didn't."

Alyssa reached up and brushed at her tears. The dark recesses in her heart, untouched for so long, were slowly being revealed to her. In these corners lived every negative word spoken against her, words she thought were forgotten, but were only pushed deeper inside where they rooted and grew.

"The other night," Tamera continued, "God touched me deep in my heart, and He healed me from all those that the enemy had sent to defile me. Even though in my heart I knew I was right before the Lord, I still lived in a wrong mentality."

Alyssa closed her eyes, allowing the truth and revelation to wash over her. It was so clear to her now. Years of words spoken over her; thousands of sideways glances belittling her; assumptions that made her less than human; well-meaning honesty of friends and family that pronounced death on all her hopes. These had all lived inside, never forgotten.

Tamera finished her testimony. "Pastor said that it was going to be a gradual healing in me—a process. He said God had to do a work in my heart. That night God led me to write a list of all the people who had hurt me mentally, physically, or with their words. He even brought to memory those I didn't realize had any effect on me. I had to forgive each of those people, then God led me to burn the list. Then I felt the heaviness lift. I know I've been set free."

As Tamera stepped down from the stage, Pastor French's voice rang out over the speakers. "He gives beauty for ashes, strength for fear, gladness for mourning, peace for despair..."

Alyssa didn't hear the rest; her sobbing was so great. Once more, God was reaching into her soul and removing old built-up junk that weighed her down. She cried over past hurts that had never fully healed.

"God, it hurts." No one heard her painful whisper but Him to whom she spoke. "It hurts so much." She felt the chains pulling tightly around her heart, put there by years of rejection, which tore at still-festering wounds, leaving her feeling like less than a woman.

She searched her heart for those who still held a place of resentment in her soul. Who had hurt her? There was no way for her to count each name, for people she had only met briefly oppressed part of her. Where were all the well-meaning Christians who encouraged her to accept herself as a cripple and praise God for such a "blessing?" Where were all her uplifting friends who helped shape her distorted self-image?

Putting those people aside for the moment, she looked deeper. Familiar faces lurked and came forward, causing even greater sorrow. Siblings' irritated faces glaring at her when she asked them to help. Taunting voices that accused her of self-pity. They had all been children and meant no harm. Yet the resentful words were not forgotten, and they gave birth to seeds in a child's heart.

Her father's face came into view, bluntly telling her she couldn't go outside in the winter like her little brother because she was different. It was another stroke of the brush that would paint a self-portrait in her mind; a picture that was ugly and repulsive, so unlike everyone else's self-portrait.

Thousands of memories of Jake came back, bringing fresh waves of humiliation. She could still hear his voice telling her he desired her, that he loved her. What a joke! The lie had cost her what little self-respect she may have had left.

Time had restored her hope, and God had given her back the promise of love. But nothing had given her back the piece of herself that Jake had taken. He was the final blow that had crippled her inside. Not only could she not walk physically but she suddenly realized that she had been crippled emotionally as well.

Lastly, her mind turned toward her mother. No matter how hard she wanted to deny it, she had never fully understood her mother's pain and suffering. Alyssa had often looked upon her mother with anger and resentment. Pridefully, she had inwardly declared that her mother had no right to feel sorry for herself; only Alyssa had that right.

Deep moans came forth as her mother filled her thoughts. Catherine had hurt her daughter with her obvious show of resentment and irritation toward Alyssa. Catherine unintentionally poured guilt upon her daughter's head, and Alyssa had been consumed by it. Catherine had spoken words in haste out of frustration, causing deeper wounds in Alyssa than either of them realized.

But how much more had Alyssa hurt Catherine?

"Oh God!" She moaned in repentance before the only One who knew the depths of her soul. How deep did her mother's wounds run? How heavy was Catherine's burden of guilt that caused her to pierce others with shame?

Alyssa determined that she would be free, whatever the cost. She *had* to forgive…she *had* to forget. Only then would she be completely delivered and completely healed. When her tears subsided, she grew quiet, soaking in the healing presence of God. A huge burden had lifted, and she felt a great peace and hope for what would be a new future in Christ. The truth of Tamera's words rang loudly in her heart—it would be a process, and the process had begun that night.

The sound of rejoicing burst forth through the sanctuary. Where just a short time before, hundreds cried out for deliverance, as many were now shouting in victory. Alyssa saw Rebecca leaping high into the air, shouting between her peals of laughter. Alyssa could not suppress her own laughter at the sight of her sister's joy.

Rebecca had never felt so free. As she listened to Tamera's testimony, she grabbed on to the truth, seeing the lies with which satan had clouded her mind. The devil had held her back with guilt from past sins, telling her she hadn't changed. He had distorted her view of what real love and intimacy was all about; for a time he had succeeded in making her retreat in fear to a bondage she did not have to bear.

But the devil had lied! "G-L-O-R-Y!" Rebecca screamed until she went hoarse. She couldn't contain the excitement she felt—she had victory! Jesus had set her free from the past, and she was a new creation in Him.

Once she had realized the lies that had held her down, it was easy to pray and release those things of the past to Christ. She was even able to forgive herself for the sexual immorality she had lived in. She had held on to the immense feelings of guilt for all she had done as a form of punishment and atonement inflicted upon herself. It was a punishment God had not asked her to endure—He had taken her guilt through the blood of His Son, Jesus.

Looking for her brother, Alyssa noticed Kristen sitting on the floor blowing her nose. The girl glowed with a new happiness shining in her eyes, and Alyssa gave God glory for the new believer. Looking to the person lying at Kristen's side, Alyssa gasped with joy. Tyler lay sprawled out under the power of God. He had seemed so bored when the service started!

By My Spirit all things are possible.

"Yes, Lord," she laughed through her tears, raising her hands in praise.

Though Alyssa saw her brother lying motionless, she had no idea what was going on inside of him. Sometime during the service Kristen had slapped Tyler's arm and commanded him to pay attention—so he did. He managed to turn his focus onto God, thinking about Him and what He wanted. It was then that Tyler fell to the floor under the power of God, where he now lay.

God was speaking to him. Tyler saw his dream again, only this time he and Kristen took the rope and tossed it to the falling people. He was amazed when person after person began crawling up the rope to the safety of the hand, each thanking him and Kristen as they came. Then the voice of God spoke so strongly it rattled through his body.

Tyler! This is what I want. I have rescued you from the world for a reason. Now go and rescue the multitudes who are dying and going to hell. Tell them about Me that they may be saved.

All Tyler could do was lie pinned to the ground as God continued to speak and lead him. He vowed that he would follow each command and surrender his entire life to Him forever.

Gradually, and long after the service had ended, the crowd thinned out. Tyler finally pulled himself off the floor and into a chair. Kristen was close by, holding his hand and beaming with excitement. She spoke to Rebecca in her usual sweet voice. "We're going to stay awhile. I want to talk with Pastor French and his wife." Her eyes shimmered with hunger for knowledge concerning what she had seen and experienced.

"OK, we'll see you tomorrow." Rebecca hugged her, then moved aside for Alyssa to do the same. They both gave their brother a satisfied teasing smile before leaving.

Arriving at their house, Rebecca headed up to the front door, then waited for Alyssa to get out of her van and follow. She was watching idly as Alyssa pushed the button to shut the remote-controlled side door when she heard the phone ringing.

She flung open the door and went to snatch the phone from its holder. She wondered briefly where her family was, before she said, "Hello?"

"You've been out quite late, my love." A melodically evil voice sounded through the phone.

Surprisingly, Rebecca felt little at the sound of William's voice. "What do you want?"

"I thought you'd like to come to the cabin." William sounded strangely hopeful at the ridiculous request.

As if speaking to an uncomprehending child, Rebecca answered slowly. "I told you, I don't want to see you anymore. You need to stop calling me and stop going to the cabin. It's over." She turned, meaning to hang the phone up when William's next statement froze her in place.

"Britney and Paige really are delightful."

Rebecca could feel the blood draining all the way down her body while cold fear poured in with William's smooth words. Alyssa came through the door and looked at Rebecca with questioning eyes.

William broke the silence for her. "Britney is becoming quite a beauty. She reminds me of you..." his voice trailed off casually, then laughing he added, "though I don't believe she's as eager for my company as you once were."

A revolting horror gripped Rebecca. Her hand flew to her mouth as she moved cautiously toward the table and sank into one of the chairs, then noticed the note lying there.

We've gone in search of Britney and Paige. Ken found Dancer near the stables. There was no sign of the girls. Send Tyler out to look when he gets home—Mom.

"What have you done?" Rebecca sounded oddly calm as she lay the note back on the table.

"Nothing—yet. I thought you'd like to join us. This party's getting a little dull, and I may be forced to liven it up if you don't." William suddenly sounded more evil than Rebecca ever remembered. Was this the same man who had spoken soft words of love to her?

"I'll be right there." Where her calm decisiveness came from she was not sure.

"Becca," he called to her before she hung up. "Don't keep me waiting. I've been waiting too long already. If you don't hurry…I can't be held responsible for what I might do."

Rebecca slammed the phone down and bolted from her chair. "What's wrong?" Alyssa asked fearfully.

"I've got to get Britney and Paige." She headed toward the back of the house. "If anyone comes, tell them I found the girls. I'll have them home soon." Rebecca disappeared through the back door and into the night.

Twenty-Nine

Rebecca ran down the dark path as fast as her legs would allow. Fear chased closely behind, snapping at her heels and whispering things she dare not contemplate. Certainly William wouldn't do what his words implied. *"Britney's becoming quite a beauty...she reminds me of you..."* His voice echoed in her head. She cried with desperation and forced her legs to move faster.

"Jesus!" she prayed with fierce urgency. "Please release every angel in heaven to surround Britney and Paige now! Lord, I pray You keep them safe! Please! In Jesus's name don't let William touch them!" She cried her prayers in frustration as she ran.

When the cabin came into view she almost shouted in relief and spent her remaining energy pushing herself to the door.

Don't be afraid, Rebecca. Stand firm, and see the deliverance I bring.

Throwing open the door, she rushed in and scanned the room. Seeing William relaxed and smiling on the couch, she spoke in a low threatening voice. "Where are they?"

His smile widened. "In the bedroom."

Rebecca's eyes flashed fire at him before she turned and hurried toward the all-too-familiar room. Inside, Britney sat on the edge of the bed cradling Paige, who was curled up in her arms. Her face lit with joy and relief as Rebecca went and knelt beside them.

"Are you alright?"

"We're fine," Britney answered bravely.

"Did he hurt you?" Rebecca pushed her question through a hoarse throat, praying to hear the right answer.

"No."

Paige's little head lifted slowly then, her enormous blue eyes peeking over her knees. "Aunt Becca, he wouldn't let us go home!" Paige threw her arms out, falling into Rebecca's embrace.

"It's OK, Sweetie, I'm here." Standing, Rebecca held the little girl close and soothed her for several minutes before looking into her small face. "I need you to go with Sissy now, OK? She's going to take you home."

"You too?" she asked plaintively.

"No, Sweetheart, not yet. Becca has to talk to William. He won't bother you again, I promise." She held Paige close once more and turned to Britney. "Can you get Paige home?"

Nodding, Britney stood, took Rebecca's offered hand, and followed her out of the bedroom. Rebecca didn't spare William a glance as she led the children to the door and handed Paige into Britney's arms. "Go straight home, and I'll be there soon, OK?" She watched the children until they were out of sight.

"That was touching." William's sarcasm came from behind her, causing her to turn her attention to the repulsive man.

"Don't you ever go near those girls again." Her voice was low and even and her eyes were leveled at his.

He merely smiled, choosing his words carefully. "I'm glad you got here so quickly—I was getting *anxious*."

Rage burned in Rebecca's eyes. She hissed at him in disgust. "She's a *child* William!" She clenched her fist in an attempt to still the urge to slap the smug arrogance from his face.

"What's a man to do when he's consumed with such a need as I have?" Suddenly his face changed from amusement to guarded anger.

"You disgust me," she spat. "To think I gave myself to you once." She mocked her own past, as if seeing him for the first time.

William's face softened into something resembling regret. "Becca," he moaned, suddenly full of emotion. "I'm sorry. I wouldn't have hurt the children. I just had to find a way to get you here."

Some of the anger drained from her, though she didn't believe a word of what he said. Somehow she knew that if pushed too far, William was capable of anything that might satisfy his flesh. He was empty inside, so empty that he struggled continually to find that which would bring peace and satisfaction. He was obsessed with the pleasures that allowed him those few precious moments to forget how completely empty he was.

William was a desperate man, she saw it in his eyes and heard it in his voice. "I need you," he pleaded, stepping toward her. "Please, stay with me tonight. I'll do anything."

"No, William." A surprising amount of compassion laced her words.

"You loved me once—I know you did. I could feel it when you touched me. Please, I'll make it better than before." William almost whined as he begged for one more chance. "Remember how good it was? Remember what you said—that you had never felt so amazing as when I loved you?"

With a small smile Rebecca easily replied. "Even when I felt I was soaring into the heavens with you, it never compared to what I have now. I realize I wasn't even alive until I left you and found Christ. I didn't know what joy was—or what real pleasure was—until I surrendered my life to Him."

Rebecca's face shone with the truth of her words, causing William's face to harden menacingly. Before she had the chance to speak further, William's hand sliced hard across her face, throwing her entire body back several steps.

Her hand quickly covered her stinging jaw and her eyes locked defiantly onto William's. He was taken back by the lack of fear in them. Enraged, he came at her again, noticing that she would not cower. "How dare you speak so flippantly of what we shared!" Grabbing her face harshly between his strong fingers, he hissed. "You belong to *me*. You surrendered yourself to *me*—over and over again. Have you surrendered your body to Christ as well?" he mocked.

Unwavering she answered, "Yes. All I have is His—body, soul, and spirit." Though her jaw throbbed painfully under his grip and his face darkened by the second, Rebecca was consumed with an inexpressible peace.

Tightening his grip, William scoffed. "You gave Christ your body? I'm surprised He wanted it after it had been used so many times." When she made no attempt to defend herself, he continued his tirade. "Does your Christ enjoy that which belongs to others?"

Without thought, Rebecca began quoting scriptures she didn't know she knew. Boldness arose in the power of the Holy Spirit, and she began to speak with conviction. "Once you were dead because of your disobedience and your many sins. You used to live in sin, just like the rest of the world, obeying the devil—the commander of the powers in the unseen world. He is the spirit at work in the hearts of those who refuse to obey God. All of us used to live that way, following the passionate desires and inclinations of our sinful nature. By our very nature we were subject to God's anger, just like everyone else."

William was stunned into silence as Rebecca continued quoting from Ephesians chapter 2. "But God is so rich in mercy, and he loved us so much, that even though we were dead because of our sins, he gave us life when he raised Christ from the dead. (It is only by God's grace that you have been saved!)"

Jerking his hand away, William stepped back and continued to stare at Rebecca, whose eyes were shining from some invisible force. "For he raised us from the dead along with Christ and seated us with him in the heavenly realms because we are united with Christ Jesus. So God can point to us in all future ages as examples of the incredible wealth of his grace and kindness toward us, as shown in all he has done for us who are united with Christ Jesus."

Rebecca's face broke out with a joyous smile despite the pain in her jaw. "God saved you by his grace when you believed. And you can't take credit for this; it is a gift from God. Salvation is not a reward for the good things we have done, so none of us can boast about it. For we are

God's masterpiece. He has created us anew in Christ Jesus, so we can do the good things he planned for us long ago."

When she finished speaking, she closed her eyes in a silent prayer of thanksgiving for the precious gifts God had given: forgiveness, salvation, and a life with no past.

William recoiled at the words she spoke. "Have you lost your mind?"

"I've found it." Her peaceful laugh infuriated him.

"How long do you expect to keep this charade up? You're forgetting, Becca, I *know* you." He grinned in arrogance. "You were made to give and receive pleasure. It's what you do best, my love." He stepped purposefully toward her, his eyes intent on her body and blazing with hungry fire. "It won't take much to remind you. I'll love every minute of revealing your true colors," he whispered, fiercely determined as he reached for her.

"No!" The force of Rebecca's voice caused William to halt in his steps. "You'll never touch me again, William!" The words were not issued as a command but as a fact. "You'll not call, or try to see me, or try to be part of my life in any way."

William's eyes narrowed and dulled at her final words. Just as he had the last time she had come, he felt unable to move or object to her refusal. His whole body screamed for her, and his mind commanded him to take her. But his feet were grounded to the floor, holding him just out of reach of his prize.

"I've told you the way to happiness—it's Christ. Now it's your decision to choose life or death." She turned and walked to the door. With one last look into his eyes, she pleaded softly before walking away forever. "Choose life, William…choose Christ."

Standing motionless, William stared at the closed door Rebecca had walked through and out of his life. Her words haunted him, leaving a strange yearning. What haunted him more was the overwhelming emotion in her face as she looked at him for the last time. She had looked at him with compassion.

Pulling out a pad of paper, Alyssa slowly began writing a list of names. She lifted each person up before the Lord, remembering the pain caused by words or deeds, then released them in forgiveness from the dark corners of her heart. Some people were harder to forgive than others. Her family came easily, for she knew they loved her and spoke only from their pain. But those who had claimed to care, then hurt her or lied, caused greater pain. Jake was the hardest of which to let go. She didn't know what had been truth and what had been lies. With all her determination she let go of everything: every look, every word, every promise—pried from her heart.

Having released every hurt to God, she ripped the paper from the pad. Under it lay a fresh clean sheet. Smiling, she realized that God was doing the same thing to her; He was ripping out those hurts and making her heart pure, clean, and empty of pain. She tore the list to pieces and threw it away, praying every negative word that had held her down would be thrown into the sea of forgetfulness.

"Thank You, Father!" she rejoiced. "Thank You that I am free from the past! Thank You that all those words spoken against me are forgotten. Thank You, that I can forgive and that You forgive me for all the hurt I've caused."

Her voice rose to the heavens. "Thank You that I am free from the bonds of unforgiveness, and You will bring healing to my life!" She let go of all the words spoken in lack of faith concerning her illness. "I am healed in the name of Jesus!"

As she prayed and meditated on her healing, the revelation of her bondage burst forth, and she saw how trapped she had been. Every negative, hurtful thing others had said was what she had believed to be true about herself. Every time she had been rejected she had become more sure that she was unlovable.

In her mind she was far more crippled than her body could ever be. Even the very word brought images of an ugly distorted thing that others couldn't stand to touch or look at. *Cripple*. How could she have expected healing when her mind would not allow her to contemplate such a thing?

Amazed tears fell as the truth unfolded. "I've been such a fool. Forgive me, Lord, for not seeing myself as You see me," she prayed. God saw her healed, but her mind had not allowed her to see that same image.

After praising Him and allowing her soul to grasp what God was saying, she started praying again, this time with boldness and authority. She commanded the enemy with a conviction she never had before. "Satan, you have lost the battle! No more will you deceive me! No more will I believe your lies!"

She moved around her room as she shouted. "Jesus Christ has healed me! I AM HEALED! It is God's will! He loves me and *yearns* for my healing! He *desires* me healed!"

Tears streamed as she continued to declare God's promise. Though the words were startlingly difficult to say, she began to proclaim the things she had never believed before. "I *am* worthy, satan! I am worthy to be healed! Jesus has made me worthy!" she cried. "I am a *woman*...I am beautiful in Christ, and you will no longer make me feel ugly! God has made me beautiful. Do you hear me, devil? NO MORE!" she declared, her voice getting hoarse. "I will have a husband who loves and desires me! I am anointed and called for a mighty ministry!"

She continued to pray and declare all the promises God had given her. When finally her prayers ceased, she quietly soaked in God's manifest presence and allowed God to speak to her concerning her relationship with her mother.

Alyssa knew there were many things she had to make right. It wasn't her mother who she needed to be concerned about; it was herself. She was aware that deliverance was for her, but Alyssa would have to take the steps. The lies would still be spoken, and there still could be hidden things needing to go before she was completely free. But she was confident that deliverance belonged to her.

Alyssa had caused reason for resentment and anger. If Catherine felt Alyssa took her for granted, then there must have been a reason given. At one time she believed that she and her mother couldn't be free from that underlying resentment until she was either healed or moved out of the house, but she knew now that wasn't true.

Gathering all the boldness she could muster, she went onto the back porch to wait for her mother's return from her morning walk. She prayed she would speak with wisdom, humility, and love.

It wasn't long before Catherine appeared on the path. "It's so nice out." She walked up the ramp and sat on the porch swing with a sigh of relief. "I'm getting too old for this," she joked.

"You're not old."

"Pretty soon you'll have to take care of me," she laughed.

Alyssa smiled at her mother. Catherine was a remarkable woman who had come through things others never see in a lifetime. There were times such as these that all seemed well between mother and daughter, times when both laid aside their defenses and became something resembling friends.

"Mom." Alyssa faltered the moment she decided to speak. "I—I want to tell you something."

"What?"

"I want to tell you that I love you."

"You love me?" Catherine looked curiously at her daughter.

"Yeah." Alyssa attempted to open her heart. She swallowed hard and forced her voice to be steady. "I don't know if I've ever told you how much I love you…how thankful I am for you."

"Well, I love you, too." Catherine waited for Alyssa to continue and reveal the reason for such a declaration.

"I haven't been the greatest daughter. I know we haven't been the closest family, and it's my fault as much as anyone else's." Was she saying the right thing? "I want you to know that I'm sorry for all I've done to hurt you. I'm sorry I wasn't a better daughter to you."

"What makes you think you were a bad daughter?"

Alyssa chose her words carefully. "I've held bitterness and resentment toward you. I knew you were bitter about my disease, and in some way you resented me for it."

She looked at her mother then. "I was selfish and didn't think you had the right to be as angry as I was. I didn't realize you were suffering as much as me. I feel guilt constantly—for everything you have to do for me, and I held that against you, too."

Tears dropped from her eyes as she revealed her soul. "I've been ungrateful and thankless for how much you do, how much you've always done for me. I want to thank you and ask you to forgive me for being so rotten. My attitude is horrible, but I'm honestly working on it."

Catherine's own eyes filled with tears. "God knows you can't blame yourself for your attitude," she said with a shaky laugh. "You come by it honestly." She was speechless in the face of her daughter's confession.

"I want us to start new. I want to get to know you—to really know you. I want us to be friends." Alyssa cried openly now. "I think you're an amazing, strong woman, and I want to learn from you."

Catherine's face contorted with emotion. "Thank you, Alyssa. That means more to me than you know. I'm sorry, too, for getting angry and resenting you. I want to take care of you and will, for as long as I'm physically able."

Alyssa smiled at her mother. "You taught me that Jesus loves me and lives in my heart. I know that's the only reason I'm here today: that, and your prayers for me."

Unsure if she should speak any more, Alyssa decided to take the risk. "I need you to believe God with me for my healing. Mom, your encouragement is so important to me. I need you to stand with me in faith, so I can stand unwavering and see God bring forth my miracle."

Catherine was moved deeply that Alyssa had admitted her dependence upon her, not just physical dependence, but emotional dependence. "I will believe God with you," she said quietly.

Alyssa knew her mother wasn't convinced of God's promised miracle. Catherine had never been persuaded that Alyssa's situation would change. But she knew her mother would stand by her now and speak words of life over Alyssa if she could.

"Thank you, Mom." She went to her mother and held out her arms. Catherine wrapped her arms around her child and held her for a long time. Finally, the two let go awkwardly. Alyssa expressed her sincere regret at having to go to work, then left feeling more free and hopeful than she ever had in her life.

That night Catherine and Elizabeth agreed to attend church with Alyssa and Rebecca. The service was powerful as the congregation praised hard and worshiped deeply. Alyssa noticed her mother crying as she worshiped the Lord with raised hands. Catherine was being touched as the Spirit poured upon her with fire and power, and a new radiance shone on her face.

Elizabeth looked uncertain at the happenings of the evening. She seemed unaffected by God's presence until Catherine asked if she could pray with her. After a time, Alyssa saw Elizabeth blowing her nose and nodding her head in answer to Catherine's whispered questions. Taking Elizabeth by the hand, Catherine led her to the altar where they knelt together. Rebecca and Alyssa looked at each other in amazement and gratitude.

Catherine's heart was changing so rapidly that she could almost feel it turn into soft, pliable flesh. Suddenly she was hungry to know more about what she was experiencing, realizing there was a lot more to learn about God than she ever thought possible. Also, she was hungry to know her family. She yearned to love them as she never had. She yearned to love Christ as she had never thought possible.

Alyssa and Rebecca joined their family up front, urging Britney and Tyler along with them. They hugged and cried and repented for the years of strife and division. The thick walls were coming down around them. Catherine felt like someone she didn't even know. The words pouring from her mouth were things she had never been able to say. If she had ever said "I love you" to her children, it was never in tears or with humility. But something took over, and at the altar, she revealed her most vulnerable emotions to her children. Though the process of loving and trusting one another would take time, each purposed to change and strive toward unity and love.

Thirty

Peter looked nervous sitting on the brightly-checkered blanket Rebecca had laid out. The surface of the lake sparkled like jewels under the bright sun and the warm June breeze made for a perfect picnic. The two were silent, wondering about each other's thoughts.

Peter twisted his hands anxiously. Rebecca watched him, judging his mood and possible reactions to what she had to say. "Peter...I need to talk to you about something."

"OK." Immediately he leaned closer.

She smiled softly at him. His eagerness to understand her and his constant attentiveness were things she had grown to adore about Peter Barton. She couldn't imagine life without him. For the last week she had rehearsed this conversation in her mind countless times. But suddenly it was real, and she wasn't as sure as she had been in her imagination.

"I know I haven't exactly been affectionate toward you." She hesitated as she tried to share her thoughts.

"That's OK, Becca. I understand."

"No," she said softly and took his hand in hers, "you don't." Taking a deep breath, she bared her heart. "I've been pulling away from you, and I need you to understand why. You see, it wasn't because I didn't want to be close to you—I did. That was the problem."

Peter's face registered a mixture of surprise, confusion, and hope all at once. He remained silent as Rebecca continued to attempt an explanation. "Before I gave my life to God...I did some things that I'm not really proud of."

Once more she gathered her thoughts before continuing. "I was in a relationship with this man I met at a party. We were involved for awhile." Her voice became distant, as though telling someone else's story. "I didn't really love him, but he made me happy in ways no man ever had. With him life seemed exciting and worthwhile."

Looking up into Peter's face, she was painfully blunt as she recounted her relationship with William. "I slept with him the first night I met him...and that's about all we did our whole relationship." A stab of regret pierced Rebecca's soul as Peter visibly flinched and averted his eyes from her.

She forced herself to go on despite Peter's obvious disapproval. "I thought the excitement I felt with him was what I had been searching for. For a time he filled a void inside me." Her voice suddenly filled with pain and regret at the memories she wished would disappear.

Slowly Rebecca let go of Peter's hand as he fidgeted uncomfortably under her confession. Clasping her hands and lowering her gaze to the ground, her voice grew soft as she revealed the extent of her sin. "At first it was exciting and new. After awhile, he just got more and more demanding." She stumbled over her words in embarrassment. How could she have done the things she now spoke of? "But I did whatever he asked."

The span of silence was maddening. Rebecca scrutinized Peter as best she could but only saw a guarded look of horror on his face as he avoided her eyes. *He's obviously disgusted with me.* "Eventually he started wanting things that I wasn't willing to do." She pressed on, breaking the silence. "The satisfaction that I thought I had found in him was wearing thin. It got so that I couldn't stand the sight of him—or myself. I grew disgusted with myself and the things I was doing."

Rebecca pulled her knees up under her chin, hugging her legs close to her as if for protection and comfort. "That's when I left him and turned to God." A small smile gently came at the memory. Peter looked at her then. His eyes had transformed from shock and horror to that which resembled compassion. He silently waited for her to continue.

"When I met you…you were so different." She searched Peter's face for understanding. "You saw something in me that I didn't see. You looked at me like I was beautiful—pure." Rebecca laughed shakily, looking away from his gaze. "I loved the way I felt with you. But I was scared of what you would think of me if you knew my past."

When Peter offered no defense to her claim, she grew more nervous and confused about his reaction. "When you kissed me it was wonderful." She bit her lip before continuing in a near whisper. "I felt alive. But it scared me, too. I was scared to feel anything for you because of what I had been in the past." A tear dropped from her eye.

"So I pushed you away," she continued, getting her emotions under control. "I thought I would be safe as long as I didn't allow you to touch me. Each time I felt myself responding to you, I felt consumed with guilt all over again."

Dropping her legs into an Indian style, she smiled the first genuine smile since she had started her confession. "But last week, Jesus set me free." She now gathered the courage to meet his gaze. "I finally saw that I was no longer guilty for the sins of my past. I had repented and Christ threw all those things away, forgetting them forever. I realized that I am pure in Christ. I realized something else, too."

"What's that?" Peter asked softly, speaking for the first time as his eyes delved into hers.

"I realized that what I feel for you is not a sin." She looked away momentarily, then her eyes locked with his again. "I can love you without shame and without the fear of falling into sin as long as I stay focused on Christ and His will. I will guard myself against temptation but allow my emotions to love freely. If you're willing Peter. If you're willing to forgive my past and walk with me in purity."

Rebecca felt like she might explode in the moments of complete quiet that followed. Peter sat still, his eyes studying her with a look that was overwhelmingly intense yet indiscernible. She wanted to scream at him to say something—anything—but forced herself to remain silent, knowing Peter would respond when ready.

When he did respond, she was astounded with his reaction to her confession. His eyes never left hers and his mouth formed no words as he reached for her, cupped her face in his hands, and leaned toward her. When his lips lightly touched her forehead, it felt to her like sweet atonement oil of love and forgiveness.

More and more frequently, God's words burned in Alyssa's heart. *I Am your Husband!*

She had done an extensive Bible study, looking in the Word of God concerning Christ's love and what exactly it said about Christ being her husband. Taking out her notes, she once again looked over the scriptures she had written down and meditated on their meaning. *Spirit, show me!*

There were scriptures that said specifically that the Lord was her husband and that God's people would call Him such. Then there were other scriptures that caused Alyssa's soul to rejoice in amazement, and she read those again:

> "...God will rejoice over you as a bridegroom rejoices over his bride" (Isaiah 62:5).

> " I will make you my wife forever, showing you righteousness and justice, unfailing love and compassion" (Hosea 2:19).

> "He will take delight in you with gladness. With his love, he will calm all your fears. He will rejoice over you with joyful songs" (Zephaniah 3:17).

As a bridegroom rejoices over his bride, Jesus rejoiced over her! She considered how a bridegroom would rejoice over his bride. A husband loved with a fierce and possessive love: a love that knew no bounds and was deeply passionate. Is this how Christ loved her?

The God of all creation loved her with a passionate, rejoicing love? The one who created the universe *longed* for her? Jesus Christ had chosen her for His bride? Such things were too lofty for her to comprehend.

I Am your Husband!

What does having a husband mean to me? Why do I so desire a lifetime mate? A husband would mean being loved unconditionally. It would mean being united with another person; two becoming one. The union that comes through marriage was born out of the heart of God, so it was reasonable to believe that God's own love reflected that of a husband's. Grabbing her Bible she opened it to the Song of Songs and began reading at the beginning. She knew that the Lover represented Christ and the Beloved represented the church, or in this case, herself.

"Kiss me and kiss me again, for your love is sweeter than wine," she read aloud to her empty bedroom. "How fragrant your cologne; your name is like its spreading fragrance. No wonder all the young women love you! Take me with you; come, let's run! The king has brought me into his bedroom." The power of the words struck her. She felt her soul stir and suddenly knew the yearning that David had written about in the Psalms. Many times he had expressed how his flesh cried out for God, how he yearned for the Lord as a deer pants for water.

David's longing for God hadn't been a simple religious twinge. It had consumed him as surely as a man is consumed with desire for his wife. Reading on, she found scripture after scripture that spoke of a beautiful, intimate love. She read where the Lover says to his Beloved, "How beautiful you are, my darling, how beautiful! Your eyes are like doves... Let me see your face; let me hear your voice. For your voice is pleasant, and your face is lovely."

As she read, tears of awe flowed. The truth was too great for her to bear. Was this the heart of God toward her? "You are altogether beautiful, my darling, beautiful in every way...You have captured my heart, my treasure,my bride...Your love delights me." Her eyes hungrily ate the words on the page. " I am my lover's, and he claims me as his own."

Alyssa continued to read the entire book of Song of Songs. After, she quickly flipped to the book of Ephesians. She searched as a starving

284

person would for life-giving food. She found what she was looking for in chapter five. There she read the instructions written to husbands and wives: "For husbands, this means love your wives, just as Christ loved the church." Skipping down she continued to read out loud. "A man leaves his father and mother and is joined to his wife, and the two are united into one. This is a great mystery, but it is an illustration of the way Christ and the church are one."

Closing her Bible she set it back on her desk then bowed her head in her arms upon the desktop. "Lord," she whispered emotionally. "This is too great a thing to be true. God, that You could have such a deep desire for me…that You actually long for and delight in me! Lord, I'm not worthy to be Your bride, but I will love You. I want to know You as my husband. Jesus, I want to be Your wife."

She began to worship the Lord with all of her heart. She yearned for what God had for her. It was time she put aside her constant longing for a man and give her entire self to Christ. As she entered into God's presence, she felt His love fall and permeate the room. His voice spoke clearly to her heart, drawing her into His chamber.

My Beloved, Alyssa! Come, My Beloved. Let Me fulfill your heart's longing. I desire to have a personal relationship with you. You are beautiful, My darling, for I created you! You are beautiful, My Beloved! Oh how I love you!

Alyssa could feel herself being drawn into a holy place. She saw Christ standing there holding out His arms with an all consuming expression of love. Jesus was pouring love upon her, overflowing her heart and soul. As in Psalm 84, her soul longed, even fainted, to enter the courts of the Lord.

"My Lord!" Alyssa cried out in a trembling voice overcome with new and powerful emotions. "I love You. Oh God, I want to love You. I want to please You. I want to adore You, to worship You, to kiss Your feet Lord."

The love of Jesus was so tangible, so real. He was lavishing His love upon her, and drawing her into intimacy with Him. Alyssa yearned to love Him back, but what could she do?

Just love Me, Alyssa. Your love brings Me great joy. Your worship brings Me intense pleasure. Each word of adoration you speak unto Me is as a kiss. I long to see your face and yearn to hear your voice. I love you with a passionate and possessive love. You are Mine—My beautiful, Beloved, Alyssa.

"Jesus," she whispered closing her eyes. "My Jesus, I love You." She had no words adequate enough to express her feelings. She had finally found and experienced true love. She now knew what it meant to be consumed by love and have absolutely no doubts as to the sincerity of the One that loved her.

It was some time later when Alyssa raised her head and wiped any leftover tears from her face. For the first time in her life she didn't feel a persistent desperation for a man of God to come; she felt satisfied. Though marriage was still a desire of her heart, Christ was now fully her delight. Suddenly her thoughts turned to Austin.

As she thought of his smile, his deep blue eyes, and his tender touch, she felt only peaceful joy. It was true that she still missed him and always would. She loved him fiercely. But she now had all that she needed in Christ. Jesus had filled a place that she had thought only Austin could fill.

She knew it was time to let go.

She had held on to a wild, groundless hope that someday he would return. She had never admitted it to herself, but she realized now just how much she had depended on that hope. It was time to let it go and say goodbye. Her heart was ready to move on into the fullness of what God had for her.

Austin had taught her so much. He had shown her Christ, opened her heart, and touched it with love. And he had brought to life parts of herself that hadn't yet been born. She would be forever changed because of him, and for that she loved him.

Closing her eyes and wrapping her arms tightly around herself, she could see Austin clearly the night she watched him walk out of her life. "Goodbye, Austin," she whispered into his eyes that were fixed as intensely on her as ever. "I love you...I always will." Alyssa then released the dream into her Lord's hands for the last time.

The Last Chapter

Staring transfixed at the end of the path, Austin watched as if in a dream. Was he really back on the ranch? He knew it had to be true, for though he had seen Alyssa many times in his dreams over the last couple of years, she had never looked so real and beautiful. His heart was beating abnormally slow, and he felt he might stop breathing at any moment.

Every inch of his flesh longed to run to her and grab her into his arms, but he was frozen in place, unable to move. "God, she's more beautiful than I remember." None other than His Maker heard his whisper. He was awed by the expression of utter peace and joy shining on Alyssa's sweet, upturned face. Her eyes were closed and her lips moved silently in prayer.

"Thank You, Lord." He prayed the same words he had prayed since the day before he left Europe. That was the day when God had told him to come back. He had been asking God about where his next mission trip would take him, when God had released him to return to Alyssa. He still couldn't believe such a gift had been given to him.

After spending hours in prayer, he sobbed crazily, for he knew God had spoken. Never did he imagine nor dare hope that God would allow him to come back. Now he was standing near the very place she was sitting. His eyes traveled over her, hungrily devouring the sight of her. Raking his hands through his hair nervously, he tried to calm his overwhelming sense of anticipation.

Alyssa hadn't changed much, though he noticed she was glowing with a new intensity. Joy flooded Austin's soul as he saw the obvious signs of how much God had been moving in her since he had left. As he continued to watch, he thought that she looked slightly taller and not quite as thin as she had gotten before he left. Still she was small, and petite, and irresistible.

Suddenly he realized she wasn't in her wheelchair. He hadn't thought of it until that moment. He briefly looked around. It was nowhere in sight, so he dismissed it from his mind, remembering how she had hated being in it. He felt a certain sense of relief to think that someone helped her out of the chair from time to time.

Unable to wait any longer, he took a deep breath and choked back the fierce desire threatening to cause him to act hastily. Taking slow but deliberate steps, he started toward what could be the beginning of a fantasy, or the end of a dream.

Alyssa sat with her legs stretched out and her head tilted back toward the late summer sun. Her white cotton skirt was pulled up to her knees so the heat would burn over her skin. She was aware of nothing but the sweet abiding presence of God that burned increasingly hotter, as surely as the sun was sending its heat and warming her body. Her face held a serenity that glowed behind her closed eyes and in her soft smile as she sat meditating on her Lord…her Husband…her Father…her Friend…her Everything.

Her heart lifted up silent praises; she didn't want to intrude with words upon the awesome communication of her spirit and God's Spirit. God's Spirit had become a drug that she couldn't get enough of, and she loved Him more each day.

So distant was the world to her at that moment that she failed to hear the approaching footsteps. It was only when a familiar voice from her past spoke that she was drawn back into the natural realm. It wasn't a voice that called her gently away but rather one that jerked her to reality, causing her heart and breath to stop in shock and disbelief.

She heard the voice. "Lyssa..." It seemed to choke on emotion.

But she knew the voice. None other spoke that name or held the same deep, soulful sound that caused her senses to quicken. Her eyes flew open and rose up to meet the face of the man in front of her, and she felt faint as she breathed his name in doubtful amazement.

"Austin?"

Alyssa was stunned into silent wonder as Austin slowly lowered himself in front of her. Was this real? Had she been caught up into some kind of vision? Certainly Austin wasn't actually in front of her smiling brilliantly.

"Surprise," he laughed gently, watching her hand fly to her mouth to muffle a cry of joy. She began shaking violently with exuberant sobs as Austin pulled her into his strong arms and held her small, quaking form. He wrapped her tightly in his embrace and buried his face in her hair, drinking in the feel and smell of her. "I've missed you." His voice was hoarse against her hair.

"I can't believe it! What are you doing here?" She managed to push out a question or two between sobs.

"God told me to come back." Austin would explain it all in depth later; right now he just wanted to hold her. As he did, he swore to himself that he would never let her go again.

It was a long time before Austin pulled away from Alyssa to look into her eyes. Her heart leapt wildly at the intensity of his gaze. She had forgotten how completely his eyes could hold her captive. "I can't believe it." She was in a dazed awe as she simply stared. "What happened? Why are you here? I mean, I'm glad you are." She had a million questions but was too shocked to ask them intelligently.

"There's time for all that later. First I need to tell you something— something I've wanted to say for so long. I need you just to listen, OK?" He smiled at her gently and touched her face as she nodded. His fingers moved along her cheek as if unsure she was real. He pulled his hand away, rested his elbows on his knees and took a deep breath, his eyes delving into hers the whole time.

"Lyssa...I love you." All the love he had held in his heart for years was evident in his voice, causing Alyssa's heart to leap into her throat. "I've loved you since the first moment I saw you. I'm totally, madly, and hopelessly in love with you." His smile, the one she so adored, beamed at her.

Alyssa bit her quivering lip as fresh tears poured down her cheeks. She had to be dreaming! Austin loved her? *Oh God, this would be too much joy for me to bear! Do You love me so much that You would give me such joy?* She wanted to laugh wildly but could only sit in awe of Austin's words.

"I want to spend my life loving you," Austin continued in a low voice. His hand went back up to cup her face as his thumb brushed across her chin lightly. "I love everything about you, Lyssa, and want to spend the rest of my life showing you how special and wonderful you are." There was so much in his heart, so much he wanted her to know.

His eyes burned with increasing intensity as they bore into hers, willing her to see what was in his heart. "I want to make you mine—my wife."

A rush of warmth flooded through her. She was completely speechless as Austin continued. "I know the doubts you have about getting married, but I swear to you I will never resent you or regret making the choice to marry you. I want to take care of you; I will love every moment that I'm able to protect and care for you."

Alyssa knew that she should say something. She should tell him that it wasn't necessary to take care of her anymore. But she was unable to find her voice. Austin continued with the words he had been playing over in his head for two years.

"I know God is going to heal you. But even if He came down from heaven and swore He would never make you walk, I would still long for you and delight in loving you for the rest of my life. You are the only thing that will satisfy me, now and forever. If all you ever do is whisper my name with half of the love and passion I feel for you, then

I'll be the happiest man alive." He spoke with such intensity that she couldn't help but believe him.

"Let me take care of you until God finishes His work. Let me love you the way I long to love you, the way a man loves a woman." He stroked her cheek adoringly, his voice almost a whisper.

She reached a small hand up to touch his face. "Austin." Her voice was barely a breath, but Austin closed his eyes momentarily and allowed it to wash over him. She had spoken his name with love and passion that said everything he needed to hear.

His free hand went to cup the other side of her face. He pulled her closer and lowered his mouth slowly to hers as he had waited to do for so long. Their lips met carefully in a silent promise. In that moment two hearts found each other and melded themselves into one. Two souls rose and mingled, becoming united.

When he pulled away from her, his eyes shone with a new light: the same light she felt surging along every nerve inside her. "I love you, my sweet, beautiful Lyssa."

"I love you." Alyssa could not help but laugh in delight as her smile spread radiant across her face. Her eyes traveled over his face, marveling in his features. His deep blue eyes were as bright and piercing as ever. His lips formed into a wide, full smile against his ruggedly sensual face. His body was clearly just as muscular and well defined. Was this man really going to belong to her? It wasn't possible. She did not deserve such a gift. She wasn't enough for him.

"I never want you to doubt my love or desire for you." As always, he read her thoughts and could reveal her heart so easily. His sincerity stung her eyes with tears, but she pushed them back with an expectant smile.

"Austin." Alyssa suddenly felt shy. She did have one gift she could give him. "I have a surprise for you."

He looked at her with a curious grin, which dropped into a stunned expression full of utter shock when she moved away from him and slowly stood to her feet. She laughed gaily at his expression. "God has healed me! I'm healed!"

Austin's gaping mouth lifted into an awed smile and tears overflowed down his face. "God…my God," he whispered hoarsely and watched in wonder as she took off running freely across the grass.

When she had gone far enough she stopped and turned around. The beauty of her shining face was so full of joy that it startled Austin. She grabbed her skirt and hiked it up to her knees. "I can dance, Austin!" she cried laughing. "I can dance!"

Austin's own laughter joined with tears as he watched Alyssa jump and twirl in wild abandonment among the bright yellow wildflowers that grew all around. Dropping her skirt she spread her arms wide and spun around like a child.

Overcome with the magnitude of the miracle, Austin fell prostrate on the ground before God. His body shook as he cried and prayed his thanksgiving. The power of God struck him like lightning and ran through his body as he lay worshiping God for the miracle given to the most precious person in his life.

Even as he praised and desired only to give God the glory He was due, God spoke to him, reaffirming His blessing upon Austin and Alyssa's love.

You were faithful unto Me, Austin. You delighted in Me above all things, and now I give you Alyssa. Love and care for her as I love and care for her. Possess that which your heart desires.

Alyssa walked slowly through the flowered grass lifting her hands to heaven as the realization of her miracle flooded her once again. She would never fail to marvel at what God had accomplished in her, always giving Him all the glory and praise.

Finally, Austin got up from the ground. His eyes caught and possessed her, causing her heart to jump into her throat. He walked to her purposefully, took her hand in his and knelt on one knee before her. "Alyssa Langer, would you do me the honor of becoming my wife?"

"Yes," she whispered in a trembling voice. Suddenly she laughed and answered once more, loud enough for the world to hear. "Yes, I will marry you!"

Austin's face broke out in joy as he stood up. Taking her face in his hands, he bent to kiss her. His tender kiss gradually turned deeply intimate, causing Alyssa's heart to race madly as he possessed her soul with his mouth. She felt her knees grow dangerously weak at his touch.

He touched his forehead to hers while they both tried to find their breath, then he gently kissed her lips once more before pulling away from her. He kept her hand in his, however, not wanting to let her go completely.

"How about we get married today?" Alyssa saw how serious Austin was as he looked down into her eyes.

"Today? We can't get married today." Alyssa laughed lightly at his request, while trying hard not to get distracted by the feel of his fingers wrapped around her own.

"Why not?"

"Well, for one thing, Tyler and Kristen just got married last month. They're planning to move to Portland and start a ministry there that will reach the unsaved. Besides, I have a million things to do! I'll have to get a dress, order the cake and flowers and..." Austin effectively managed to cut her words off by capturing her lips with his once more.

When she had become silent, he grinned down at her adoringly. "I can't wait, Lyssa. I want to do this God's way, which means I'm not going to be able to keep kissing you if I want to keep my flesh under control." His expression was so boyishly charming and open that Alyssa's heart melted once more. "I can't stand the thought of not kissing you."

Alyssa couldn't argue with that. She didn't like the thought any more than he did, and she would come to find out that Austin was true to his word. He didn't kiss her again until the vows were spoken.

"I'll give you one month—then I'm making you mine." His rough voice left no room for argument, and Alyssa offered none.

"I like that," she said. "I like the thought of being yours—of belonging to you."

"Me too." Austin marveled at the gift that God was offering him. God had picked Alyssa from the beginning and saved her for him until now. She was completely and truly his.

The wedding day came quickly. Having married Peter just months prior, Rebecca had walked Alyssa through the whole planning process for the last four weeks. Now the bride-to-be stood in a small room in the back of the church, looking into the full-length mirror. Alyssa's wedding dress was simple but elegant. The bodice fit and curved around her frame and rested slightly off her shoulders. It was embroidered with intricate pearl beads and lace overlay that sparkled in the light.

Her dress had no train, and she chose not to have a veil. Instead, she wore a delicate headpiece with white flowers and pearls worked around it. Rebecca had styled her hair into soft curls that hung down her back, with several strands falling around her face.

When she was ready, she left the small room and went to where her father stood waiting to walk her down the aisle. Ken looked down on her with a smile as he took her arm, and Alyssa noticed the light that shown in them. It was the same light that had shone since he had gotten saved after seeing the miracle of Alyssa's healing.

Alyssa felt she had entered a dream from the moment she walked down the aisle to the time Austin took her face in his hands and sealed their vows with a thorough kiss filled with promise.

Before she knew it, Pastor French was announcing, "Mr. and Mrs. Austin Jacobs!" They walked with clasped hands and beaming faces, through the rejoicing congregation and out of the sanctuary. The reception flew by quickly with an increasing sense of giddy expectation filling Alyssa's stomach.

Finally they left the gathering of well-wishers with Alyssa throwing her bouquet to Kristen. They drove to their destination where they would stay for two days before leaving for their honeymoon. Alyssa could not help but recognize the fire of expectation in her husband's eyes as he looked over at her.

Her own excitement over the last few hours was almost too much to bear. As they neared the place where they would spend their first night together, she felt the warmth of her excitement change to an undefinable fear. She forced herself to breathe deeply, trying unsuccessfully to ease her increasing tension.

When they arrived at the small log home along the lake, Austin picked her up in his arms and carried her over the threshold. The cabin was cozy and nicely decorated. It would serve as their home until they started traveling. Word of Alyssa's miracle, and the hundreds of others healed through her testimony, spread quickly. She was scheduled to share her testimony in churches all over the country in the coming year. Austin's ministry was also demanded in many countries. The two newlyweds looked forward to combining their ministries together and going forth to spread the gospel.

Closing the door behind them, Austin kissed Alyssa thoroughly before letting her down. He grabbed her hand and drew her along with him. "Come on." He grinned and led her toward the bedroom. "I have a surprise for you."

When he opened the door, she cried out softly in wonder. "Oh Austin, it's beautiful! How did you do all this?" Her eyes took in countless candles and a fire in the fireplace that lit the room in a soft glow. A big four-poster bed stood regally amidst it all. To the side of the room was an elegant vanity with a large mirror reflecting the light of the candles and fire.

"I had some help." Standing behind her, he wrapped his arms around her and placed a sound kiss on her neck. "I wanted it to be nice for you."

"I love you." She turned to him with a grateful kiss. He returned her kiss with quick passion. His desire seemed to overwhelm him instantly, and he pulled himself away to regain his control. He didn't want to go too fast. He couldn't forget that this was all new to her, and he must be sensitive to that. But with every fiber of his being he longed to love her completely.

Alyssa stepped out of her shoes and went to the vanity mirror. She drew in several shaking breaths as she removed the pins and headpiece, allowing her hair to fall in soft curls around her face. She placed a quivering hand on her stomach as she looked at herself. *Oh*

God, what's wrong with me all the sudden? Why I am so nervous? Help me, Lord! Help me not to disappoint him.

She watched him in the mirror as he removed his shoes and socks then his tuxedo jacket. He pulled off his tie and unbuttoned several buttons on his shirt before untucking it. He looked completely comfortable. He glanced up and saw her watching him in the mirror. Standing and going to her, he slid his arms around her waist affectionately.

"Do you know how beautiful you are?" His eyes locked with her reflection in the mirror. He was awestruck by the woman who was now his wife, standing in front of him clothed in sparkling white with her hair spilling around her shoulders.

"So you've said." She gave him a half-hearted smile. He lifted her hair off her neck and kissed her bare shoulder and the curve of her neck. His hand moved across her throat, then held her chin and turned her face toward his in a tender kiss.

Suddenly her fear increased drastically. He was so wonderful! He deserved so much, and he was now stuck with her. What did she know about making a man happy?

Taking her hands and lacing his fingers around hers, Austin pulled her away from the vanity. "Come here," he said quietly. She was surprised when he knelt on the floor and pulled her down with him in prayer. "Lord, we come to You before we start our lives as husband and wife. Lord, before we give ourselves to each other, we offer ourselves to You. Right now, Lord, we once again consecrate our lives, our marriage to You—this day and forever. May we glorify You in our marriage."

He paused in his prayer a moment to gather the many thoughts that surged through him. "Father, I ask that You would cause me to be a good husband to Lyssa. Let me love her as You love Your people. Bless this night, Lord…grant me wisdom and sensitivity that I might bring pleasure to my wife."

When Austin opened his eyes Alyssa's wide eyes and rosy cheeks amused him. "Did I embarrass you?" He brushed her cheek with his fingers and grinned.

"No…I just didn't expect you to…to ask God for something like that," she said stupidly, growing redder as she spoke. Wasn't that her own heart's cry? *Yes, Lord—if it's all right to ask, than please help me bring pleasure to my husband.*

"God already knows my heart Lyssa. He just likes me to say it. Besides, He created us in such a way that we delight in one another. I delight in you, Alyssa Jacobs." Austin cupped her face in his hands and drew her close in a long kiss. Her hands went around his neck. He could feel her respond to him, but something was holding her back. Even as she trembled under his touch he could feel part of her retreating.

Still holding her, he looked down into her eyes and spoke gently. "Are you nervous?"

"It's not that," she said quickly. "It's just—I…" She stopped and bit her lip shamefully.

With his fingers under her chin, he lifted her head up to look him in the eye. "Lyssa, talk to me. Tell me what's wrong."

Her eyes lowered away from his again as she spoke barely above a whisper. "I just want to make you happy. I—I don't want you to be disappointed."

As she spoke, God opened his eyes to see her soul. She was still afraid of rejection. Austin saw that there was a part of her left scarred by the years of feeling like less than a woman. She still looked at herself and saw an ugly disease when it came right down to being intimate. He couldn't believe that she still saw herself incapable of pleasing him.

"Alyssa, why would you think that? I love you. I could never be disappointed with you. Sweetheart, you make me happy just kneeling there," he said quietly, praying he could make her understand.

"But I…I'm not like other girls." Her eyes pleaded with him to understand. "Austin, you've had so many beautiful women who knew…I'm scared that…what if…?" Alyssa went silent, not knowing how to voice her fears.

Austin felt a fierce stab of guilt for his past wash over him. The realization that his former sins were now causing his wife pain was almost too much to bear. How far and long reaching were the roots of sin? Reaching out, he pulled her into his arms and held her for a long time.

"Lyssa." He spoke through her quiet tears. "I'm sorry. Forgive me for giving away what was meant only for you. I'm so sorry I hurt you." Releasing her, he tilted her head up to face him. "Now listen to me." His voice was quiet but firm. "That man, the man who was with those women—he's dead. Do you understand?" He waited until she nodded. "That man is not here tonight. He's not in this room, and he's not the one who is going to love you. I am."

He brushed the tears from her face, then continued. "I am your husband. I love no one but you. I want and desire no one but you."

Alyssa was crying openly now. Austin's words were like healing balm over old wounds. "I *know* no one but you."

"I'm sorry, Austin." Alyssa felt great guilt over making such a mess of what should have been a perfect night. As he watched her face lower in humiliation, he knew that his words alone would not be enough to erase such deep roots.

"Don't," he cut her off quickly. "You don't ever have to apologize or feel ashamed with me. No more guilt, no more shame, no more fear, and no more feeling unworthy or inadequate." He pulled her quietly shaking form into his arms once more. *Lord, what do I do? How can I make her see?*

Love her Austin. Love her completely and unconditionally.

Austin knew then what he was to do. Love her unselfishly, unconditionally, as Christ had loved him—perfectly. He would make her see once and for all how truly beautiful she was to him. "You're my wife now. I want you—I want all of you. I'm going to adore you until you're so full of my love that there is no room for any other thought but of how much I love you." His voice was hoarse with the fierceness of his emotions.

Rising up, Austin pulled Alyssa to him and, with hands full of adoration, began to repaint the self-portrait in Alyssa's soul. He loved her so completely that she could not help but see herself through the eyes of her new husband—as one who is truly beautiful.

Under Austin's gentle hand, she learned something more about the love of Jesus. God's passion for her was even stronger than the fires that burned within her husband. The love she and Austin shared was but a reflection of the love and intimacy that God desired to share with them. If Austin took such delight in her, how much more her Creator?

She rejoiced in this truth! She rejoiced in Austin's love! Giving herself fully to her new husband, she felt her spirit rise and soar with his until they were dancing on the edge of heaven.

About the Author

Kimberly M. Millard was born in Pottstown, Pennsylvania and raised in Fort Fairfield, Maine. Although limited physically by a spinal muscular disease, she did not allow her mind or spirit to be limited. Kim excelled academically and overcame many challenges. Graduating as Salutatorian at The University of Maine at Presque Isle, Kim was an inspiration to all.

Upon graduation from college, Kim went to work writing articles for various newspapers. Her most beloved articles where those written about real people making a difference in their communities or in the lives of others. In 2003 she became the editor of the local newspaper, *The Fort Fairfield Review*.

I Can Dance- A Soul's Cry of Freedom is Kim's first and only completed novel. Her life on this earth ended before she was able to finish the task of publishing this book. This is a fiction novel, but the essence of the story is very true to life. Kim drew from her own emotions, experiences, and relationships to create this story. It is one all can relate to on one level or another; it is inspiration for hope and freedom in the midst of one's circumstances.

Kim cherished the time God granted her on this earth. Spending time with friends and family brought her great joy. She appreciated the simple things in life like reading a novel underneath a beautiful sunny sky, watching the leaves change in the fall, and seeing the bright eyes of her nieces and nephews light up when she came for a visit. Kim was an active member of her church, Celebration Center in Fort Fairfield, Maine. Her faith in Jesus Christ and the freedom she had inspired all who knew her.

A Message from the Author

Dear Reader,

God has blessed me so greatly through the writing of this book. I was able to relive all the glorious ways in which He has delivered me out of a life of darkness. Though fictionalized, I Can Dance is a personal testimony of how God has worked in my life. Every thought, emotion, fear, breakthrough Alyssa experienced came straight from my own experiences.

I was born with a spinal muscular disease that is much like Muscular Dystrophy, but a much greater bondage then that of my body was that of my soul. Without God's saving grace, I don't believe I would be here today.

This letter to the reader was found in Kim's files. It is probable that she had intended to write more to each of you. Though incomplete, it was felt that you should have this short piece of what she wanted to share with you. Knowing Kim, she would have continued with a beautiful exhortation to look to God the giver of all life and freedom.

A Word From the Publisher

Thank you so much for taking the time to read one of our books. I hope you enjoyed it! There is something else I would like you to read, and it will only take a moment of your time. You see, I am alive today because Jesus changed my life!

By the time I was two years old, I was given only six months to live due to a life-threatening blood disorder. It was at this time that my parents took me for prayer at their home church, calling on the name of the Lord. Shortly after this prayer, God intervened, and I was divinely healed just two weeks later. Jesus changed my life!

One afternoon in 1992, just three weeks before my high school graduation, I died of a drug overdose. This one event caused me to see Jesus face-to-face and also witness my dead, lifeless body down on earth. Through this incredible encounter I was brought back to life and instantly set free from drugs. Several weeks later, I gave my heart to the Lord in a county jail cell late on a Friday night. It was there that God called me by name and set me free from alcohol. Within one year, God sent me to Bible college where I met my wonderful wife, Cathy.

In my freshman year of college I was placed in remedial English due to my lack of skill in reading and writing. I certainly was not college material back then, but once again God had special plans. In 1999 I had another encounter with God that lasted nearly two and a half hours. This is when the Lord imparted to me the ability to prophesy and gave me the anointing to write. This is when the passion for creative media all began.

In the year 2000, I got involved with publishing, often working late evening hours to volunteer with media efforts behind the scenes. In 2005 I started writing a small, encouraging e-mail to five people each week. (I think two or three of them did not even care to read them!) This small beginning was discouraging, but God told me to keep on writing. I began writing on an international scale in 2008 and have continued to do so. Depending on what venues take these writings God gives me, they are sent to well over three hundred thousand potential viewers worldwide.

Not only did the Lord implant in me a desire to prophesy and write, He also put within me a longing for knowledge. After earning a bachelor of arts degree in Bible from Central Bible College in Springfield, Missouri, I continued my studies at Freedom Seminary in Rogers, Arkansas. There I received my master's degree and doctorate in Christian education, earning the status of summa cum laude and President's honor roll. Once again, Jesus changed my life!

These are some of the many reasons 5 Fold Media, LLC was founded. We are passionate about creative media and seeing lives changed for Jesus. God broke my addictions and then took my inability to write and turned it into a promising opportunity to touch the world for Him. God has changed my life!

God bless,
Dr. Andy Sanders
Publisher, 5 Fold Media, LLC

More Titles by 5 Fold Media

The Light at Hope's End
by Kathy Dolman
$16.00
ISBN: 978-0-9825775-2-3

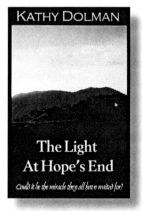

Ray Weber peers out through the darkness, mesmerized by a mysterious light on the mountainside opposite from his home high above the town.

A struggling small-town pastor with a crumbling family and fading ministry…A distraught, lonely waitress facing her dying mother's last days alone…A desperate young black man in the grips of a street gang teetering on the brink of destruction…A twenty-something party boy hovering over the line between the need to survive and a life of crime… What do they all have in common? They've reached hope's end in the town of Hope's End and are desperately in need of a miracle.

Master of the Dance
by Sharon Smith Myers
$15.00
ISBN: 978-0-9825775-6-1

As eight grandchildren sing and dance freely with Grandma and Pappy in the living room, miraculous things happen and their faith is unleashed to a new level. Join Grandma as she captures the heart of her grandchildren through enchanting allegories symbolizing God, His love and His Kingdom.

This heart-warming fiction will bring you back to a childlike wonder and awe of the Kingdom of God. The King is after you, fighting for you, inviting you to dance. Won't you join Him?

Visit www.5foldmedia.com to sign up for **5 Fold Media's FREE email update.** You will get notices of our new releases, sales, and special events such as book signings and media conferences.

5 Fold Media, LLC is a Christ-centered media company. Our desire is to produce lasting fruit in writing, music, art, and creative gifts.

"To Establish and Reveal"
For more information visit:
www.5foldmedia.com

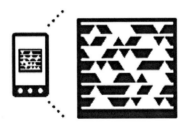

Use your mobile device to scan the tag above and visit our website. Get the free app: http://gettag.mobi

Breinigsville, PA USA
14 February 2011
255553BV00002B/4/P